
Praise for *This Knot of Thorns*

"Packed from cover to cover with nuggets of God's unconditional love, His unfathomable faithfulness and unfailing promises, *This Knot of Thorns* is a masterfully written story following one girl's relationship with her God, and the effect that such a relationship has in the lives of those she meets.
This book is a beacon of light and a challenge to the believer not to let our faith grow dim, even in the midst of our worst nightmares. I promise that you cannot read *This Knot of Thorns* and come away untouched by the Spirit of God!"

Abigail Sarah, author of The Guardians of Tawaii

"*This Knot of Thorns* is a book that will break your heart and then sew it back together again. Faith has woven together a tapestry full of life's ugly truths and illuminated them with God's redeeming love. *This Knot of Thorns* is a beautiful depiction of how light overcomes darkness, piercing even the blackest night. It's a perfect illustration of beauty from ashes, and it's a book that will stay in my heart for a very long time."

Kaelin Scott, author of Kissed by a Rose, Worthy of Love, and Game Set Love

"*This Knot of Thorns* is a beautiful, transportive read back into the past where the people of old faced the same struggles many do today. Mathewson digs deep into biblical themes and shines a redemptive light on difficult topics while telling a compelling story. This book, the characters, and lessons are all ones you can root for."

Caitlin Miller, author of The Memories We Painted and Our Yellow Tape Letters

"Poignant and powerful! *This Knot of Thorns* invites you to step back into the riveting atmosphere of the first century, yet its stirring truths of guilt, shame, and grace remain timeless in their portrayal. In the darkest of moments, hope's healing embrace can still be found. A beautiful addition to any history lover's shelf!"

Morgan Taylor Giesbrecht, author of The Lies We Live

This Knot of Thorns

Faith R. Mathewson

Grandma Sally,
Thank you for always being my first reader
and my biggest encourager.
This one's for you!

"Do not rejoice over me, my enemy; When I fall, I will arise;
When I sit in darkness, The Lord will be a light to me."

Micah 7:8

Glossary of Terms

Imma (EE-MAH) — Aramaic term for Mom/Mama

Abba (AB-BAH) — Aramaic term for Dad/Papa

Peristyle — A section in a Roman home that surrounded a courtyard.

Triclinium — Dining Room

Tablinum — An office or Study

Atrium — An open central court

Lararium — A small room or space reserved for Idol worship

Popina — A Roman tavern or pub

Cubicula — A roman bedroom

Part 1

48 AD

I

Iulius
Nazareth, Galilee

When the sun set and the world went to sleep, the demons in her mind came out to play. All she needed to do was close her eyes and they pulled her back to that day—back to the well and the memories that caught and tangled like fish in a net.

Jubilee had avoided sleep in the beginning, choosing instead to keep her mind alert and ready to ward off the darkness that awaited her. But rather than find relief, she had only served in making the memories stronger against her fatigue-softened mind.

Sniffling, she rolled over and stuffed the blanket in her mouth —stifling the scream that was building in her throat. Her screams would tear through the quiet when sleep finally gripped her. Not a day went by when she wasn't woken by her parents, her limbs entangled in her blankets, her throat raw and voice hoarse. Freeing her, her father would let her rest against him, refusing to return to his bed until her tears subsided. He too had suffered from the nightmares once. Only he had moved on. In less than a month he had left that day in the hands of the Lord, while three years later his daughter relived night after night the feel of a man's hands.

Though she had tried to fight it, God had become a question to her that nothing could solve. No matter the time spent thinking about it, she couldn't grasp how the God she had loved and trusted so dearly had allowed something so terrible to take place in her life.

Her father's words came to her—firm but gentle. *"Have faith, Jubilee. When you have nothing else, have faith."* Biting down on the pillow, Jubilee resisted the urge to scream. She wanted to drown out her father's voice and curse the very words he spoke. What good were Scriptures now?

But no amount of effort could erase the truths etched deep within her. From the very moment of her birth, the Lord and all His glory had been engraved upon her heart. Jubilee—their Joyous Jubilee. A celebration of joy, she had been named for the Lord himself, for not once had her faithful parents doubted their Messiah would rise again.

Why must she question and doubt when her parents had remained faithful, even in the face of certain defeat?

...

Jubilee kept her head down as she and her father slipped out into the morning air. She had enjoyed the walk to the shop when she was younger, with the cool air and the sounds of neighbors' sheep banging about in their pens. But in recent years she had begun to wish the shop had been built closer to home, where she could avoid the looks that followed her—whether looks of pity or mirth, the stares she collected grated on her like sand in the wind.

Hugging herself tightly, she quickened her step before remembering her father. Coming to a stop, she waited, using her covering as a curtain between her and those who wandered by.

Her father's limp was worse that morning, and as she watched, she could see the trouble he was having not to become tangled in his tunic as he moved. As he neared Jubilee a little girl ran from a small, stone home, nearly knocking him to his feet.

Coming up on her, her father pushed her dark hair behind her ear before touching her cheek, easing the ache that had made its home in her chest. "You didn't sleep," he noted quietly. "You know it will only be made worse if you fight it, Jubilee."

"I wasn't fighting it, *Abba*." Like a child, she crossed her arms over her chest. "I simply couldn't sleep."

Malachi touched his daughter's forehead, checking for tell-tale signs of fever. "Go home and sleep, Joyous. The shop will be waiting for you."

"I'm all right, *Abba*. I want to work. I need to work." Brushing his hand aside, she started walking. "Besides, I will wake up once I am busy."

...

Biting his tongue, Malachi followed after her. It would serve nothing to fight her—nor did he wish to. Not when medicine proved one of the few things that lured her from the catacombs of her mind. At eighteen, the girl had already faced more than a parent could fear—they both, together, facing a tragedy that, three years later, still held his daughter captive.

How can she move on when she looks upon your face each day, knowing what you witnessed? His wife's words, though spoken with love, felt like an iron down his throat. Could he truly play a part in why his daughter still suffered so greatly?

Juliana had used her thumb to wipe the tears that dripped down his cheeks. "It isn't your fault, *carissime.* But perhaps to be in a new place—one that holds none but the good parts in her life, she will finally be free of her pain." Juliana had smiled tremulously. "The Albanus' will care for her. This is the right decision, Malachi. I can feel it."

He had felt no will to fight her then. He couldn't deny that Juliana's lifelong friend would care for their daughter, and in their twenty-nine years of marriage, he had learned never to doubt his wife's feelings. Whether he wanted it or not, they had never proved wrong. But as he watched their daughter walk, her arms wrapped protectively around herself, the curls of her dark hair concealing her face, he began to question the woman's gift of feeling.

How could sending her away be helpful? The girl had never spent more than a night away from them, let alone been to a city like Rome.

Reaching the shop, Jubilee braided her hair before setting the table with their most commonly called upon instruments. Simply entering the shop, she seemed to awaken—her black eyes seemed brighter if not livelier.

Jubilee had loved the shop from the time she had first stepped foot inside, the draw of medicine calling her at the tender age of three. He could still remember the way her wide, innocent eyes had watched in fascination as he worked. Nor would he forget all the days he had caught her sneaking into his shop. No amount of discipline could discourage his normally subservient daughter from watering the seed that had been planted within her.

It was in the shop that the decision to send her to Rome became unbearable. They had worked together since she was ten years old, when he had finally given in to her pleas. She was to be his inheritor when the time came—a time he feared was coming far too quickly.

With the shop ready, Jubilee opened the door before returning to Malachi. Her eyes narrowed as he eased himself down behind the table. "Are you all right?"

"I am afraid you will have to face most of it today, Joy." It had been two years since the pain in his joints had begun its course through him, making his profession near impossible even at the best of times.

"But what about—"

"I will handle the men, Jubilee. You focus on everyone else." Malachi ran a hand over his face. The child was not ready for marriage. Not even to someone like Atticus Albanus.

...

Sleep weighed heavily as Jubilee ate that night. The thought of the demons awaiting her was enough to keep her from curling into the blankets that beckoned to her—an all too convincing tool of the enemy.

"There is no sense in delaying it, Jubilee." Setting her hands on Jubilee's shoulder, her mother guided her to the thin, worn out quilt that was her bed. "Go to sleep." With a quick kiss, her mother stepped outside.

Crawling under the covers, Jubilee stared up at the ceiling, waiting for the tendrils of sleep to pull her under. Though her eyes weighed heavily, she couldn't sleep. The smell of cooked grains hung heavily in the air from the dishes that still sat on the table. Through the window, she could hear parents calling for their children to come inside and sheep moving about. Sighing, she turned over when her parents came back, their night preparations quiet as they tried not to wake her. When she knew they were in bed, she rolled back, her chest tight with fatigue. She wouldn't be able to hide another night's sleep from her parents.

When an hour turned into three, Jubilee heard movement from her parent's mat as her mother eased herself off of it, careful not to wake her father.

Sitting at the edge of the mat, Juliana brushed her daughter's forehead. "Why aren't you sleeping, love?"

Jubilee shrugged. "Why aren't you?"

"I never sleep, Joy. Not until you have woken up."

Guilt washed over Jubilee as she learned she was not the only one missing a week's worth of sleep—not if her mother lay awake waiting for her daughter's inevitable fit. "I'm sorry."

Juliana tucked her daughter's hair back. "Do not be sorry, love. It isn't a new thing. I haven't had a decent night's sleep since Abel was born. I used to stay up with each one of you, waiting for you to fall asleep—and even then I stayed up longer just listening to you breathe in and out." She smiled. "And back then I couldn't take a nap during the day."

"We were children then, Imma. You shouldn't have to worry now."

Moving the blankets aside, Juliana slipped in beside Jubilee. When the Jubilee curled up against her, she kissed her hair. "I will always worry, Jubilee. Do you think because your brothers are out on their own, I do not still worry over them?"

Jubilee shrugged. "It's different. They're not burdening you all hours of the night."

At her words, her father groaned. Sitting up, her mother squinted into the dark. "Malachi?"

Malachi waved off her concern as he shuffled to them. Sitting up, Jubilee went to her father—burying her face into his tunic. Rather than force them apart as Juliana had feared, their shared experience had only served to draw them closer, Malachi being the only one who truly knew the horrors Jubilee had endured.

Fighting to breathe against the onslaught of images and sounds that edged the outskirts of his memory, Malachi kissed his daughter. "You were assaulted, Jubilee. I don't ever want you to see your struggles as a burden to your mother and me. What happened was not your fault. Do you understand?"

Jubilee sniffled. "I am so tired, *Abba*."

Malachi swallowed. It was not the first time his daughter had spoken of the tired ache that had filled her soul. In the weeks that followed her assault, his daughter was not the only one who found herself plagued by memories, and more often than not, the two had found themselves together in the dark, dreading the images that awaited them.

"I am tired, Abba."

Thinking she yearned for sleep, Malachi urged her to rest. "Sleep, Joyous. I will wake you when the nightmare comes."

Her hand slipped from his and her arms wrapped themselves around her knees. "You don't understand." She croaked. "This is not the sort of tiredness that sleep will diminish. Not the sleep you speak of."

Her voice was hollow—so unlike the bright tone she always carried. Though she never mentioned it again, it was clear that the life that had once lived within her was gone. Stripped away with everything else she held most dear.

Pulling his daughter closer now, he held her tight. "You have come so far, Joyous girl. You must not let the enemy win."

"He already won, *Abba*. He won the moment that man touched me, and I have come nowhere." Pulling away from him, she began to pick at the soft skin on her wrist—a habit she had developed when memories overwhelmed her. "I can't handle male patients. Each time I try, I feel as though my heart is going to rip from my chest."

"That does not mean you have not improved," Juliana interceded. "You wouldn't let Abel or even Nathanael touch you in the beginning. Do you remember that?"

Jubilee remembered. She remembered the pain in each of her brother's eyes each time she pulled her hand from theirs. Nathanael had always been her dearest friend and even he had brought nausea to her stomach when he came too close.

Taking Jubilee's hand, her mother pressed it to her cheek. "Please do not give up hope now, love."

Jubilee glared out the window. "Why am I the only one questioning Him? Why do I feel as though I am being sentenced to Hell for something I had no control over?" She couldn't understand it. Her faith had been strong once—unshakable even when neighbors mocked her and her belief in a risen Lord. She had unequivocally loved the Lord with her entire spirit. Now she couldn't find God in the simplest of places. Among the peaceful hills of Galilee, she had once felt comfort. Now they only held memories of that morning.

"Jubilee," Juliana whispered.

"Jubilee, you are never going to move forward if you keep fighting this on your own." Malachi brushed her cheek. "You have to trust Him to lead you through."

Jubilee looked at him miserably and sobbed. "I don't know how." When she had calmed, she pressed her palms to her eyes. "I don't know what to do."

"What are you willing to do, Jubilee?"

"Anything."

Juliana glanced toward Malachi who nodded. "Jubilee, when the merchant's ships rolled in, I received a letter. From Sibyl." That caught the girl's attention. Though she didn't voice it, they knew she thought of Atticus. "She says that Atticus has been struggling as well."

"Why?"

"She did not specify. She only said he was married and that he has not been the same since."

Jubilee's lip quivered noticeably. "He was married?"

"That isn't what's important right now, love. Sibyl thinks, and I agree, that you two would serve each other well."

Jubilee looked back at her mother before the meaning of her words settled. "You mean you want me to—no." Ripping her hand from her mothers, Jubilee stood and paced. "No. How could you even think I would do something like that?"

"It is only a suggestion, Jubilee. We only wish to see you happy—healed."

"And your answer to that is to send me away?" she said. "To force me into a marriage I do not want?" The moment the words left her tongue, she felt the color drain from her face and she hung her head. "I'm sorry. But I can't be with a man—not even Atticus."

Malachi stood and tucked her hair from her face. "I understand your aversion to marriage and what it entails. Your mother and I could never force you into a marriage. I could never force you to ever have to know a man in that way again. But you are drowning, Jubilee. Before Ju—" He paused at the way she winced. "Before it happened, you wanted marriage. You wanted children. You wanted Atticus. Now I know those desires have not left you. I see the way you hold your nephews. The way you look at the children who come through the shop." He took her face in his hands. "I see the way you look at your mother and me."

Jubilee nodded tearfully. "I have thought about it," she admitted quietly. "I want it, *Abba*. But I can't. Not when I know that I can't face what it would take." She began to rock slowly. "I think about marriage and children and I think about *him*."

His willowy frame and the scars that marred his body. He was so unlike Atticus' fullness or the dimples and unblemished skin and yet she didn't know that she could move past *him*.

"But it doesn't have to be that way, Jubilee. You have the power to change that. To enjoy a God-given gift." Malachi missed the days when the topic of intimacy had made him squirm—all barriers between them had been broken that day. "You have always loved Atticus. Do you think he could be enough?"

"He would be more than enough, *Abba*. It is I who would not be enough. Not now."

At their daughter's words, Juliana tucked her face into Malachi's neck. He could feel her hot tears pooling on his skin. "Don't you ever speak like that again, Jubilee. Ever." He choked.

Jubilee shook her head. "It's true. I won't be able to give him anything. Not like a wife should."

"Jubilee, please." Juliana moaned. "Do you think I did not have the same thoughts when I married your father? Coming to him as I did? I didn't even know if I would be able to give him a child. But Atticus has always loved you, Jubilee. He will wait for you—just as your father did me."

Jubilee looked toward her. "I don't want to disappoint you, Imma."

"Oh, *Mea Puella.*" Taking the girl's face in her palms, Juliana found her eyes. "You could never disappoint me, my love. Least of all in a decision like this."

"But you want me to go."

"I want you to move forward, Jubilee. I know what it's like to look upon your home with disdain. To see only the terrible parts of it. But I also know what it's like to come to a new country, and I could never be disappointed that you do not wish to add that weight upon yourself."

…

The topic of Rome and marriage was not brought up again. *Abba* most of all seemed pleased with her decision. When the shop closed each night, the two spent hours poring over the writing of fellow physicians, as well as the words Malachi had gathered for himself over the years. He taught her to mix herbs and other plants to create medicines and oils when supplies ran low.

The quiet moments with her father made the decision to stay easy. She had spent seven years gaining the trust of their neighbors to let her touch them. She couldn't imagine starting over now—in a city as vile and godless as Rome.

Following her decision, her father had left her the responsibility of helping children be born—a job that had previously been forbidden by her mother, who feared her being scared unnecessarily.

"It's a cruel thing, I know," Juliana admitted to Malachi one night. "But I hope that seeing these mothers will give her a change of heart."

She was not wrong. The more Jubilee assisted with the birthing and the children who came through, the deeper the ache in her chest grew. It seemed as though everywhere she looked there were mothers with their children. Wives with their husbands.

With the memory of him freshly stirred in her mind, Atticus came to her frequently. It had been Atticus whom she had most craved after the events that took place. Her protector. Her friend. Though she loathed to admit it, the craving still lived within her. It came to her at the oddest times—her stomach fluttering as it used to when she thought of him. She had felt nothing since *his* hands had grazed her flesh and it was always at the thought of *him* that the flutter would disappear and nausea took its place, reminding her that no matter how much she wanted Atticus, nothing could erase the feel of *his* flesh against hers.

When she wasn't working with her father, she busied herself with her mother in the garden or took care of her nephews, giving Abel and Rebekah time for themselves.

It was watching them play that she felt the familiar ache in her chest, deepening each time one of them giggled.

Blinking back tears, she left them to play. *Lord, why are you doing this to me? I can't marry. Take this desire from my heart.*

Waddling over to her, Isaac perched himself in her lap. After a moment, he touched her face, his chubby fingers catching and smearing the tears that trickled down her cheeks. "Why are you crying?"

Wrapping her arms around him, she forced a smile. "Don't you worry about it, dearest."

Rather than run off as she had expected, the boy curled deeper in her chest, one hand patting her shoulder. Holding onto him, she buried her face in his thick curls. *God, please!*

Across the room, she could see her parents, the ache in her chest deepening as she watched them together. *Imma* was massaging a salve into *Abba's* hands, stiff and immovable after a long day's work. She could see by the smile on her mother's face that *Abba* was telling her a story. At the look in her mother's eyes, Jubilee felt sick with loss.

For three years, despair had been an ocean she was merely treading. Clinging to the words of God as her parents had always taught. But she was sinking. If she refused her parents' proposition, would she drown in her pain?

She thought of Atticus again, tears burning her eyes. She hadn't realized how deeply she missed him until his name entered their home once more. She hadn't allowed herself to miss him for the pain it would cause. Atticus had been her refuge. She had needed him in ways she had never needed anyone else. Even as a child, it was him that she went to. Could he truly hold the key to her freedom?

Urging the boy to go play, Jubilee looked at her parents. "I want to go," she whispered, surprising even herself. "I want to go to Rome."

From her spot across the room, Jubilee could see her father's lip quiver, though he was quick to cover it.

"Are you sure, Jubilee?" Standing, Malachi made his way to his daughter. "Won't you think on it a little longer, Joyous? I don't want you making any rushed decisions."

He knew it was selfish, discouraging his daughter. He had watched Nathanael go off into the world with confidence, and though he missed him with each day that passed, he trusted that he was well, sharing the word of God with those in need of it.

It was a courtesy he seemed unable to offer his Jubilee. Though he loved his children equally, he knew his relationship with his daughter to be of great importance. *Oh God, I don't think I can lose her.*

Nor can I.

The words felt like an iron against his heart. His daughter struggled greatly and he knew the war that raged within her. Though he knew his daughter loved the Lord, it was clear that the relationship she had once shared with her heavenly father had been weakened. Could she truly stay on her path without her brothers and sisters in Christ to guide her?

They didn't even know where Jude had gone after he had assaulted Jubilee. What if they were sending her straight back into his grasp?

"I don't want to live like this anymore, *Abba*."

Looking at his daughter, Malachi felt sick. He had always thought it impossible for the girl to look anything more like her mother, but in the years since Jude had taken her, stress had grown continuously in her young face, showing to him his younger wife in the circles growing steadily darker under her wide, prominent eyes.

The tears started of their own accord and then it wasn't him comforting Jubilee, but she comforting him. "I only trust Atticus, *Abba*."

Drying his tears, Malachi pulled away. "I will make the preparations tomorrow."

II

Rome

Atticus Albanus swirled the wine in its cup, his muddled mind hypnotized by the subtle undertow of the blood-red liquid. When the liquid settled, he held the goblet to his lips, the bitter scent of it making his head spin. It was his third glass, and he could hear that cold voice in his ear. *Wine leads to fat, puppy.*

It had been two years since Aelia had left him, and he could still hear her voice, as clearly as the crystalline waters of Greece. He could see all too well how her dark eyes would patronize him —one eyebrow raised in disdain as he poured another glass.

With a click of her tongue, she would run a delicate finger over the fat of his stomach, a sly smile tugging at her lips. *I say it because I care, puppy. We wouldn't want anyone looking upon you as an animal, now would we?* The woman had been skilled in the abuse that ran off her tongue.

In the end, it was his father's voice that drove him to pour another glass. Slamming the cup onto the table, he poured another generous helping, ignoring the way his mother watched him. Perhaps a few more drinks would drown out the noise of his father's ramblings. "You never agreed to my marriage with Aelia, but you would have me marry a Jewess?" Atticus laughed dryly. "I think your standards are somewhat misplaced, Father."

"That *Jewess* is family, Atticus. Not to mention she comes from a very prominent line in Rome. Which is more than we can offer that harlot you picked up off the streets." Glaring back at his son, Regulus took a deep breath before continuing. He had promised his wife a peaceful meeting, but he no longer had the patience with his son that he once had. "Perhaps next time, you may want to stop and think before using Aelia as a defense."

At his side, his wife set a hand over his own—ever the peacemaker between father and son. She had remained silent throughout dinner, stress marring her pretty face as the conversation moved to battle. "Atticus," she said softly. "Won't you at least listen to what your father is proposing?"

"I have no desire to marry again, Mother. Once was more than enough for a hundred lifetimes."

Moving to sit beside her son, Sibyl bushed a finger over his rough chin. She had been happy to see him return from Greece with his whiskers grown out again—just as he was before Aelia had come and demanded change, erasing all traces of their summers in Galilee and Atticus's love for Jubilee and her culture. But even that small act of rebellion against her had not been enough to erase the damage his wife had inflicted. "Life has been unkind to both of you."

At her words, Atticus straightened. For just a moment, the hollow look left his eyes—a poorly concealed fear taking its place. "What do you mean? What happened to Jubilee?"

"Nothing, Atticus." Regulus's voice was considerably softer than it had been before. "Your mother only meant to say that you two have grown in the years you have been apart. You have had your mishaps. But," he emphasized. "As your mother has said, we all believe the two of you would do each other well."

"Jubilee is beautiful," Atticus said. "She always has been. How has she not married by now?"

"They say she does not desire marriage."

"Then we do share something—if the poor girl does not want to marry, then leave her be." Atticus knew Jubilee. Even a stubborn nature as strong as hers had its limits—her parents. If they wanted it badly enough, she would do it. No matter the pain it caused her. "Jubilee and I are too mismatched."

"And you and Aelia were kindred, were you?"

Sibyl glanced toward Regulus, her eyes silencing him. "I see why you fell for Aelia." The words grated at her throat—aside from her face, the girl had nothing a man could truly love. "She was very beautiful, and you did always have a weakness for those dark eyes."

"You remember where that weakness started, don't you?"

Atticus turned away as he found himself staring into Jubilee's dark eyes, as real and as vivid as though they stood nose to nose. He knew exactly where that weakness had started—in eyes so black, he was brought to question the existence of her pupils. He had fallen prey to those eyes the moment he had laid eyes on them—first as a protector. A friend. Until the feelings that overwhelmed him at the mere thought of her had become frightening. "It's as you said." He croaked. "Jubilee is family. The love I have for her is that of a friend. A brother. The girl is a child I held in my arms as an infant."

"You were ten, Atticus. Your mother is eight years younger than me. Do you hold fault to me? Or perhaps you hold fault to Malachi and Juliana and their twelve years?" His father watched him coolly. For all his brazen talk, Atticus could never succeed in hiding his feelings and it was no different now as he shifted uncomfortably, green eyes narrowed. "As for Jubilee." Regulus continued. "She is eighteen. That is hardly a child any longer."

As though sensing rising tension, Sibyl stepped in, her eyes holding more stress than either man cared to see in them. "Atticus, you know we only wish to see you happy."

"I know you do, Mama. As for father, he cares only for name—we are to forget happiness in the process."

"Atticus."

"Stop acting clueless, Mother." Atticus glared back at his father. "You know he has been anxious to fix me ever since Aelia."

Regulus leveled his gaze with his sons. "You will not speak so disrespectfully to your mother so long as I am around."

After a long moment, Atticus took a deep breath before turning from his father. Taking his mother's hand, he brought it to his lips. "My apologies, Mama. You are not the one I should be aiming my misgivings toward." Taking a deep breath, he turned back to his father. "Why is this union so important now? If you wanted to combine our families, why didn't you do it sooner? *Why now?*"

"Jubilee's parents believe she needs a change—a husband who can care for her." His father's voice had taken on another tone of gentleness that made Atticus uncomfortable. "Your mother and I believe the same in you."

"I have no desire to force a girl's hand. If Jubilee does not wish to marry, I will take no part in this arrangement."

"I had no desire to see my only child throw his life away for a harlot, but we do not always get what we want."

"Regulus, I disliked Aelia as much as anyone, but we will get nowhere if we keep going in circles like this." Turning back to her son, Sibyl smiled softly. "We have no plans of forcing anyone's hand, Atticus. We simply wish to see you two move on from your pasts. You cannot keep going on in anger and fear, my boy. This is Jubilee we speak of—you have loved her all of your life. Are you to tell me that love has vanished?"

Atticus ran a hand over his face, his thumb and forefinger putting pressure on his eyes. "I will always love Jubilee. But too much has happened since we have known each other. She deserved better."

His mother touched him gently. Even his father seemed concerned, if only for a moment. "You have made mistakes, love. But they are not you."   Tears filled her eyes. "Please, Atticus. If not for Jubilee, then for me? I can't bear to see you go on this way—I won't."

Atticus frowned at her. Tears were a weakness that not even Aelia could break him from. He knew his mother wanted what she believed was best. She wanted a daughter she would love and grandchildren to fill the home with what it now lacked. "I will think on it, Mama. But I make no promises."

...

Regulus watched his wife pace the inner permitter of the peristyle, her fingers absentmindedly grazing the freshly bloomed flowers. Her hair, once a pale blonde, shone white in the sun—its light catching the graying strands. As he watched, she took a shuddering breath before wrapping her stola tighter.

His wife's behavior was beginning to worry him. She was no longer the young bride he had married so long ago. After twenty-nine years of marriage, they had faced more trials than they cared to admit, but always his spirited young bride had taken it and done away with it. Only once in their years had she been so quiet and often sullen—shutting him away as she did now.

She worried about their child—they both did. But he knew it to be something far more for her. After two miscarriages and a difficult labor that had nearly taken her life, Regulus had not seen it worth the risk of losing his beloved wife, leaving Atticus to be their only child.

She longed to see him happy. To see the boy she had raised wed. It was a desire that seemed less likely to transpire with each day that passed. Even if the two did agree to the arrangement, the idea of their once tenderhearted child coming back to them seemed all but unattainable.

When her rounds brought her closer, he took her waist and brought to her him. Her face had rounded in the years since they had married, deepening the dimples in her cheeks. His fingers brushed where the dimples caved, drawing a reluctant smile to her lips. "It will be all right, Sibby."

Sibyl refused to meet his eyes. "Are we doing the right thing, Regulus? In doing this, how are we any different than Julius or your father?"

Regulus sighed. Though the idea had been her own, he had feared how she would feel when it was done. "What they did was out of greed. What we are doing is out of necessity. Atticus was blind when he married that woman and if we leave him alone now, he will destroy himself in his anger." *And you with him.*

Sibyl sighed as her husband pressed his lips to her forehead. Her love for him had only seemed to deepen with each year that passed and she loathed being the reason for the concern that filled his dark eyes. Though she longed to erase it, she struggled to find the words to do so. She could not explain for herself the dark cloud that had seemed to take rest over her.

Pressing her face into his chest to hide the tears, she decided on a half-truth. "Have we made a mistake, Regulus? The two have had such horrible histories since separating. Neither is the person they were when they knew each other." She thought of their son, who slept by day and drank himself sick by night. Where he had once been shy and kind, a deep seeded anger had taken root—alongside a sadness that broke her heart in two when she looked into his eyes. "Do you think he will be understanding if she struggles in the beginning?"

Regulus was silent. Though he hoped some semblance of their son still loved within him, there was a fear of how deeply Aelia had changed him. "Atticus has always loved Jubilee. No matter how angry he might be, I cannot imagine him treating her poorly." He brushed away a strand of hair that had caught in her lashes. He hated the way her eyes stared down at her hands, twisting and turning restlessly. There was something more to her pain—something that had been growing long before Atticus had strayed away from them. "Why don't you visit the temple of Angerona?" The goddess of pain and sorrow.

Sibyl shook her head. "No. No, I don't think that would do." As of late she had no longer felt the same satisfaction she once had when visiting the gods. Her most recent visit had left her with a strange sense of unease. An unease she had yet to shed since her last visit.

"Have you finally given up on your gods?" Regulus teased. "You know I don't believe in those things. But I don't want to see you lose your belief."

"I don't know what I believe anymore, Beloved." She smiled slightly, bringing back the old, playful mischief that, in better times, still filled her olive eyes at the age of forty-five. "Perhaps I must go out and find it."

…

Jubilee stayed on his mind in the days that followed—the more she filled his mind, the deeper the ache grew. Atticus had grown used to her absence over time, but the mention of her had stirred up the feelings he had stuffed away.

Did he truly want his Jubilee in the hands of a stranger? One who didn't know her as he once had? Surely the years could not have changed them so much that they wouldn't still fit one another?

Rolling out of bed, he went to the kitchen that acted as his tablinum. Sitting at the table, he fussed over the array of tools. He imagined Jubilee's face—the way she would smile curiously as she watched him pick over the herbs and minerals. Not settling until they were in their proper places. He had accumulated new habits since he had last seen her—ones he knew she would frown upon.

Pushing Jubilee from his mind, he looked over the notes from the day before. During his years in Greece, he learned that simply practicing medicine was not enough. He enjoyed the science behind it. The creation of the medicines they called upon, and it was there, he learned, that his talent lay.

Filling a goblet of wine, he went to work, sorting out different portions and grinding them before writing them down, working until the remaining light of day disappeared in the horizon.

Atticus stepped out onto the street, breathing deeply of the night air. Free of the circling smoke that filled the *popina.* He had given up on his work when the wine had run dry—not even medicine held a distraction as it once had. Not when it was Jubilee's love for medical art that had pushed him toward it. Not when he had once imagined working with her by his side.

He cursed his parents. He didn't want to think of Jubilee. He didn't want to think of their childhood summers. He most certainly didn't want to think of their last night together—Jubilee in his arms with nothing more than the stars for their company. He wouldn't be if his parents hadn't forced her name upon him with the promise of food and drink. Oh, he had drunk all right. By the time they had finished, he had drunk them dry and it still hadn't been enough. Not when memories of Jubilee haunted him. He couldn't think of marriage again. Not even to his Jubilee— least of all to Jubilee. He had seen the true colors of marriage and he would not let those colors blur the image he saved of his Jewess.

Atticus stumbled toward his apartment, a straight walk ahead. He had promised his mother to stay within the confines of his apartment when he drank, to evade the thieves that wandered the streets at night. But he had been out of wine and the torment she had caused had been enough to drive that promise from his mind.

How long are you going to stay drunk? Atticus swung at the sound. The voice had been so clear—as though its body hid among the shadows.

The memory came slowly, drifting through the fog. The memory of Jubilee reading aloud from her scriptures as she had often done in their time together. "Throw away your wine."

Swearing, Atticus tore open the bottle he carried and drank deeply of it. He knew the words Jubilee would have for him. She would repeat scripture, as though old scribbles could erase what had been done.

Reaching the step of his apartment, a slight shift to his right caught his attention. Dropping his wine, Atticus reached for the dagger he carried. Pain exploded at the back of his head before his fingers could graze the hilt and he dropped to the ground. Still grappling for the dagger at his thigh, he felt them picking over him—looking for coins they wouldn't find. Realizing their mistakes, they beat him until at last, he slipped into a haze of darkness.

When he roused, he could hear what he thought to be two men fighting over the few things they had managed to get off of him. His family ring. His mother's pendant. He bit hard on his tongue as they jostled him, sending shocks of pain through his battered body. When they had finished they cut the clothes off his back—a simple act of humiliation to finish it.

"Hurry up," one whispered frantically. "The sun is rising. We need to dispose of him before people find him."

"He is no one." Another spat. "A drunkard."

"*Stultus.* That is an Albanus."

The second swore. "Why didn't you say something before? We could be hung for this."

Atticus felt the dagger ripped from its sheath and waited. When the pain didn't come, he moaned inwardly. Would they take their time with him? "Be ready to dump him in the sewer." The cold edge of the knife grazed his neck before the sound of a window opening above him brought it back. Cursing, the thief jumped back as the slop rained down on them.

Unwilling to be caught, the men ran.

Groaning, Atticus rolled to his stomach, and using all his strength he pushed himself to his knees. Stripped of his clothes and now drenched, he wanted nothing more than to reach his room unseen by the neighbor's eyes.

Again, Jubilee's scriptures pounded at his mind. *How long will you go on this way?*

He moaned at the thought of his Jewess seeing him now. She would be horrified. He couldn't marry her. She wouldn't understand. Where Jubilee was untried and without fault, he was nothing but faults. The things that had transpired in the years that had separated them had left nothing of the man she had known.

Life has been unkind to both of you, his mother had said. All the more reason to leave Jubilee where she was. If she truly was struggling, she needed someone better than himself.

III

Augustus

Jubilee stared into the darkness, focusing her mind on the moonlight that shone through the cracks above her, snuffed out each time a crewman moved across the deck. The gentle creak of the wood grated against her tender nerves.

The ship had entered the outskirts of Rome and by morning she would be walking the stone-cobbled streets to a life that sent her trembling at the mere thought.

Why had she thought she could do this? *He* had instilled a fear in her that not even Atticus's gentle way could touch. *Atticus.* Would the man even want her after all these years? Would he still want her after that last night? She was drowning in unanswered questions. If Atticus still wanted her, why hadn't he come back? Did he know the truth about what kept her with her parents? Was it disgust that kept him away?

Jubilee had thought nothing of the first absent summer. There had been summers before that had found them without the Albanus'. It was the second summer without so much as a letter that Jubilee gave way to the horrible gnawing in her soul—Atticus had moved on without her. Perhaps with someone older. Someone cleaner.

Hugging herself tightly, she wanted nothing more than to be wrapped in her mother's arms.

As the time had neared for them to leave, it had been decided that her mother would stay behind, when the prospect of seeing her father again had confined her to their bed for a week. *"I thought I was past this," she had cried. Malachi had held her, whispering comforting words Jubilee couldn't hear.*

Jubilee sat behind her, brushing her hair in the same way her mother did when she cried. "You can forgive him without forgetting what he did to you, Imma." Whatever that may have been. Though her mother rarely spoke about Julius Aquila, Jubilee and her brothers had pieced enough together to know that their mother had lived a childhood far from the one she had given her children. "Stay here, Imma." The words were out of her mouth before she could stop them.

Juliana had watched her incredulously. "I most certainly won't stay here, Jubilee. You are getting married—a girl needs her mother there."

Jubilee could have taken it back—she wanted to take it back. But the words wouldn't come. "Not if her mother will suffer." She breathed. "You wouldn't expect me to face him. So how could I ever ask you to face your father?" The words burned as they clawed their way up her throat. "I'll be all right, Imma. I'll have Abba with me."

Perhaps regret was the cause of her sickness.

Across the room, her father snorted loudly, drawing Jubilee back to the cabin and the sick feeling she had made a mistake. Her father appeared to sleep soundly, one arm slung to the side, as though her mother lay beside him.

Careful not to wake him, Jubilee traveled by toe to the stairs, holding her breath each time the floor creaked beneath her. Feet touching the deck, she rushed to the side, reaching it in time to be sick into the rushing water below.

Resting her arms against the side, she let the cool sea foam splash her face. When the feeling of sickness passed, she turned her back to the sea and slid down the rough wood, grateful for the cool air that caressed her skin.

Over the violent pounding of her heart, she could hear the nervous whispers of the crewmen, but she couldn't bring herself to care for what they might be saying. "I'm not strong enough for this," she cried, ignoring the wide-eyed stares of the crewmen. The sobs broke free in floods. Why had she made her mother stay back? Why was she on this god-forsaken ship? What had made her think she could leave home? To marry, of all things?

"Are you all right, my lady?" The voice came from one of the crewmen. "Are you sick? Should I be getting your father?"

"No." She cried. "No, don't wake him." She had to gain control, but the sobs kept coming. Her nails dug into the wood beneath her, cutting into her skin.

"Now, my lady." The man tried again. "Are you sure I shouldn't be getting your father?" When she didn't answer, the man set a hand to hers, prying her fingers from the rough grain of the wood.

The recognition of a man's skin against her settled slowly as she stared at her light brown hands, small and fragile against the dark, work-blistered hands that held them. There was no fear at his touch. She glanced up then. It was a young man, no older than fourteen, with black skin and eyes like the rich soil of her mother's garden.

Jubilee forced herself to breathe as the boy pressed a rough rag against her wounds, gently working the splinters from her skin. He must have thought her insolent at the way she watched him.

What was it about this man's touch that didn't ignite the bile that always rested just below the surface? In three years there had been four men who touched her, and only one stood outside of her family.

Catching her stare, he smiled, letting a sudden and overwhelming calm settle over her. He was a brother. Squeezing her hand, he lifted her to her feet. "Take courage, sister. The Lord goes before you."

Jubilee didn't move as the man moved away. *Take courage, sister. Take courage.* Hadn't her mother made the very same journey to Galilee? Sick and broken, with no idea of whatever trials awaited her. Her mother had been ridiculed—belittled and spit on her for her Roman name and still, she had faced each with courage. "Oh God, give me strength. Give me the courage of my mother. I can't do this without you."

...

Her father walked with purpose through the people-heavy streets of Rome—his feet sure of the path he hadn't walked for nearly thirty years. How anyone could grasp direction in such a mess, Jubilee didn't know.

Rome was a mess of narrow avenues and cobbled streets that rose and fell and twisted at random. Above their heads, windows opened with shouts of warning as water and waste rained down around them. Each time her father pulled her away to safety, narrowly avoiding whatever foul stench hit the ground.

"You never forget the first time you don't move fast enough." Her father warned. "Best learn to listen." Despite the disgust she felt, Jubilee could hear the smile in her father's voice. Rome had been his home for half of his life. The busy streets and even the smells gave him the very things Galilee did for her. Had her parents felt as overwhelmed as she when they walked the streets of their new home?

The moment she stepped off the ship, she was met with shops of all sorts. Bakers and butchers. Idol makers and stone cutters. Everywhere she looked, people rushed about, buying and selling from stalls covered in bright fabrics, jewelry, and miniature idols.

Children chased each other through the streets, pushing and shoving their way through the crowds. Turning down a narrow shop street, she stumbled as a dirty-faced child ran in front of her, a loaf of bread tucked under his arm. Two small fish hung from a line around his neck. As she watched, an angry-faced vendor followed closely on his heels, not slowing until the child slid into the close-packed quarters of an alleyway, too slim for the plump-bellied vendor. Screaming a string of curses at the boy, he turned back and returned to his stall.

"We're almost there," Malachi told her. "Regulus acquired us a carriage to carry us to the Albanus Domus."

Following his gaze, Jubilee peered through the crowd, making out the shape of the small carriage. As they grew closer, she could see the driver leaning against the side, his foot tapping the ground lightly.

Seeing the man himself, her father laughed. Still holding her hand, he cupped his mouth. "Leopold."

The man jumped before smiling in return. "Malachi." Finishing the final steps, the two embraced, kissing the others cheek in greeting. "It's good to see you, Malachi."

"And you. I wasn't sure I would be seeing you."

"Yes well, when Julius Aquila learned of your impending visit he insisted you stay with him. I requested that I be the one to deliver you to him."

Jubilee held herself tightly as the two spoke. She had not missed the way the man had paused in his explanation and she knew her father had not either—their staying with her grandfather was not a request but a command. Despite the rising uncertainty, she felt the residual regret of her mother's absence fade away. It was right to have her mother stay home. Even if she must now face it alone.

The man's eyes shifted to her often as the men spoke. She could feel his eyes on her as her father lifted her into the coach, unwavering in his curiosity.

...

Leopold couldn't take his eyes off the girl. He had nearly lost his footing when he had seen her walking beside her father. She was small. Even hunched over as he was, her father towered over her. What she lacked in size, he noted, went to her black eyes. So wide they gave her a look of perpetual innocence. She chewed her lip, a habit Julius had been unable to break in her mother. "Just like Juliana." He laughed. "I missed this face."

Malachi ran a hand over the girl's hair. "I cannot say I blame you. I have myself two beautiful women."

Leopold nodded, the momentary joy that had filled him at the sight of them was fading fast as he took in the absence of his Juliana. "How is she, Malachi? Really? I have read the letters over and over of her health, but Juliana was never one to complain." The girl had often hidden the extent of her pain from those around her until it became too much for her to bear. "I fear that she has embellished, knowing I cannot see the truth for myself."

"She's perfect, Leopold. She finds herself in better health than me in recent years." He nodded toward the cane that supported his weight.

"How can that be? The last time I saw her she was only deteriorating more."

Malachi watched him a moment, his dark eyes concerned. "You have read the letter, Leopold." He replied patiently. "All you must do is believe it to be true."

…

Julius Aquila was just as she had imagined. Though well-aged and sickly, his skin shriveled and spotted, his eyes discolored and nearly blind, the old man was not so feeble as he seemed. When anger roused him his voice sent chills down Jubilee's spine.

They had not stepped into the room before her grandfather was screaming obscenities at her father. "Filthy Jew." Worn from his tantrum, Julius slumped back against the pillows. He was quiet for only a moment before his eyes fell on Jubilee, half-hidden behind her father. His face darkened as he took her in. "Let me have a look at you." His voice was thick and coarse. "Closer girl. I cannot see."

Slipping her hand from her father's, Jubilee lowered herself onto the bed, holding her breath as he studied her. "How old are you?"

"Eighteen, my lord." She felt feverish as he looked her over, his milky eyes staring into her own. Tearing her eyes away from his she glanced towards her father, wanting to see him. To know that he was there.

"You seem healthy enough." Her grandfather rasped. "You have meat on your bones. Unlike your mother." His hand gripped her chin and turned her to him. The feel of his aged hands, the scar that marked his palm rough against her skin, made her stomach jerk. Pulling back she hit the floor hard.

Scrambling away from him she found herself at her father's feet. "That is enough, Julius." There was an irritation to his voice that Jubilee had never heard in him before. Lifting her to her feet, her father kissed her forehead before turning to Leopold. "Would you mind showing my daughter to her room?"

"Of course, my lord." The man smiled kindly.

Surprising even herself, Jubilee took the man's outstretched hand without hesitation. Her mother had told her many stories of the man she had called Leo, and as she followed him from the room, the remaining fear fell away.

Left alone, Julius sensed more than saw the man's eyes follow his daughter. With Leopold gone, his awareness of the Jew became unbearable. "Why is it she has never married?" He demanded. "As far as beauty she is as lovely as Juliana ever was. Too dark, but I suppose that can't be helped. At eighteen she is already older than her mother was when you stole her away from Regulus."

Malachi closed his eyes, praying for patience. None had ever tested him like Julius Aquila. "It is not in lack of interest, I assure you. She has had many prospects." He did not mention Juliana. Nor did he mention the true nature of their daughter's circumstance. He knew the sort of vile things the man would say over his daughter's prolonged grieving.

"None of them good enough for you?"

"Jubilee has chosen to focus on medicine until now. She has quite the talent for it."

Julius shook his head. "It isn't right for a woman to practice such things. She should be home caring for a husband. Giving him children."

"I will not force a child of mine into a marriage they do not want."

"And yet that is what you are doing now," Julius smirked, his eyes malevolent.

Malachi bit down on his tongue. *God, let him finish or give me strength.* He needed rest. His back ached miserably and the bones in his palm ached where he held the cane. "To guide and to force are very different things." He breathed. "If Jubilee chooses to deny the plan laid before her I will respect her decision."

"Because you know she won't. A young, unwed Jewess denying the wishes of her parents? What would the neighbors think of you?"

"Jubilee knows her rights within our family. What neighbors think means nothing to me."

"I remember," Julius replied. "You never cared much for what anybody thought, did you? Not even your father? I believe he frowned upon your choice of a Roman girl as well, did he not? The man hated the Romans nearly as much as I do your kind."

"My father is not the one we are discussing." Malachi's calm demeanor was dissolving quickly. He had been hesitant to leave his wife behind, knowing the heartache she would suffer not knowing how her child was. Now he was grateful for their child's selfless act. Juliana had suffered unimaginably at the hands of her father. She need not face more. "Why are we here?" He demanded.

"I wanted to offer my granddaughter all of this." Julius waved a hand around, signifying the room and beyond. "Upon my death, all my possessions will be placed into the hands of your daughter. My money. My estate." The man smiled. "My shop. To do with as she pleases. From what I understand, Atticus Albanus has just returned home from studying under the influence of Aretaeus of Cappadocia and is looking to set up his practice. Should you agree to my terms, I am willing to hand over mine as Jubilee's endowment. The moment the contract is signed he may set up his practice. The boy has always been an odd one, I am sure he would allow Jubilee to assist him. Until the children come of course."

"Your terms?"

"She will sign her name as Jubilee Aquila."

"You want me to hand my daughter over to you?" The words brought goosebumps to Malachi's skin. "So that you may treat her in the same fashion you did Juliana? I would die before I let you lay a hand on that child."

"That can be arranged, Malachi." Sighing, Julius rubbed his temples. "I don't want your sullen-faced daughter, Jew. I want what is owed to me. The thing you stole from me when you

36

corrupted my daughter. I want to see my name alongside an Albanus. Using my name will be in practice only. Though she will be known as an Aquila, the rights to her will remain with you and Atticus."

"That is too simple." Malachi breathed. He had seen with his own eyes the lengths Julius was willing to go to achieve his goals. Deceit was not below him. "What are you not saying?"

Julius leered. "There will be no practicing her faith while I live."

Trust, Beloved. Malachi paused, his mouth open and ready to object. Trust? Trust the man who wanted to tear down the little faith that remained within his daughter? *What do you want, Lord? How can I trust a man such as him?*

Trust me.

Swallowing back the urge to fight, Malachi met the man's eyes. "What does that entail?"

"There will be no visits to the synagogues. I won't be humiliated in such a way again." Julius warned. "There will be no special meals made in her honor. She will eat what is prepared for her or she will not eat at all. Any mention of this faith and its god and I bear the right to punish her as I see fit." He glared at Malachi. "I made the mistake of allowing the Jewish faith to enter my home once before. I will not make it twice."

...

Leopold moved silently as the girl walked beside him. She had not been ready to resign herself to her room. She wanted to walk the peristyle and the garden and all the things her mother had told her about. The girl seemed especially fond of the gardens, as her mother had been.

"*Imma* loves to garden." She whispered. Tears still trickled down her honey-brown cheeks. She was a brown-skinned picture of her mother and after only moments of knowing her grandfather she was taking on the stance Leopold had so many times seen his Juliana in. "She would spend all day there if she could. She says it is where she feels the Lord the most."

Tears stung Leopold's own eyes. He had not realized until he had seen the two alone how set his mind had been on seeing Juliana in Rome once more. "I often found her here at all hours of the day. When she was a child she would slip away from Sonali at night just to sleep among the wildflowers." He had been sure to keep the wildflowers growing in her absence. "It used to drive Sonali mad, waking to find the child gone every other night, what with her poor health and all."

"Who is Sonali?"

"Your mother's nurse. You would know her as Amma, I am sure. It was your mother's name for her."

Sitting among the flowers, Jubilee closed her eyes, wiping the remaining tears from her cheeks. "My mother doesn't speak much about her old life."

"Understandable of course."

"She has told me about you though. You and Amma are the only things she speaks of. Apart from Sibyl of course. She told my brothers and I about how you saved her life. How you raised her as though she were of your flesh." The girl smiled. "How you used to surprise her with charcoal and paint and pieces of papyrus. She was always afraid you would never know how grateful to you she was for such a gesture."

The lump that had formed in Leopold's throat grew. "She had incredible talent." If Julius wouldn't encourage such a talent in her, Leopold knew he must. He still carried each of the girl's drawings in a chest, from the ones she had done as a child to the ones she had sent of her children. "And I always knew her gratitude, my lady."

"I am sure you did. My *Imma* is rather a worrier where her old life is concerned."

"Your mother was my light, my lady." The tears were falling now and to his surprise, the girl gripped his fingers. "She was a child like any other. She could be selfish, but I always felt it was well deserved on her part." The child had suffered unbearable pain from the moment she entered the world. She could have called for his death and Leopold would have walked proud, knowing a quick death would be nothing to what she faced. "Would you mind my asking, my lady? What they say about her health? Is it true?"

The girl smiled. "If it weren't so, I wouldn't be here."

Leopold didn't feel sure. He had read the letter until the words were nothing more than smudges on the page. He had listened to Sibyl's stories of her friend until her throat was raw. He had accepted Malachi's reassurances and still, he could not believe it as truth. That the delicate child he had sent away no longer lived at death's door. How he wished he could see for himself the miracle graced upon her. "I was afraid when I didn't see her that perhaps it was due to me. To hide the truth."

"She wanted to come, my lord. But circumstance forced her to stay back."

"Her father." It was not a question. If anything was to keep Juliana from Rome and her child, it was Julius.

"The memories are not so distant as they once seemed, I am afraid." Quick tears gathered in the girl's eyes. "Is this truly the life she lived? Walking on ice to keep her father happy?"

"She was well loved, my lady. We kept her from harm as often any slave could." Noticing something more in the girl's eyes, Leopold smiled. "Take comfort, my lady. Let me show you to your room. Your mother's room."

IV

Malachi watched as his daughter worked her fingers through her thick curls, her fingers expertly adding pieces to the already intricate braids. When she finished, multiple braids hung down her back, resting on the blanket of tight curls she had left loose. "Did your mother teach you that?"

Tucking a gold-leafed comb into the thick braid that wrapped around her head, Jubilee smiled. "Yes. She asked that I wear it this way. Do you like it?"

"Very much, Joyous. Your mother made the right decision."

Jubilee ran a hand over a small box, containing several jewels. "She instructed me to borrow a few things from Sibyl, but I found this." Waving to the comb and simple earrings she wore, she smiled. "I think these were her favorites. See where they are scuffed?"

"I believe that she was wearing those exact pieces the day I met her." He remembered it as though it were yesterday. Nearly thirty years and he still felt that same brainless smile tug at his lips.

It was a look he had seen growing in Atticus's eyes in their final summers. Would that love still hold even now?

Avoiding his eyes, Jubilee rose and moved towards the bed. Her plain tunic was tight and hung a couple of inches too high. It seemed a strange contrast against her gold-adorned hair and the simple jewels she had found in her mother's arca. His daughter had never complained about the old tunics she wore, even when they grew small and worn thin. But still, he wished now that they could have afforded her a new tunic. The wedding tunic she would have worn under better circumstances.

"I wrote *Imma* something." She pressed a scroll into his palms. "Would you give it to her for me?"

Her voice cracked, threatening to bring Malachi more tears of his own. He had done his crying in the night before her nightmares had woken her. He must be strong for her now. "I will make sure she gets it, Joyous."

"You'll say another goodbye to Abel and Rebekah for me as well? And the boys?" The sudden realization that she might never see her nephews again proved too much and again the tears were falling.

"Jubilee." When she looked at him he brushed the tears away. "You do not have to do this, Joyous Girl. Your mother and I will hold no fault to you if you choose to come home."

"Why do you still call me that?" The girl whispered. "It isn't truth anymore is it?"

Malachi lowered himself onto the bed and forced his daughter's eyes on his. "You think you no longer bring joy to me, Jubilee? Do you think that I can no longer look upon you with the same sort of love and pride I have felt all your life?"

"I thought it was for how I was before." Her fingers twisted a small length of her hair. "I am not her anymore."

"There are so many reasons the word joy comes to mind when your mother and I think of you, Joyous." He pulled her hands from her hair and held them tight. "The events that took place on the day of your birth are the very reason we chose your name. Your fitting it was nothing more than a happy accident.

And I believe that you will find your way back to that girl one day. With or without Atticus."

Lips locked tight, Jubilee stood and began to pace. "Does he know? About what happened?"

"No. Sibyl didn't have the heart to tell him when she learned of it."

"Good." She whispered. "I don't want him to know."

"Jubilee, if you go through with this he will need to know. As your husband he will deserve that much."

"Because I can't give him anything else?" She demanded. "Because I can't give him the one thing a woman is supposed to give her husband on their wedding night? I don't want him to know. There is no need to burden anyone else with it."

"Do not pretend that that is your reasoning, Jubilee. I understand your feelings, but I will not condone your keeping such a secret from a man you will be spending your life with."

"You want me to tell him that I am not the perfect little Jewess that he left behind? So that I can have another person look at me with pity?" She laughed. "What is the point of all of this then? If I cannot truly start over?"

"There is no true way to start over, Joy. There is no changing what happened."

"I don't want him to look at me differently, *Abba*. I couldn't stand it if he looked at me like everyone else does. Like I am fragile."

"Don't you think he will find out eventually?" Malachi demanded. "He is going to wonder at your new behavior toward him. You may be able to fool him with the timidness of a new bride at first, but don't you think he will ask questions when you wake up screaming for the fifth night in a row?"

"*Abba*!"

"He deserves to know the truth, Jubilee. From what Sibyl has shared, Atticus has experienced many sufferings of his own. How will you feel if he decides to keep his secrets from you?"

Jubilee felt a shaking begin within her. A bone-deep shake that made her heart race in bubbling beats. Her parents had mentioned the sufferings Atticus had experienced in the years that separated them and each time she felt a bone-deep shake appear. She could see within herself the changes her experiences had wrought. Could Atticus's own have changed him as well? Would they even recognize one another through the layer of dirt and grime that covered them?

…

Sibyl felt the need to move as she waited, her heart pounding wildly in her chest. She felt as though she were awaiting the long overdue return of her own blood. When at last she saw them enter the tablinum, Regulus was forced to take hold of her arm in the way a father held an excitable child from running off. "We do not want to overwhelm her, Sibby."

It was Jubilee who ran the final steps, throwing her arms around Sibyl and holding her tight. "I missed you."

Pulling away, Sibyl kissed both cheeks before taking her in. Her round face had thinned out since she had last seen her, enhancing the cheekbones Sibyl had always admired in Juliana. Despite her small stature and childlike eyes, her little girl had become a woman.

Letting her go, she watched as Jubilee hesitated with Regulus before rising on her toes to kiss his cheek. Though she couldn't be sure, she thought she had seen him blink back tears as he wrapped her in his arms.

When hello's had been said, Sibyl saw the girl's eyes sweep over the room. Not finding what she was looking for, her eyes fell back to the floor. Her hands wringing at her tunic. "Atticus will be here shortly. He may have been held back with a patient." Or a bottle of wine. Excusing herself, Sibyl made her way to the window that overlooked the street. She feared her son walking the streets alone after what had happened—thieves could smell drunkards the way a lion smelled its prey. *Let this work.* She begged. The boy needed Jubilee. He needed someone to care for him. To love him. To manage him in a way she no longer could.

…

Back in the room, Jubilee listened quietly as her father spoke with Regulus. Inwardly she wished Atticus would hurry. Despite the fear there was an underlying anticipation at the idea of seeing him and the longer she was kept waiting the more violent the butterflies in her stomach became. What would his experiences have left her with? Someone hard and cruel? Would he still love her despite her changes? The thoughts made the bubbles in her chest rise until she felt she would choke.

God, please! Let him be as he always was. Only then can I do this.

Joining Sibyl at the window, she felt the ache for her mother ease as the other woman took her hand in hers. "He will treat you well, Jubilee. Like yourself, he may struggle, but I know he will treat you well."

"I am sure he will. I only hope I can treat him well." She had found herself stepping out in the days since leaving Galilee. Since the crewman had held her hand in his, never once igniting her nausea. She had allowed and even welcomed Leopold's friendly touch. Had felt little fear in welcoming Regulus's embrace. She knew it to be of God. A gift of faith. But was she ready for what marriage would entail? It was one thing to welcome a touch of comfort. The hug of a man who had always been a father in her eyes. But what Atticus would expect was so much more than a simple touch.

"There he is." Sibyl stared down at the street, watching a thin figure enter the Aquila grounds. Pressing the girl's hand, she led her back to the party. "You will serve him well, *Puella*. You have always treated him well."

Jubilee watched through her lashes, fighting the sudden, unexpected urge to cry as she watched Atticus move. His waist was considerably smaller, she noted quickly. His once round face had thinned to an almost sickly state. Deep, yellow circles framed his eyes. She had expected change in him. She had been warned not to expect too much before leaving for Rome. But she had never thought to worry over his physical form. She was glad to note that he at least still adorned his facial hair. Though a rarity in Rome, it was now the only thing she recognized about him.

Upon reaching the small party, she watched curiously as Atticus's eyes carefully glanced over his father, giving nothing more than a quick cursory nod in his direction.

Atticus smiled at his mother. "Mama." He leaned over and kissed her cheek. "Malachi, my deepest apologies for my tardiness. I hope you were not too inconvenienced."

Malachi shook his hand. "Not at all, Son."

With all others greeted, Atticus turned his eyes reluctantly to Jubilee, fearing the effect she would have on him after so long apart. He had spent the night and all that morning preparing himself. He would not let her sway him from the decision he knew was right. It was only after the fourth cup of wine that morning that he truly felt confident in his abilities. Even Jubilee's beauty had its limits.

But by the gods, she was beautiful. Too beautiful. Even bare-faced and dressed in a plain tunic she was ethereal.

She bowed her head at him, uncharacteristically formal. "Atticus."

"Jewess." That coaxed a small smile. "Why don't we walk?"

Stepping outside the Domus walls he watched the way her eyes roamed over the view. It felt strange to see her in Rome, learning about its sights and culture for the first time. He had known all there was to know of her home since he was a child. From the Sea of Galilee to a small, mundane home in Capernaum, where her mother was touched by the Man they called Jesus. He had loved her country. What would she think of his own?

"Have you been able to explore much since you arrived?"

Her eyes flickered to his for just a moment. "No. Julius- my grandfather wanted us here straight away. After he finished with us *Abba* needed to rest."

"You will have to remind me to take you." No. No, she would be leaving. He couldn't let her get to him.

"That would be nice. You owe me after all those tours of Galilee." She began to count them off on her fingers. "There was

Nazareth of course. Shimron. Cana." A small smile pulled at her lips. "Capernaum."

"Every year," Atticus replied. It was the tradition of her family to make the nine-hour walk to Capernaum each July, to celebrate the new life both Juliana and Nathanael had found there. "Do you still go? With your father as he is?"

"Of course. *Imma* would stop, but *Abba* insists on continuing the tradition. He says it's only right. She was in worse condition than he when she made the walk."

They walked in comfortable silence before the woman's eyes went a shade brighter, as they always did where medicine was involved. "Leopold says that you have only just returned from studying under Aretaeus. What must that have been like?"

Atticus felt the uncertainty in his chest ease at her words. No more than a few moments and already they were slipping back into their old, easy ways. Perhaps the two could grow back together.

"It was an experience. Trying. I don't have the natural talent for it that you do."

"It's not natural, Atticus. I simply started younger."

Atticus kept quiet. She was too humble for her good. He had watched her suture her father's face when she was only six. The child hadn't even flinched when Malachi pressed the needle and thread into her small palms. "He would have liked you."

She smiled again. But it wasn't the sort of smile he had come to expect of her. She was not the bright-eyed girl he had watched her grow into. "My parents said you were married? My condolences."

"Aelia didn't die." He replied sharply. "She left."

"Oh." Was all the woman could muster. Her eyes glanced around them, looking for conversation. Finding none she sighed. "Our parents want this."

Our parents. Not we. Not I, Atticus thought. "What do you want, Jubilee? I do not want to hear about what your parents want. I want to know what you want."

Jubilee stopped so suddenly, Atticus walked past her. Turning back, he found her staring past him—her eyes on a slow procession of slaves being marched toward them. Thick tears trickled down her cheeks. "I want to be free," she whispered.

Moving her aside, Atticus forced her eyes away from the sight. "Free?" he questioned. "Free from what?" He knew it couldn't be her parents. Juliana and Malachi were two of the most loving parents, treating him as their son.

"I have my secrets and you have yours, Atty." Atty. It was a name she had bestowed upon him when Atticus was too big for her tongue. "I know that you have been hurt in the past. But if we must marry, shouldn't it be to someone we know? Someone we trust?"

"I suppose."

"We were friends once. I see no reason why we couldn't be so again. Friends."

"Friends who share a bed." Atticus couldn't help but smile at the way she shivered. For just a moment she was the Jewess he once knew.

"That wouldn't be necessary. This is not your idea, I don't expect you to find your pleasure in me."

"Do you expect to find your pleasure in another?"

Her dark eyes widened and a deep blush filled her cheeks. "Of course not." She breathed. "I am simply stating that you are used to other things, I am sure. Things I cannot give you. I would not expect more than what must be done on the first night." She swallowed. "Or what must be done for children."

"Jubilee, if this is not what you want then you must not give in to them. Do what you need. I know that your parents will not force you."

"I am doing what I need. I need this. I want this. I *want* this. I just-I am scared." Her eyes traveled back to his. "Can you understand that?"

Atticus frowned as he watched the tears pool at her lips. Despite the years that had pulled them apart, he still felt that old, familiar pull toward her. The desire to comfort her. He had come with the notion that he would turn her away and he found himself unable to do so as he looked at her. "Scared of what, Jubilee? Of me?"

"Of you. Of me. Of everything."

Without thinking he touched her cheek, wiping away the tears. "There is nothing to fear from me, Jewess."

"I know." Her hand touched his briefly, but her eyes stared past him. "If we do this, can I make one stipulation?"

"Of course, so long as you listen to mine."

Jubilee was quiet, her eyes glued to the passing procession. "I won't ask questions if you don't." She blurted. "When and *if* we decide to share things, we, on our own, make that decision."

As he watched, her nail dug deeper and deeper into the flesh of her wrist, drawing a small drop of blood that hit the ground between their feet. The girl never even flinched. "Jubilee, what happened to you?"

"No questions." She insisted. "You want to know my past and I get to know yours, and I know you don't want me to."

"And what makes you say that?"

"Because you would have told me by now. We used to tell each other everything." Wiping her face she started walking again. "What was your stipulation?"

Atticus faltered as he followed after her. "I-" He shook his head unsure of how to continue. "If I agree to this, I want a real marriage." He had done a fake marriage. He wouldn't settle for such a menial life again. Not with Jubilee. "If that isn't what you want then perhaps we should reconsider."

Jubilee slowed to a stop now. "It is. I just- I don't know how to do that."

"Neither do I," Atticus replied honestly. "But we will figure it out together."

...

There was no true ceremony. Only the simple handling of the dowry and the requirement of both parties to give their consent. As requested, Jubilee signed with the Aquila name.

With each passing moment, Jubilee felt her nerves rubbing raw. The sooner it was over the sooner she would leave with her new husband. The sooner her father would leave her.

When the contract had been signed, Julius ordered everyone to the triclinium, where a small meal had been prepared. Malachi felt Julius's eyes on them as the food was placed before them. A wide assortment of foods graced the platters—pork and sausages placed most prominently among them.

Ignoring the man's smile, Malachi took his daughter's hand to say grace over the meal. Afterward, Jubilee took up her fork and ate without hesitation.

Though the selection was small, Jubilee had never seen half the foods that graced the table. From dormouse to beef to a wide array of fruits, most were a delicacy that her family could never have afforded had she married back home.

"Well, Malachi," Julius announced, drawing the attention of the others in the room. "It seems as though your daughter has taken quite easily to her limitations. Perhaps your little Jewess is not so faithful as you would hope."

"Quite the contrary, Julius," Malachi replied. "Jubilee is very faithful. As for your rules, she will keep them, for it matters not what we put into our mouths, but what we let come out. As you requested, my daughter will not be practicing her Jewish faith, my lord, but Christian." Smiling, Malachi took up his utensils and cut into the pork.

Julius glared at him, his face red. "A technicality." He hissed. "It doesn't change anything." When Malachi refused to answer, Julius demanded Leopold carry him to his room.

As things settled, Atticus watched his new wife carefully. His father had warned him that she would not be as Aelia had been when she came to him.

"You mean she is a virgin? I expected nothing less from a Jewess."

Regulus had taken him by the wrist, drawing him closer. Despite the tight hold, his father had looked more desperate than angry. "I mean to say that you must be gentle with her. Patient. If she hesitates, which she will, you let her. Do not rush her."

Atticus pulled back, pushing down uncertainty that was beginning to grow in him. "What sort of monster do you take me for? That I would think to mistreat a virgin girl?"

"Atticus, there are things involved here that you do not understand."

"I will give her all the time in the world if that is what she needs."

And he would.

As the time neared for the two to make their leave, Atticus could see the fear mounting in her wide, black eyes and he urged her to drink. Perhaps wine would ease her mind.

…

She had made a mistake. Jubilee's stomach rolled dangerously as she made her way through the dark corridor on trembling knees. She could still feel *his* fingers against her skin. She could still feel *his* breath against her lips. *His* voice was in her ears. *Atticus.* Her mind screamed. *Atticus. Not* him.

But it was useless. The moment he had touched her he had ceased to be her Atty. Her sweet, precious Atticus. The hatred that filled her at each stroke of his gentle hands had felt like a weight against her entire being. He had not pushed her. He had not forced himself on her. He had been gentle and patient. He had told her she could wait. He had been the man she had always known and yet in that moment she hated Atticus as much as she hated *him.*

Couldn't he see her pain? Her fear? Why had he done it? Couldn't he see she didn't want to?

But she did want to, didn't she? Had that not been why she came to Rome? To put what had been done to her behind her? To know what true love was? Had she not urged him to continue when he hesitated at her resistance? Had she not urged him to continue when he waited at each tear on her part?

Deep down she knew it was not Atticus she despised but *him*. She knew and still, she hated Atticus. To lay beside her husband was to lay beside *him*.

V

October

Jubilee hurried down the corridor, the tray she carried teetering dangerously as each step threatened to spill its contents onto the pristine floors.

Her grandfather had already called three times, his insults growing cruder with each second that passed. She had not thought it possible for her grandfather's behavior to worsen, but with her father gone Julius's abuses had only grown worse, many having turned towards her.

After their revelation of faith, her grandfather had turned his former rules around. Rather than forbid her to practice her faith, she was forbidden to practice medicine and despite Atticus's protests, the man would not relent—not if Atticus wanted to keep the shop. So while Atticus ran the shop, Jubilee cared for her grandfather, leaving him to be her only access to medicine.

"Jewess!"

Two months, every second spent by his side and she had yet to hear him speak her name. She was *Jewess* and nothing more. What had always been a term of endearment from Atticus was nothing more than an insult in the eyes of her grandfather.

With the room in sight, she quickened her step, only to slip on the fabric of her tunic. Landing hard on her backside she watched the tray clatter noisily as its contents spread across the floor, soup and watered wine staining the mosaic of Fortuna. The goddess of luck.

Kneeling to clean the mess, Jubilee felt the woman's marble eyes mocking her as her grandfather cursed her. "So much for luck." She muttered.

Ignoring the man's foul screams she hurried back towards the kitchen, muttering her own words under her breath.

Leopold watched her with knowing eyes as she entered. "Pace yourself, my lady. It will not hurt him to learn patience."

Dumping the contents of the tray into the washtub, Jubilee began preparing another tray. "How have you not run off like the rest of them?" After only two months she could not find it within her to fault the servants who had run away, the risk of being thrown to the lions less daunting than Julius Aquila. Had it not been for her vows to Atticus, she would have tucked her tail and swam back to Galilee.

"You must not let him frighten you, Jubilee."

A truth easier said than done. To stand where her mother once stood only solidified the fears she had always held over her mother's past life. Lowering herself to the floor she rested her head against the wall. "He *is* frightening. And cruel. I can't help but picture my mother with him, listening to every hate-filled word he had for her."

"You will learn to manage him. Or to tolerate his words at the very least. He can't hurt you. Not now."

Not now. Jubilee thought. *Not like he hurt my mother.*

"Give it time, my lady. You may just come to care for him."

The idea seemed as far stretched as the entirety of Rome embracing the Jews. Or better yet, the Jews embracing the Christians. The man was vile and cruel. In two months she had yet to hear anything more than words of hatred and vile curses spill from the man's mouth. She knew she should be speaking to him—sharing God's word with him where she could. But each time she was in his presence she found herself unable to speak more than a simple greeting. And why should she? This was the man who had tried to take that faith from her. The man who had abused her mother and cursed her father. The man didn't deserve the word.

...

Carrying the tray, Leopold led the girl into the hall, keeping her at a steady pace. It had taken only a few days to learn that for all her mother's beauty, the girl held none of the woman's nimble grace.

Julius's eyes followed the girl as she entered the room after Leopold. They narrowed as she took the tray and sat beside him. "My apologies, *Avus*."

Leopold watched as the girl fed the man, noting the stiff way she held herself—sitting so near the edge, any sudden movement would land her hard on the floor. Any movement on Julius's part and she held her breath, her stomach tucked tight as she leaned from his reach. Like her parents, he had hoped that her time with Atticus would free her from the hands of the man who had taken her, but still, she remained distant from all but Leopold himself.

Julius cursed. "You are a married woman now, girl. Must you still act like a wide-eyed virgin?" Leopold cringed at Jubilee's sharp intake of breath as Julius took her hand and held her in place. "A man's touch will not hurt you."

"*Avus*, please." The girl's voice cracked miserably, toeing the edge of hysteria.

Stepping in, Leopold eased her hand from Julius and lifted her carefully from the bed. "I'll take it from here, my lady. You go rest now."

Sitting beside him, Leopold adjusted Julius's pillows—waiting until the sound of the girl's footsteps fell away. "Do you have to be so hard on her, my lord? She is young and away from all she knows."

"She is an ungrateful brat. Like her mother. Like the Jew."

"She is suffering." From what, Leopold knew he could never admit it aloud. He had grieved long when Sibyl had passed Juliana's letter onto him. To think of the vile things his master would have to say was too much for him. "Give her time to adjust before you judge her so harshly. She could have walked away. She could have married under her father's name. Do not push her away."

"The girl wanted riches. Signing the contract as she did was for none but herself."

"Jubilee doesn't care for riches."

"Everyone cares for riches, Leopold. All women want to adorn themselves in fine tunics and jewels. Even a humble Jewess."

"You have her wrong, Julius. Just as you always had her mother wrong." Leopold had to believe there was more to the decision that led to her being there. More than jewels and riches. "She still wears the tunics she came in, despite the condition of them. If she cared for riches she would have spoiled herself with new things by now."

"And she will, just as soon as she feels comfortable. You can hold onto all the misconceptions you want about my daughter, but she was as vain a girl as any. The girl liked her jewelry and judging by the pieces the girl stole from her mother's arca, I would say her daughter is no different."

"I have no misconceptions held about Juliana. The girl was most certainly spoiled in her ways." He bit his tongue against the words that threatened to spill out of him. *But unlike you, I choose to see past such things.* "Won't you be good to her, Julius? Do not drive her away as you did Juliana."

"Juliana left because she was a traitor of her kind." Julius spit. "Twice over it seems. I will not sit here and take the blame for the choices Juliana made."

Leopold held his tongue as he finished feeding the man. It was useless to argue with a man like Julius Aquila.

…

Atticus couldn't understand it. Why had she married him only to shut him out? Since their union had been made, he had found himself missing her far more than in the years they had been apart. In the two months they had been married, they had spoken very little. Most nights finding her in bed, sound asleep before the wine dried out.

Forbidden by her grandfather to assist him in the shop, communication between the two was limited to meals and the middle of the night, when her screams tore through the air like knives.

To have her so close and yet so far seemed a twisted sort of fate. Though he tried not to, he felt a bitterness growing toward her. He had not made love to her in weeks. He couldn't—not when he knew the thoughts that crossed her mind. The disgust she held toward him was obvious in the way her eyes glazed over, fixed on something just beyond his ear. Nor was he so oblivious to the way she slipped from the room when she thought he slept. He had thought nothing of it in the beginning. She was as free to roam as he was. It was not until he had chosen to go in search of wine that he discovered where she went each night. Distracted by the harsh sound of her sobs he had found her tucked away in the gardens—retching into the dirt.

You see what you do, Puppy? You make her sick. You make everyone sick.

She did not return immediately after her late-night sickness but rather stumbled into her old room, where she cried longer, clutching the blankets to her chest as though they held the comfort she needed.

Atticus longed to go to her. To hold her in the way he always had before. But if she wanted comfort she would come to him. She wouldn't tuck herself away in the dark.

It wasn't until she had cried herself dry that she crept back into the room they shared and even still she would lay as far away as their small bed allowed.

What did you expect? That she would love you? That she could look at you with anything more than disgust? Look at you.

Pushing his meal away from him he stood, grabbing the bottle of wine.

"Aren't you going to eat?" Jubilee's voice was soft. When he found her eyes they were sweeping over him. Inspecting him.

"I'm not hungry."

"Atticus, you've not eaten in days. Look at you."

Look at you. How many times had Aelia spat those words at him? Her face twisted in disgust as her eyes roamed over him. "Look at me?" He hissed. "Look at me? When was the last time you looked at me, Jubilee? Do not pretend you care what happens to me."

Jubilee's lips parted. "I do care, Atticus. None of what I am going through has anything to do with you. Not directly, anyhow." She began picking at the skin of her wrists. It was as though she didn't realize she was doing so. Not until her nail broke the skin, drawing her eyes away from him and to the bloody, crescent shape on her wrist. "I need time, Atty. I need patience."

Snatching a cloth from the table he pressed it to her bleeding wrist, ignoring the sharp intake of breath as his skin brushed hers. "I have been patient, Jubilee. I have been patient and all I get in return is a door slammed in my face."

"I know you have been patient, Atticus. More than I could have hoped but I-"

"Why did you agree to this if it wasn't what you wanted?" He demanded. "And why me? Was it not enough to torture yourself, you had to torture me as well?" He winced at how pitiful he sounded.

Who would expect anything more, Puppy?

"I chose you because you are the only one I could face this with. Because you are the only one I trust."

Trust? Where was her trust in him? "Why marry if you didn't want it, Jubilee? Your parents never would have forced you so don't lie to me."

"Because I had to." Her voice trembled. "I couldn't keep going as I did before. I don't want to live the rest of my life trapped in my dark mind with no one to run to."

Atticus's eyes met hers. "Then stop running from me, Jubilee."

"I want to. I do." Taking his hand in hers she held it tight to her chest. "It is hard to explain. It is a lot to adjust to. But I'll get used to it. I promise." Jubilee looked up at him. "Do you remember that summer when I was thirteen?"

"Of course." It was their one summer that rather than run to him as she always had, she had instead remained stiffly by her father's side as Atticus made his way off the ship. She had flinched then too when he touched her—tugging a small strand of her hair in greeting. As he had done since she was a child.

She had never told him what bothered her, but just as she did now she had shied away from his touch. Nothing more than the innocent touch of a friend in those days. It had been a month into their summer before she had grown comfortable with him once more.

"It's like then," Jubilee whispered. "You were patient with me, remember? You never made me feel guilty for avoiding you. That is why I trusted you with this. Because I know that this can work, just like it did then. Because you're you." She touched his cheek tentatively. Almost curiously. "I just need time, Atty. Please understand that."

Atticus curled his fingers through hers, still resting against his cheek. "You never told me what it was that kept you from me then."

"Someday I'll tell you. I promise."

Atticus watched her through narrowed eyes. Those godforsaken tears. They would be the death of him. Hadn't that been Aelia's way? Pushing him away and then drawing him back with a few forced tears? Only Jubilee's tears were not forced. She was fighting and failing to keep them back. She blinked rapidly against them and with each tear that managed to fall she wiped it away quickly.

He could walk away. Break the union and send her back to her family. Was it truly his fault that his parents insisted on ties that were bound to break? But one look at her and his resolve would crumble, and it was all in the visible way she was fighting those miserable tears—he couldn't send her back to her country in shame.

Ignoring the revulsion, he sat back down and pulled his plate towards him again. He couldn't send her back to her country with that sort of shame. No matter who she appeared to be now, she would always be his Jewess.

...

Placing the tray on his knees, Leopold was careful to avoid Julius's eyes. He was not willing to speak on Juliana and her family again and the anger that lingered within him would show all too clearly in his eyes.

"Why do you avoid me?" Julius's voice was low. Inviting. Threatening to break away all the defenses Leopold had prepared himself with.

"I do not know what you mean, my lord. Would I have offered to take the girl's place if I were avoiding you?" Leopold met the man's eyes only momentarily—long enough to please Julius.

Satisfied, Julius began to eat. "I was wondering why you were here instead of that Jewess." *That Jewess.* Would he ever say the girl's name?

"Jubilee is with her husband at the moment."

"I prefer it." Setting a hand over Leopold's, Julius smiled. "You have always taken better care of me."

Leopold glared back at him, ignoring the subtle hints in the man's voice. "Then why make her serve you? Why treat her like a slave? Why not let the poor child have one piece of her old life?"

"I have, Leopold. The girl has her faith. Do you think that I couldn't have taken that too? The Jewish and Christian faith are very closely intertwined. They come from the same beginnings do they not?"

"I wouldn't know, my lord."

"Of course, you wouldn't." Julius smiled. "You are too clever for such ridiculous ideologies. You know you would only be hurt in the end."

Unlike Julius, who could read all about the hatred that the people of Jubilee's faith held toward men like them, Leopold feared such words and Julius knew it. Could the scriptures they shared be true?

Julius touched Leopold's cheek, his normally hard, dark eyes softening as they looked into Leopold's blue ones. "I know you have missed Juliana, but tell me you have not seen the good in her being gone? With her mother dead, she was the last thing forcing us to hide. You saw how Juliana looked at us. That Jew had gotten into her head and turned her against us and she tried to get into yours. She whispered lies to you, Leopold. She tried to pull you away from me. This girl will do the same in time. Once she is comfortable.

"Do you think she doesn't know, Leopold? Do you think Malachi would not have told them of *vile* acts committed between us?" Julius laughed. "You think they didn't command their daughter to preach fire and brimstone if you didn't listen? Look at who the girl's grandfather is! Do you remember what he did to us? He threw stones at us, Leopold. That child will prove no different. Not in the end."

"You're wrong." Leopold croaked. "Juliana only meant to help."

"She meant to destroy, Leopold."

He was wrong. Juliana wouldn't wish any ill on him, no matter the circumstance. Nor Malachi, who had proved kinder than his father from the beginning. Two beings who carried such dark ancestry had never meant any harm to him. Surely Jubilee, created of their perfect mold couldn't be as Julius described. "You are wrong."

"Will you tell her then, Leopold? If you believe so strongly that the child is made of the love their kind preach, will you tell her what you are?"

No. The thought came before he could stop it. He knew Juliana would never have spoken of such a private thing with her daughter, and neither would he. Even if she chose the path her parents had, he knew the thoughts that would run through her mind were too much for him to bear. She would worry for his eternity and insist on speaking of her God in earnest, rather than the idle chatter while they prepared Julius's meals.

She would want to sit with him and speak in depth, insisting that to wait was to risk. She would not understand that he only had so much time left with Julius and did not want to spend it fighting him.

VI

Careful not to make any noise, Atticus eased the door closed, grateful for the soft light of the candle Jubilee left burning.

She slept facing the door and for the first time in months, she looked peaceful—her hands tucked up under her cheek, her dark hair fanning out around her. Moving closer, Atticus brushed her cheek. Traced the full set of her lips. In the soft light of the flame, she looked angelic.

Since their night in the triclinium, the walls that surrounded her were slowly beginning to crumble. She was opening up, revealing to him the parts of herself that he recognized as his Jewess. But still, she was hiding the very thing that had taken her away. Despite his patience, she still avoided his eyes. She didn't pull away from him but still, she flinched at his touch. Why? She allowed Leopold's touch. She allowed his fathers. But it was his, the one whose touch she had always welcomed before, that she shuddered at now. Was his touch truly so horrible as Julius Aquila's?

Did she ever truly welcome your touch, puppy, or were you simply blind to the disgust you brought her?

Despite her constant reassurance, the way she avoided him felt like the sharp blade of a knife to his chest. This wasn't like that summer when she had been a girl whom he was just beginning to see in a different light. Her rejection of him then had been softer. Innocent. He remembered the way she had taken his hand in hers, holding it to her chest just as she had in the triclinium. *"I'm sorry."* She whispered. *"I don't mean to do that."* She had curled her fingers through his, a smile twitching at the corner of her lips. *"It's not you though. I promise."* The smile had reached her eyes in a way he had yet to see since she had come to Rome. Whatever had haunted her in Galilee was nothing of what kept her from him here.

Atticus tried to focus on her words, rather than her body. It hadn't been him then and wasn't him now. But Jubilee's rejection brought more pain and doubt than Aelia ever had. Aelia was cold. Cruel. She lived to please herself and no one more. But not Jubilee. He had never known his Jubilee to be capable of cruelty. But neither had he ever known her to shut herself away so entirely. Even in Galilee, she hadn't hidden away. She had simply avoided his touch. What held her mind so tightly that she woke struggling in the dark of night, sweat glistening on ghostly white skin and a scream on her lips?

He had asked her once when she had escaped the dream entirely. "You never had those dreams before."

"We never slept in the same house, Atticus. How could you possibly know that?"

Was she accusing him of something? Was she implying he watched her? "Because you would have told me, Jubilee." It struck him that it was the very thing she had said to him in the beginning. The years apart had separated the both of them, destroying more than themselves. It had destroyed the only true relationship he had ever known. "There was a time when you wouldn't keep anything from me. Nothing, Jubilee. No matter how embarrassing or terrifying—no matter how much it hurt you to tell me."

Except for that summer.

"Please do not pretend that you haven't kept things from me, Atticus. And I do not mean since I came to Rome." She pressed her lips into a fine line to hide the trembling. "Do you know how that made me feel? To learn that you were married from my parents? You should have told me, Atty. In a letter at the very least. So I didn't spend three years of my life thinking I did something to drive you away."

Atticus's mouth opened and then closed again. Thick tears dripped lazily down Jubilee's cheeks. "What could you have done to drive me away, Jewess?"

Jubilee said nothing but turned away, her eyes shut tight against the tears. He knew what she was thinking. The well. "I would have been happy for you. So long as you were happy."

Sitting next to her, Atticus massaged his eyelids. "I wasn't happy, Jubilee. Not once in that accursed marriage was I happy. If it helps, I wish I had gone back."

"I wish you had never left."

I wish you had never left. There had been no anger in her voice. But still, there was something more than the brokenness. A resentment? Did she resent him for leaving? It seemed a rational answer. Through all the changes he could see in her, the stubborn will she had always possessed was still in her grasp and he was glad of it. Even if it was that stubborn will that kept her from him.

As he readied for bed, Atticus heard Jubilee move, her breath shifting from its steady rhythm to one of harsh panic. Turning he found her entangling in the blankets as she struggled. A small whimper escaped her lips.

Unwilling to face the screams again, Atticus let his hand graze across the stand, sending a heavy basin shattering to the floor. A small yelp escaped her lips as she sat up, her dark eyes wide. "Sorry."

Bending to retrieve the broken shards of clay he watched her draw her knees to her chest. Setting her chin on her knees she watched him. "I'm keeping you awake. "

"No. I don't sleep well at night." The ache in his stomach worsened, as it always did when he looked at her. Whatever she dreamed of drained all color from her skin and left her trembling visibly. "Will you still not tell me what those dreams are?"

"I told you, Atty. They are just dreams."

"Are they? Or are you too ashamed to admit the truth to me?" Dumping the shards onto the stand, he got into bed beside her, ignoring the way she inched away from him.

She is disgusted, puppy. Look at you. Pulling the blankets over himself he turned away from her.

"Goodnight." She said quietly.

In the following moments, he listened to her soft sobs chip away the silence. Despite their parent's hopes, the old friendship they had once shared was slow in its coming. Never had he hesitated to comfort her. To take her in his arms and hold her until her cries had ebbed. They had never even fought.

His heart ached for her. No matter the distance between them it couldn't stop the pain from rising in his chest to see so easily, in her eyes alone, the pain she carried within her. Whatever secrets she kept were eating at her, and no matter how hard she pushed him away he couldn't let her suffer alone.

Turning to her he touched her shoulder, desperate to ease her pain in any way he could. To his surprise, she didn't flinch but quieted. "I'm sorry. I'll be quiet."

"Don't be. I only wish you would trust me. Perhaps telling me would help."

Turning to face him she watched him through narrowed eyes. "Would speaking about your wife help you?" The words weren't spoken in cruelty but curiosity. "You hide your secrets as well as I do."

"I suppose I do." They settled back into silence, the few inches between them feeling like a crater. "Perhaps it would be best if I slept elsewhere."

Jubilee's hand was on his before he could move. "No." She breathed. "I don't want to sleep alone."

Before Rome she had never slept on her own, having always slept opposite her parents in their one-room home. She had neglected to realize before then how fearful of the dark she was. It was what drew her back to Atticus after her late-night wanderings.

The memories of *him* lurked in the darkness. When she wandered the Domus at night she could swear she heard *his* footsteps following her, watching her as she suffered from the very thing she had always wanted. The thing *he* had stolen.

She had taken to sleeping with a lit candle, trusting Atticus to extinguish it when he came to bed. "I don't like the dark."

Atticus stared back at her before answering. "I do not like it either."

"You don't have to lie to me, Atticus. I am not a child."

"I am not lying, Jubilee." Lying back against the pillows he watched as a sheepish grin turned her lips.

"Can I ask why? I mean will this venture into questions?"

"I don't know. It just started one night." Blood started to pound in his head. "There is a presence in the darkness. Something that makes me feel helpless."

"Anything can happen in the dark. Without anyone even knowing." She spoke so softly that Atticus had to lean it to catch it.

Ignoring his uncertainty he touched her cheek, grateful for the way she leaned into it rather than away. "Do you want me to keep the candle burning until you fall asleep?"

She shook her head, silent tears pooling on her cheeks. "I am all right. I just don't want to be alone in it."

Doing his best to ignore the quiver in her voice, Atticus turned to extinguish the candle before something stopped him. "Jubilee?" He tried again. "Would you like me to keep the candle burning?" She bit down hard on her lip and nodded, thick tears blurring her eyes. "I'll put it out after you have gone to sleep."

Laying back he noticed the way she twitched, looking very much as though she were going to lean in but caught herself. Lying back against the pillows she curled under the blanket, her wide eyes watching him almost childishly. "Thank you, Atty."

...

Atticus woke early the next morning, only to find Jubilee had already left. Stifling the expected disappointment he prepared for the day before hurrying towards the gardens, where she prayed before tending to her grandfather.

Not finding her in the gardens, he made his way to the shop.

What did you expect from one fruitless night? She doesn't love you.. Not after what happened.

Shaking his head, Atticus forced the thought away. They had both been responsible that night. Jubilee knew that. Pressing his fingers to his temples he groaned. His head pounded and he yearned for wine. To forget Jubilee in that bittersweet liquid.

Thoughts of wine carried him to the shop, a few hours of work and he could reward himself that delirium. Lost in the thought, he almost missed the faint sounds of someone rummaging through the bottles and shelves drifting from the shop. Cursing, Atticus ripped the curtain back—the intruder yelped and spun to face him, her dark eyes wide.

"Jubilee? What are you doing in here?"

"I needed fennel." She replied. "I'm happy to see you awake. I didn't want to disturb you but I cannot seem to find it on my own."

Moving past her, he combed through the shelves. "Is everything all right with Julius?"

"He is complaining of pain in his lower back." She muttered. "He will not let me examine him but I believe it may be stones."

Finding what she needed, Atticus turned to find her walking the room, new tears dripping down her cheeks. Catching his eye she dried them quickly, a shy smile pulling at her lips. "I miss it. I don't know who I am without medicine."

"I am sorry. He shouldn't be doing this to you."

"I'll survive." Taking the fennel she quickly sorted it out. "It's worth it, knowing that if I cannot be with my family, I at least have a way of feeling closer to my mother."

Atticus followed after her. "And what about your father? Medicine was always what you did with him."

"And I will practice it again. But I have to be patient now."

Nearing the room, Atticus stopped her. "Do you want me to help with him?"

Jubilee smiled. "You have an entire shop, Atty. I have him." Turning her back to him she bounced into the room. "*Salve, Avus Carissime.*"

Atticus's lips twitched at her tone. *Hello, Dearest Grandfather.* He could hear, rather than see the mischievous smile on her lips. For just a moment his old Jubilee was shining through the cracks of the stranger he called his wife.

For the first time, the man was speechless as his granddaughter sat carefully at the edge of his bed. "You will have to drink this, *Avus.*"

"I do not want that." The man was too weak to feed himself, but with one feeble hand, he could easily slap a cup from the girl's hand. "Leave me be."

Sighing, Jubilee kneeled and mopped up the mess with the ends of her tunic. "Well if you want to be comfortable you will need to take it." None of the irritation in her voice was visible on her face. "Unless of course, you would prefer Atticus perform a *Lithotomy.*"

"Or Jubilee," Atticus spoke up. "From what I remember she has far more experience in such things than myself." He met Jubilee's eyes and noticed the small smile on her lips. "Though of course, it would be rather silly to submit yourself to an operation when you can simply take the fennel."

Julius glared between the two. "I'll take the fennel."

Atticus was gone a moment. One mere moment and as he neared the room, fennel in hand, the all too familiar sound of Jubilee's tears met him.

Only now they were tears of anger. "I won't."

"I won't touch the fennel until I have paid my respects to the gods and seeing as I am unable to do so on my own, you will have to do it for me."

"Well, then I am afraid you will have to suffer. Because I will not do that."

"Then perhaps you and your husband should begin thinking of another place to call home. How would your husband feel to know you lost his shop?"

"You wouldn't do that."

"Oh, I would." Julius's voice was dangerous. "We made a deal, Jewess. You take care of me and everything I own becomes yours."

"On the basis that I still get to practice my faith. I will not pay tribute to a false god."

"I'll do it." Pulling Jubilee aside, Atticus grabbed a reed.

"You shouldn't have to do that." Jubilee's hand rubbed at her arm, which he had grabbed too roughly in his anger. "It doesn't need to be done."

"It will not hurt me to do it." He lit the reed swiftly and set it to the emblem as he had seen his mother do so often growing up. "There. It is done." Avoiding his wife's eyes, Atticus left the two alone. The brief glimpse of his Jubilee was gone and the hollow look had crept back in.

But that glimpse had been enough. No matter what it took he would bring out the Jubilee he now knew still lived within her.

...

Atticus found himself watching Jubilee wherever time allowed. Despite her desire to be in the shop, she was devoted to her grandfather. She went to him in the night when his pain worsened. She seemed to sense any shift in him and was ready with whatever he called for. Julius was cruel and demanding, but Jubilee never faltered. She never grew angry but served with inhuman humility.

But she was not immune to the words the man spat. Each morning she was found in the gardens, her forehead pressed to the cool stone. "Oh God, I don't know how much more I can take. He is cruel, Adonai. He is so cruel. I have tried to share You with him but he refuses to hear."

The tears confused him. He knew she was no stranger to the thoughts people carried toward her faith. She had known adversity from the time of her birth, her family being one of the original traitors of the Jewish faith. They were a family who not only turned their backs on the Laws of Moses but walked with Romans, welcoming the Albanus's into their home even before the Jesus had called to them.

"Give me strength, God. Give me the patience to show him who you are."

As each morning passed the words changed—her mood shifting from one of defeat to one of obedience. "Give me the words he needs to hear. I won't reach him without You."

When they dined together she spoke with increasing grief of the decreasing health of the man who despised her. There was love in her voice. Love for a man who had never spoken a kind word to anyone.

"Why do you dread it, Jubilee? You will be well served when that man is gone." They all would be. "The man is a devil."

"And so I should turn my back on him?" Jubilee replied. "Because he is cruel? What if it had been that way with the Messiah? Turning His back so easily on those who curse His name?"

"Don't bring your faith into this. What sort of god demands someone love a man who only spews hatred upon them and their family?"

"Jesus was killed, Atticus. He suffered so that people like my grandfather could hope for peace. I will not give up on him."

"Your Jesus didn't know Julius Aquila. The man deserves all the fires of Hell."

Shaking her head, Jubilee set aside her cloth and stood. Without a word, she left the triclinium. Atticus watched her go, unwilling to stop her. If she wanted to spend her life doting on a devil, let her.

Taking up the wine he made his way to their room. The woman was too kind for her good. But it wouldn't last. Not with someone like Julius Aquila. The man would break her and her faith if she wasn't careful.

When the wine was finished and Jubilee hadn't returned he went in search of her. She was his wife. She should be caring for his needs. Not the demands of an incessant, overgrown child.

He found Julius asleep in his room with Jubilee nowhere to be seen. When he didn't find her in the gardens or her mother's room, he knew of only one place she could be.

He found her in the shop with her back pressed tight against the wall. Her face pointed upwards toward the sky as her lips moved silently. A candle sat on either side of her, illuminated the tears on her cheeks.

Careful not to disturb her, Atticus lit the remaining candles and waited. He wondered if she would be angry to know how often he listened to her prayers. Somehow he knew she wouldn't. She would be glad of it, thinking he listened in yearning. She would speak of her god the way she used to.

The thought struck him odd. They had been married nearly three months and he could count on one hand the number of times her faith had been brought to his attention from her lips. In their summers before she had never let a day go by without mention of her god. She had shared her prayers with him willingly. Now, along with the other pieces that made her his Jewess, she kept it tucked away.

Was he to blame for her newfound shame in her faith? He tried to remember the last time he had asked her about it—the last time he let her know that he cared to hear what she believed in.

Cursing under his breath, Atticus stood and removed things from their shelves.

"Do you wish Hell upon Aelia?" Her voice, though little more than a whisper, was enough to make his fingers twitch, sending a glass bottle shattering across the dirt floor.

Avoiding her eyes, Atticus bent to retrieve the broken pieces. "I wish a thousand Hells upon that wench."

"Atticus." Jubilee breathed. "You admit that so willingly. Does it not scare you? To feel such hatred?"

"You didn't know Aelia." He spit. "Now get over here."

Standing she joined him at the table. "I have known evil men, Atticus. Men far worse than Julius." Taking in the supplies on the table she raised an eyebrow. "What is this?"

"Your grandfather may have denied you the ability to practice medicine, but he said nothing about helping me formulate them. I am running low and need your help."

The girl appeared to vibrate with excitement as she drew the chrysanthemum to her, her right hand already waiting with mortar and pestle, and Atticus found himself watching her—head bowed and her eyes narrowed in concentration.

"It's not easy for me, Atticus." She said suddenly. "To tend to a man who is joyful to share the hatred he has for my father. To love a man who speaks of the things he did to my mother when she wasn't what he wanted her to be? There is no regret in him. But I can't turn my back on him. It is not what my mother would do and it isn't what my father would do. You heard the things he has said about *Abba*. He said those things to his face and still *Abba* continues to hope for good in him. And I will do the same. For *Imma* at least."

"There is no good in him, Jubilee. Not everyone is you."

The woman sat back, abandoning the powders she had yet to sort. "What of me, Atticus? I am not perfect. If you knew anything about me, could you ever wish Hell upon me as gleefully as you do Aelia?"

"No."

"Why?"

Atticus swore. How had he managed to find himself in a debate of Eternity? "Because you are good, Jubilee, even if you aren't perfect. You are kind. You have your god."

"By luck of birth, Atticus. Who is to say what I would be elsewhere? Who is to say I wouldn't be Julius? Or those men who nailed Jesus to a cross?" She shook her head. "I know I wouldn't be."

"You're perfect, Jubilee. Do not compare yourself to—"

"I have wished a person to Hell." She told quietly. The words seemed to have poured out of their volition. When he glanced up at her, her dark eyes were wide and blurred by tears. She pinched at her wrist before Atticus took her hand. "Just like you do. I know you won't understand why it is such an awful thing. But it is, Atticus. To hope that someone would spend eternity in misery is the lowest thing you can do to someone." Her voice had drifted to nothing more than a whisper so low Atticus had to lean forward to hear the rest. "I know that and I still hope for it even now. I know that I shouldn't. But I do. I take relish in thinking of it, and it scares me how easily I can picture it."

"That isn't the same, Jubilee. You would never truly hurt another."

"Wouldn't I?" She croaked. "The Lord says that to hate is to have committed a murder and I hate this person. I have murdered him a hundred times in my anger. In a hundred different ways."

"But you are still good, Jubilee. Even without your god, you are incapable of the sort of cruelty that Julius breathes. There are plenty of Romans who deserve well. My parents deserve well. Some people are evil, it has nothing to do with where they come from."

"But does that mean we should consign them to Hell so easily?"

"I don't know, Jubilee. Speak of your faith, but do not ask me to agree with it." Atticus pressed a finger to his temple. "Please, just enjoy your time here."

Jubilee returned to her work, leaving the only sound to be the subtle scratch of tools against the wood. "Thank you." Her eyes met his, new tears blurring the dark circles. But a hint of a smile shone through. "I needed this."

"Sometimes you have to break a few rules." Atticus smiled. "Get out of that room and I can give you a lot more than this."

VII

Sibyl watched as the darkness crept in, moving through the Domus walls like the thick fog of morning. It snuffed out the freshly lit emblem of the *lararium* and the candles that surrounded it. It kissed her like hot, fetid breath, drawing beads of sweat to her skin. She wanted to move. She wanted to run. But she couldn't. She could do nothing but let the darkness wrap around her like a blanket of isolation.

Her heart roared in her ears, making her head pound. Sweat soaked through her tunic. Her hair. It dripped down her skin in streams. She had always imagined the darkness as cold. But this was hot. As though an unseen fire surrounded her.

From the darkness came the sound of something scraping against the marble floors. "Regulus?" She breathed. There was no answer. Nothing but the harsh scratch of iron against the marble. "Regulus! Regulus, please."

Sibyl felt the blood drain from her face in the following silence. Regulus would never ignore her now. By the gods, where was he? What dreadful creature lived in the darkness?

Forcing her leaden feet forward she could walk only a few steps before she found herself falling into the darkness, hurtling towards the invisible floor. Tears stinging her eyes, she dragged her hands across the marble, searching for anything that might banish the darkness. Finding nothing she let out a small sob. The darkness was suffocating. Getting shakily to her feet she stumbled toward the wall, and the candles of the *lararium*, she groped for the flint.

The laugh started quietly. Soft and near unrecognizable for what it was. It built slowly. Ominously. Until it rang through the corridor, echoing off the walls and surrounding her. Using the wall as her guide she pushed forward into the darkness.

Hot burning breath licked her neck like fire and she screamed. The laughing heightened. Dark and cruel. Picking up her tunic she ran blindly but the fire stayed at her heels, burning the hairs of her neck.

"Sibyl." Stumbling over her feet in the darkness she fell to the floor, hitting her head against the wall.

"No." The heat licked at her skin. "No." On hands and knees, she hurried forward, only to have her feet pulled out beneath her. Her chin hit the marble floor. Sobbing, she wrapped her arms around herself, shielding her face against the unseen flame.

"Sibby." Something soft touched her. Something cold. Her eyes fluttered open hesitantly to find Regulus looming over her, his handsome face creased with worry. In one hand he held a burning candle, its warmth kissing her cheek. "You hit your head." He said, touching a tender spot on her forehead. "And your chin."

"I was running." She whispered. "It was so dark. And hot. I tripped."

Regulus raised an eyebrow but said nothing as he pulled her into his arms, lifting her easily despite her weight.

Looking around she found herself in her room. "I was dreaming?" It had felt so real. "Oh, it was horrible, Regulus." Feeling the weight of the darkness closing in on her she pressed her face into her husbands neck.

Setting her on the bed, Regulus tucked the blankets in around her before climbing next to her. "Why do you keep them from me, Sibyl? Why won't you share what haunts you?"

Sibyl thought about the darkness. Of the hopelessness. The anguish. Regulus didn't believe in the unseen world that often hid themselves within dreams. Not like she hoped Jubilee would. Would the girl believe her if she told her what she felt the dreams were telling her?

"You have been having those dreams for months, Sibyl. But never like that. I tried waking you for five minutes before you fell. You hit your head on the stand."

Her hand went to her forehead and she winced. It was no wonder the pain had been so real. Already she could feel the beginning of a goose egg protruding from her skin. "What about my chin?"

"You tried to crawl away and got tangled in your tunic. I couldn't catch you before you hit the floor."

Sibyl could only nod as she remembered the heat. Holding her breath she touched the back of her neck, where the fire had licked her skin. It was soft and smooth. Untouched by the evil one's breath.

Lying back against her husband's chest she let the steady rhythm of his beating heart calm her own. Despite the two burning candles the room still seemed too dark. It cast shadows upon the unlit corners of the room. "Will you light another candle?"

Regulus lit three more candles before opening the window, allowing a small shaft of moonlight to reflect off the marble floors. Crawling back under the covers he pulled her to him and stroked her hair. "Will you still not tell me, Sibby?"

"I am not sure that I can. It is too confusing."

Regulus pressed his forehead to hers. His dark eyes watched her curiously. "Why don't you go for a visit with Jubilee tomorrow? You have been saying for weeks you want to."

"I don't want to bother her, Regulus." Her voice was small again. "What would she want with an old bat like me?"

Regulus cuffed her chin. "Jubilee loves you, Sibyl. The girl lives in a home full of men, she may appreciate some lady time." Bringing her eyes to his he watched her sternly. "You are going and that is an order."

"Since when do you order me?" She asked in a halfhearted attempt at jest.

Laughing, Regulus kissed her. "Roll over." When she listened he pulled her to him, wrapping an arm around her waist. His breath was hot against her ear as he laid his head on her neck. "Now go to sleep."

…

"That wretched, foul excuse for a man." The words slipped from Sibyl's mouth not for the first time that morning. She had long ago stopped feeling guilty for the thoughts she held toward Julius Aquila. Her father had despised the man. "That wretched, foul man." The letter she held felt like a weight in her hands. Twenty-nine years and the damage her father had inflicted upon Juliana still crippled her at the idea of seeing him.

Sibyl ached to see her friend now more than ever. She had looked forward to seeing her when they watched their children marry. Instead, she had been left with a letter, explaining why the woman was forced to stay back. When would that wretched man die?

Setting the letter aside she took out the old letters the two had passed. Slipping them out of their wrappings she bound the letters the two had passed as children and set them aside for Jubilee. Perhaps seeing them would bring the child comfort in her mother's absence.

Moving to the ones they had shared after Juliana's move, she pored herself into the pages, reading again Juliana's words of faith. She hoped to comfort the broken child within her, still haunted by the darkness.

She admitted to feeling the call to her friend's faith long before the years had separated them. But always it left her when she left Galilee and Juliana and the constant reminder of what their faith provided. It was when the boat hit the open sea and the shores of Galilee could no longer be seen that the questions would come and doubt drowned out everything she had learned. How could an unseen god serve as any source of comfort? But somewhere in the years they had been apart she had found that old curiosity seeping back. Along with a bone-deep ache within her.

Unfolding the latest letter once more, Sibyl read it through. "You must think me so cruel asking Jubilee to put her faith in the Lord when I can't face a simple fear of my own." She heard the woman's voice as clearly as though she sat beside her. "But in some way, I feel as though I am not supposed to be there. It's so strange. At times I feel myself drawn to Him when the memories come. Others I feel as though I don't even know Him. As though I have never known Him. I think I am drifting, Sibby. I always do when I think of returning to Rome. Jubilee needs Rome. She needs to breathe new air. It is the very thing that will renew her faith. But I feel as though my faith will suffer if I leave Galilee.

I love my father, Sibyl. Despite everything I have always loved him, and I will pray until his last breath that he finds his way. But I know that I cannot see him again. Too many things happened in those final days that are best left untouched.

I can only hope that you understand. I need to be here. Here, in solitude is where I'll find my peace."

Sibyl frowned. Juliana loved to speak of the healing she had found in their god. She spoke of freedom from not only her past sins but pain. And yet the pain her father inflicted still clung to her like a stench that wouldn't fade. Why hadn't her god healed her of that? Why did he let it pull her away from him?

Binding the letters once more she set them back in their casing. Regulus would insist she saw Jubilee if he found her poring over old letters. She had been able to skirt around his orders once, but if her disposition didn't resolve itself he would leave her no choice. He wouldn't understand that she wasn't ready—that she wanted to be sure of her decision before she disrupted Jubilee's life again.

Dinner that night was a quiet affair. At Sibyl's request, Regulus put on his best face with their son. When forced to fill the silence they spoke of supplies for the shop.

When the people of Rome required anything, they went to Regulus. Beginning with the small ship his father had gifted him, he had sailed from Germania. To Ephesus and China. Building from the small fortune he had been given, until he was the owner of an entire merchant fleet, surpassing his father's success with ships sailing across the world. Beef and corn from Rome. Pottery and papyrus from Britannia. They brought back medicines from

Greece and sent them to Jerusalem, India, and Sicily. It was something that never ceased to amaze Sibyl. That the quiet, working-class man she had fallen in love with had worked his way to equestrianship, providing for her in ways she knew a senator never could.

"Write down what you'll need and have Leopold bring it over." Regulus kept his eyes on his food as he spoke. "I'll visit the warehouses in the morning."

Kicking him under the table, Sibyl glared at him.

Sighing he tried again. "I have been telling your mother that Jubilee is sure to be anxious for time with a woman. Perhaps you might be able to distract Julius long enough to give your wife a chance to visit."

"Slip him a vial of Valerian," Sibyl muttered. "Let him sleep and give everyone a chance to breathe."

Atticus snorted. "The man would smell it. The old man is becoming paranoid in his old age. He doesn't let anything pass his lips without Jubilee first taking a share of it."

"That man is going to run Jubilee mad." Regulus spit.

"He already has. The woman is delusional. She believes there is good in him." Atticus scoffed. "Julius Aquila. What will it take for the Christians to learn that not all can be saved? It wasn't enough to watch their prophet hang from a cross?"

"They believe in hope, Atticus." Sibyl blushed as both pairs of eyes found hers. "I find that rather beautiful."

"Don't tell me your new god is the god of the Jews." Rather than his usual teasing smile, Regulus watched her intently. "Are you chasing after a god unseen now?"

"Would it be so wrong if I was?" Her heart had begun to pound hard against her ribs. She had never known Regulus to be put off by her gods.

"Only that there is a level of danger in believing those things, Sibyl," Regulus spoke softly, as though he feared being overheard. "You have heard the things being said. How long do you think it will be before the recognition between Christians and Jews becomes evident? Their kind will never be accepted, Sibyl."

"There is talk among the people that Claudius will make the decree in time," Atticus added. "If the Jews don't settle down there will be riots on his hands. He'll have no excuse but to ban them again."

"And what will you do if this comes about?" Sibyl demanded. "Will you follow Jubilee?"

Atticus laughed. "The girl looks as fitting of a Roman title as you do, Mother. She'll remain in Rome."

"You think she will turn her back on her people, Atticus? Whether the two see eye to eye or not, the Jews and the Christians share the same core values. Many share the same ancestry. If her people go, Jubilee will follow. You best hope the rumors are just that unless you desire a new life in Galilee."

"Give the boy a break, Sibyl." Regulus sighed. "Atticus never said he agreed it was right. As for me, you know my stance on Jews. They are free to worship as any. But it doesn't eradicate the fact that a war is brewing. Their people bring violence to the streets daily. I won't ask Jubilee to deny her faith but I will be asking her to be careful. Her parents entrusted her in our care and I will do all in my power to keep her from harm. Even if that means being silenced in public."

"The woman won't keep silent, Father. She speaks of her faith with Julius daily. It's as though she doesn't hear the words he spits at her and her god. If she continues on it's only a matter of time before he sends the Romans after her."

Sibyl scoffed. "Julius would never do such a thing. He fears embarrassment."

"Even so." Regulus intervened. "The girl must remember that she isn't in Nazareth anymore. Faith like hers is dangerous to the people of Rome and it will get her killed if she isn't careful."

Sibyl glared across the table. "I think I am done here. Atticus, it was lovely to see you. Please wish Jubilee well." Tossing her cloth down she left the room, ignoring Regulus's call for her to come back.

It had been years since the two had agreed on anything and it took the abuse of the Christian faith to bring them together. It was laughable. Her son had been raised among them. He had fallen in love with one and there he sat, mocking them. What would they say if they knew she truly felt drawn toward the religion herself?

She walked the peristyle, breathing in the scent of roses from the courtyard and letting the sound of bubbling water calm her. When she could trust her temper she went in search of her husband. Nearing the tablinum she heard him curse. Entering she found Regulus crumpling a letter. "Is everything all right?"

"It's nothing, Sibby. It's only work." He tucked the letter away before she could reach for it. Seeing she wouldn't relent he went on. "There was some rain in Ostia. One of the warehouses was flooded."

Sibyl followed after him. "Will they be needing you there?"

Regulus avoided her eyes as he moved to his desk. "I will have to go and help them sort it out. Will you be all right while I am gone?"

"Well, why don't I go with you? It's been years since I have accompanied you."

"This won't be like the other times. I am going to be busy most days and you won't have Juliana there to keep you occupied."

"Which leaves plenty of time to shop." Sibyl smiled. "I have been meaning to get Jubilee some things. From what Atticus has said it seems as though Julius keeps her too busy to replace the few tunics she brought with her. She'll be needing more."

"Really, Sibyl. It is a short trip. I will be back in two days."

Sibyl felt her blood run cold in her veins as her husband avoided her eyes. "If I didn't know any better I would think you were hiding something. This is your third trip to Ostia in six months, Regulus. I have begun to lose count of your trips over the years. None of which you have wanted me on."

Regulus slammed his fist on the desk. "Do not start this again, Sibyl. We are finally past it."

"What is in Ostia, Regulus? And do not tell me it's work." Her voice quivered miserably. "Every time you come back you are shaken. You're irritable. You can barely look me in the eyes. I know you, Regulus. I know it isn't a woman, so what is it?"

Regulus glared back at her, his breath harsh. Cursing, he lowered himself into his seat, looking as though he had aged a lifetime. "This stays between us, Sibyl." The man's voice was nothing more than a whisper. "You must promise me."

Kneeling beside her husband, Sibyl took his hand. "I promise."

VIII

November

Though she remained silent, the shift in Jubilee was audible. She no longer pushed him away when he wanted her but went willingly. She aimed to please without taking any pleasure for herself. She invited him in and closed herself away.

It had been the night in the shop that had sparked the sudden change within her—moving with him as they walked towards the cubicula. Allowing his hand on her back. Letting him kiss her goodnight. It wasn't until they had climbed into bed that she drew away from him.

Settling in beside her, Atticus stared up at the ceiling, watching the flame of the candle cast shadows across the room.

He couldn't get it out of his head. Each time he felt the space between them grow smaller, she pulled back. Why marry him if it wasn't what she desired? Even if it was something her parents had wished for, it would not have been enough to push her.

"I'm sorry." Jubilee's voice was small and though he couldn't see the tears, the sound of her voice told him they were there. "I don't want to push you away. I love you, Atticus."

"Then why, Jubilee?" He couldn't bring himself to comfort her now. He wanted answers. A reason for the constant push and pull that Aelia had been so fond of.

"I don't know." She cried. "I don't know" And she didn't. She would trust Atticus with her life. Hadn't she once trusted him with the very thing that was stolen from her? The thing he now expected? She loved him. She wanted him. Her body cried out for him, only to be quieted when his touch became anything that hinted at his desire for her. Why must her past cling to her like a blood-sucking rodent to its prey?

God, release me from this burden. Destroy this spirit of fear within me. Don't let him win. Please don't let him win.

Opening her eyes, she rolled over to find Atticus watching her. He had inched closer and when he spoke the wine on his breath made her dizzy. "What do you feel when I touch you?" She let his fingers trace down her side, making her shiver.

Clinging to scripture she pressed closer, unwilling to push him away. His thumb traced her cheekbones. Her jaw. Her lips. Heart pounding she let his lips graze hers, waiting for the scream of fear that would pull her back. When it didn't come she let Atticus fill the gap. His hand resting on her neck, his thumb caressing her cheek. She let him draw her closer until no space was left between them and for one beautiful moment, she let the world fall away, enjoying the soft, comforting moment she knew would end.

Atticus felt the subtle change in her. Whatever had shifted in her had been broken. As his fingers grazed her hip he felt her jerk, before taking his hand and putting it away from her. Pulling away he grazed her cheek, waiting until she found her voice.

"I'm sorry. I'm sorry." Those two words poured from her, tumbling one after the other until they were unrecognizable.

He kissed her, quieting the steady stream of shame. "Don't be sorry, Jewess. All I want is to see you trying. Don't shut me out."

Though still hesitant of his touch something within her had broken away in that moment. She did not simply tolerate his touch but seemed to welcome it. Their nights in the shop had become their little secret. His glimpse of his Jewess had ignited a fire within him to bring her back out and it was in the shop, nothing but candlelight and their work, that she slowly began to emerge. Drawn out by the stories of the patients who came to him.

Atticus loved watching as she leaned forward, a soft smile on her lips. She never hesitated to jump in and give her guesses as to what ailed the patient, nor did she shy away from telling him what she would have done differently. Together they lived for the nights that found only them in the dim candlelight, the old threads of their friendship weaving back together.

…

Atticus smiled as Jubilee entered the shop, sending a slight shiver up her spine. "I'm almost ready."

Taking her spot at the table, Jubilee couldn't help but watch the way his bones moved sickeningly beneath the translucent skin of his wrists. He had lost more weight in their three months of marriage. His face continued to thin underneath the whiskers that covered his chin and his tunic hung loosely. She had always known him for his round face. She had loved him for his soft and gentle hugs and the way his dimples caved deeply in his plush cheeks. To be in his arms now was terrifying in ways beyond the memories of *him*. He was like bone—hard and cold.

Excusing herself, Jubilee hurried back towards the kitchen. Putting meat over the fire, she cut up fruits and vegetables. Cheese and bread. Retrieving the meat from the fire she cut it into sections and placed it among the other foods. With a jug of watered wine, she hurried back to find Atticus still arranging the table.

Setting the food among the supplies, she watched his eyes graze over the food and go to the wine. "It's watered." She told him. Cursing, Atticus went back to work. "You can't live off wine alone, Atticus. You need to eat."

"Eat it yourself, Jubilee. You could serve to put a little meat on your bones."

His words, rather than hurt her as he intended, made her eyes narrow angrily. "I'm perfectly comfortable, thank you. As I remember you to be before."

"It's hard to keep confident when your wife can't stand the look of you." He spit carelessly.

"I apologize if my indifference has caused you pain," Jubilee replied quietly. "But please don't pretend this started with me, Atticus. This change in you was the first thing I noticed."

"Because it was a change that was needed, Jubilee."

"Is that what Aelia told you?"

The muscles in Atticus' body went tight. His fingers gripped the edge of the table until they ached. "Don't mention her name to me."

"I'm sorry. I shouldn't have said it." Moving beside him, Jubilee took his hands, gently easing them from the table. "But you really must eat, Atty. Please?"

Atticus glared down at their hands. He could feel the few tendrils that had begun to connect them beginning to fray once more. Why must she continue to pester him over food and wine? He had lost all control when Aelia came into his life. What he did. Whom he saw. He would not let it happen with Jubilee. Not when she remained turned off by the idea of him and sex. Not when food and wine remained his only choices even now. He had gone to Greece at his father's demand. Came home at his mother's plea. He had married Jubilee at the first few tears on her part. This was his very own and it would not be taken away from him.

Picking at the food, Jubilee watched as Atticus continued working on the instruments. Even the items she placed herself were taken back up and moved meticulously until everything was as he wanted them. None of this man she called her husband was the man she once called a friend and she needn't ask to know that the woman who came before her had brought about the change in him. The thought was frightful.

I know that I am failing him, Lord. But I am trying. I want to let go of what has been done to me, but it clings to me even now. Even as I long for him. Oh God, I love him. Let him see it. Let him see that I mean what I say. I beg of you do not let me lose him now. Not like this.

Setting her hand over his, she clasped it tightly. "Atticus. It's okay. It doesn't need to be perfect."

"You don't understand." Snatching his hand back he started over.

Taking his hands once more she pressed them tightly to her chest, holding him in place. "I do." She had picked up her own mindless ticks in their years apart. Hand wringing. Washing three times when she bathed. She had sent the neighborhood boys to the well every day for three months after it had happened. Often twice in one day. She bathed until her skin was red and raw, bleeding at the slightest touch. "I understand, Atticus." Shaking back her tunic she showed him the skin of her wrist, marked with bruises and red crescent moons.

Atticus stared at the wounds on her wrists before clearing his throat. "What does that prove, Jubilee?" He croaked.

"That life is cruel. We do not always have control of most, if any of what happens to us. So we look for the littlest things that we can control and when we find it we abuse it." She glanced down at her wrist. It had once been a simple habit of nerves that had quickly become a means of comfort. A way to keep her mind present. It gave her something to feel besides the overwhelming nothing that threatened to overcome her. "That is why you do this, is it not? I mean you have always been a bit particular but nothing like this. And you never once worried over food and wine. It isn't healthy, Atticus." Traitorous tears burned her eyes and her voice quivered.

Reaching up, Atticus wiped the tears from her cheeks. Jubilee leaned into his hand, her eyes closing at the touch. "Just let it go, Jubilee." Taking the wine he left her alone, forgetting about his stories.

Extinguishing the candles she followed after him. "God show me what I must do. Tell me what I must do and I will do it." She would do anything to see him healthy and whole as he once was.

Carry your cross, Beloved.

Jubilee stumbled in the dark. Her resolve wavered at the gentle voice that nudged her soul. *Carry your cross.* Was that what it would take? Must she truly offer herself up to him to heal him?

Fear gripped her chest like an iron chain. Each step to their cubicula leaden as fear told her to walk past. To spend the night in her mother's cubicula. Why must she carry her cross when he refused to carry his own? Why must she put herself aside when he refused to do the same?

Has he not?

The thought stopped her only feet from their room. *Has he not?* She remembered their first night. Of all the nights she pulled away. Denying him the very thing a wife was called to gift her husband. He never grew angry with her. No matter the pain her rejection caused him he left her to herself when she drew away.

Forcing back the voice that threatened to pull her away, she pushed forward.

Atticus sighed as Jubilee came into their room, her arms wrapped tight around herself. She trembled as she slipped the carafe from his fingers. "How long are you going to pretend wine is all you need?"

"As long as it takes for you to realize your god is no more helpful than wine."

Rather than fight back, Jubilee pressed closer to him. Her fingers grazed his chest. "Come to me instead." The girl looked as though she were ready to keel over but she didn't recant. "Be with me."

"You don't want me, Jubilee."

"I do." She kissed him hard, her fingers curling into his hair. When he tried to push her away she pressed closer still. "I want you, Atticus."

"Don't do this to me, Jubilee." He wouldn't open himself up to her only to have another door slammed in his face.

"Please, Atticus. I'm trying."

He glared back at her. "I don't want to see you slipping away when we finish. Too sick to even look at me."

A touch of fear seemed to melt away from her as the words slipped from his mouth. His voice was small and shameful. "I won't, Atty. I won't leave you." Her fingers caressed his cheek. "I want this, Atticus. I want you."

Unable to bear it anymore Atticus closed the space between them. She kept her word. She didn't pull away. But neither did she take any pleasure.

Atticus could feel the way she shook as he lay back beside her, her fingers tangling and untangling in the blankets. True to her word she didn't leave. "Why, Jubilee?"

"Just leave it, Atticus." Pulling the blanket to her chin she turned her back to him.

Why had she done it if not of her own accord? Why let him take her all those nights if it was something that disgusted her? Had he demanded it of her? Had he made her feel obligated? No. He knew he hadn't. He had given her the option to stop their first night and she refused. Even as tears spilled down her cheeks she had urged him to continue.

Again and again, the same questions plagued him. Why marry him and then shut down? Why make love to him but escape into her mind? Why had she done it all if she hated being with him?

Not you, Beloved.

...

Atticus couldn't get the thought out of his head. *Not you, Beloved.* He did not take comfort in the thought. Each night, when he woke to Jubilee's screams, horrid images pressed in on him. If not him then who? What could have created such fear in her that the moment a touch turned to intimacy she fell apart? She was fine. She kissed him and she didn't shrink away as she often had before. It wasn't until he laid her across the bed that her trembling began.

It hadn't been like their first night when she jolted at his simple touch.

"I'm sorry." She said, moving back toward him.

He said nothing but stood patiently, waiting for her to move first. When she merely stood he sighed and sat at the edge of the bed. *What would she want with someone like you, puppy?* Pushing back the voice he stood once more and took her arms, holding her in place. "Look at me." He breathed. "There is no rush. Now just sit and breathe. We won't do anything until you are ready."

Sitting and drawing her knees to her chest she closed her eyes.

She sat there for hours. Frozen. The thought had crossed his mind then, as it often did when she fought him but he had pushed it away, just as he did now. That couldn't be it. Not his Jewess. It was him. It had to be him.

...

Julius sighed as Jubilee entered his room. The smile she tossed his way grated his nerves the way Juliana's tears always had. She was worse than his daughter. Juliana may have been weak, but she never bothered to hide her distaste for him. She never hid her anger behind sugar-coated smiles and false kindness.

Where her mother had been docile to a fault, his granddaughter refused to falter in her ways. No amount of words deterred her. No threats on his part could make her turn away from her ridiculous god. She spoke of her god as she cared for him, telling stories of expectant virgins and men who fathered nations. She gave him a headache.

Ignoring her, he focused on the pain in his hand, clasping and unclasping his palm.

"Does that still bother you?" She nodded toward his scar.

"On occasion."

Abandoning the tray at his side she held out a small, brown hand. "May I?"

Julius hesitated, unsure of what she planned. But there was no malice in her eyes and when he relinquished his hand to her she held it gently, examining the scar that covered his palm. Thick and pink and blistered.

"Do you want something for it? I can get aloe."

When he refused to answer she stood. "I'll be back in a moment." She returned with a small vial. Taking his hand in hers she began to massage the oil into it. The air was quiet between them as she kneaded the skin.

Julius couldn't understand it. He was at her disposal. She could easily cause him pain rather than relief and yet she didn't. She worked gently, as though she feared hurting him. It made him uneasy.

The girl's eyes found his. "Do you mind if I ask what happened?"

Pulling his hand free, Julius tucked it out of sight, the memory of the scar burning behind his eyelids. "It doesn't matter. It was a long time ago."

Jubilee watched him, her eyes grazing over his arms where old scars were visible. "I suppose your job would have been rather dangerous, wouldn't it?"

"It could be. If you aren't careful."

"Is that what you always wanted? To create idols?"

"Yes. I loved the gods from the time I was a boy. My mother used to take me to the temples with her. She used to take me by the shops each year to show me where the idols were made." The words seemed to flow from him of their own volition and he hated himself for it. Why must she ask him questions? So that she might condemn him further?

"My mother said you were very talented. The best in Rome."

Did she? He hadn't imagined his daughter speaking of him at all with her children. "Your mother hated idols from the time she was a child. She hated anything to do with the gods. Any god." He emphasized the final words, so that she knew just what her father had done, worming his way into her mother's delicate mind.

"It doesn't mean she didn't notice the talent that went into them." She said quietly. "They are still beautiful."

"And visible," Julius muttered. "Which is a lot more than you can say for yours."

"We see our God in different ways, *Avus*." To his surprise, there was no malice in her voice. "We may not see him physically but we still see him. We see his hand in the things he created."

"Your father said something like that once. Something about seeing him in the mountains." He knew the humor in his voice did not go unnoticed, but the girl remained unfazed.

"That's one place we can see him. I see him in people. The way my parents never hesitate to welcome those in need into our home. The way my *Abba* will accept nothing more than wood for the fire in payment for his services." The girl smiled hesitantly. "The way *Imma* prays for you from sun up until sundown on the sixth of January."

"The sixth?" Julius breathed. "Why the sixth?"

"She wouldn't say. Except that it holds an important event for the both of you."

"It was the day she left." Julius snapped. "If she is praying then it isn't for my salvation I assure you."

"*Avus*."

"Leave it be now, girl." Why had he spoken? Of course, the child would want to speak of her god. The girl was relentless. Like her father. Like her grandfather.

IX

J ubilee woke to a figure looming over her. She sat up, a sharp
cry breaking through her lips.

"It's all right." Atticus's voice washed over her in the
darkness. Soft and reassuring. "It's just me."

Jubilee set a hand to her chest as Atticus lit a candle. "What
are doing?" She spit. "You scared me."

Sitting beside her, Atticus brushed her cheek, catching stray
tears with his thumb. "I'm sorry." He murmured. "I didn't mean
to frighten you. I was going to wake you when you woke on your
own."

"I wasn't dreaming." Irritation still lingered in her voice,
making him smile.

"No. But I have been called out and I was hoping you would
accompany me."

"You want me to come?"

"I am not the one keeping you from medicine, Jubilee. If I
had my way you would be working by my side every day." He
couldn't bring himself to admit to her that his Jubilee was shining
through the cracks of the broken girl she had come to him as.
Piece by piece his Jewess was coming back to him and he looked
for any reason to bring that girl back out. With only the stories of
his day bringing her such pleasure he was desperate to get her
away from Julius and back into real medicine. If a smile were to
reach her eyes it would be there.

"My grandfather." She moaned. "If he finds out we will lose the Domus." She couldn't imagine Rome without Leopold or the Domus she now called home. If she must be away from Galilee and her family, she found solace at least in the fact that she was surrounded by the very walls that had held her mother as a child. "I want to, Atticus. But you must understand that I can't risk losing this. I need this piece of my mother."

Atticus put a finger to her lips. "He won't find out, Jubilee. We will be back long before he wakes." He could see the excitement growing in her eyes before he could finish, drowning out all fear.

Smiling she threw the blanket to the floor, nearly tumbling off the bed in her hurry.

"I will be in the atrium when you are ready."

When Jubilee made her way into the atrium she wore an old tunic and her hair was bound at the back of her head. It never ceased to amaze him that in such plain wear, she could outshine all the women of Rome. She smiled as she met him. After a moment of silence on his part she let out a nervous laugh. "Are we going?"

Blinking, Atticus nodded. His hand on her back he guided her out the door. "I warned Leopold. If your grandfather wakes, Leopold is to tell him we are busy."

Atticus could feel the excitement radiate from her as they made their way through the silent streets. There was a new bounce to the way she walked, much like the one she had when teasing Julius. Even to himself, her love for medicine was astounding. She held no fear of what the night might bring them.

"I am not sure what to expect, Jubilee." He warned. "The neighbor is the one who came for me. He says the child has been ill for some time but he would not give me anything more."

The smell that hit them as they neared the home was putrid. Both in turn came to a sharp stop, unable to breathe for the smell.

"Jubilee." Atticus motioned for her to come closer before taking a piece of eucalyptus-soaked fabric from his bag. Turning her around he placed it over her nose, tying it off behind her head.

"What about you?" She asked. "You can't go in with nothing."

Taking a scalpel from his bag, Atticus cut a strip of fabric and tied it securely over his nose. Moving deeper into the home he felt his eyes begin to water. Without the oil to mask it, the smell still found its way to his nose, though it was no longer overwhelming.

He watched Jubilee. Would her months away have weakened her? Though she blinked rapidly against the stench that burned her eyes, she showed no signs of hesitation as she reached the small child. Leaning over him she spoke softly, reassuring him before tentatively pulling back the filthy sheet that covered his leg—careful not to cause him further pain.

Atticus felt his stomach knot at the gruesome sight. "What happened?"

"He was climbing." His mother sobbed. "He loves to climb but he fell and sliced his leg."

"How long ago did it happen?"

"Two weeks. Asclepius promised to heal. Why didn't he heal him?"

Jubilee was quick to comfort the mother, assuring her they would do what they could. But it was clear she knew the outcome would not be good. There would be no saving the leg. Even if the mother allowed amputation it would take a miracle to save the child. The boy was pale and his breaths labored. Perspiration poured down his feverish face. Having put it off, the wound had festered and maggots had found home. It was a wonder the child had not gone before they arrived.

Despite his hesitation, Jubilee had taken charge immediately. First calming the hysterical mother before setting out to remove the maggots that lived in the wound. Atticus couldn't help but watch her as she worked, her face set in a determined mask—not the slightest hint of the disgust he felt at the mother showed on her face. When the boy started to whimper she told in hushed tones a story from her scriptures, a gentle smile in her voice that turned the boy's lips.

With the wound cleaned, Jubilee stepped aside to let Atticus look it over as she continued calming the mother.

Atticus bit back a curse as he examined the leg. Gangrene had set in, turning the leg a repulsive black. Motioning for Jubilee he leaned in. "There will be no saving this. You know this don't you?"

"Of course. I'm speaking with Camila now."

Turning back to the boy, Atticus brushed the dark hair from his clammy face. "Don't you worry any," He said quietly. "We're going to do all we can. Once we take care of that leg you'll feel much better." The boy watched him through foggy, distant eyes. He showed no signs of the pain he must have been in. "You must be very brave, you know. Not many people can handle it like you are. I bet you didn't even cry when you fell." That warranted a smile.

Sighing, Atticus relaxed, grateful he had brought Jubilee along. He much preferred the children to their well-meaning but altogether brainless parents. Children, for all their frailties, were tougher than they appeared.

...

Jubilee didn't mind the parents. It had been the reason that her father had brought her to the shop so often as a child. To comfort and distract those who needed it. She never shied away from a parent's hysterics.

"Let me pray, Camila." She urged softly.

Camila shook her head stubbornly. "Aesculapius has denied me. What makes you think he will listen to you?"

"I do not mean to Aesculapius."

"Then to who?" The woman demanded. "I have prayed to all. Hygeia. Panaceia. Still, Decimus grows sicker. They made their choice with him."

"The God I pray to isn't counted among the gods of Rome, Camila."

There was silence as the woman eyed Jubilee, her face growing steadily tighter in the passing seconds. "Aquila." She breathed. She stumbled back. "You are Juliana Aquila's daughter, aren't you? My father told me about your parents. How your father corrupted your mother and stole her away. Your kind is always stealing others away. Corrupting. Cheating. Your mother was sick and your father fed her lies. I won't let you do the same thing with me."

"My mother yearned for something more and she found it, Camila, and she is better because of it. She loved and still loves my father just as he loves her. You mustn't listen to rumors." Taking the woman's hand she squeezed it. "Please, I am not trying to corrupt you. I'm not asking you to give your life to God if you are so against it. All I am asking is that you let me pray with you. What will it cost you in the end?"

Camila frowned. "You are not like they say the Jews are. My husband says your kind is hateful."

"Rumors and gossip are not much to trust in." Jubilee smiled. "Jews have their own rumors of what the Romans are. It doesn't make either true."

"No, I suppose not." The woman closed her eyes. "If you think it will help my Decimus, I will do anything."

Jubilee took both hands in hers. She could feel the woman's body relax as the words flowed over her. When she finished, Camila's eyes were wide.

"What is that?" She whispered.

Jubilee smiled. "I think you know, Camila."

The woman nodded, her eyes still wide but relatively free of fear.

Atticus jumped to his feet as they entered. The mother walked past him and kissed her son's cheeks. "You stay with me and your father, Dec. You hear me? You don't leave me." Standing she looked at Atticus. "You do what you must. So long as you think you can save my boy."

"I can't make any promises." He replied. He wouldn't be held accountable if the boy didn't survive.

Sending the mother out of the room, Atticus ordered Jubilee to the other side of the table. "How did you calm her down?"

"I prayed." She said simply. She brushed the boy's hair back as the valerian pulled him under. "It was all I could think of."

"I am surprised she listened, most people of Rome would have your head at the simple mention of your god."

Jubilee watched him a moment, her head tilted. Sighing she went back to work. "She almost didn't. It is why I was gone so long. I asked what it would cost her in the end."

"Doesn't she have to believe?

"She trusted, Atticus. Even if only for a moment she put her faith in something she couldn't understand." They lapsed into silence, her eyes flickering to the boy every few moments to ensure he was sleeping. "They always believe, Atticus. Even if they don't truly recognize it for what it is. It is what keeps them going. People spend their lives looking for something, most not even realizing it is God they are chasing after." Again she pictured her mother within the walls of the Domus, paying tribute to the gods, her heart always pulling her towards something she couldn't even name.

...

The sun was rising steadily as they made their way home, setting the morning fog on fire. Jubilee walked with her head up, breathing in the scent of chimney fire and freshly made breakfast.

Wrapping her palla tighter about herself she urged Atticus to walk slower. It had been months since she had left the four walls of the Domus and she felt no desire to rush back to them. "Do you think he will adjust well? Camila said he was always climbing."

"He will survive. That is what matters now."

Seeing the Domus, Jubilee took Atticus's hand, bringing him to a stop. "Thank you for including me tonight. I don't want to disobey my grandfather again but maybe...maybe you could show me around Rome? Get me out of those walls again."

Bringing her hand to his lips, he promised to take her the moment she asked.

The Domus was silent as they entered. Julius was still asleep. Taking advantage of the quiet, Jubilee broke away from Atticus. "I am going to take a bath."

Easing out of her tunic, she slipped into the water, ignoring the sound of Atticus behind her. She had expected it. She wasn't the only one who needed to clean up after their night.

Turning to face him she felt her heart ache as she took in his wet tunic. How long had she been denying her fears and she still hadn't eased his own? "Atticus." She breathed. "What can I do?" What could she do to make him see that she wasn't ashamed of him?

Atticus laughed softly. "I could ask you the same thing, Jewess."

Despite the ache in her chest, Jubilee couldn't help but return his smile. "I suppose. But I mean it, Atticus. I am trying to make you see that it isn't you."

Atticus considered her a moment. "I know, Jewess. But you have to understand that it works both ways."

"It's not me." Jubilee had a good idea of who it was, but she kept quiet. She wasn't ready to share her miseries and she wasn't about to force his. "Would you tell me someday?" She asked quietly. "What happened while we were apart?"

"Will you tell me?"

Jubilee could do nothing more than nod.

"Then someday." Atticus conceded. "But I am not sure you would look at me the same after."

"And you me," Jubilee replied. "But I could never look at you differently, Atty."

"And I you." When Jubilee smiled, Atticus felt his lips turn. It still wasn't the smile he longed to see, but it was a smile.

"Someday."

"Whenever you're ready, Jubilee. Not a moment sooner." Pulling her gently to her he kissed her forehead. "You owe me nothing until you're ready, Jewess. But please don't keep it from me because you think that I couldn't love you after."

"I could say the same to you, Atticus." Wrapping her arms around his waist she toyed with his tunic. "You don't have to hide from me. I don't want you to be afraid of me. I-I don't want to hide from you."

"Nor I you."

...

Jubilee woke to the cool morning air drifting in through the open window, enveloping her like a loving embrace. She had always loved morning. That love had only deepened as she took care of her grandfather. Julius Aquila rarely woke before noon, leaving her most of the morning to do as she pleased.

Rolling over she watched Atticus, still sleeping soundly, his mouth hung open, one hand slung over his face. She felt the flutter in her stomach that had become a new normal.

After her late-night adventure with Atticus, the draw to medicine had become too overwhelming to ignore. She found herself sneaking down to watch him work until Julius called for her. She met him when Julius was napping. An occasion that was happening more as time passed. She justified that he had only forbidden her to practice. He had said nothing about listening.

"I won't disobey quite so directly again." She had told Atticus before a small smile curved her lips. "But he said nothing about watching you."

After catching her three mornings in a row, Atticus had placed a stool for her in the corner and though he never asked her outright, he would often hint at her. She knew he was simply pretending to be stumped. That he could handle the patient as easily as she could. But he knew the hunger that roared inside of her and he fed the beast. For that she was grateful.

Reaching out a tentative hand she touched him curiously. It was an odd sensation to her, when only months before she had been unable to think of touching a man. The time they shared was drawing them back. Leading them slowly toward the relationship they had once shared. Though her longing for him was only in thought, she took it as a hopeful promise that her parents had been right—Atticus held the key to her finally letting go of *him*.

It had been almost a month since that small voice had urged her forward and already she could see color returning to Atticus's face. With the meals she made him each day, she could see the weight coming back to him, lessening the sickly color to him. He still clung to wine as one clung to life. But he was coming back to her.

As she watched, he stirred, and catching her stare he smiled, pulling her down beside him. "Are you coming down again today?"

"If I can." Despite the initial jolt at his closeness, she settled against his chest. *This is Atticus. Remember Galilee and all the times he made you feel safe.* "*Avus* had a fever last night. I think I should stay with him."

"Very well." Had she only imagined the disappointment in his voice? "You will come and get me if you need any help?"

"I won't."

"Of course not." Atticus laughed.

Despite her confirmation that Julius needed her, Atticus found himself glancing toward the corner, where Jubilee had taken to watching him. Unlike her presence, her absence was loud. He had grown used to her quiet presence. His little mouse in the corner.

She's using you, Atticus. Just like Aelia.

Atticus sighed. His mind had become muddled where his wife was concerned. She had offered herself up to him, despite the anguish that nearly crippled her. She had laid herself down to raise him up. And for what? A few measly meals?

When meals came now, wine was cleared and replaced with honeyed water or milk. A beverage she had sent Leopold to fetch, despite its rarity in Rome.

"My father used to encourage my mother to drink milk." She explained, pouring him a generous helping. "It helped her maintain her weight when she was too sick to eat."

The woman left no stone unturned. Each night he entered the tablinum to find the table full of platters, each one filled with different meats, cheeses, and fruits. Many platters contained the meals which she knew to have been his favorites in Nazareth.

"Why are you doing this, Jubilee? What does it serve you?"

She turned to him. "Because it isn't healthy, Atticus. I am not telling you to go back to where you were before but you cannot stay here. You're sick, Atty."

She doesn't want what you were before. Each day he sat with her and picked at the food. But without the wine to blur his mind it was becoming harder to ignore the voice that taunted him.

X

December

Julius watched his granddaughter through narrowed eyes. She was no longer the sullen-faced girl she had come to them as. If not entirely happy, she seemed content. The shyness she had shown had eased until she shared her stories with confidence, continuing even when he mocked her.

Despite himself, he had begun to tolerate her presence and even her stories. A child defeating a giant. A man in the belly of the whale. Her latest had three men tossed into a blazing furnace, only to come out unscathed. If not entirely ludicrous, they were entertaining.

She spoke now of a man named Daniel, who had been tossed among the lions. He had expected more of such a story.

"You have been busy lately." He rasped, tired of the story. "Finally taking to your role as a wife, are you?"

Ignoring him, Jubilee continued as though he hadn't spoken. "It is only right." He pressed. "As a woman of your faith you wouldn't want him turning to another would you?"

Sitting straighter, Jubilee looked him straight on. "This is personal, *Avus*." Though she spoke softly, she had taken on the stern tone of a mother with an uncooperative child. "My relationship with Atticus is a matter between him and myself."

"Would you like to go back to your family in shame, girl? The things your neighbors would whisper about you would drive them out of town."

"My parents pay no mind to what neighbors say. Nor are they strangers to it." There had always been the few who blamed her and her family for what had happened.

What is a man to do with a girl of such beauty who held her head too high? Had her family not guarded her like a queen perhaps she would have had the decency to accept the man's proposal, rather than lead him to sin. They had seen the way she went off with the Roman boy. A family who flirted with Romans held no morals. The number of those who held her responsible had always been few, but they were the loudest in her ears.

"I'm sorry." She cried into her mother's chest. "It's all my fault."

"It isn't your fault, love," Her mother had soothed. "You did nothing to provoke him."

"I angered him. I shamed you by going alone with Atticus."

"You and Atticus did nothing wrong, Joy." Her father stepped in. "We trust what you say. If nothing happened then that is that."

"But Abba, we-"

"Enough!" Her mother shouted. "Enough. I will not stand to hear you go on blaming yourself. Jude was a sick man who took you as he pleased. He would have done so with or without your and Atticus's actions in the mix."

Julius watched the girl carefully. Whatever plagued her had turned her face tight. Her lower lip trembled as though she would cry. "Well, you do not have to bring them shame." He said. "Treat him well and a girl with your face could keep any man."

"I can't." She cried. "I don't deserve him."

"A virgin undeserving of a man?"

"I am not what you think, *Avus*." The pain that saturated her voice touched him strangely. Without his own consent, he reached forward and touched her hand.

She pulled away harshly. Picking at her wrist she glanced back at him. "I'm sorry." She whispered. "I don't mean to offend you. But I-I can't let you touch me."

Julius felt a strange pity for the girl as the months fell together. The stiff way she held herself. The terror-filled screams that woke him in the night, drifting from the room beside his own. "You weren't a virgin." Her head shook rapidly. "Oh, child." Before he could say anything more Leopold was entering the room.

Looking at Jubilee, Leopold frowned. "Are you all right, child?"

Wiping quickly at the tears, Jubilee smiled. "I'm quite all right, Leo. *Avus* and I were simply talking."

"And now we are done," Julius announced. "You may go, girl." When she had gone, Leopold set out to rearrange him on the bed. "Do you know about the girl's past? She wasn't a virgin when she came to Atticus. Does anyone else know?"

"She was attacked." Leopold sighed. "Juliana sent letters to the Albanus' and me when it happened. But I do not know that Atticus knows. She was keeping it secret the last I heard."

Julius glared back at him. "And you didn't think it necessary to tell me that my granddaughter was raped? She is my family, Leopold."

"I didn't think you needed to know." Leopold was infuriatingly calm. "Nor did I think you would care, Julius. I watched you mistreat Juliana all her life. Belittling her. Beating her. How was I to know you would care about her daughter?"

"I would have cared if a man violated my daughter, Leopold. You can call me a monster if you like but what I did with Juliana was a matter of love. The Jews were a people I wanted her kept from."

"You call that love, Julius? Whipping her raw? She was sick and you chose to make her pain worse, all because she didn't hate the Jews."

Julius glared back at him. "I would have killed any man who dared to touch her." Seeing the man refused to waver, Julius took the man's hand, desperate for him to meet his eyes. "Don't let me lose you to the Jews as well. I thought bringing a piece of Juliana back to you would set things right. Not draw you further from me."

"You drew the line, Julius."

"Mistakes were made, Leopold. I apologized." He could feel tears beginning to prick in his eyes. This disease was making him soft. Grinding his teeth he glared up at Leopold. "I prayed to the gods that my mistakes would not end your life as well as mine. It is because of me that you aren't dying a painful death."

All anger melted from Leopold's features. "Are you in pain now? I can get Atticus."

"I don't want Atticus, Leopold." Like words on a page, Julius could read the emotions that crossed Leopold's face. His granddaughter was getting to the man, just as Juliana had tried. He believed the words her people spoke of them. But he loved Julius. That he was sure of. If he wanted to know Jubilee's god he would be unable to do so until Julius had passed.

Closing his eyes, Julius tried to see what he saw. The appeal of the thing that drew his daughter away. Jubilee preached love. But what he saw of their god was nothing but his wretched memories. "I couldn't have her sympathizing with Jews." He breathed. "Not after Tobias."

"And yet she did," Leopold replied. "You drove her to them and in the process you managed to miss out on a wonderful child. A beautiful child. Do not do the same with her daughter."

"Will that earn your forgiveness?"

"You already have it, Julius. You are the one who can't leave it behind."

…

Julius could feel it within him. The disease growing. Spreading through his body like cancer. If only it were so simple.

He knew he could only keep his secret for so long. He couldn't rely on Leopold's assistance forever. The man was only three years younger than Julius, and though he found himself in good health, his bones were growing brittle with age. Before too long the boy would need to step in and then the boils that covered his skin would be discovered. How long would it take before the true nature of his illness reached his granddaughter's ears? What would the girl think of him when she discovered the boils? Despite all the foul words he had thrown at her she continued to treat him with a kindness that made him uneasy.

A *Christian*. The thought made him groan. He had thought it terrible that his daughter had run off with the Jews. Now he must swallow the idea that she followed a man who died and rose again. The idea was ludicrous.

As Jubilee entered the room, he worked to hide his discomfort from her all too observant eyes.

"Morning *Avus*." Her eyes grazed his and she smiled in a way that nearly drew a smile to his lips. The power this girl was having on him was inconceivable.

"Morning girl." The words were weak even in his ears.

Jubilee turned toward him, her dark eyes concerned. "Are you in pain?"

"I'm fine." He spit, hoping a foul mood would turn her away. He could see that she did not believe him. Nor did she scare so easily. So long as she wasn't touched the girl seemed made of stone.

Sitting beside him she began to feed him. He focused on her to divert his mind from the pain. It was a shock even now to look at her young face and see his daughter. Had it not been for the darker shade of her skin, he would swear it was Juliana beside him.

You missed out on a wonderful child. Leopold's voice whispered. *Do not do the same with her daughter.*

"Why Jubilee?" He wondered aloud. It was a question that had plagued him from the moment he had heard it spoken.

"Pardon?"

He breathed deep against the pain. "Your name. It isn't a common name even among the Jews. At least not the ones I have known."

"No, it isn't." Setting the tray aside she sat beside him. "My father wanted to name me Joy. It was my mother who chose Jubilee. In our Jewish faith, there is a special holiday called the Year of Jubilee. It is a celebration that occurs every fifty years."

"And you were born among it?"

"No, my lord. I was born the day our Lord Jesus rose."

"The very same?"

"Yes, my lord. My name was Joy for five days before the news reached Nazareth that our Lord had risen. Just five days before."

"Then why the name? If you already had one?"

The girl bit her lip just as Juliana had always done when she worried or pondered. "My mother said that she had felt unsure for days after my birth—that no matter how much she loved it, Joy wasn't my name. Upon hearing the news she knew why. She said the moment she heard, it clicked that my name was to be Jubilee, due to what is celebrated in its times. During the Year of Jubilee, slaves are freed, debts are forgiven, and God's mercy is upon us. Just as it was with the Lord's death and ultimate resurrection." She smiled. "And thankfully for my father, the word Jubilee, to many, has come to mean joy, which appeased him."

"With no proof?" Julius demanded. "Did they see him for themselves?"

"No. Not for several weeks. They were told by a woman who saw Him. My parents did not need to see Him to believe it, *Avus*. They had listened to his preaching. They knew the scriptures had promised a Messiah and knew it to be Him."

"Of course, your mother never needed much proof to believe in such nonsense."

"My mother had been touched and healed at his hand not even a year before, *Avus*. To her and my family that was proof of who He was."

"Leopold told me my daughter had been healed," Julius said quietly. "He never said how only that she and her newborn son had been brought back from the brink of death."

"By Jesus. My mother traveled nine hours in a very blind hope that this man would save Nathanael."

"And he did it? For nothing? No sacrifice?"

"He required nothing but her faith, which had been proven."

"These are nothing to you, Jubilee." Julius shook his head. "Nothing but stories. How can you believe them so easily?"

"Because I wouldn't be here if those stories weren't true." She said simply. "Even those who don't believe in the Lord have been unable to deny the miracle of my mother's life. Not when they knew her before."

Julius closed his eyes, trying to picture a whole and healthy Juliana. The image wouldn't come.

"You don't believe it?"

"No." He replied. "But the name is beautiful and it is a lovely story nonetheless."

Tears filled the girl's eyes but she said nothing. Julius couldn't explain the emotion he felt looking upon her. He had thought it pity over her past. But as he watched her grow into her new life he knew it to be something more.

In the past weeks, he had seen sparks of joy in her. Sparks he knew came from her work with her husband. It hadn't taken him long to learn that she often stole into the shop. If the girl refused even the most innocent of touches then he knew of only one thing that could bury that sadness even for a moment. "Go to him." He told her. "Go help your husband."

"It isn't a woman's place."

"It is a woman's place to assist her husband where assistance is needed." He spit. "Now go before I change my mind."

A shy smile played on the girl's lips. "Thank you, *Avus*"

Jubilee forced herself to walk until her grandfather's cubicula was behind her. Picking up her tunic she ran through the atrium and out onto the street, running headlong into another body. Landing hard on the floor she felt her face drain.

When a hand was offered to her she took it reluctantly, her eyes flicking up to find Sibyl smiling at her. "I see nothing has changed with you in that aspect." She dusted at Jubilee's tunic. "Are you all right, *Puella*?"

"Yes, my lady." Tossing a wistful glance toward the shop, Jubilee invited Sibyl in. "Are you all right, Sibyl?"

"Regulus thought it would do me good to see you." After he had revealed the truth of what awaited him in Ostia her constant unease had deepened.

The story had spilled from her husband as though every day had been a losing battle fighting them. Aelia. Of course, it was Aelia. Even gone she wasn't truly gone. She never would be.

"You thought it would end there?" Sibyl demanded. *"Pay her off and we never see her again?" She swore. "Honestly, Regulus! You judge our son for his mistakes and here you are in the same position!"*

"I am in this because of our son." Regulus spit. "I am here because he was stupid enough to get himself into a situation he couldn't get himself out of and I was willing to pay the price to do it for him! And you! I saw the toll it took on you, watching him struggle. Why do you think I kept this from you? I wanted this woman gone from both of your lives even if she couldn't be gone from mine."

"And she won't be, Regulus. Until the day we die."

Pressing her fingers to her lids, Sibyl forced her mind away from the conversation. Regulus was right. She needed to speak to Jubilee.

"I have been meaning to send Leo for you, but *Avus* keeps me busy. I've hardly had a moment."

Sibyl waved her off lightly. "No worries, sweet girl. You mustn't feel pressured to spend your days with me. You are young."

"Nonsense, Sibyl. Denying you would be like denying my mother."

As they made their way around the peristyle, Sibyl felt the ache in her chest ease. Away from the consuming walls of her Domus, the nightmares seemed like nothing more than that. Nightmares. Nothing of the strange foreboding she always felt when she woke.

Speaking with Jubilee held the same air of comfort that Juliana's presence always had. "How is your mother?" She asked quietly. "I was heartbroken to see you without her. I never stopped to think she might not come."

"She is well, Sibyl. There were simply too many memories here that kept her away."

Sibyl swallowed. "It's understandable of course. I feared at first it may have been me who kept her away."

Stopping, Jubilee frowned. "Sibyl, why would you be her reasoning? She was never angry about your visits ending if that is what you are thinking. She only ever worried about you."

"Yes well. I would understand if she was angry. It was terribly cruel of me to cut her off so suddenly."

"Do you mind if I ask why?" Jubilee asked. "I mean I understand now why Atticus didn't come back. But I can't figure yours out."

Sibyl massaged her temples. "That first summer we were having so many troubles with Atticus that leaving seemed impossible, and then we received that letter. About you and Ju-"

"Please." Jubilee interrupted. "Don't say his name."

"I'm sorry, *Puella*. I wanted to write back but I couldn't seem to find the words. Your mother had always been a sister to me, and you and your brothers, all of your family really, were my family where I had none." She looked at her hands. "How do you respond to something like that? In a letter?" Sibyl quickened her pace, unwilling to face the girl. "I tried a hundred times to respond to that letter but the words wouldn't come. Hearing about what happened was simply too much on top of everything with Atticus. It felt like I was losing both of my children."

The sudden harshness of her sobs surprised even herself. Dropping to her knees, Sibyl keeled forward, her arms wrapped around her torso as though she could hold herself together. It was all too much. Atticus's continued spiral. Regulus and Aelia. Jubilee and Juliana. The nightmares that haunted her every moment and the unending, unbearable ache of her soul.

Jubilee was on her knees in an instant—her hand on the woman's back. "Sibyl."

"What sort of friend am I? That I left her alone when she needed me most? I let her write me every year begging for a response."

"Sibyl, she never held an ill thought towards you. *Deliciae*, she knew that whatever kept you from her was bigger than a simple growing apart. She knew something was wrong."

"And you?"

Jubilee let out her breath. "I suppose I was more confused than anything. I missed you. I missed Atticus."

Sibyl looked up at her, her cheeks wet and her voice thick. "Do you resent my bringing you here?"

"Not most days," Jubilee replied honestly. "Things have been difficult. I won't deny that. And I do question whether I will ever truly move beyond what happened. But I love your son, Sibyl. I always have. Whatever problems we have now, I have to believe that things will grow." Sibyl nodded, fresh tears building in her green eyes. "Sibyl, is there something more that is bothering you?"

"Are you sure I haven't bothered you enough for one day?"

"Of course, Sibyl. Come on." Helping the woman to her feet, Jubilee led her into the gardens.

When they were situated, Sibyl toyed with her hands. "Bringing you here was not entirely what it seemed, Jubilee. I was worried for Atticus, that much is true. I wanted to see him wed again. Wed to someone worthy. But Jubilee, it was for my selfish gain that I found the courage to write. To bring you for Atticus just seemed the perfect way to bury three problems." She was quiet for a long moment, silent tears cascading down her cheeks. "I have been having nightmares, Jubilee. Terrifying, horrible nightmares."

"Oh, well Sibyl, I am not a prophet. If what you want is for me to explain them to you, I am afraid I will be of little help."

"I know what they mean, Jubilee. Believe me, I know what they mean."

"Then I am not sure what you are asking of me."

"I need you to tell me about him. About your god."

"Oh." Jubilee felt her face drain. "Oh, Sibyl." How could she be so selfish as to keep to herself the words of God? Her father would be humiliated to know. "Of course. Whatever you want to know."

"I don't know what that is." Tears choked the older woman's voice. "I am so confused."

"Then we will start from the beginning. But do not be afraid to ask whatever questions you may have."

...

Jubilee was beginning to grow restless. In four months she had left the Domus walls only once. She longed to explore her new home. To visit the places her parents had spoken of. Atticus had known every crevice of her home country. She had shown him all the places she found solace as a child and she knew none of his.

When Leopold encouraged her to accompany Atticus on a walk she could not find it within her to deny him. The man knew Julius better than she did. He could care for him long enough to allow her a breath of fresh air.

Atticus let Jubilee keep hold of his hand as they walked the street. He loved the feel of her closeness. The way she fit him in ways Aelia never had. When would she realize the same?

Nothing had changed since she had offered herself to him. She still shut him out when it came to love, never allowing herself the pleasure he longed to offer her. He wanted to shake her. To do whatever it would take to wake her up to him. To pull her mind from whatever held her in its clutches.

Again and again, images would threaten to undo him. Not his Jewess. Not with the level of protection that had been offered to her. So what was it that kept her from him? What could she have in her past that she feared sharing with him? He could think of nothing but one horrible thought and the images that accompanied it.

As they worked their way through the crowd Jubilee pressed closer to him, her nails digging into his hand. "You're shaking." Moving her out of the crowd he touched her cheek. "Are you all right?"

Without a word, he watched as her eyes found a man's innocent stare. Heart pounding in his throat, Atticus let his own eyes roam over her in a way that suggested his desire for her and watched her recoil, further cementing his fears. "Jubilee."

Going into Atticus's arms, she buried her face in his chest. "I think I would like to go home now."

"It's been too long since you have seen any company outside the four of us." He rationalized. Kissing her forehead he turned her in the direction of his parent's Domus. "I'll leave you with my mother while I get the supplies we need."

Jubilee stayed close to Atticus's side, refusing to allow an inch of space between them as they pressed through the crowd. Every nudge against her body, every stare from the men they passed made her heart race quicker until she was lightheaded and grateful for Atticus's arm around her waist.

I go before you, Beloved.

"I go before you." She whispered, aware of Atticus's eyes on her. "I will give you rest." Though the scripture didn't bring to her the peace it once had, it carried her to the Albanus Domus.

Away from the crowd, Atticus allowed Jubilee to move back into his arms. "I have a few things to discuss with my father." Waving his mother over he handed Jubilee off to her. "Just rest now, Jewess."

Accepting Sibyl's hand, Jubilee followed her through the peristyle and into the garden. "I'll have Layla get you a mug of honeyed water." Patting her hand she left her for only a moment before returning, urging Jubilee to rest her head against her shoulder. "Does Atticus still not know?"

Jubilee shook her head. "I can't tell him. Not yet."

"You do realize you will have to tell him eventually, *Puella*? Secrets don't do marriage anything but trouble."

"I will tell him. Just not yet. I can't."

Sibyl rubbed circles on Jubilee's back as she waited for the tears to subside. "I understand keeping secrets, Jubilee. I kept more than my fair share in the beginning. But it only made it worse, and the only way I was able to move forward was when I told Regulus. I had someone to share the burden with and my husband to give me comfort. That could be Atticus, Jubilee. If you told him."

"I'll tell him when I'm ready. It's not like he isn't keeping his secrets."

Sighing, Sibyl bit her tongue against pushing it further. She knew the truth would come out eventually and she could only hope they didn't tear themselves apart before it did. "I have something for you, *Puella*. Come on." Pulling the girl to her feet she led her to her childhood room. "Your mother and I spent endless hours in here. She spent countless nights here."

"*Imma* said she used to stay here as often as she could manage it."

"It was always better for her than her own home. Even my mother adored Juliana." Ordering her to sit, Sibyl retrieved the bundle of letters she'd prepared. "I don't have the letters I sent your mother anymore. I left them with her one summer. But I thought you might enjoy the ones she wrote."

Jubilee chewed her lip, her fingers toying with the ribbon. "Thank you, Sibyl." She turned away as her eyes burned with tears. Her mother had shared many of Sibyl's letters while teaching her to read in Latin, but she had never seen the letters her mother had written. She had been missing her mother especially lately. Her time with Sibyl, though filling a small part of the ache could only do so much. Her motherly touch made her long for her mother's way.

Seeing her aching, Sibyl ran her hand over her hair. "You will see her again, *Puella*. Just ask Regulus and he'll arrange a spot on one of his ships. I am sure Atticus will approve of it."

"Perhaps someday." She conceded. Tucking the letters away she stood. "I think I should be going back now. I don't know how long Leopold can handle *Avus*."

Meeting the men in the atrium, Jubilee met Atticus with a gentle touch. "Are you all right?" She asked, looking at the tight line of his lips.

"We're leaving." He spit.

Sibyl glanced at Regulus. He stood with his arms crossed at his chest. He muttered something under his breath as Atticus set a hand at Jubilee's back.

With goodbyes said Sibyl followed after her husband, the look on his face keeping her quiet throughout dinner. He would share when he was ready.

Regulus closed his eyes, forcing his mind to focus on the gentle, soothing tones Sibyl played for him. Evenings had always been his favorite time of day, laying across the lounge as Sibyl played the harp. Now his mind was caught on other things.

He worried for his son. He missed their quiet, innocent child. He had been handsome. Intelligent. Now the boy was quickly becoming nothing more than bone. He didn't know where his temper came from when it came to their son. Never had he yelled at Atticus as a child. He wanted to sympathize with the struggles he knew his child faced, and yet the moment he laid eyes on his son he was reminded of the waste the boy had brought into their lives. Of the trouble he now found himself in, all to keep his son out of it.

Sitting up he watched Sibyl's fingers move across the strings with all the grace of a well-trained harpist. By the gods what he wouldn't do for her. He had seen the sadness in her eyes when he had fought against the Christian faith and why? He had never found fault in his friends for the god they chose to follow and despite his fear, he had been unable to deny his wife that same right if their god was what she wanted. Anything to fill the hole he knew was widening.

He should have given her more children when they had the chance. It had been selfish to deny a woman of her love the children she had desired. He could see the anticipation in her eyes when she left for her visits with Jubilee. She hoped for grandchildren.

"Have I failed you, Sibyl?" He was all too aware of the emotion that filled his voice. "Have I failed the both of you?"

Leaving the harp, his wife came and planted herself in his lap. "I can truly say you have not failed me, my love. You were everything I ever wanted. No amount of children could compare to it."

"Atticus can't stand the look of me. Even Jubilee seems distant with me now."

"If that's so it has nothing to do with Atticus. Jubilee isn't so petty as to let that sort of thing stand in the way. She has always adored you. As for Atticus, he is hurting now. But he loves you, Regulus. Give him time. I can already see a difference in him. Jubilee is changing him. Perhaps not as quickly as we would like, but she is bringing him back to us."

XI

"Are you spending the day with *Avus* again?"

Leopold couldn't look at the girl as he readied Julius's breakfast. Was she beginning to question his devotion? "It doesn't seem right to leave him alone. His health is only declining."

"Of course, Leo," Jubilee said softly. "I think it's good he has had someone like you all these years."

Leopold turned toward the girl, looking for any sign of disgust or condemnation in her eyes. He found nothing but a subtle fatigue that made her eyes droop. "Are you spending the day here again?" It was her Sabbath—the one day the girl requested for herself.

Jubilee sat curled by the fire, a piece of papyrus in her lap. "It feels the closest to home here."

"Well if you can, find some sleep. You can take the blanket from my bed if you want to sleep by the fire."

Leaving her alone, Leopold hurried down the corridor. He had begun to look for any way to spend his time with Julius. He sent Jubilee on errands, saying it was time she knew her home. He had taken to the nightly duties so that he may stay with Julius until the sun had risen. Then he would sneak from the room before Jubilee could find her way there.

As Julius's health declined, Leopold found it harder and harder to remain indifferent. He had spent so long being angry at the deception that led to the man's illness. Now he wanted nothing more than those months back. Why had he wasted the little time he had left fighting? Why had he spent all those years fighting who he was?

He remembered the way Julius treated him when he came home that night. He hadn't looked guilty. Julius would never allow himself that sort of shame. But he had lowered himself that day and no matter the anger that roared in his chest, Leopold could not deny him. For all the man's faults, he had remained faithful until that one night.

"I don't want to live without you." He whispered. The thought of his days with Julius soon coming to an end was enough to make him sick. He had never known a day without Julius by his side.

"You will do fine without me, Leopold. You'll find Jubilee's god and soon enough you will hate me for all the things we did."

"I could never hate you, Julius."

Julius struggled to sit up, his eyes closed tight against the pain. "You have always been more resistant of what we are, Leopold. Ever since Tobias. Once I am gone you will jump at the chance to cleanse yourself of the disease he claimed was within us."

Leopold sighed. "You can't keep holding Malachi and his children accountable for what his father did, Julius. You will be no different from Tobias in the end—hating Juliana for nothing more than blood."

"I will grant that Jubilee is kinder than her grandfather. But she doesn't know what goes on behind closed doors. She would be just as disgusted to learn it as he was."

"Perhaps," Leopold said. "But it doesn't mean she would torment you. Malachi knows of us and he has never treated me any different because of it."

Unable to bear it any longer, Julius slumped back against the pillows. "It doesn't matter. Her belief is nonsense."

As Julius drifted to sleep, Leopold listened to the silence. The voice that had started within him at Jubilee's appearance was getting harder to hear the longer he spent with Julius. He hadn't heard that soft *Beloved* in days and he wasn't sure he wanted to. What sort of god condemned one for who they loved? What sort of loving god let one of his people beat another for whom they disagreed? They had been children when Tobias had sent wild dogs on them for what he merely suspected them of. But behind his eyelids, he saw Juliana and Jubilee. *No.* He wanted to tell them. He had thought he wanted to know their god. But the nearer that time drew, the lesser the desire became.

…

Regulus stood in the doorway of the quarters, waiting for Jubilee to notice him. Curled by the fire she looked too peaceful to disturb. In her hands was one of her mother's childhood letters. As he watched her eyes began to droop, the letter dropping to the floor.

He made to leave when she jumped awake and rubbed the sleep from her eyes. "Does *Avus* need anything?" She stopped short as she glanced up, realizing her mistake. Her look of surprise turned to horror as she took in his blood-soaked tunic and the fabric he held to his nose. "Regulus. What happened?"

She rushed over to him, a fresh rag ready to replace the soiled one.

"Leopold told me I could find you here." He explained. "I took a fall at the gymnasium. I know it's your Sabbath but I was hoping you would fix me up."

"Of course, Regulus." She led him to the table before moving a bucket of water over the fire. "Atticus is in the shop now. Why didn't you see him?"

"Atticus and I are not on the best of terms at the moment. I think it may be best that we stay away from each other."

She eyed him as she pressed the wet rag to his nose. Her left hand was gentle at the back of his neck. "I was wondering why we never see you for dinner. I have been telling Atticus we need to have the both of you over, seeing as I can't make it over when he visits."

"Atticus hates those visits." Regulus flinched as she dabbed at his face. "We have told him he needs to take Julius off your hands one night so that we can have you. Sibyl has seemed much happier since she started visiting with you."

"Good." The girl smiled. "It's been a gift having her with me so often. I only wish you would show your face more. I have been here four months and I have only seen you twice."

"I didn't want to overwhelm you, *Puella*. Your father said you have struggled with men outside himself and your brothers."

Jubilee stopped working, her face serious. "You count among my father and brothers, Regulus. I could never be scared of you."

Grateful for the girl's distraction, Regulus closed his eyes, hiding the tears that threatened to spill. How long had he feared her repulsion of him?

"I don't think it's broken." Jubilee's voice drew his eyes open once more. He noticed the tears in her own eyes. "The cut won't need stitches either." Washing her hands in the basin, she glanced back at him. "Do you have to go now that I'm finished?"

"I can stay if that is what you wish." He wanted the bleeding to be done before he went back to Sibyl.

As though hearing his thoughts, Jubilee eyed the blood-soaked front of him. "You should change into one of Atticus's tunics. I can get that washed for you before you go home. Keep you from scaring Sibyl too much."

"That isn't necessary, Jubilee. I can't ask you to do that."

"Please. I miss the normalcy of home. It feels strange having someone else do so much for me."

Seeing she would not back down, Regulus went in search of their cubicula. He returned to find her hovering over the boiling water. Taking his tunic from him she went to work immediately.

He watched her quietly, even in silence her faith seemed to emanate from her. Remembering the conversation he'd had with Atticus, Regulus hoped he could reach her. "Jubilee, do you share your faith with your grandfather?"

"Of course I do."

"And are you aware of the dangers in that? You aren't in Nazareth anymore, Jubilee. These people do not take kindly to the people of your faith."

"It was dangerous at home, Regulus. Perhaps even more so. You must remember that it was my father's people that ordered the crucifixion of Christ. In their eyes we are traitors."

Regulus sighed. He ought to have known it wouldn't be easy to convince the child to remain quiet where her faith was concerned.

Seeing his discomfort, Jubilee set a hand to his. "I'll be careful, Regulus. But if I feel myself called to say something I cannot deny it."

"And I won't fault you for that. I just don't want you looking for those calls. If you feel you must then you must, all I ask is that you hide as best as possible. I have asked the same of Sibyl, should she continue this route." They hadn't made it this far for him to lose her to a god unseen.

Jubilee smiled. "My grandfather isn't so terrible, Regulus. Not when you get to know him. When he found out what happened he was kind. Sad even."

Regulus chucked her chin. "You, *Deliciae*, could see good in the darkest of people. But the truth you'll soon learn is that he is no different than Aelia. He'll tear you apart as she did Atticus if you aren't careful."

"Stop." The word was sharp on her tongue. "Please. I can't hear about her. Atticus and I have agreed to keep our secrets until we are ready. It wouldn't be fair to know his when he knows none of mine."

"*Puella*." Regulus chastised. "A marriage cannot survive on secrets. It's no wonder you two are still so separated."

"I don't think I am ready to tell him."

"Secrets are not meant to be kept between man and wife, Jubilee. They only create distance." He thought of Sibyl and the secrets that had separated them in the beginning. Of those, he had kept most recently. "You'll find that telling him will ease some of the pain."

"I will tell him eventually, Regulus. When I am ready. I just..." She shut her eyes. "I'm not ready to see that look on his face." Hanging the tunic she sat across from him. Tired tears had begun to drip down her cheeks.

Looking around them, Regulus searched for something to bring her mind away from that day. "You know I spent my entire childhood in the quarters? We didn't have a lot of money but my parents made sure to have at least one servant. My parents never were ones for children and they needed me out of their way. Your mother and I share that in common."

"My grandmother died when my mother was born, didn't she? Toxemia. It's why my mother was sickly?"

"I believe so. I suppose I can't truly speak for what her life would have been like had her mother lived, but I have heard stories of what Imogene was like."

"So my mother was just born without an ounce of love in her life?" Jubilee asked.

Regulus set a hand over hers. "Your mother wasn't unloved, Jubilee. She had Leopold. She had Sibyl. She had Sonali. I don't think a more devoted mother lived than her Amma. The woman devoted all she ever made to bettering your mother's health. Not to mention she was the only person who ever stood up to your grandfather." He gave her a small smile. "I was raised primarily by servants and I don't regret it. I had a father in my life but I still see Nehemiah as my father." Regulus gave a bleak laugh. "You look at our lives and we do seem perfectly matched, don't we?"

"In a terrible sort of way." Jubilee shook her head. "I never realized how much my mother hid from us."

"I don't think she was hiding it, Jubilee. I think she simply didn't feel the need to speak about it. Do you think you will feel the need to talk about what you faced with your children?"

"I do not mean it the way it sounds," Jubilee assured. "I only mean that it seems like a lot to keep to yourself. Especially when we saw her struggles but didn't know how to comfort her." A deep ache was beginning to form in her stomach as she remembered her mother. "Did you know that she never spanked us? She never let *Abba* do it either. Instead, she would simply talk to us. Taught us in other sort of ways. The one or two times she was forced to let *Abba* move past conversation she would always hold us afterward and cry. I never understood why until now. I mean we never held an ill will toward her for it. We knew why she disciplined us and we even told her so, but still..."

Jubilee let her words dwindle, searching for any piece of conversation to latch on to. "So it's true then?" She breathed. "That you and my mother were to be married?" She'd known it her whole life, but it wasn't spoken of often in their home and no matter how hard she tried, she struggled to see the truth in it.

Regulus laughed. "I was thirteen when the truce was made, we were betrothed for nine years. There is no greater burden than to be pledged to someone you don't want." He let out his breath, realizing too late how it had sounded. "That is not to say that I did not love your mother, Jubilee. I did. In many ways. Nehemiah and Sonali made sure we knew one another from the beginning and for that reason, she was one of my closest friends. There are parts of our history that will keep her with me forever. But she wasn't Sibyl." He had known Sibyl almost as long as he had known Juliana. From the moment the two had met the girls had been inseparable, with Sibyl attending every meeting arranged for him and Juliana—her hand always glued to the other girls.

"You don't have to explain, Regulus. You aren't supposed to love her in that way."

He laughed. "She would have been a lot more docile than Sibyl has been, I am sure. I don't think your mother has a fighter's bone in her body."

"No." Jubilee agreed. She could think of only once when her parents had ever fought and it had been before her time.

The two fell into silence as Jubilee rose to throw out the blood-red water. "My mother wouldn't be alive right now." The words were spoken so softly, that Regulus wasn't sure he had heard her right. "If she had married you."

Regulus nodded. "Neither would you. And what sort of world would that be?"

...

Coherent thought had died days ago. Jubilee struggled to remain upright as she said her prayers, but closing her eyes only reinforced the idea of sleep. Pushing herself up she paced, forcing her mind to focus. It was pointless. She repeated herself. She trailed off. Even standing, her sleepless mind slipped away into strange dreams. Giving up she hurried to meet her grandfather. Finding him resting she found Leopold in the kitchen.

Leopold watched as she slumped against the table, her head against her arms, the effort of keeping her head up proving too much. "You should be resting, my lady. I can handle dinner on my own."

"And what of you?" She yawned. "You wanted to talk." As did everyone. She split her time between Julius, Sibyl, and

Atticus. All taking different parts of her day. Sibyl came in the mornings, with a hundred questions and a thirst for knowledge. Atticus took her in the evening. Julius called on her at all hours of the day for nothing more than entertainment from the pain that was becoming consuming. Leopold stole her time when time allowed, always asking the same questions about her mother.

But none was she willing to give up. Her grandfather was warming to her and when she allowed to herself to do so, she even believed he was beginning to love her in his way. He asked questions of her brothers and her mother. Even her father wasn't forgotten. He listened again and again to the story of her mother's healing—questioning but never contemptuous. What had started as a tolerance for her grandfather had become a love so deep she feared the thought of losing him.

She loved watching Sibyl learn. She loved watching the transformation the Lord was making within her with each answered question.

She had adored Leopold from the moment she had met him and her fondness for the man could only grow as he spoke of her mother.

Atticus. How she adored Atticus most of all. Tucked away in their little sanctuary, all the pieces that bound them in Galilee had found their way back. She loved him with her entire soul.

Leopold placed his hands on her shoulders and steered her toward the door. "I will sleep well knowing that you are rested, Jubilee. We'll speak when you have accomplished that."

"Tomorrow morning." Jubilee insisted. Sibyl would be in Capua with Regulus.

"Tomorrow." Leopold agreed. "Now go."

Jubilee moved slowly. The walls swam before her and the marble floors felt soft. For a moment she wished she had allowed Leopold to walk with her. How many nights of sleep had she lost now? She tried to remember when her grandfather's night terrors had started, but couldn't remember. Her mind was slow and murky now. She felt almost feverish as she reached her room.

"Jubilee!" Her grandfather's pained scream pulled her out of her tired haze.

Picking up her tunics she ran to the next cubicula. Her grandfather was curled in on himself, his hands clutching the sheets. Startling her to her core, he was crying.

...

"Atticus!" Jubilee's voice came from the hall, high and frightened.

Forgetting his work, Atticus hurried to meet her. Her eyes were wide and strands of hair stuck to her tear-streaked face. "Are you all right? Are you hurt?" His eyes grazed over her looking for any source of pain.

"It's Julius. He's in so much pain, Atticus. But he won't let me help him. He is asking for you.

Coming up on the room they could hear Julius's pained moan. Rushing through the door, Jubilee took his hand.

"Get away from me." The man shouted. "Get out."

Glancing pleadingly at Atticus, she left the two alone. With the door closed Julius glared miserably at him.

"Do you want to tell me what is ailing you?" Though he needn't ask to know just what sort of disease was spreading before him. Atticus had his suspicions about the man and his slave. If the man wouldn't allow Jubilee to handle him there was only one answer.

"First you must promise to keep this to yourself. You hear me?"

When Atticus nodded, the man eased the blanket away from him. Internally, Atticus recoiled at the boils that covered Julius's transparent skin. "Is that what I think it is?"

"It started a few months ago. But it is spreading quickly."

"And Jubilee doesn't know?"

"I don't see why she needs to know." Atticus raised an eyebrow. It seemed just the sort of thing he would want Jubilee to know. That her now beloved grandfather was not who she thought him to be. Nor Leopold. "There is no need to hurt the poor girl further."

Poor girl? Atticus glared down at him. What was he playing at? "What do you mean further?" He spit.

Julius met his eyes. "She truly hasn't told you?"

"Told me what? Why does it seem everyone knows what hinders her but me?"

Julius bothered to look concerned. "Nothing." He said quietly. "It isn't my place to say."

Atticus felt uneasy as he covered the man, careful not to cause him any more pain than was expected. "I am afraid there is nothing I can do for you. The infection has spread too far."

"So I have been told. I don't expect you to save me now. I have something else to ask of you. Something that mustn't reach Jubilee's ears."

Atticus rubbed his eyes as he made his way back to Jubilee. She paced the length of the corridor, her fingers picking at the already ravaged skin of her wrist. What was he supposed to tell her? That her grandfather laid with men? That he had weeks if not days? How would he explain that she would no longer be caring for him?

Reaching her, he noticed the flush in her cheeks. Her eyes drooped miserably and she couldn't have been bothered to braid her hair, allowing it to fall down her back. She went to him as he neared, allowing him to close her in his arms. Even through his tunic, he could feel the heat that came off of her.

Her eyes closed as he brushed her cheek, feeling the hot skin beneath his fingers. "Are you feeling all right?"

Her eyes opened again, embarrassment coloring her cheeks. "I am only tired is all."

"You haven't slept in days." She was spreading herself thin. Worshiping her god until his mother came to walk the peristyle. Caring for Julius all hours of the day. Between Leopold and himself she could talk hours into the night. "You need sleep, Jewess."

"No." She whispered. "*Avus* needs me."

"And you need sleep. Go, I'll handle Julius."

She glanced up at him, her eyes misted. She set his hand over his, still pressed against her cheek. "Are you sure? I know that he can be troublesome. I know how to handle him now."

"I'll figure it out, Jubilee. Now go." He kissed her forehead, feeling the way her skin burned against his lips. "I want to keep an eye on that fever."

She nodded. "Thank you."

...

Atticus jumped awake, unsure where he was in the dark. Blinking against the sleep, he focused on his surroundings. Julius's sleeping figure made itself clear as another terrified scream echoed through the open door.

Blurry-eyed and stumbling, Atticus hurried towards his room, where Jubilee arched on the bed, her fingers clawing at the blankets.

"*Abba*!" She screamed. "*Abba*!" The sound tore at his ears.

First moving the candle from her way, Atticus knelt next to her and touched her forehead. Her skin was like fire. "Jubilee." He breathed. It had never taken much to wake her before. Nothing more than her name or touch to cheek. "Jewess." Her cries persisted. No longer curdling screams but a soft desperate sob as she called for her father. "Jewess."

She began to repeat something, too mumbled by her tears to make out. "Jubilee." He pleaded. The minutes seemed to drag as he stroked her hair, resisting the urge to shake or even slap her. Her screams ripped through him, tightening every muscle in his body. "Come on now, Jewess."

Finally, her eyes fluttered open and then she was choking, too dazed to move. Rolling her over the bed, Atticus held her hair back as she was sick.

"*Abba*." She cried again, her mind still ensnared in the dream.

With her sickness over, Atticus held her to him, unable to control his shaking. By the gods, it couldn't be true. It couldn't be true.

XII

❝ Won't you at least tell me what is wrong with him, Atticus?"

Jubilee had yet to let go of her grandfather's dismissal, and the rejection was clear in her posture. But there was a worry in her eyes. "I am his granddaughter. I have a right to know, do I not?"

She stepped back as Atticus reached for her. She wasn't letting him distract her now. "No, Jubilee." He sighed. "You don't, not if Julius has requested I keep this information to myself."

"But maybe I can help him?" Tears filled her eyes and she turned to hide them.

"I assure you, Jubilee. There is nothing *you* can do to help him, there is nothing anyone can do for him. There never was." It had been two days since Julius had revealed the truth to Atticus and already the disease had spread like fire. The sores, hidden from sight, had begun to fester and ooze. Ulcers marked his skin and dark bruises covered the entirety of his body like a second skin. He hoped sincerely that Jubilee never knew what it was that ailed and would inevitably kill the man she mindlessly loved. "You must prepare yourself, Jewess. He hasn't much time left."

Jubilee shook her head stubbornly. "No. No, I need more time with him. He isn't ready. But he is close! I can feel it. Atty please." Her voice rose hysterically. "Let me see him."

Atticus bit back a retort but still, he couldn't let it pass entirely. "Julius Aquila is beyond saving, Jewess." He said, not unkindly. He couldn't fault her for her heart, no matter how naive it might be where Julius stood.

"No one is beyond saving, Atticus."

Without warning, Aelia came to his mind. She was wrong. Some people were beyond saving. Ignoring her expectant stare he snapped at her. "Get to work. I don't want to lose business because of you."

The words had been cruel but they worked. Blinking back tears, Jubilee left the room.

Slumping onto the bed, Atticus put his face in his hands. Their relationship walked a fine line between love and fear. Pleasure and discontentment.

Jubilee had changed. She met him each day with love-filled kisses. She no longer slept at the edge of their bed. But still, the doubt crept in each time she pretended to sleep. Each time she averted her eyes and drifted away into some distant part of her mind when he made love to her. Whatever held her mind had consumed every piece of her, and no matter his efforts he couldn't rid himself of the memory of that night. How long did she expect him to believe they were only dreams? Whether dreams of fear or grief, he knew they were more than figments.

Standing he forced himself to move. Julius would be calling him by the time he had shuffled his way to the cubicula.

...

Julius moaned loudly as pain seized him. The pain was becoming unbearable and unrelenting. Would it never end?

"Atticus!" He screamed. Where was that insolent child? "By the gods, boy! Get in here."

"I told you there is nothing I can do for you." Atticus snapped. "I don't see why you feel the need to scream my name every few seconds." He was tired. Dark circles framed his eyes. As he reached the stool beside the bed, he slumped onto it. "Would you like a bedtime story? Because there is little more that I can offer you."

"Is that how you treat all your patients?" Julius retorted.

"Only the ones who remind me of you."

"And Aelia?" Julius smirked as the boy cringed. "I wonder what your new wife would think of the things your first wife was known for. From what I hear, we had something in common."

Atticus glared at the man. "Do not forget what I have, Julius."

"Is it not the truth? She made her way around all of Rome, that wife of yours. She left a trail of broken hearts and an even longer trail of bodies. Why is it, do you think? That she chose to leave you alive when so many others who graced her bed, later met their maker?"

"I own you!" Atticus hissed. "If you want me to keep my promises you will stop talking."

"It's because she thought you would kill yourself, isn't it?" Julius continued. "Does your Jewess know? About the poison you fed your body? All because your spineless father never taught you to handle a woman? Like all Albanus men, you let your woman rule over you."

Atticus upturned the stool as he stood. "That is enough. Unless you want Jubilee to know what you asked of me?"

Satisfied, Julius smiled. "I want Gentian."

"You said it doesn't work, I won't waste valuable herbs where it isn't useful."

"You're useless."

"I have done all I can. What you are suffering from cannot be undone. Perhaps you should have thought about that before going against the natural order of things."

"Get out!"

Gladly. Kicking the stool aside, Atticus stormed from the room. The man could suffer alone if that is what he wanted. He had had enough of him. If Jubilee wanted to waste her efforts believing good lay within him, let her. He didn't have to. The man was nothing but a sore.

Reaching the baths, he dived in without bothering to remove his clothes. As the water rushed around him he worked to dispel from himself all the memories Julius dredged up. *She got around, that wife of yours.* It wasn't news to him. Aelia had taken many lovers within their marriage—a fact she never felt the need to hide. Even with other men she was capable of bending them to her will. But Atticus, she knew, was weak and easily daunted.

"What will you do, puppy?" She smiled coyly, her head tilted seductively before glaring at him. "Nothing. Because you're a coward." She had been right. He had let her walk past him night after night, someone new on her arm. Like his father, he had never been one for confrontation and for that reason, he found himself where he was now. Caring for a diseased man and married to a woman who cringed at the mere thought of intimacy.

...

As Julius's health declined, so it seemed did Atticus's. The man's skin paled in the passing days and his feet dragged. Where he once stayed awake until late into the night, he now slept long before Jubilee could make her way to bed, and slept longer than what seemed a healthy number.

He had Jubilee worrying in ways that distracted her from the work she thought she wanted. When Atticus had left to assist her grandfather, he had left the shop to her, entrusting to her all that he had built in their months of marriage, and though she feared failing him, she feared more his rapidly declining health.

"Have you eaten recently?" She asked, finding him dressing before dinner. He had been doing well. A healthy fat had been finding its way back to him, filling his face and giving him color. If he continued as he was he would be back to where he had been before. "You will feel better if you get something in your stomach."

"I am busy, Jubilee." He spit.

"You're always busy, Atticus. That isn't an excuse for starving yourself."

Atticus glared at her. "I eat, Jubilee. Now get out."

Standing her ground, Jubilee watched him. "Do not lie to me. I am not stupid, nor am I blind. Look at you! You are killing yourself!"

"Perhaps it would be better that way, Jubilee. You want nothing to do with me anyway. If I die you can be free to go back to your family without shame."

"You think that is what I want? To see you die? To see you die at your hand because you are too stubborn to see reason?" Tears filled her dark eyes. "I don't like this. I don't like seeing you like this."

Did she think he liked seeing her as she was? Cringing at the mere thought of his touch? Screaming for her *Abba* in the dead of night? Sighing he took her hand. "Don't worry about me, Jewess. I'll be fine."

Rather than take comfort in his words, she pulled her hand free. "No. You won't." Skirting past him she fled the room.

Cursing her wretched tears, Atticus followed after her. Snatching up a plate he forced down the food. "Are you happy?"

Jubilee simply shrugged, her eyes on her food. Throwing the plate against the wall, Atticus left, ignoring the apology she cried after him.

Hidden behind the privacy of a bush, he stuck his fingers down his throat, lurching the small meal onto the ground.

Panting he wiped his mouth on his tunic, fighting the emotions that came with the ridding of his food. In his mind, that dreaded voice cooed. *That's it, puppy.*

He felt a small hand grip his shoulder gently and then her arms were around him. "It's okay." She breathed when he tried to pull away. "It's okay." Tears soaked into the back of his tunic, where she rested her cheek.

They sat in silence, Atticus's chest rising and falling from exertion. From the tears that spilled of their own accord. Shaking her off, he stood.

"Why do you shut me out?" She cried.

"Why do you?"

"I don't-" She closed her eyes, swallowing another round of tears. "I don't mean to." She said. "I have tried every day to tell you but I freeze. I don't want you to look at me differently. I don't want you to know that I am not-" She shook her head. Her fist pressed to her mouth.

Atticus felt the urge to laugh. "After everything you just witnessed, what can you be hiding that would change the way I see you?"

Jubilee shrugged. "It's not you, Atticus. This has nothing to do with you. I'll love you no matter what. I just want you healthy. Happy." Moving closer, she wrapped her arms around his waist. "Won't you try and listen to me?"

Disgust filled him at her touch and he pushed her from him. "Get away from me." He spit. "When you want something from me you find it within you to push past your disgust! You're no better than-than everyone else." He stuttered. "You are all the same, using pleasure to gain what you want."

Jubilee's lips trembled and she didn't bother to hide her tears. "Atticus, that isn't what I was doing."

"You are all the same." He repeated. "I should have known you would be no different. You are nothing like the girl I knew."

"Atticus!" Jubilee's sobs trailed after him but he didn't stop. Let the little harlot cry on her own.

Jubilee remained on the garden floor until her knees burned and her body ached. No matter her effort the sobs kept coming even when her ribs throbbed and nausea roiled in her stomach.

She had almost told him. She had wanted to tell him. More than anything she had wanted to finally rid herself of the sickening reason why she still trembled at his touch. But she didn't. Again she let fear rule over her and she had hurt Atticus in doing so. "God, where are you?" She cried. "Why am I here?"

Images of Atticus's hard, cold face played over in her mind, only creating more tears. *You're no better than-than everyone else.* He had stuttered. Changing directions. She was no better than who? Aelia?

Until then, she had grown used to forcing out any thought of her husband's first wife, feeling a strange wave of insecurity and jealousy when she slipped into her mind. Why had he chosen her? After everything, why had he left Jubilee for her? But as she thought of Atticus's shaking voice, guilt weighed on her chest like a brick as she remembered all the times they were together. He never allowed her to see him. When he finished he was quick to grab his tunic or slip beneath the covers. All because of one woman.

You are no better. Look at the way you treat him. You are just like her.

I'm not. She wanted to cry. *I am nothing like her. It isn't even him that disgusts me.*

Surely he knew that. She had seen the look in his eyes when she came out of the dream. She had felt the way he shook as he held her. She had tried to convince him they were only dreams. But she had seen in his eyes that he did not believe her and why should he? She had given him no reason. She could not lie but she had known she couldn't tell the truth either. She wasn't ready to see that look on his face. The look that said she was no longer a person worthy of being treated like any other.

And so you let him go on as you do, feeding all his insecurities. You are a coward, Jubilee.

...

Atticus felt as though he walked on glass as he made his way to his room. The wretched man hadn't let him sit once. He was hot.

Cold. Hungry. Nauseous. Like an incessant child, the man demanded everything.

Let him die already. He thought miserably. Unable to stand any longer he fell into the bed, nearly crushing Jubilee as he did so.

She gasped as she sat up, her hand clutching at her chest. "Are you all right?" The stress of their earlier fight remained in her dark eyes, begging him to talk.

"I'm fine." Ignoring her anxious gaze, he rolled to his side of the bed and closed his eyes. What was there to talk about? She had at last shown him her true colors. This was not his Jewess.

"It's not you," Jubilee said quietly.

"What?"

"You think that my lack of enthusiasm is because of you. You think I am disgusted by you. Atticus, I don't know know what she did to you, but if you listen I-"

"Quiet." He spit. "Stop."

"Atticus, listen to me. I want-"

"Stop acting so innocent, Jubilee. You think you can hide behind your questions while trying to trick me into sharing my troubles."

Jubilee glared back at him. "I am not trying to do anything. Pardon me for being attentive enough to put things together. Meanwhile, you are too caught up in your mess of problems to know that you already know my secret." She stared back at him, eyes blazing. "You say I am nothing like the girl you knew? What of you, Atticus? You are not the Atticus I grew up with. The Atticus I loved. That Atticus was kind and gentle and beautiful."

"Jubilee was fearless." Atticus spit. "She never let anything hold her back." He watched the downward curve of her lips and swallowed. "She was happy. You never saw her without a smile."

She nodded, nothing but fresh anger in her teary eyes. "Atticus never would have hurt me." Turning away she pulled the blankets to cover her face. "Perhaps you were right. This marriage was ill-advised." It seemed that no matter how close they grew their pasts pulled them apart once more and she wasn't going to share hers now. Not so long as he hid his own. Not so long as he remained so deeply in his that he left himself blind to hers.

Atticus hovered over her, his lips grazing her ear. "Jubilee wouldn't give up so easily."

"Neither would Atticus." She blew out the candle and the conversation was over.

XIII

The tension between the two persisted as the days blurred into one. Atticus spent his days from dusk till dawn with Julius. Unable to do more than watch him worsen with each day that passed, knowing it was only a matter of days until the disease took him.

When forced to spend the night with Jubilee, his mind played, again and again, the words she had thrown at him. *Atticus was kind and gentle and beautiful.*

Kind and gentle. He knew Aelia had hardened him. He had never been blind to the change in himself. But had he not tried to be kind to Jubilee? He had given her time. Space. He had given her patience time and again and still, she pulled away from him. And yet over and over her words played themselves for him, guilt gnawing at his core. *You already know my secret.* By the gods, he could shake her. Scream at her. *How can I know what you keep from me?* But always something stopped him from voicing his frustration. He could not deny what he had seen in her as she had spit the words at him. Despite the fire that had filled her eyes, her voice had been small. Pain oozed through the shattered pieces of her. *Atticus never would have hurt me.*

How many times had he been sick at those words? By the gods, why had he done it? Even through the anger that consumed him now, he could think of no reason for the things he had done that night. They had had a day of peace. They had walked the streets of Rome, Atticus showing her all the places he had loved as a child.

And it had all fallen away with a few words on his father's part.

"Do you think a woman like Jubilee will ever truly love you if you go on this way?" His father demanded. The words had pricked at his mind as they made their way home, Jubilee close at his side but still so distant in spirit.

By the gods he loved her. He wanted her. And he would have her. He needed his wife to love him as one should.

She hadn't fought him when he pulled her to him. She went willingly. As she always did now, she participated until finally he felt her retreat into her mind, shutting him away.

Tears had pecked his eyes again as his father's words repeated themselves, blending all too well with each word Aelia had taunted him with when it came to love.

He wanted his wife to look at him. To say his name. To love him the way he loved her. Grabbing her chin, he forced her to look at him. "Do not fight me, Jubilee." His voice shook miserably. By the gods he was pathetic. "Say my name, Jewess."

She had obeyed, her voice little more than a croak as her eyes fixed on the ceiling.

He turned her chin back to him, as gently as his own shaking hands could manage. Still, she avoided his eyes, keeping her stare past his ear. He spoke softly, his fingers caressing her cheek. "Look at me, Jewess."

"I can't." She sobbed. "Atticus, please. Don't do this."

"Do what, Jubilee?" He demanded. Laying next to her, he put pressure on his eyes, forcing down the emotion that was building in his chest. "Is this the way our marriage is going to be?" He

demanded, the emotion still clear in his throat. "Making love to my wife while she slips into some strange world in her head?" When the woman said nothing, Atticus cursed. "I ask nothing of you, Jubilee. Nothing but this."

She glared miserably back at him. "This is everything, Atticus. Don't you see that? You don't know what you are asking of me." She had begun to sob in earnest but for once he couldn't bring himself to care. Did she not see his pain?

"I am asking my wife to say my name. That shouldn't be too much to ask for. What are you so afraid of?" He demanded. "Is it your god?"

Jubilee sniffled. "God created this. He gave it as a gift."

"Then why do you fight it?"

"Because it is not a gift to me, Atticus. Not anymore." She stared upwards once more. "Now, please. I know it must be done, but don't ask more of me."

"It must be done?" Atticus spit. "What is this to you?" Closing his eyes he willed himself to calm. "I want to give you pleasure, Jewess."

"You can't." She sobbed. "It's too late."

"It doesn't have to be." He touched her cheek. "Please, Jubilee. Don't hide away from me." She could only shake her head. By the gods, how could he reach her? "Just try, Jewess. You have come so far. Just try."

She was shaking violently now, making the bed tremble beneath them. "No." Slapping his hand away from her, she scrambled away from him.

Nausea swept over him as he watched her move, the realization of what he had done washing over him like cold water. The way she shook as she dressed cut him. Why had he pushed her? Why had he demanded so much of her?

His face fell into his palms. "What is this, Jubilee?" It was his turn to beg. "I can't take this anymore. The constant push and pull. Do you not see what you do to me when you pull away? Do you think I don't notice when you go somewhere else? Do you think I don't know what that looks like, Jubilee? I know all about that." He swore as old memories closed in on him. Images he had long since forgotten.

Jubilee watched him silently, angry tears still pooling down her cheeks. "Don't touch me." She didn't say another word as she climbed back beside him, the old crater between them.

They lay in silence until Atticus felt ready to burst. "I want you to feel what I feel when I am with you, Jubilee. Don't tell me that your god gave man and wife sex and then tell me that it's not meant for you. It can be beautiful, Jewess. If you would just stop fighting it."

At his side, Jubilee closed her eyes tight. Her lip trembled. "I know it can be."

The thought found its way to him at every hour. *I know it can be.* Her voice had been distant. Wishful. Was it not fear that kept her from him at all? But rather, grief? The images that had so previously haunted him were replaced. She no longer struggled against him but went to the faceless man willingly, enjoying all the things Atticus couldn't give her. When her screams ripped through him each night, he imagined her discovering him. The man she loved dead on the floor. It was an easier thought. But it didn't ease the pain. He wasn't the man she wanted.

Pulling the blankets over his head he blocked out Jubilee's presence.

. . .

Jubilee felt Atticus's presence at her side like one felt a tumor. His very presence was suffocating. Easing herself off the bed she hurried across the cold floor and out into the hall, but his presence followed her.

Jubilee was happy. Fearless. He had spit the words at her. He had hoped to cause her pain. The intent was clear in his eyes and he had succeeded.

But though his words had stung, she knew the truth of them. She knew she had been changed that day. Even she didn't recognize the person she had become at times. But could she ever truly be that girl again? Fearless? Joyful? Someone worthy of the name her parents had chosen for her?

The idea seemed ludicrous now. Had she not tried every day to reach that point? Only to be pulled back in by the memories that haunted her mind? Bringing back all the pain she was now pushing onto her husband, the very person she had once trusted more than any other being?

Slipping into her cloak she hurried out of the vestibulum. She did not know where she was going, but she needed to get away from the claustrophobic walls of the Domus. Away from Atticus and the overwhelming failure that clawed at her at every hour.

God, what am supposed to do? Why have you brought me here if only to keep me where I was? Why bring me this far from home if I am to stay trapped within myself? I am hurting him, Lord, and I don't know how to stop it.

She didn't know how long she had been walking when she heard it. The ghostly echo of voices drifting through the darkness. After another few steps, she could hear the sound of voices melding together in praise, and despite the heaviness that pressed against her she felt a flicker of hope.

Tripping over herself in the darkness, she hurried toward the sound, the seedling of hope growing with each step. Heart pounding furiously, she approached the home where the music flowed. A humble, inconspicuous Domus.

Jubilee nearly pounded at the door in her excitement and heard the singing cease before the sound of wood being removed from the door.

Keeping her face hidden, a woman peered out at her. "May I help you?"

Jubilee felt her heart skip at the familiar accent. This woman was a Jewess. "Oh thank you, God!" She breathed. To have even the slightest bit of home. "I heard the music and I..." She trailed off feeling unsure. Perhaps it wasn't a church at all. She had not heard the words they sang but the simple beauty of them.

"Might I get your name?"

"Jubilee."

The woman's eyes narrowed. "You belong to the idol maker."

"Yes, my lady. Please do not turn me away." Tears filled her voice and the woman smiled pitifully.

"We do not turn away those interested in learning of the Lord." Opening the door wider, the candlelight shined on the woman's ruddy skin, revealing the thick, silvery scars that etched her flesh, disfiguring the left side of her face. Her left eye was clouded with blood and drooped lazily. Already pulled into a permanent smirk, the left corner of her lips pulled up only slightly when she smiled. But it wasn't the scars themselves that kept Jubilee's stare. It was the woman. She knew her. Only she didn't know how. The woman held out her hand in welcome. "I am Tamar."

Tamar led Jubilee into a small Bibliotheca, where the people were gathered. When the woman introduced her, she was welcomed with open arms. She was surprised to recognize many faces. The man from the ship, whom she learned was Mathias. Helena, who had brought her daughter Julia to the shop only days before. Elizabeth and her husband Remus. Even Camila sat among them with Decimus in her lap.

The mother smiled widely as she recognized her. "Jubilee!" She welcomed her into a tight hug. "I was hoping I would see you here. I thought you must come here since I couldn't find you at the synagogue. But when I came none had ever seen you."

"Yes, Camila has been quite fond of speaking of you." A man stepped forward, a gentle hand on the woman's shoulder. "I was wondering when we would meet the woman who brought our Camila to us." Leading Camila back to her seat, the man smiled. "I am Solaris."

Jubilee felt lighter as she made her way through the night. It had been so long since she had been in the presence of another believer. So long since she had felt the breath of God in its overwhelming magnitude.

As if the weight of it all had fallen upon her at once, she sank to her knees. The unfamiliar words poured over her until they poured from her lips.

But the moment she stepped back into the dark corridors of her new home, she felt that cold and lonely force take hold once more. Just as it had at Galilee. In the euphoria and security she found in the church, surrounded by those who shared her faith, she had felt the presence of the Lord upon them. Only when she was alone again did her faith dissolve. The Lord was not with her. He was with others. She was simply a bystander to his presence—an intruder.

Heart sinking, she hurried back toward her cubicula. *Oh God, why is it I can feel you so strongly there and yet feel none of you here?*

She was nearing her cubicula when she heard it—a sharp cry drifting from her grandfather's open door. Peering in she found him thrashing. Tiptoeing in, she took a seat next to him and patted his hand. "*Avus*." She whispered. "Wake, *Avus*." It was several moments before the old man's eyes peeled back, one at a time.

He stared up at her and then he was howling. "I told you to stay out of my room." He bellowed. "What did you see?" Despite his frailness, his hand was tight against her throat. "Tell me! What did you see?"

Jubilee felt her heart pounding wildly in her chest. "Nothing, *Avus*." She couldn't breathe. Her nails clawed at his hands. "Julius, please!"

"I swear by the gods, that if you tell anyone of this, Juliana, I will kill you!"

Juliana? Jubilee shook her head. The man was crazy. "I won't tell anyone." She croaked. "I promise."

When at last he released her she scurried away from the bed, nearly colliding with Leopold as she fled the room.

"What's going on in here?" He asked quietly. His eyes went to her throat. "By the gods, Jubilee. Are you all right?"

"I'm fine." Her throat burned and the words came in an inaudible croak.

Unwilling to face Atticus now, she ran past their room and into the one she had slept in when first arriving in Rome. Fighting back tears she climbed into the bed, her mother's bed, and slipped beneath the covers.

Her mother had slept on those very blankets, as the room had been wholly untouched in her mother's absence. It was where she came when she needed a piece of her. Had her mother, like herself, cried herself to sleep?

All her life she had listened to the shocked comments of her resemblance to her mother, but inwardly she had felt more like her father. It was not until Rome that she recognized the parts of her inner being that belonged to her mother. Both were two lives changed forever by one simple vow. With only one detail of change. For her mother, marriage had brought her out of the darkness. For Jubilee, marriage had only served as a way to drag her deeper into it. As if she was destined to finish out the life her mother had escaped.

Tears cascading down her cheeks she searched for any remnants of what she had felt in the church, but nothing remained.

Do not be ashamed of your tears. Her mother's voice whispered. *They are your heart's prayer when you can't find the right words to say.*

A fresh round of sobs burst from her lips. It had been almost thirty years since her mother had slept there and yet she felt closer to her as she curled beneath the covers. As if she were wrapped in her arms, the way her mother so often held her as a child. The way she had the day Jubilee left. *It's all right.* She would whisper. *You are not alone.*

XIV

Julius couldn't move. It had been three days since a stroke had left him to lay limply on the bed, the left side of his face drooping. Unable to speak he was left to listen to his granddaughters preaching. Rather than share her simple stories she had taken to repeating sermons from the church she had found. Her last, desperate attempt at saving his soul. At first, he fought her, moaning his objections as his hand flopped on the bed like a fish out of water. But as the days passed, he found himself listening.

"I know you don't believe in these things and I suppose I can't blame you." She was quiet for a moment. "It is difficult to believe in something unseen. Something unheard. I know that, and I could never pretend that it is easy. But *Avus*, I ask that you listen. That is all. Just listen to the stories I tell. The songs I sing. The prayers I pray. I won't ask for more than that. I won't force it on you or make you feel pressured in any way. I just want to know that I did my best. That I did my best by you. For *Imma*. Because whether you believe it or not, she loved you." She took a shaking breath before leaning in and kissing his forehead. "*I love you, Avus.*"

He didn't believe the words she spoke of her god, he couldn't, but the soothing tone of her voice took his mind from the pain that overwhelmed him, and he found himself waiting for her visits.

She sat now with her head bowed low, her hand clutching his as she breathed a prayer in an unknown tongue. Tears rolled down her cheeks, startling him. Did she truly cry for him? He only knew one other to cry over him and he did it in the solace of night, when no one would see. This girl cried without shame.

From the doorway, Atticus watched in disgust. He loathed the way Jubilee fawned over the man. Even after all the words Julius had thrown at her, she continued to care for him. Crying over him. He had hoped the bruises that marked her neck would have been enough to pull her away and yet there she sat, her head bowed before him, praying unceasingly for the soul he didn't have. "You may go." He ordered.

She jumped, her hand dropping Julius's. "I am fine here." She scooped his hand back into hers and proceeded to pray.

Even now anger from the nights before kept them apart, only further proving how far gone this woman was from the girl he had loved. For all her stubbornness, his Jewess wasn't spiteful.

Julius' eyes opened and he glanced between the two before focusing on Atticus. He moaned, his eyes glued to Atticus's hands.

Jubilee followed them to the small vial clutched in his palm. "What is that?"

"Before I started caring for him, your grandfather made me promise not to let him go on if he came to such a state."

Jubilee watched him, the words coming together slowly. "No." She grabbed his hands, covering the vial. "Please, you can't do that."

"It will be quick, Jubilee. His suffering will end."

"You don't care about his suffering!" She spit. "You only care about yourself. You said it yourself you want him dead." She knelt beside Julius, once again taking his hands in hers. "*Placere, Avus*. Don't do this."

Her grandfather watched her, his dark eyes softening. For a moment it seemed as if the man was considering her words before his eyes turned to Atticus. He lifted a finger.

Atticus set a hand on Jubilee's shoulder. "You should go, Jubilee."

She stared up at him, her eyes wet with tears. "I know you didn't want me." She whispered. "So don't think of me now when I ask this. Think of Galilee. Of Nazareth and Cana. Of Magdala and Capernaum. Or how you used to kiss my nose when you got off the ship every year and how you changed to tugging my hair as we got older. If you ever loved me, even a little, you won't do this. Please, Atty."

It was the first time she had called him Atty in days. The sound of it on her lips, mixed with the soft tears stirred his stomach. For the briefest moment, his walls fell. Atticus brushed her cheek, wiping away the tears. "I made a promise, Jubilee."

Her mouth set angrily. "Promises can be broken." She replied. "Every promise he ever made was broken."

Atticus watched her silently. He knew there was a chance she would never forgive him if he followed through with Julius's request. But that was just as well. Taking a deep breath, he turned and called for Leopold. "Would you escort Lady Jubilee out of the room please?"

"Yes, my lord." Leopold was gentle with her as he pulled Jubilee to her feet.

Jubilee glared up at Atticus, hurt tears dripping down her cheeks. "Atticus, please." She breathed.

Atticus turned away as Leopold wrapped an arm around her waist. "Come along, my lady."

She spun on him now. "Do you agree with this?" She demanded. "You care for him. I know you do, so stop him!"

Leopold frowned. "There is nothing to be done, Jubilee."

"There is everything to be done." Pushing away from him, Jubilee kissed her grandfather's cheek before leaving the room.

…

Sibyl stroked the girl's hair from her tear-streaked face. Jubilee had not stopped crying since Julius's death.

It had been Leopold who came for Sibyl. *A girl needs a mother at such a time.* It had seemed a strange thing, to think of someone mourning the passing of a man like Julius. She felt more than sure that the man was no less cruel with his granddaughter than his daughter, and still, there the girl was when she arrived, tears streaming down her cheeks.

"He went of his own accord, as he wished it. It is not an uncommon thing in Rome."

Jubilee shook her head but said nothing. *God, what use am I? What purpose did you have in bringing me here? Of asking me to sit with him day after day, listening to his cruelty of you and Imma and everything? And for what? I did nothing! I have reached no one.*

"It's my fault." She cried. "I didn't fight hard enough."

"Nonsense." Sibyl comforted. "You cannot blame yourself for what happened. He was dying, *Puella.* No amount of attention could solve that."

They don't understand! God, I tried! I tried!

Sibyl exhaled as the realization came upon her. "You are thinking about his eternity. His soul?"

Jubilee turned to glance at her through wet lashes. "I tried to help him. But he wouldn't listen. He thought they were only stories."

"I know that I don't know much, Jubilee. But everything I have heard from you and your parents is that he is a loving god. Would a loving god blame a child for failing to reach a man as stubborn and set in his ways as Julius Aquila?" Sibyl brushed the girl's tears. *"Puella,* it would have taken a miracle to see any change of good in him."

"But there was good in him, Sibyl. He was kinder near the end. If I only had more time with him I know he could have been saved."

"Atticus did what he thought was best, Jubilee. He made a promise."

"He played a part in killing him, Sibyl. He and Leopold both. They just let him kill himself without any regard for his soul."

"Because they don't believe in those things."

"And you?" Jubilee whispered. "Please tell me I have at least reached someone. Please tell me there is a reason for all of this."

"I am trying, Jubilee. But I need my time." Encouraging Jubilee to rest her head in her lap, Sibyl began to sing softly.

…

Atticus stood in the doorway of the cubicula, listening to his mother's soft voice. Her hands played delicately with Jubilee's hair, braiding it away from her face and the tears that stained it. He was grateful Leopold had thought of her for Jubilee. No matter his feelings for her grandfather, the girl deserved comfort in her grief and she would not have taken it from the one who had taken him from her.

When the song finished, his mother spoke more with the soothing tones only a mother could carry. Atticus had always resented the fact that his mother had borne no children after him. She was a mother to her core and she had been denied the right to any more than one. He knew it to be the reason for her urgency in his finding another wife of suitable merit. She longed for grandchildren. New babies whom she could hold and love.

Aelia had denied her that right on more than one occasion. A truth which he sincerely hoped his mother never knew. *I will not be a mother, Atticus. I will not be tied down.*

Atticus rubbed his eyes. Some days Aelia's voice was so clear in his mind he could swear she was in the room with him. Three years gone and she still managed to play with his mind.

He stepped back as his mother came towards him. Jubilee remained in the room, her fingers pinching at her skin.

"Will she be all right?" He asked.

Sibyl sighed. "Do you truly care, Atticus?" The words were out of her mouth before she could stop them.

"I am not without a heart, Mother." He snapped. "Whether the rest of you choose to see it or not." His mind went back to Aelia and the things he kept from his mother for the sole purpose of protecting her.

"I am sorry, Atticus. But you cannot hold me to blame for your shortcomings. Aelia changed you." Her eyes looked him over and she shivered. "Would it truly have hurt to give Jubilee more time with him? The man was delirious. He was dying anyway, what would a few more days have mattered?"

"I gave my word when I took over his care."

"Do not pretend that is your reasoning with me. You were done with him. I understand that. That man has had people wishing for his death since before I was born. But it doesn't make it right, Atticus. One day you will have to stop thinking about yourself and start thinking of your wife. It is not always about you."

"It has never been about me where my wife is concerned, mother. Not with Jubilee and certainly not with Aelia."

Sibyl shook her head. "You two have got to stop keeping so many secrets before they become your undoing. Do you want another marriage to fall through the cracks, Atticus? Do you want to send that poor child back to her family in shame?"

"If Jubilee leaves in shame it is not due to me. I have tried with her but she is impossible."

"She is broken, Atticus. In horrible ways. Ways that you will never fully understand." She took his hand. "I know she may not seem like the woman you loved before, but she is in there. Think of her before you fight more, and remember that you are far from the man she loved."

Atticus ripped his hand back. "I did not come back to Rome to listen to you and Father insult me. I did not marry a prudish Jewess so you can continue to point out my mistakes."

His words hung in the air before settling heavily between them. "Sometimes I do not even recognize my son anymore."

"It seems no one is happy with me here. Perhaps I should take my practice back to Greece."

"Atticus, wait." Sibyl's fingers brushed his arm as he moved away from her. "Atticus." Her arm fell to her side as he disappeared around the corner. She swore for the first time in weeks.

Atticus felt the full weight of his exhaustion as he entered his cubicula. His heart seemed to race in his chest and for a moment he feared he might not make it to his bed. His head spun miserably. Ashen-faced and shivering violently, he curled under the blankets. He was asleep before his head hit the pillow.

Part II

49 AD

XV

Ianuarius

G rief welled within Leopold with every breath he expelled from his lungs. The emptiness that had taken hold of his heart threatened to send him to his knees. He had never known a man so long as Julius. To listen to the hatred that was spread about the man was sickening. The man was dead—not yet in his grave. Could they show no sympathy even then?

He kept his mind on his work to distract himself from the pain. Knowing Julius best of all, he had requested he be the one to put everything in order. A way to honor the master he had always served, one last time. He liked to believe it was what Julius would have wanted. A friend. Not a practical stranger without a kind word to say in his honor. Had they known him as he had, perhaps they could have seen the good that lay within him.

"How is he?" Sibyl's voice broke through his thoughts. The woman's eyes were on Jubilee as she entered the tablinum. Atticus, after Julius had passed, had fallen asleep and had yet to wake for more than a few moments of fit-like nightmares.

"Still sleeping," Jubilee replied softly. "But you mustn't worry, this is to be expected after the amount he was drinking. But I believe his fever will break soon."

"Will you go back to him? I don't want him alone."

"Of course, Sibby. I'm only going to fetch fresh water and rags."

Sibyl nodded before turning back to the harp, a special favor for Jubilee. Julius had enjoyed the harp.

Leopold had been sure to thank the girl when given time. Unlike the others, she shared in his grief. Her dark eyes had softened when she smiled at him—a strange sort of softness that made him wonder if she knew. "Of course, Leo. If there is anything else you would like do not be afraid to ask."

Leopold had had to work to push back the tears that threatened to reveal him. The girl was too innocent to put together something so sinful. She wouldn't know. She couldn't. She would never look at him again if she knew. "It's good to see someone honoring my lord." He said quietly. "He was not all that he seemed, my lady."

"I know he wasn't, Leopold. But don't let their feelings get to you. He did hurt a lot of people, Leo. It is hard to let such things go sometimes."

Leopold watched the girl now as she crossed the room, her mind too set on her husband to notice him. *He did hurt a lot of people,* Leo. How he knew. He often hated the way he served the man so loyally.

...

The quiet creak of the door clawed at the inside of his head. Couldn't they see he wanted to sleep? Had he not earned the right to a few hours of peace?

Pulling the blankets above his head he willed himself to sleep longer. When the presence in the room stayed, he sighed and sat up, instantly regretting it as his head spun. When he stretched he felt every aching bone in his body. When his head had settled, he looked up to find Jubilee beside him, her fingers wringing out a rag.

When she noticed him, a small smile played on her lips. "You're awake." Relief coated her small voice.

"I am." He replied shortly. Could she not handle a few hours without pestering him? Could she not leave him in bed for even a moment? His head pounded and the pain in his stomach was blinding, he wanted to be left alone.

As he stretched, he could feel Jubilee's eyes on him. "What?" He demanded.

"Please can we just stop this?" Her voice was small. "I don't want to fight anymore."

Atticus turned to look at her. The dark circles that framed her eyes had deepened. She looked the way he felt. Tired. "Neither do I." He replied hoarsely.

Without a word, she moved to hand him a goblet of water. Gulping down the water he asked for more. "Drink it slowly." She said quietly. "You have been asleep for nearly for nearly two days, you will be sick if you drink too much too quickly."

Two days? He rubbed his eyes, still begging for more sleep. It explained the empty ache in his stomach. The stiff muscles. "Who took care of everything?" He didn't think Jubilee would be capable of putting together a Roman funeral. Least of all one as lavish as Julius Aquila's was destined to be.

"Leopold and your father worked to get everything Julius desired." She smiled. "It will be interesting I am sure."

The two lapsed into a comfortable silence, the sort that they had always enjoyed in Nazareth. It was several minutes before Atticus felt the woman's eyes on him. Glancing up at her he frowned at the worried look that had crept back into her eyes.

Would life ever find its way back to those eyes? "What is it, Jubilee?"

"I don't want you to be angry with me." She pinched at her skin.

Taking her hand in his, he held it tightly. "Stop that."

She bit down on her lip instead. "I never meant to make you feel used. When I touched you. I have never meant to use you. I have only ever worried over you."

"Jubilee stop." Could she let nothing rest?

"Please do not get angry with me again!" She cried. "It's only that you said a lot in your sleep. A lot of things about me." Her lip trembled and she pressed his hand to them. "I can't take this anymore, Atty. Here I am sitting next to you and I somehow feel myself missing you far more than before. I felt closer to you when you were delirious because at least you weren't hiding your pain behind anger." Hesitantly she leaned in and kissed him softly. "I am not asking you to share your secrets if you aren't ready. I have tried and failed to tell you mine. All I am asking is that we stop trying to hide our pain from one another. All we have managed to do was hurt the other."

Atticus watched her and the stiff way she held herself away from him. As though at any moment he would pull her down beside him. "What happened to you, Jubilee?"

"You truly don't know?" She whispered. "Please think, Atticus. I have tried to tell you but I don't think I can bring myself to say it. Not to you. Please just understand, that I am trying to give you what you deserve." She kissed him once more before grabbing the damp rag. "The funeral begins in an hour, so I want you to rest while I'm gone."

Atticus's eyes closed as she pressed the rag to his forehead. Why was she being so kind to him? He had thought that to abide by her grandfather's wish would be the final thread cut. "I had hoped you would be glad to see him gone."

"Pardon?"

"Your grandfather was as cruel as a man can be. I have heard the stories of the things he has done. Even if you loved him, you should be thankful to be free of him and yet you mourn him even now."

Jubilee's eyes narrowed. "Who could ever be glad to see someone gone? To see someone take his own life?"

"He was dying, Jubilee."

"It makes no difference to me."

"He put his hands around your throat, Jubilee." Atticus pressed. "He could have killed you."

"He was delirious, Atticus. He didn't know what he was doing."

"He called you by your mother's name." Atticus pleaded. "He wasn't simply delirious, Jubilee. His mind was in the past. Do you think he didn't do that to Juliana?"

Jubilee opened her mouth but couldn't deny it. She had thought the very same thing after it had happened. How often had he taken her mother that way?

"I heard the things he said about you." Atticus continued. "They were nothing compared to the things he said when you weren't there. How can you mourn a man like that? How can you say you loved him?"

She bit her lip. Her eyes blurred. "He was my family, Atticus, and I saw a different side of him. He was kind when I needed him to be."

"He hated you, Jubilee. A man like that doesn't deserve your love."

"Nor do I the love of God." She replied. "Whether we wear it on our sleeves like Julius or hide it away, we all carry something ugly within us. Something deemed unlovable by one person or another. So I ask you if we loved only those who deserved it, who would be left?"

Atticus shook his head. "There are plenty of people who deserve your sort of love. Many far more deserving than he."

Jubilee's eyes softened. "I pray someday you will understand, Atticus." Tucking the blankets in around him she kissed his forehead before leaving him alone.

...

Jubilee walked with Leopold as they made their way back to the Domus. The burial had taken place in the form of cremation. Something near unheard of in Galilee. The differences in the places she called home would never cease to amaze her.

The urn containing her grandfather's ashes rested in Leopold's hands, ready to be placed in the *lararium* as Julius requested. Jubilee couldn't help but watch as Leopold clutched the ashes to his chest.

An unease had begun to form in her stomach as she watched the man mourn. Tears still streamed down his cheeks, leftover from the service. The man had been unable to control himself during the service and had leaned on Jubilee for comfort.

"What will happen to you?" She asked. "Now that he is gone?"

"As of your grandfather's passing, my life now rests in your hands, my lady."

"What does that mean?"

"It means I now belong to you. You may keep me or sell me."

"I would never sell you, Leo. You know that."

Wouldn't you? A dark voice whispered. *Don't pretend you don't know what he is.*

No. No, she could never sell him, no matter what he came to be. She took his hand and squeezed it tight, fighting back the fresh tears that stung her eyes. What she had seen was wrong. She had seen it wrong.

Leopold gave her hand an awkward pat as he juggled the urn. "I would not blame you, my lady. Most people are looking for younger, more useful slaves."

"I am not looking for any slave, Leopold. We'll keep you with us because we love you."

The voice came unexpectedly. *Let him go.*

"That is if you want to stay with us?" The words seemed to claw their way out of her. "I can always free you if that is what you want."

Leopold was quiet. His eyes glossed and when he spoke there was a strange pitch to his voice. "It is all I have ever wanted, my lady."

"Then that is what you will get." Jubilee breathed. "Where will you go?"

"I have not thought that far ahead in a very long time, my lady. I was born into slavery. I worked for your grandfather's family. We grew up together."

"Did you?"

"He was only three years older than I. We were friends. My mother was his mother's lady's maid, and they were quite close despite the rank between them."

"You cared for him didn't you?" She hoped he could not hear the tremble in her voice. "Even after everything?"

There it was again, a strange flicker in his eyes. "He was not always so cruel, my lady. I still remember a time when he was kind."

"What happened?"

Leopold looked down at her, the corners of his lips curving sadly. "You're grandfather has not lived an easy life, Jubilee. It doesn't excuse what he became, but it does explain it." The man bit his lip. "It would have broken his mother to know what her boy became. There was no kinder woman than his mother, and she loved Julius more than anything."

Reaching the Domus, Leopold separated himself from Jubilee and hurried toward the servant's quarters.

Jubilee watched him go, his head bent over the urn. *How can you ask that I send him away if that is the life he will live?*

Trust, Beloved.

Going the opposite way, Jubilee quickened her step, anxious to check on Atticus. She found him asleep, the blankets wrapped tightly around him. Sitting at the edge beside him, she brushed his forehead. His eyelids dragged open at her touch.

Groaning, he sat up with help from Jubilee. "How long did I sleep this time?"

"The funeral only just ended." She assured him. "How are you feeling?"

"Better." The queasiness of his stomach had settled, as well as the miserable spinning in his head.

"You had me worried. I thought I was going to lose you." She bit her lip. "Atticus, I know you don't want to hear it, but-"

"I need to eat." He interrupted.

"Yes."

"Would you mind getting me food? I don't think I could make it."

"You're going to—I mean yes. I'll go put something together." She returned quickly with a tray of assorted fruits and meats. Sitting from him on the bed she placed the tray between them. "Eat up."

Helping herself, she kept her eyes averted, for which he was grateful. When they had finished the tray she watched him nervously. "Are you going to…"

"No, Jewess." He assured. "I mean I-I don't want to."

Setting the tray on the floor she crawled over the blankets and rested next to him. "Don't listen to whatever voices have been put into your head, Atty. Just listen to mine." She stroked his hair. "You do not need to harm yourself to be beautiful."

Ignoring the fear that made her heart race painfully, she curled closer to him and wrapped her arms around his waist. If he was to face his demons, she too must face hers.

XVI

Februarius

Leopold felt as though the world around him was caving. It would only be a matter of time before the girl learned the truth behind his grieving. How long could he continue in his grief before she admitted to herself the truth of what he was?

The girl had offered him his freedom more than once, but fear held him back. He wanted it. More than anything he wanted it. So long as he resided in this home, so full of memories and secrets, he would never move on from what he was. But could he avoid temptations on his own? All the things so previously denied him would be laid at his feet and without proper knowledge of the god he wished to serve, he knew he would be all too willing to accept them. Betraying Juliana again and again with each small choice.

But fear alone didn't keep him. Just one look into those dark eyes and he felt himself being pulled back in, just as he had with Julius. He could see the girls suffering. Just like her mother, she held no secrets from him. She had shared her struggles with him, her desires to please her husband and the fears that held her back. He couldn't leave her. Not as she was.

Leopold kept his head down as he hurried through the street. He could not fathom what he was doing. Any other servant he knew would be punished for his late-night adventure. But he knew the masters he served, as well as those he intended to meet. Knocking at the door, he pulled the cloak tighter about himself.

A servant opened the door. The tall Egyptian girl he remembered tending to Sibyl during the funeral preparations. "I must speak with Lady Sibyl." He announced.

"You are from the Aquila Domus." She eyed him, her lips turned in a distrustful frown. "Is everything all right with the lady's son?" No servant wanted to be the bearer of bad news.

"Yes. Yes. He is fine." Leopold waved her off impatiently. "It is a personal matter."

Eyeing him a moment longer, the girl motioned for him to step inside, leaving him alone in the atrium. It was several minutes before Sibyl appeared.

"Leo." She smiled. Taking his arms in her hands she looked him over. "I hope everything is well. You? The children?"

"It is, my lady. Thank you."

Pacified, Sibyl looped her arms through his as she and Juliana walked as girls. "Why don't we move this to the peristyle? Layla has told me you had something personal to speak of?" Sending the slave girl for cheese and crackers, Sibyl walked him through the triclinium and into the gardens. Taking her seat she urged him to take the place beside her.

"I would prefer to stand, my lady."

"Oh please, Leopold. I have known you since I was seven years old, it's absurd to be so formal with one another."

Leopold frowned. It did seem rather strange now he was to be a freeman. He had watched the woman grow up, always so forcefully protective of Juliana. The woman was one of only three to call him Leo. He lowered himself next to her, thankful to rest his legs.

"It seems such a trivial thing now that I am here." At her soft smile, he continued. "Jubilee has offered me my freedom, my lady."

"Leopold that's wonderful! You have more than earned such privilege."

"Yes, my lady."

She took his hand in hers. "Aren't you at all happy?"

"You see, my lady, I have taken quite a liking to Jubilee. I worry what will become of her when I am gone."

Sibyl sat up straighter, her face pinched. "What do you mean, Leopold?"

"It is not that I do not trust your son, my lady. I can see that he loves her and is more than capable of taking care of her, and I know the two have a history. But I feel that what Jubilee needs now is more than a husband."

A smile eased across Sibyl's face as she began to understand. "She needs a lady's maid." She laughed, all the previous worry gone from her eyes. "Of course, I don't know why I didn't think of it sooner." She had grown close to the woman who had tended to her after she had married. She had become a friend when she had lost Juliana. "But who? It can't be just anyone."

"If you do not mind my saying so, my lady. That Egyptian looks to be near Jubilee's age?"

"You mean Layla?" Sibyl frowned. "Yes, I suppose she would do quite nicely." She had grown to like the Egyptian girl very much. She was hardworking. Respectful. "I think I could part with her for Jubilee's sake."

"I hope I have not overstepped my boundaries, my lady."

"Not at all, Leo. You are right, it is difficult to find someone who will serve loyally. Jubilee needs a friend and Layla is the perfect girl." At that moment, Layla entered, her dark eyes curious at the mention of her name. "Thank you, Layla, dear. You are free to join us if you would like."

Knowing the woman would not take no for an answer, Layla knelt beside them on the ground. Her stomach rolled nervously at the conversation. Was she truly going to be passed off again? Like nothing more than a child's plaything? They couldn't. She had made herself a home with the Albanus'. Her old mistresses and their husbands had been cruel and petty. The Albanus', for all their beauty and successes, were neither vain nor biased and the servants that came through their home were treated with the kindness and respect of any freeborn civilian. Sibyl had taken to treating Layla as nothing less than a daughter when it was only the two of them. It was an honor she was not ready to give up. Not for another spoiled bride.

…

The air was unusually hot as the two made their way down the street. Sibyl had insisted on walking to her sons, regardless of the sun.

Sweat beaded on Layla's lips and brow. She rubbed at her scalp, blistering in the heavy heat, despite the wrap that covered it.

Regardless of how the sun bothered her, Sibyl seemed unbothered. She walked with her head held high as the sun shone off her blonde hair. The woman glanced toward her now and again, her green eyes seeming to glow in the bright sun. "You will like Jubilee very much, I think. She is nothing like Aelia." The woman's voice took on the tone that only came with the

189

mention of her son's first wife. Regaining her composure she patted Layla's hand. "You will like her. She'll be good to you."

Layla kept her tongue. She had grown accustomed to Sibyl and now she was once again being passed off. No matter the mistress's assurances, she was certain she would be handling another young and spoiled bride. She took comfort that if this Jubilee was anything like the master's first wife, she would be back serving Sibyl once more before the month was through.

Ushered into the Domus, Layla let her eyes roam. One could tell a lot about who their owner would be by the state of their Domus. The place looked wholly unchanged since the original master's death.

The vibrant purple curtains still separated the atrium from the rest of the home. The tapestries of the Roman god still hung along the yellow walls. The small table that sat to the right of the entrance still held the red vase with a new arrangement of roses. None gave her a sense of who this new mistress might be.

When the girl entered, Sibyl took her hands in the way a mother would. She had never handled her son's first wife in such a way. Even if she would have liked to, Layla was certain Aelia would have held her off. Turning to her, Sibyl set a hand at Layla's back with all the kindness of a mother, and she felt an unwelcome pang in her chest. "I wanted to introduce you to Layla. I never got the chance before."

Layla moved forward and bowed her head. "My lady."

Jubilee smiled warmly. "It is nice to meet you."

"I thought she would suit your needs quite nicely."

The girl raised an eyebrow at the woman's smile. "I wasn't aware I had a need." She said quietly.

"A lady's maid." Sibyl frowned. "Did Leopold not warn you?"

Jubilee's face fell. "Oh no, my lady. Please." Her eyes flickered to Layla's and her cheeks went pink. "Really." She said quietly. "I can care for myself."

"Every young lady needs one, Jubilee. They are much more than help. They can also be great friends."

Layla glanced between the two. Born into servitude she still felt anger at how she was little more than an object to play with when bored. The girl didn't need her, did she? Was she already not good enough? Inwardly she begged Sibyl to keep her, at least with the Albanus' she was human.

The girl chewed her lip before turning her dark eyes on her. She was smaller than her husband's first wife. And those eyes. Never had she seen eyes so dark. But as dark as they were they held no malice. Rather, there was a shyness to them as she smiled apologetically. "I am sorry if I have offended you. I have never required a lady's maid before."

"A fine lady of Rome not needing a maid?" The words left her lips before she could stop them, carrying with them the anger she felt at her rejection. Her eyes darted toward Sibyl and she cursed herself and her quick tongue. She had never wanted to embarrass Sibyl. But there was no change in the woman's round face. Nor resentment in the younger girls. "Please forgive my tongue, my lady."

Sibyl laughed softly. "My quick tongue has gotten me into trouble more times than I would like to admit."

"There is no need to apologize, Layla," Jubilee assured. "But to answer your question, I am not from Rome. I was born in Galilee. Nazareth."

Layla raised an eyebrow. A Jewess?

Taking Jubilee's hand, Sibyl pulled her aside. "Please take her in, Jubilee. I think it would be good for the both of you." She frowned as she glanced back to the slave girl. The girl was hard. Closed. She had been with them for three years and despite the obvious warmth she held toward them, she had yet to even smile. "I believe she needs you as much as I know you need her." Perhaps Jubilee's heart could ease whatever filled the girl's soul.

Squeezing Sibyl's hand, Jubilee turned back to the girl. "I do not wish to disrupt your life, Layla. If you have made a home for yourself with Lady Sibyl I will not be offended if you wish to stay."

"This is not my choice, my lady."

"It is with me."

"If my lady wishes for me to serve you, I will do so."

"Very well then," Jubilee said. "Let me escort Sibyl out and then I can show you to your quarters."

Walking Sibyl back through the Domus, Jubilee took hold of the woman's hands. "Will you come again?" She had missed the woman's visits. Their meetings had started daily until they had tapered off into nothing. "I still have so much to tell you of the Lord."

"All you have to do is send Layla and I will come."

Jubilee nodded, fresh tears filling her eyes. Sibyl touched her hair softly. "Jubilee, you know you are always welcome in our home. Do not be shy." She smiled. "Our visits do not always have to be your stories, you know. I have quite a few stories of your mother as well if you would ever like to hear of the mischief the two of us got into as girls."

A light smile touched the girl's lips. "My mother could be mischievous?"

"There are many sides to your mother that you probably do not know about, *Puella.* If it weren't so, she may never have met your father."

Meeting Layla back in the peristyle, Jubilee motioned for her to follow. "I am afraid there is only one bed." She said quietly. "But Leopold will be leaving soon, which will leave you with the quarters to yourself." Entering the quarters, Jubilee stopped at the door. "I'll leave you to settle in then."

With the girl gone, Layla walked the Domus, as she always did in a new home. She wanted to know every corner before she began her official work. Tears pricked at her eyes and she beat them back. Sibyl's tenderhearted nature had softened her, but she wouldn't cry. Just as with any other transition, she would hold her head high.

XVII

Aprilis

S ibyl picked at her food—her stomach turning miserably. "How long will you be gone?" She hoped her voice did not betray her. She knew Regulus struggled to bring himself to Ostia and she needn't make it worse. Having finally shared his dealings in Ostia, the man no longer tried to hide the frustration he felt at what awaited him. Nor his dread. She had never known her husband to be daunted by any, but even he wasn't immune to Aelia. He had returned from his last trip pale and agitated despite the hours that had passed. Wrapping his arms around her waist he had set his head to her abdomen. "By the gods, the way she makes me feel, Sibby. If the devil is true he lives in that woman."

"Would it truly be so terrible to tell her no?" She asked. "To cut the girl off?"

"Yes. I will not have her coming back into our lives. Especially not when we have Jubilee to look after." Regulus watched her a moment. "I shouldn't be gone more than the day."

Taking another bite, Sibyl forced herself to chew. She had grown used to Regulus's frequent trips in the past, but it had been ten years since he had entrusted his workers with the task of deliveries, and in those years she hadn't suffered from the nightmares that now haunted her nightly. "I suppose that isn't so terrible."

"Don't do this to me again, Sibby. I want to know that you are well while I am away."

"I didn't say anything, Regulus." Abandoning her food she moved to sit beside him. "I will be perfectly fine, I'm simply going to miss you. Our bed is lonely without you."

"Why don't you stay with the children while I am away? You always seemed happier after speaking with Jubilee."

"The girl has only just gotten back to medicine, I hate to bring her away from it so soon."

"A few hours are not going to hurt her, Sibyl."

Sibyl brushed at the corner of his mouth, where crumbs had gathered. "Will it make you feel better to know that I am with her?"

"You know it will. I hate to think of you alone when I am gone. I know how your mind gets when you are alone." He watched the way her eyes glanced down. Her hand was on her stomach. "I know you think of them."

"I'll go after lunch." She said quietly. "But you really must stop worrying over me."

"You cannot blame me, Sibyl." Pulling her closer, Regulus set his forehead to hers. "You have given me quite a lot of trouble in the past. All I can do is worry when I am gone."

"Well, those days are long past, Regulus. As is the need to worry over those issues. What troubles me now is entirely different."

Regulus sighed at the sudden change in her tone. "You truly think that what bothers you will be fixed with Jubilee's god?"

"I don't know anything yet, Regulus. But I am willing to try anything to rid myself of those terrible nightmares."

"I thought you said they have worsened since listening to Jubilee's stories?"

Sibyl shrugged. "Perhaps that is something I must speak with Jubilee about." Her fingers toyed with his hair, her eyes distant. "I do remember Juliana saying her bouts of sadness worsened when she first started listening to Malachi's stories. I don't know what it means but I know it didn't last."

"Juliana continued meeting with Malachi."

"Why are you so concerned?" Sibyl asked. "I thought this was all foolishness to you?"

"I do not believe in an all-powerful being, Sibyl. Nor do I believe an ordinary Nazarene rose from the dead. What I do believe in is the power of one's mind. When you believe to need something, finding it will more often than not cure you of whatever ails you. Even if only by your determination."

Sibyl raised an eyebrow. "You do realize I am not your son?" She retorted. "Would you mind explaining that again?"

Laughing Regulus started over. "Jews and Christians and even the believers in Roman gods, believe so strongly in their respective gods, that it is by their own minds that they create the things in which they believe to be from their gods. If you look at Juliana and the sadness that followed her in life, you can believe as she does that it was her god who changed her. Or you can look at it discerningly. Juliana wanted to rid herself of those feelings so strongly she was willing to believe this god held the answer."

"You believe she cured herself of those feelings? By nothing more than desire?"

"That or simply being free of her father. There are many reasons why things change people, Sibyl."

"But what can you say of Juliana's health?" Sibyl demanded. "She had been sick all her life, Regulus. She was practically on her deathbed that summer. She should have died after Nathanael was born. Nathanael should have died with her or at least have had the health Juliana lived with and yet they didn't. That man laid his hands on them both and they were healed. That isn't something that the power of the mind can control. Is it?"

For once, Regulus stumbled. "I am not saying you shouldn't believe in it, Sibyl." He replied. "If it brings you the peace you are looking for then I will be happy. But I do not believe in it. Whatever healed those two was not of a supernatural cause."

Sibyl walked Regulus to the coach, before wrapping her arms around him, reluctant to let him go. "Just one night."

"One night." Kissing her flushed cheeks, Regulus boarded the carriage.

When he was gone, Sibyl walked the expanse of the Domus. Already his absence was deafening. One night without Regulus to wake her. One night without his comforting arms to hold her. Tears trickled down her cheeks and she worked to staunch them to no avail. The first night was always the hardest.

The moment the tears subsided, Sibyl stood and readied herself to leave. She wouldn't last until lunch, not when the walls already threatened to consume her. She needed something to keep her mind off Regulus and the nightmares and all the history that haunted her in Regulus's absence. Within the walls that held such a prominent place in her dreams was no way of doing so.

When Layla opened the door her dark eyes widened with surprise. A small dimple on her cheek revealed the smile she fought to hide. "My lady." She said quietly. "I wasn't aware that Lady Jubilee was expecting you."

"She isn't, love. I'm afraid my visit is very last minute. When you fetch her, let her know it isn't urgent."

Escorting Sibyl to the garden, Layla hurried toward the shop. She could hear the two voices floating through the curtain before reaching it. They sounded happy. She had never heard Atticus laugh, nor had she heard such kindness spoken between him and his first wife. Pushing the curtain aside she found them huddled together as they prepared for the day. "My lady?"

Jubilee turned, her eyes bright and her lips smiling. "Yes, Layla?"

"Lady Sibyl is here to see you."

Glancing back at her husband, she whispered something that made him smile before hurrying after Layla.

"Would you like a tray of food and wine for the table?"

Jubilee's mouth opened to protest before deciding against it. She had learned early on that the woman preferred to be moving. Before his leaving, Leopold had warned her that to deny her work was a disservice to the girl. "That would be lovely, Layla. Thank you."

Meeting Sibyl in the peristyle, Jubilee smiled. "One of these days I'll make it to your Domus." She said. "So you can tell me all about my mother's days of troublemaking."

Sibyl smiled. "Yes, I am very anxious to squeal on your mother. Though she was most certainly the good one of the two of us."

"Why do I not find that surprising?"

"My child." Sibyl laughed. "Your mother was certainly no angel, I assure you."

Jubilee laughed tearfully. "I do need to see you more, Sibyl. You have been a great comfort where my mother cannot be."

Sibyl patted the girl's hair. "I love you too, *Puella*." Taking Jubilee's hand the two talked quietly until Layla returned with the tray.

"Is there any particular reason for your visit? It has been weeks since we spoke of the Lord."

"I am afraid I began to feel discouraged," Sibyl said, before explaining the increase in her nightmares. "Is there any reason that would be?"

"Satan doesn't want you coming to the Lord." The girl said simply. Seeing Sibyl didn't understand, Jubilee smiled. "It is perfectly normal, Sibyl. The evil one has had you in his grasp for so long and now he is losing you. He will do whatever it takes to keep you, especially if it means making you think your nightmares are because of God. He takes relish in making you think terrible things come from God."

"It is all so confusing. None of what you say makes sense to me." Sibyl set her head in her hands. "Am I hopeless?"

"No, Sibby. Scriptures can be nearly impossible to understand at times. It is why we have teachers. I don't understand half of what I have been taught. All that matters is that you believe them to be true. That you believe Christ is Lord."

"How can you believe in what you do not understand, Jubilee?"

"Well." *Oh God, how do I witness when I don't understand? I need you!* Jubilee felt sick as the seconds passed. She was going to fail Sibyl just as she was failing Atticus. Just as she had failed her grandfather. *God, give me the words to reach her.* Taking a deep breath she tried again. "If you do not mind my asking, Sibyl, do you believe the commandments of Moses to be true? That one shall not commit adultery. Nor should we steal or covet?"

"Of course?"

"And you believe and understand God's other laws? His laws over marriage and intimacy and loving one another?"

"Yes."

"Then you understand enough, Sibyl. You know his laws. You know the commandments. Keeping those is what matters in God's eyes. Reading scripture is what keeps you accountable. Prayer is a way of building your relationship with the Lord and learning to trust him and his ways, rather than your own. Simply struggling in those areas does not make you less in his eyes. So long as you understand the most basic parts of his teaching and follow them, I don't think God will hold any fault to you. I mean if that were so, only the priests and pastors would be saved, and even their eternity would be in question."

"How can that be?" Sibyl asked. "I look at your father or your mother and they seem so sure in what they believe."

"In what they believe, not what they fully understand, Sibyl. Nathanael has written us stories of his encounters with the apostles Peter and John and both admit to having not understood what Jesus said to them. Now if those who studied beside Jesus himself and knew him couldn't fully understand, what chance have we?"

Sibyl's lips trembled. "I want to believe you, Jubilee. Truly I do. But it all seems too good to be true. That all seems too simple."

"It sounds simple, Sibyl. But to truly live for the Lord is of great difficulty. An enemy is roaming this world who wants us to fail, and he will do anything in his power to make us stumble. He will use your weakness against you. He will bring you new weaknesses when you conquer the old ones. But so long as you fight for the Lord and what you believe, the evil one will not defeat you."

"It all seems so easy for you."

"It is far from easy for me, Sibyl." Jubilee turned her hands over in her lap, pinching at the soft flesh before Sibyl took hold of them. "Truthfully I feel as though you deserve a better teacher than I. The Lord is a curiosity to me now and I often find myself asking the same questions you do. But I know that I can't turn my back on Him."

Sibyl was quiet as she wiped gently at Jubilee's cheeks. "I did always wonder." She said softly. "How one continued in faith after something so tragic. Especially one of your age."

"It is not without effort."

Sibyl squeezed her hands. "That only makes you all the more faithful in my eyes, *Puella*. To struggle as you have and still see you believe as you do. I wouldn't ask for anyone else to teach me."

XVIII

Maius

Jubilee ran a hand over her abdomen, as flat and barren as it had ever been. It had been Sibyl who first brought to her attention her lack of a child, unwittingly planting a new fear in her mind.

The woman had been beside herself when she had arrived to find Jubilee laid out on the lounge, uninterested in walking the peristyle, as was their tradition. "Layla tells me you haven't been feeling well lately." She set a hand on the girl's pallid forehead. "I hope it isn't serious."

Jubilee felt herself blush. "I wouldn't worry, Sibyl." She spoke quietly, unable to admit that her time of month had found its way to her.

But the embarrassed smile that pulled at the corner of her lips brought a smile to her mother-in-law's face. "Oh, Jubilee! Are you with child?" The joy that had filled the woman's voice made Jubilee's heartache at the idea of breaking her hope.

"No, no, no, Sibyl. It isn't that."

"Oh." The woman's face fell. Moving Jubilee aside, she let the girl lay her head in her lap. "I am sorry to get so excited." She said quietly. The air was silent as Sibyl began to play gently with Jubilee's hair. "Aelia never conceived." The words were spoken so quietly that Jubilee almost missed them. "I never liked

the girl much, but a child is always a blessing. Atticus has always wanted to be a father."

Jubilee's stomach turned. "Should I have conceived by now?" Closing in on a year of marriage, surely she should be with a child by now?

"Oh no." Sibyl waved her off. "Women are all different, you know that. I conceived my first two easily, but it was over a year into my marriage before I came to expect Atticus." Seeing the fear still hung in the girl's eyes, Sibyl kissed her forehead. "You are young, Jubilee. I see no reason for you to start worrying now."

It had been three weeks since their discussion and Jubilee had yet to show any signs of a child growing within her. Not days before a patient had been kind enough to remind her that one was not truly married in Rome until the conception of a child. What would Atticus say about her lack of children? Since Sibyl's acknowledgment, Atticus had spoken many times of the family they would make and all the grandchildren they would give his mother.

"You mustn't worry, my lady," Layla said softly. Taking the woman's hand from her stomach she pulled her away from the mirror. "You will conceive in time, and your worrying will do nothing about bringing it any faster."

The woman didn't understand it. Not when she didn't face losing her husband if her body refused to produce a child.

"You don't need to worry about your husband, my lady. The master is a good man."

"I know he is, Layla. But he wants a child, it is all he has spoken of for weeks now. Who am I to deny him such a blessing?"

"It is not your doing, my lady. The master's first wife denied him children on many accounts and still he stayed." Layla's hand went to her mouth. The months with Jubilee urging her to speak her mind had served to worsen the girl's quick tongue.

But the girl didn't look angry, only horrified. "Are you telling me she aborted his children?" She whispered.

Layla took a deep breath. "I shouldn't have said anything, my lady. That is not my place."

"No, you shouldn't have. But it is too late now." The woman sounded tired. "You can go now, Layla."

"Are you angry, my lady?" She cursed herself for the emotion that filled her voice. Why had she allowed herself to care so much about another mistress? It would only make it harder when she found herself sent away once more.

"Oh, Layla." Jubilee' voice softened and she took her hands in hers. "Of course, I am not angry. I have encouraged you to speak freely and I hold to that. But let's keep Atticus and Aelia's affairs quiet?"

"Of course, my lady. As you wish." Turning away, Layla hurried away before the childish tears could fall. She couldn't remember the last time she had cried and she refused to give in to the tears now.

Her time with Sibyl and Jubilee was breaking down the walls she had so carefully built up around herself. She had served many ladies in her years and had hated each one more than the last. It wasn't until serving Sibyl that she learned not all women of wealth were without a heart. Sibyl had treated the slave girl like nothing less than a daughter. Choosing to spend her time with her when Regulus went away. Layla had grown to love

Sibyl and even Regulus in time, and if it were possible, she loved the young Jewess even more.

Love is dangerous, Layla. She'll sell you off in time. Even Sibyl grew tired of you over time.

No. Sibyl wouldn't have sent her away if not for her love for Jubilee. Jubilee was too kind to sell her off. She had proven that in the first few days of using Layla. Her soft-spoken manner reminded her of a woman she had known so long ago she seemed nothing more than a long-ago dream.

When Layla was gone, Jubilee settled onto their bed just Atticus entered. Seeing her tears, he knelt next to her. "What is it, Jewess?"

"It's nothing." She assured him. "I'm worrying over nothing."

The man hmmed as she stood and began to ready herself for bed. "Jubilee, how long are we going to go on with our secrets separating us?"

Jubilee frowned, Layla's words bouncing around in her head. "Are you ready to tell me yours?"

"Are you?"

"I want to be." Turning to him, she met his eyes. "I hate hiding from you. But I don't know how to tell you."

Atticus stroked her cheek. "Maybe we can start slowly. A question for a question."

"One day at a time?"

"If that is what you need." Kissing her forehead, Atticus settled into his side of the bed. "Do you want to start now or tomorrow?

"Tonight is fine, but I want you to go first."

Atticus watched her slide under the covers, curiosity driving away the burning questions. "Why me?"

Expecting her to make excuses, she surprised him when she answered immediately. "Because I already know something of yours." She looked like a caught child as she explained the mistake.

"Layla told you this?"

"Please don't be angry, Atticus. It was an honest mistake and she was mortified when she said it. It's my doing really, I told her that with me she is more than a simple servant." Jubilee stared at the clothing by the door, waiting to be tended to. "I don't like the idea of treating them the way some do. They are people, Atticus. They deserve to speak without fear of punishment."

"I am not questioning you, Jubilee." He'd been surprised to see her keep the woman at all, to know she intended to treat her as a free-born however was of little surprise. "Treat your servants as you wish."

"I did tell her that you and Aelia were off limits and she understands."

"All right." Atticus blew air from his mouth, trying to shake off the upset Jubilee's confession had set in him.

"So it is true?" She whispered. "About Aelia?"

"Yes. She conceived twice and aborted both."

Tears bit at the back of Jubilee's eyes. "I'm sorry." It seemed a strange sort of thought to her. That Atticus could have been a father. That his children ran the fields of heaven now. She wondered if he would believe her if she spoke of it—would he take comfort in it or would he laugh?

"I comforted her." He said suddenly. "While she killed our child." He toyed with her fingers, curling and uncurling them in his hands. "The first time she passed the child without a sound. It was early enough, I think, that it wasn't as painful. But the second one." He swallowed. "The second one was farther along. When I heard her screaming, when I found her, I thought she was miscarrying. She was nearly four months along, I never thought that she would rid herself of a child that late. It was the only time I ever saw her cry. The only time I ever saw her afraid. I held her hand and she let me. I comforted her." Atticus blinked, his eyes drifting back to the present. "The next morning, when the shock of it all had worn away and she returned to herself, she told me it wasn't a miscarriage. I could beg all I wanted, threaten all I wanted, but she wasn't going to be a mother. She left a week after that."

"Atticus." Jubilee's hand touched his cheek, wiping away the tears.

"It was a girl."

"Did you give her a name?"

"She was dead, Jubilee. She didn't need a name."

"But you needed it, Atticus. I know your mother has names for the two she lost. My grandmother named every child she lost. And I know you named yours."

Atticus felt his lips quiver as he remembered the child, no bigger than an apple. The name had found its way to him of its own accord. "Amabel."

"Lovable," Jubilee whispered.

"I would have loved her." Quick tears pooled on his cheeks. He had never truly mourned the loss of either of his children. The daughter he had held in his hand—the one he had buried himself, unable to share his grief with anyone. He let that grief poor out of him now as Jubilee held him, for once unafraid of their closeness.

"I know you won't believe me." She said when his tears subsided. "But know that they aren't gone. They play in heaven now." She smiled. "Perhaps even with Abel's children."

"Do you truly believe that, Jewess?"

"I have to. It is what makes loss bearable when it seems like it may crush us. To know that my grandmother still lives in Heaven was what helped me when she first passed."

"I suppose it is better this way then," Atticus said. "I hate to think of what sort of mother she would be. Nothing of the kind I know you will be."

Feeling the tears coming, Jubilee buried her face into his chest. "What did you want to ask me?"

Atticus startled at the abrupt shift before clearing his throat. He had only one he could think to ask. "Your dreams? Are they are more than dreams?"

Jubilee was still against him, her breaths shallow. "Yes."

XIX

Atticus sensed the change in Jubilee's sleeping form before it happened. Opening his eyes, he listened for the soft moan that meant she was dreaming.

"No." Before he could touch her, she began to thrash, her body twisting as though trying to free herself from someone's grasp. A horrible, guttural scream broke from her lips.

Remembering the last night she had struggled to wake, he moved hesitantly—fighting his rising panic. "Jubilee." Not wanting to frighten her further he spoke softly, hoping to ease her from the dream. "Wake up now."

"*Abba*!" She screamed loud enough to hear the tear in her throat as the word slipped from her mouth again and again before she again was mumbling something. Too smothered by tears to be understood.

He tried again, running his hand across her forehead. "Jubilee, wake up."

Her eyes popped open, wide and clouded, still caught in whatever horrors haunted her dreams. Screaming she pushed Atticus from her and brought her knees to her chest.

"Jewess, it's me." His voice was soft and slow, as though he spoke to a child. "It's just me."

"Atticus?" She croaked. Large tears dripped down her cheeks. "Atty." She repeated the name as though it were a lifeline.

Moving towards her slowly, Atticus brushed the hair from her face. "You're all right now."

Setting her forehead to her knees, Jubilee began to mumbling something in the strange language he had heard her speak in Galilee. A prayer. When she glanced up, the tears remained, but she no longer shook so violently.

Crawling back under the blankets, he watched her do the same. "Come here." When she hesitated he took her hand. "Trust me, Jewess. You said once that I made you feel safe. Let me do that again."

Leaning into him, she set her head on his shoulder. He could feel the way her heart raced against his side. Pressing his lips to her hair, he curled his fingers through the hand that rested on his chest.

"Do you know?" She asked quietly. "What my dreams are about?"

Atticus remained quiet. He had a hundred different fears waging war on his mind. Fears that kept him up at night. Fears that kept him from touching her. That much was certain, and if the worst of his fears were truth, he was not sure he wanted to know. *I have known evil men, Atticus.* "Do you want to tell me, Jubilee?"

It was Jubilee's turn to remain quiet. She knew the power telling him would have on her. Images flashed in her mind. A dark face. The glint of a knife, shining in the moonlight. "I can't."

"Jubilee." Atticus felt the words choking him. "Is there someone else?"

"Of course not!" She breathed. Betrayal seemed to drip from her tongue. "I would have thought you knew me better than that."

"I don't mean now. I mean in Galilee. If you were married I need to know, Jewess." He cursed the way his voice trembled. He had no right to be jealous. He had married. The woman had had every right to marry in his absence. He had hoped for it. "You cried, Jubilee. For the first several nights you were with me. Then you seemed to resign yourself to it. You didn't cry anymore but I know you hated it. Now you participate but you don't enjoy yourself."

Sitting up, Jubilee peered down at him. "How do you know I don't?"

"Do not pretend with me, Jubilee. I know you." Tipping her chin, he kissed her lightly, aware of the way she leaned in naturally. "I know what your joy looks like." He swallowed. "I know what passion and pleasure look like on you. So if you were with someone else just tell me. If you loved him and lost him. Or if he was cruel to you, whatever it was, I'll understand your hesitance with me."

"There was no one else!" She cried. "How many times do I have to tell you that none of this had to do with you or love? Why can't you get it? You know it."

"Was it Jude?" He didn't know where the memory came from, but now it was there it seemed only too possible. "You said he asked for your hand."

"That's the part that you remember?" Her face washed white with rage. "I'd marry any foul wretch on the street before I married him. I would kill myself."

"Jubilee." He understood little of their faith but he knew to take one's own life was not a sin their people touched. Not when they couldn't take it back.

"You know how I felt about him."

"You were young, Jubilee. Feelings change."

"Not with him." Her eyes were glued to something distant. Lost somewhere in her memory. When she spoke again it was nothing more than a whisper. "He touched me, Atticus."

"He touched you?" Atticus spit. "When?"

"Anytime he could." Hugging herself tight she turned away from him. "I don't remember when it started. At first, it was nothing more than simple things, on the street when no one was looking. But when I was twelve, I woke to something on my leg. I thought it was a spider or a beetle, so I didn't pay it much mind. I just brushed at it." Her nail dug into her wrist, turning it a sickly shade of purple. Catching his eye, she pulled at her fingers instead. "That was when he put his hand over my mouth and told me not to scream. His hand was under my dress."

"You were twelve?" He breathed.

"Two days before I turned thirteen." She watched him, knowing what he was thinking. It had been a mere month before he came to Galilee.

"What was he doing in your home, Jubilee?"

"His father was cruel. He was known for beating his sons, but he was worse with *him*. My parents used to let him stay with us when he was younger, on nights when his father was especially mean." Jubilee lowered herself into Atticus's arms as the memories overwhelmed her.

She had hissed at him to go away, and when he hadn't, she had taken a breath to scream for her parents. The glint of the knife in the moonlight had been blinding. Her fingers brushed the skin of her neck, where the blade had rested.

"Don't go waking them up. Do you want to get into trouble?

"He told me that my parents would blame me if they knew. They would say I tempted him. That I flirted and used my femininity to lead him to sin with me. He said his mother had done it with a man who wasn't his father, and that he had her stoned."

She hadn't wanted to wake them. She didn't want to see the looks on her parent's faces. She didn't want to feel shame as she walked the streets to be stoned.

"You believed him?" Atticus whispered. "Jubilee, your parents never would have blamed you."

"I know that now." She cried. "But I was young. I didn't understand what was happening. I didn't know what it meant to draw a man to you. For all I knew, I had."

Atticus watched his wife. She seemed so small, curled up as she was. Wrapping her tightly in his arms he kissed her hair. "Did they ever learn of it?"

"I told them of it a few weeks later. I came home one night to find *him* at our table. My parents thought I was being rude when I refused to sit next to *him*. I told my father when he took me outside to speak with me." Her fingers wrapped in his tunic. "That is why I was never allowed to go anywhere without a man. My parents feared my being alone."

Atticus lay awake long after Jubilee had fallen asleep. *He touched me, Atticus.* He felt sick. How had he not known? How had he not seen it that last night in Galilee? Was he truly so focused on himself that he refused to see the pain she had been in?

But he had not forced her hand. She hadn't seemed frightened in any way of him.

That you know of.

He thought of the way she offered herself to him now, regardless of the pain it caused her. No matter the fear that raced through her veins, she thought only of pleasing him. Had it been so that night, while he was too bent on pleasure to notice her fear?

...

So long as she slept in Atticus's arms the nightmares evaded her. Each night she curled close to him, her fingers curled in the fabric of his tunic.

Those darker images were creeping in on him, but he couldn't bring himself to ask. It was the one question he couldn't bear to have answered. By the gods how he wished she had loved and lost before him. The images that pressed in on him now threatened to undo him. He felt uncertainty with every brush of Jubilee's skin. She had long since stopped backing away from his advances, but no matter how close she drew to him, she still seemed miles away. She welcomed his touch. His kiss. She initiated love and then drew away or crawled within herself when it came to it.

Would he ever truly be enough for her? Would she ever truly trust him enough to share whatever it was that kept her from him, or were they destined to live apart from one another? Each of them trapped in their knot of thorns? Despite her reassurances, he was beginning to question her honesty. It would be like her to spare his feelings. Their night by the well played itself for him. Could she truly blame him for that night as he had always feared? Did he remember it wrong? Had he pushed her? *He touched me, Atticus.*

He clutched a fistful of hair, heart pounding painfully. So many memories had become mixed up in his mind since then. By the gods, he was losing his mind. He had been warned of this, warned of the effects it could have on him but he hadn't believed. He didn't want to believe. He would be lucky and his mind would be unharmed.

By the gods, why had he let Aelia ruin him so completely?

Each night they asked their questions, each one growing closer to the ones they most feared from the other. How long would it be before Jubilee asked how it was he came to know Aelia? His stomach churned violently at the thought of it. What would she say when she learned just how cowardly he was?

XX

Iunius

Jubilee felt her growing attraction toward Atticus beginning to eat away at her. She loved him with every fiber of her being and desired more than anything to feel his kiss against her lips and to be touched and held in his gentle way.

When nightmares woke her each night, he was there waiting and she fell back to sleep in his arms, comforted by his embrace. She loved his closeness, but to make love to him brought about the harsh memories that haunted her dark dreams.

She could see the pain her pushing and pulling was causing and yet she found herself unable to stop. So many times the truth of her hesitation nearly slipped from her lips but fear held her back. How would he react? Could he ever truly look at her the same if he knew that she wasn't the virginal girl he had believed to have been marrying? Already he hesitated in touching her, knowing the story of *his* first exploration of her body. Would he ever touch her again if he knew that it wasn't the worst *he* had done?

Again and again, her father's words came back to her. *He deserves to know the truth, Jubilee. How would you feel if he kept a secret like that from you?*

Each time the words played themselves for her she cursed herself for not telling him sooner. How could she ever tell him now? They had stuck to their agreement of one question a day and she felt his questions growing closer to the one she feared. *Does it have to do with Jude?* There would be no way of finding a way around it, not without lying and she would never do that. She couldn't. Even if she wanted to, her very reaction would give the truth as easily as speaking it. The name made her stomach jerk violently and thick sweat broke out over her body.

Ready or not, it was only a matter of time before the truth came to light and she had to prepare herself for the consequences.

Jubilee stared at the goblet of wine before her. She had had two and she could already feel its effect on her. She had never indulged in unwatered wine. The room seemed to tilt just slightly and her tongue felt almost heavy. What would it do for her if she continued to drink? *Do not overindulge.* Her father's voice whispered.

Ignoring the gentle warning, she picked up the goblet and took another tentative sip. She thought of Atticus and the way she yearned for him in a way that threatened to send her to her knees. Why must she be so weak? Why couldn't she let go of the past and give in to what she so desperately wanted? If she kept drinking, could she let go of it all and be with her husband as she was meant to?

Just one month and it would be a year of marriage. A year and still she couldn't face the very thing she wanted. She longed for nothing more than one fearless, love-filled night with her husband.

Gulping down the goblet she refilled it and drank again. By that night she would be ready.

...

Atticus kept a ready hand at Jubilee's back as they made their way to their room. She walked crookedly, her feet stumbling beneath her. Turning into their room, she shut the door noisily before turning to face him, a coy smile playing on her lips.

When she kissed him the thick smell of wine burned his nose. "I don't think so, Jewess." He muttered. He put her away from him, keeping sure to leave one arm around her waist. "You drank half your weight in wine and now you are going to sleep."

"No." She moaned. "No."

"You're drunk."

She smiled. "Just a little." She brought her fingers together. "Like you have never been drunk before."

Atticus felt himself smile. "See now that isn't fair. I am me. You are Jubilee, and Jubilee doesn't get drunk."

"I think she does. See you're thinking of the old Jubilee. No, she would never get drunk. But see now, I am not the girl you knew in Nazareth. That girl was good. Faithful." Her breath was hot on his ear as she wrapped her arms around his neck. "She was a virgin." She nodded. "Untouched by anyone. Mostly." The joy left her face as tears filled her eyes and she turned away. She started to cry then, her fist covering her mouth to staunch the sound. As she sagged against him her tears soaked through the front of his tunic. "Why can't you see?" She cried. "I want you to know but I can't say it. I can't stand to say it. Not to you."

She sounded lost. Broken. "Jubilee, you need to sleep now." He tried to soothe her. "You will feel better in the morning."

Stepping away from him, Jubilee glared up at him, her eyes holding anger he had never seen in her before. "You act as though I am the only one miserable here!" She spit. "As if I am the only one that didn't want this. As though I am the only one who hides away in this marriage. You hide from me too."

"You are the one who agreed to this Jubilee. I would have gladly said no to this plan."

"I didn't want marriage! I hated the idea of marriage. Why would I want marriage when the very idea of being touched by a man made me sick?"

Atticus laughed bitterly. "So that is what this is about? I didn't take advantage of you, Jubilee. You kissed me, remember? You told me it was all right to keep going. I did *not* take advantage of you."

"I never said you did, Atticus," Jubilee swore for the first time in her life. "How many times have I told you that none of this has to do with you?"

"What am I supposed to think when you tell me to remember that night, Jubilee?"

"I don't regret that night, Atticus." Her voice softened. "I suppose I probably should, but I don't. I loved that night. Back when you were still you and I was still me. No stupid questions separating us." She took his hand and held it to her chest. "I wasn't talking about you and you alone, Atty. None of this has to do with you, I promise you. With every fiber in my being, I promise you that it was never you. This isn't about what *happened* that night, Atticus. It's about what was said. I know you remember. You have said it, all you have to do is admit it to yourself."

When he didn't answer she scoffed. "I wanted to marry you once, did you know that? All growing up I imagined it. I thought it would happen then. That last time you visited." She laughed dully. "Isn't that stupid? I thought—no, I had convinced myself that that was the year it would happen. You would stop seeing me as a child and instead see me as the woman I had become, and then I kissed you and you didn't stop me." Her lip quivered, her eyes closing at the memory. "You would have let things go much further if I hadn't stopped things. That just made everything so much more real in my mind. You would ask my father for my hand and I would go back with you to Rome as your wife. Only you didn't."

When Atticus opened his mouth, Jubilee spoke over him. "I mean what was it? Were you angry that I stopped us? Do you know what that felt like to stop? Do you think that because of my upbringing or because of my faith it was easy for me? I loved you, Atticus. I wanted to make love to you then more than I had ever wanted anything in my entire life, and I so wish that lapse in judgment would have lasted just a little longer. Maybe if it had, none of this would have ever happened." She scoffed. "But I was and still am just a prudish Jewess. I couldn't give you pleasure. Not like Aelia and I am sure countless others have given you since then."

"Jubilee."

"No." She spit. "No. You act like you're the only one with demons. Like you are the only one that suffered any injustice while we were apart." She glared up at him. "You have no idea." She ground. "You have no idea of the things I experienced while we were apart. Things I needed you for and you weren't there. You were just gone when I needed you most. So you don't get to be angry with me. You don't get to push me away. I needed you, Atticus, and instead, you were off with other women. I needed you. *I needed you* and you weren't there." She choked and her knees gave way beneath her. *"I needed you."* The words flowed from her mouth like sick.

"No." Atticus lowered himself beside her before his knees could give way. All the fears that had been building in him crashed down at him at once. He remembered the way she had jumped each time he touched her. The way she had cried, not from pain as he had thought. As he had hoped. But something else. She hadn't reacted that way in Galilee. She had been calm. Assured.

She was a virgin. Her voice had been small.

Tears filled his eyes. "No." He moaned. She glanced up at him, a brokenness he had never seen in her drowning in her eyes. "Jude."

"Don't say it." She cried. "Please don't say it."

This couldn't be right. Not Jubilee. Not his Jewess. "But you were never alone." At his words, her face crumpled into something unrecognizable. "You weren't alone." He choked.

She shook her head. "*Abba*." She sobbed. "The morning after you left. When *Abba* and I went to fetch water we found *him* and two of *his* brothers waiting there. My father told me to run but *he* caught me and brought me back. He brought me back, Atticus." She was shaking now. "He could have done it there when he caught me but he didn't. He knew exactly what he wanted. It was like some twisted sort of game to him." She was quiet as she worked to calm her tears. "He saw us that night. At least some of it. He was angry that my father would allow me to go around sleeping with a Roman heathen but wouldn't allow *him* even thought of marriage." She pressed the heel of her palms into her eyes as her fingers pulled at her hair. "He wanted to hurt us both, so he made me tell *Abba* that we had slept together, and then his brothers held my father down and made him watch as... as he did it."

"By the gods." Atticus croaked. He felt as though he would be sick. Not only for Jubilee but for the father who had been forced to witness it.

The air was quiet as the words settled around them. Jubilee sat with her head hung, picking again and again at her skin until a dozen crescent moons bled at her wrists. "I waited for you." She whispered. "I waited all year for the day you would step off that ship and make it better. Because you would. You were Atticus. You were safe." She sat up and ran a hand through her hair. "You always made things better."

But you left, puppy, and you didn't come back.

Atticus' hands shook violently as his mind conjured the image that had haunted him for nearly a year, only now the man had a face. "I'm so sorry, Jubilee."

Jubilee didn't look at him when she spoke. "I know."

The words were another blow. She blamed him and he couldn't even blame her for it. He had left.

Jubilee took his hand and pulled him closer to her. "Please don't leave me." She cried. "I don't mean to blame you. I know you aren't responsible. I know it."

Without a word, Atticus held her tightly to him, his lips pressed to her hair. When he could trust himself to speak, he said. "I'm not going to leave you, Jewess."

...

Jubilee woke late the next morning, her head pounding. Moaning, she rolled over and made to nuzzle into Atticus's side.

It wasn't until she discovered his empty space that pieces of the previous night began to creep back. The wine. The tears. Her outburst.

Her stomach rolled painfully. He had left her. Just as she had feared. Head pounding, she stood and hurried from the room. Turning the corner she collided with Layla.

Layla took the girl in, her chest rising and falling quickly and her hair slick with sweat. She looked as though she would be sick any moment.

Her dark eyes were wide and almost crazed. "Layla, have you seen Atticus?"

"He left early this morning, my lady." She ran a hand over the girl's pallid face. "He warned me you might be sick and asked I keep an eye on you."

"Oh, God." Jubilee sunk to the floor. "What have I done?"

Layla stood shocked. She had never seen Jubilee in such distress. The girl seemed unable to breathe around her sobs. Kneeling beside her, Layla stroked the girl's hair. "Just relax, my lady."

Picking her up off the floor, Layla led her to the baths. Jubilee didn't fight her as she peeled the tunic away from her and led her into the water. "What have I done?" She sobbed.

"Just relax, Jubilee," Layla repeated. Lifting her head, Layla poured the water slowly over her head, brushing her hair back just as she had done with her mother in the end. "The master will come back. He needs time, surely you can understand that."

"You don't know. You don't know what happened."

"I know, Jubilee. I hear the way you scream at night. I have seen the way you thrash in your sleep and the way you cry out for your father. It isn't hard to put it together."

Jubilee's lip quivered. "So you do know. It seems everyone was able to put it together but Atticus."

"Atticus knew Jubilee. He simply loves you too much to want to believe that sort of thing could be true."

"Loved," Jubilee whispered. "He'll never forgive me now. Not after I kept it from him. Oh, God." She repeated. "What have I done? What have I done?"

Layla shook her head. "You must stop letting that man win, Jubilee. You are stronger than that." *You are stronger than her.*

"I am not strong, Layla. If I were I wouldn't be here now. I would have told Atticus sooner. I would have all of this behind me and I would be enjoying a true marriage with my husband." She let out another small sob. "You don't know how desperately I want to let it go and love him in that way but I can't."

The room was quiet as her words sunk in. Layla had hoped she was wrong. She had hoped she was simply seeing her mother where she didn't belong. "I love him," Jubilee whispered. "Oh, I love him. But he deserves more than what I have given him."

"The master has had more when it comes to what you speak of, my lady, and he was miserable. So stop pitying yourself. It doesn't suit you."

"I am failing him, Layla. I can see the disappointment in his eyes when he looks at me. I can't give him pleasure. Not now."

"You can and you will," Layla commanded. "But first you need to know him."

Jubilee turned to look at her. "I know Atticus. I have always known him."

"You know who he is, Jubilee. That isn't enough now. Not when you are letting the man before him get between you. Before your husband, the only man you knew was the man who raped you. You can stand and even crave Atticus's kiss and his touch because they were parts of him you knew before. The parts of him that can't be overshadowed by the man who hurt you."

"I don't understand."

"I have only ever known one man in such a way. But just as there are differences between you and me, there are subtle differences in one man's body from another, my lady. Study him. Get to know his body and separate it from the one that was used to hurt you."

XXI

Atticus shook as he stumbled through the empty streets. It had been nearly twenty-four hours since Jubilee had confessed her secret and he still couldn't stop the way his heart raced. Each time he thought of going back to her he saw her struggling in Jude's arms. He heard the way she begged him to stay that night, silently begging him to keep her safe.

Could she be blamed for finding fault in him? He was supposed to marry her. To protect her and he had failed in the worst possible way. He wanted to go to her. To comfort her as best he could, but the thought of touching her brought about the images that made his stomach lurch painfully. No. He couldn't go to her. Not yet. Not as he was. He needed to sober before he saw her and there was one thing he needed to do before going back to her.

Entering the Albanus tablinum he found his father laid out on the lounge, his eyes closed while his mother played the harp. Both were unashamed of how they deceived him. "Why didn't you tell me?" He demanded.

Sibyl's fingers stumbled, slicing her skin on one of the strings. Waving off Regulus's concern, she looked back at her son. "She told you."

Regulus eyed the bottle clutched between his son's fingers, explaining the pungent smell that filled the room. The boy rocked where he stood. "Sit down, Son."

"No. I want an answer."

"You loved her, Atticus. Maybe not in the way you do now, but there was always something there. Your mother chose not to tell you because she feared how you would react."

"Don't you dare blame this on Mother. She tried to tell me before, and you wouldn't let her."

"Because by then we assumed it was better that Jubilee told you herself. We had no way of knowing that she would choose to keep it from you."

"Why not tell me when it happened? I could have gone to her."

"You were recovering, Atticus. We didn't want to hurt you or ruin your progress." His father set a hand on his shoulder, sudden tears filling his eyes. "Hearing about what that man did hurt all of us. That girl means something to more than just you, Atticus. Your mother didn't eat for a week. I didn't sleep. You had enough things going on in your life and we didn't want to push you further."

"I deserved to know the truth. I don't care what she meant to you. I don't care how you felt. I loved her!" He couldn't stop the tears from falling and for one solitary moment, he welcomed the way his father's arms took him in. "I loved her and she was hurting and I wasn't even allowed to know it. She was hurting and I wasn't there and I should have been. I should have known that every time I touch her she feels another man's hands."

"And what would you have done, Atticus?"

"I would have waited. I would have given her time. Space until she was ready for everything marriage entails."

"Her parents wanted this for her," Sibyl said gently. "Someone she knew. Someone she loved. Someone they knew would treat her with the gentleness she needed. Atticus, since

Jude, Jubilee has let no one close. She never allowed men to even attempt to know her. The fact that she agreed to marry you, that she let you touch her in any way was a miracle."

Atticus glared at her. "You should have told me."

"Jubilee wanted to be the one to tell you when the time was right."

"Jubilee wanted it a secret because she blamed me. She had not intention of telling me until she was too drunk to realize what she was doing." It was that very thought that had driven him out of bed once she had fallen asleep. How much longer would she have waited to tell him had she not had too much to drink?

Sibyl frowned. "The girl is confused, Atticus. If that is what she told you I am sure she didn't mean it."

"She meant it, Mother, and she has every right to. I let her kiss me that night. I knew I shouldn't have but I let my feelings overwhelm my judgement. I made him think that I-that we..." He pulled at his hair. "I have to go."

"Atticus wait." Sibyl caught his hand. He didn't fight her as she took his face in her hands, bringing his forehead to hers. "Stay here tonight. Calm down before you speak with her again." When he made to protest she hurried on. "I don't want either of you doing something stupid. She isn't Aelia, Atticus. Jubilee never meant to hurt you. So sober up and then talk to her. Let her explain before you judge her any further." She closed her eyes before continuing. "There is so much more to what she went through that you don't know yet."

...

Jubilee closed her eyes against the harsh ache behind them. Sleep was beginning to press in on her like a heavy fog, slowing her heart until she felt like it would stop. But she couldn't sleep. She wouldn't.

Layla had succumbed to sleep long ago, her light snores filling the dark room. Jubilee had spent the hours since counting the tiles of the ceiling, fighting the hours until Atticus would come home. Losing her place she would start over.

In the silence of the night, their words hung over her like a sword, waiting to cut the final thread that held them together. *Don't fall asleep.* The moment she fell asleep she would be pulled back into the nightmare's cold embrace and without Atticus to wake her, she knew the dream would play itself over again and again. Without Atticus, she would have no one to ward off the dreams as she drifted back to sleep in his arms.

Outside the sun was beginning to peak through the clouds, shining its light on Atticus's spot, filled now by Layla. Sitting up, she put pressure on her eyes before pushing the blanket aside. She couldn't face the nightmares alone.

In the hopes of running into Atticus, she dressed slowly, braiding her hair twice before leaving it down. Approaching the gardens she stopped. "I told him." She whispered in prayer. "I told him and he left me. You brought me here and you let him leave me." Turning her back to the garden, she hurried towards the shop.

The morning moved at the slow beat of her heart. With each hour that passed, the pain behind her eyes grew stronger. By mid-morning she let her eyes droop shut, her chin against her palm.

She jerked awake when a man entered the shop. His body blocked the sun, casting his face in shadows.

"Atticus?"

"Please." The man begged. "I need a physician." The man clutched his side and as he moved closer she could see the sweat that dripped down his forehead.

Standing, Jubilee smiled reassuringly. "How can I help you?"

The man stared incredulously. "I need a physician. Get me a real physician. Get me the man. Albanus."

Jubilee took a deep breath. "I am afraid I am all there is today. Now I will be glad to assist you." The man shook his head and she sighed. "You are clearly in pain. Now please, I would like to help you." Moving around the table she took a step toward him.

"Stay back." The man doubled over, a sharp cry escaping his lips.

Ignoring his revulsion, Jubilee set a hand on his shoulder. "Please, Domine. Let me help you."

"Don't touch me." Standing straighter, he shoved her back into the wall.

Her head struck the wall and her vision went black. When it faded back in, a sharp, sickening pain made her hand throb. Moaning, she turned to see Atticus yelling as he kicked the man out. Though she couldn't hear him over the ringing in her ears, she could imagine the words. Vision fading once more, she closed her eyes.

...

Atticus shook violently as he pulled the man from the shop. From anger or fear, he didn't know. He had entered the shop in time to see the man shove Jubilee violently, sending her into the shelves that held the instruments and equipment.

Turning back to her, he swallowed hard against the bile that rose in his throat. After hitting the shelf, she fell to the floor, the surgical tools spread out around her, including a now bloody, upturned scalpel.

She hadn't screamed or even cried out, but it was evident by her wide eyes and tight lips that she had been hurt.

Kneeling beside her, he touched her face, urging her to open her eyes. She did, but he knew by the glaze of her eyes she was not truly there. He couldn't say whether she even saw him. The shock of it all was numbing her mind.

Reaching tentatively for her hand he braced himself for the damage. No sooner than he grazed her hand, did she gasp and lean forward, her body lurching as her stomach emptied itself of its contents. Finished, she leaned back and moaned loudly, her eyes closed against the pain. Silent tears were beginning to spill quickly down her cheeks. "I'm sorry, Jewess. But I need to look at it."

She nodded, her breathing quick and heavy. Prying her fingers from her palm he swore. A deep cut began between her middle and index finger, before going on to peel away the flesh that covered her palm.

Scooping her up, he placed her on the table before hurrying to gather everything he would need. When he took a seat in front of her, her eyes had lost their shine and she was shaking. A new layer of sweat glistened against her skin. "I'm so sorry, Jewess." He whispered as she turned away. "I should have been here."

She tried to speak but gave up quickly, unable to spit out more than a single word after each haggard breath.

Jubilee kept her eyes on Atticus as he worked, fighting the urge to look back at her hand. She sewed people back together daily without batting an eye, yet it made all the difference when she was the one being sewn back. One never expected to see their bone.

Her free hand clutched Atticus's tunic, her fingers digging into his leg until she could feel his skin beneath her nails. She knew she must be hurting him and yet he didn't show it. When he apologized for the fourth time she lifted her hand to his cheek and smiled weakly. For the moment, all their problems were behind them.

Gently nudging her knee with his own, Atticus encouraged her to look at him. ”Do you remember the summer we spent your whole visit suturing corn bags?"

Jubilee smiled, remembering how excited she had been to show him her new trick. She had been five, and it hadn't been long before she managed to talk him into trying it with her, again and again until he had gotten it right. “I loved that summer.”

"Did I ever tell you that that was when I decided to become a physician?" He asked quietly.

"Is it?"

"I had contemplated it many times, having spent every summer of my life watching your father. But I was always too timid to ask him if he could teach me anything."

"He would have loved to you know? As much as he liked to discipline me in those earlier days, I think he was happy to see one of his children showing an interest in what he did. He enjoyed having someone to teach." She was quiet a moment, her face thoughtful. "Perhaps if you had asked you could have stayed in Galilee."

"And you wouldn't have been raped?" Atticus asked. The calm that had settled between them shattered like glass.

"You know that is not what I said, Atticus. I know how much you loved Galilee."

"No, but you were thinking it." Snipping the strand of thread, he grabbed some gauze. "Stop lying to yourself and admit you blame me, Jubilee. I do."

Her eyes went wide. "Atticus, stop. I don't mean to—"

"Why didn't you tell me sooner, Jubilee?"

She glared back at him. "You don't get to be angry with me now, Atticus. Do you want to know why I didn't tell you? This is why. I told you I was raped and you walked away. You left me. Would you have still married me if you knew the truth before?"

He sent the box of tools flying into the wall, making her jump. "I deserved to know this, Jubilee. As your husband, I deserve to know what my wife is feeling every time I touch her."

"You did know." She spit. "You just didn't want to believe it."

"You told me there was no one before me, Jubilee."

"No one I loved. You never asked if I was a virgin. If you had I wouldn't have lied. But you didn't. You asked about marriage and love and I told the truth." Jubilee glanced up at him. "I never would have lied. Not if you asked."

"You told me your dreams were nothing but dreams," Atticus said. "But they aren't are they? They are of that day."

She shrugged. "I didn't mean to lie. I think a part of me thought that maybe if I said it enough I could believe it. That they were just dreams."

Atticus scoffed. "You didn't fool me, you most certainly couldn't fool yourself, Jubilee. Stop lying to me. Stop lying to yourself, when you can't even hear his name without flinching."

She glared at him. "Leave it be, Atticus."

The next words were cruel but he couldn't stop them from coming. "Jude." He spit.

"Stop!" She crumbled in on herself, her hands covering her ears. "What did she do to you?" She sobbed. "This isn't you. You're not mean. You're not spiteful."

"What is it about his name, Jubilee? Why of all things is his name the thing that paralyzes you?"

"Questions." She spit. "You ask questions, I get answers. That's the deal, remember?"

Atticus kicked the discarded box. "You want answers? Fine. My family didn't come back to Galilee because I was addicted to Opium." He heard her sharp intake of breath and smiled. "That's right, Jubilee. Can you still look at me after that?" He laughed. "And Aelia? You wanted to know about her right?" He hesitated. He had never admitted aloud the things Aelia had said and done.
"Aeila liked to play games." He said simply. "Men and love were her favorites. She thrived on seeing how far she could make men bend to her will. She pushed. Pulled. Kicked. Screamed. Sex was her weapon. She knew how to make you think you wanted it even when you didn't."

Jubilee's lips parted. "She-"

"It was not uncommon," He interrupted. "For me to have to drag her off of men and women when we went to parties. Not uncommon to see her slipping away with them." He laughed bitterly. "She didn't even try to hide it. She wanted me to see. She wanted me to see who was in control. She had me so wrapped around her finger that I let it happen. I made excuses. I took my opium, drank my wine, and pretended I didn't know what was happening in the room next to me."

Jubilee chewed her lip. As each word had left his lips, she had felt them settle on her shoulders. She had only herself to blame for the images that played themselves for her now.

Her arms wrapped around her legs, hugging them close. "He made me say it." She said quietly. "His name. He made me say it as though it was what I wanted." Her body jerked violently and she covered her mouth. "I can't hear his name, Atticus. I can't say it. I can't."

"And I made you say mine." Atticus slumped down beside her. "Jubilee, I-"

"It's not the same thing, Atticus." She took his hand. "I am not angry anymore. Saying your name, Atty? It wouldn't have felt the way it did to say his. I do love you, Atticus, and I want to please you. But to do that. To do what you wanted me to do meant staying with you. It meant facing what we were doing." She shook her head. "I can't. As much as I want to I just can't."

Jubilee was quiet a moment, her eyes glistening with tears. "I blamed you because you didn't marry me when you could have. I blamed you because you didn't come back when I needed you." She set her forehead on his shoulder. "I blamed you because it was easier than missing you. It was easier than sitting around waiting for you to come and make it better.

"I didn't tell you because, even though I blamed you, I only wanted to protect you. I wanted to believe it wasn't important enough because it was in the past. But it's not in the past." She gave a bleak, humorless laugh. "I planned on going to my marriage bed clean and whole and in one second it was ripped away. I wasn't clean. I wasn't whole. I was defiled and dirty and broken. I was soiled and that will never change." Her voice broke and she curled forward.

From his place on her wrist, he could feel her pulse begin to race. Lingering anger falling away, he pulled her into his lap. She shook violently as she clung to him, her tears soaking his neck as she buried her face in his shoulder.

Taking her uninjured hand, he wove his fingers through hers. "Jubilee, I planned on coming back the next year. I wanted to marry you, Jewess. From the moment I stepped off the ship that last time and saw you, I knew it. You were beautiful. Smart. Familiar." He rocked her as she cried, the taste of salt on his tongue as his tears pooled on his lips. "I shouldn't have left you." He whispered. "I never should have left you."

XXII

Iulius

Atticus watched the gentle rise and fall of Jubilee's chest as she slept, safely tucked into his side. Her hand rested lightly on his chest. Taking it in his own, he curled his fingers through hers.

She had opened herself up and bled for him, pouring from her heart all the horrors from their time apart and even those before.

How could he have looked upon her face each summer and not have seen the truth of what she had hidden beneath? How could he have walked away that final year knowing the fear she held towards Jude? He had seen it in her eyes. He had heard it in her voice that last night and still he had walked away. *"There's a man named Jude."* She had curled closer to him, drawing warmth from him. *"He frightens me, Atty."*

Atticus felt his stomach roll as it often did when he looked at her. He had scarcely touched her since that night. Only at night, when she relied on him to keep the nightmares away. To touch her invited all the horrid pictures of the events that surrounded her. *He made me say it.* She had whispered lifelessly. *His name.* All the desire he had ever felt for her fell away when those words whispered themselves in his ear.

At his side, Jubilee moaned. "Atticus." He glanced down to find her watching him. "You're crying." Reaching up she wiped the single tear from his cheek. "Why aren't you sleeping?"

He couldn't. It was in his sleep that her past haunted him, as her nightmares became his own. Night after night, as she drifted to sleep in his arms, safe from all the ghosts of her pasts, he felt himself instead drift back to that awful moment. Hovering above the horrid scene, unable to do anything but watch helplessly as she struggled in Jude's arms. It was a vision so clear he never knew until the moment he woke that it was a dream. Half a dream.

"I should never have accepted the questions, Jubilee. I shouldn't have let myself live in denial for so long." *I should have stayed in Galilee.* "If I had known, I wouldn't have forced myself on you."

"Atticus stop." Propping herself on her elbows, she frowned at him. "You didn't force yourself on me. You're my husband. I never fought you. I never told you no and when I did you left me alone."

"I should have seen, Jubilee. I did see but I refused to accept it. I came up with so many reasons as to why you hated being with me. I told myself it was your faith. Your god. Sex was the first great sin. I told myself your dreams were nothing more than guilt or grief. Anything but what they were."

She watched him a moment, one eyebrow raised. Suddenly she laughed. "I'm sorry." She smiled. "I shouldn't laugh. But my parents have three children. Two of which are less than ten months apart. Did you truly think my parents wanted to conceive me when Nathanael was only three weeks old?"

Atticus laughed. "How am I to know what your god does and doesn't allow?"

"*Our* God created sex, Atticus. He created it and gave it as a gift. All he asks in return is that we save it for marriage."

"Do you see it that way, Jewess? As a gift?"

"I want to." Jubilee's fingers toyed with the front of his tunic, for once avoiding the soft, scarred skin of her wrist. "I think about that night and what I felt and what I know it would have been. What it should be now. But I don't feel anything, Atty."

"Nothing?" The words left him hollow. *You give me nothing, Puppy.* Aelia's voice came of its own accord, picking at the wounds that refused to heal. She felt nothing.

As though sensing the turn of his mind, Jubilee frowned. "Not nothing." She breathed. "I shouldn't have said that. It's not that I don't feel anything, Atty. But I don't feel what I felt that night and I don't know that I ever will." She shivered and drew the blankets tighter about her shoulders. "I want to." She whispered. "Sometimes I think I can. When you kiss me or even touch me I feel okay. I feel wonderful even. I feel every desire I felt that night and I find myself wanting to make love to you. But then it happens and I can't see anything but *him*. All I can feel is *him*. *His* hands. *His* breath." Her breath came in quick spurts. "I hear *him*. I even *smell him*. All there is is *him*."

She was quiet as she struggled to catch her breath. "I don't know how to change that, Atty." Her eyes were deep with pain and sorrow he couldn't bear to see in her.

"Stop looking for what you felt that night, Jubilee. That's a night that was squandered by Ju-*him*. You aren't going to feel what you felt before *him*, any more than I will feel what I felt before Aelia. You aren't untouched." The words were cruel, even in his ears, but Jubilee merely nodded. "Don't think, Jewess." He trailed his fingers down her arm, feeling the way she shivered at his touch. "Trust me." As he spoke her eyes fluttered shut. "You aren't a virgin, Jewess. That isn't going to change no matter how hard you try to make it so." He didn't know where the words were coming from. Nor where he was going. But he knew neither would feel what they felt that first night. What they had felt then was new. Exciting. There had been no fear. No insecurities. Nothing but a naive expectation. "But that doesn't mean we can't have that gift. Tell me what you need, Jewess."

Her eyes found his. Her voice was no more than a whisper. "To feel safe."

The words seemed to fall from her lips. They slithered across the space between them and wrapped themselves around Atticus's heart. They were the unashamed confession of a child. In that moment she ceased to be his wife. She wasn't even the fifteen-year-old, stripped bare and broken. She was the twelve-year-old girl who had seen the simplest of childhood innocence taken from her. Instilling within her the belief that even in her own home. In her own bed. She wasn't safe.

Unsure how to answer, he leaned in and kissed her hair, noting the hungry way she shifted closer, her arms wrapping around his waist as she clung to him, trusting him to provide that safety.

...

"Atticus." Jubilee's soft voice echoed through the corridors, light and full of life, beckoning him to follow her. Glancing behind him he saw a glimpse of her long, dark hair as she disappeared around the corner.

Smiling he followed after, turning the corner to find her disappearing around another. "Jubilee?" He was answered with a soft laugh that trickled down the corridor like music. He kept running until he found her disappearing into the garden. Out of breath, he slowed to a walk as he entered after her. "Jubilee." When no answer came he called again, receiving only silence in return. Rounding a hedge he swore as he nearly stumbled over her. "Jubilee."

Again she ignored him, her eyes on a wall, thick with thorn-covered vines. Spinning to face him, she glared up at him, tears blurring her dark eyes. "Why do you still hide so much from me?" Before he could stop her she dived at the wall, tearing at the vines. Blood trickled down her arms as her laughter turned to tears.

"Jubilee." Grabbing her by the waist, he pulled her away from the wall. "What are you doing?"

She stared down at her blood-soaked tunic. "I have them too." She whispered. "You know mine and still you don't trust me."

"Jubilee, what are you saying?"

"Thorns. I've shown you mine. Why must you hide your own away from me? I bled for you, Atticus! I bled for you and you still hide away from me." Tears pooled at her lips. "Bleed for me, Atticus. Bleed for me."

"You know mine, Jubilee. What more do you want?"

"Everything." She whispered, her arm waving at the thorn-covered wall. "All of you." Pulling away from him she tore once more at the thorns, turning her pale, flawless skin into ragged flesh.

Atticus sat up in bed. Sweat drenched his hair and he was shaking. At his side, Jubilee slept. Pushing aside the blanket he took up her arm and looked it over. Finding it smooth and unblemished. Laying back he held her hand in his, his fingers brushing the perfectly unblemished skin. He almost wished she would wake up as she so often did when he found himself restless, as though even in sleep she sensed his struggles. But now she slept peacefully, her breaths deep and rhythmic.

Don't be pathetic, puppy.

He pressed a hand to his eyes as Aelia's voice toyed with him. He could imagine the sneer that would mark her face if she could see him now, left shaking from a dream that meant nothing. *Do you want your Mama too?* She would whisper.

Groaning he pulled Jubilee to him, feeling the way she moved with him even in sleep. Tucking his chin in the crook of her neck he tried to push the dream from his mind. It was a dream. Brought on by his worries over Jubilee. *I need to feel safe.* They were taking steps, slowly moving forward as each worked to give the other what they needed. But still, Jubilee remained wrapped in the very thorns she had torn at in his dreams. The dream was nothing more than his guilt at being unable to rid her of them. He knew it, but even still he felt the logical mind his father instilled in him falling away as the dream clung to him.

Thorns. I have shown you mine. Why must you hide your own from me?

"What am I hiding from you?" He whispered into the darkness.

Everything.

XXIII

As Jubilee had made her way toward Tamar's the sunset had bloomed across the sky turning the white clouds into a brilliant mix of pinks and oranges. During her visit the white clouds had faded away, giving way to the dark storm clouds that took their place. A crack of thunder echoed through the empty streets, followed by a brilliant flash of lightning that lit up the night sky and cast shadows in alleyways.

Denying her fear, Jubilee had turned down the offer of Solaris accompanying her home. An offer she now wished she had accepted. It had been storming that night when she had found *him* in her bed. Wrapping her cloak tighter about herself she quickened her steps, telling herself it was the thick smell of rain that pushed her forward. *He isn't here*. She knew it and yet her mind played tricks, placing his long, willowy frame in every alleyway she passed. When the first drop of rain splashed her cheeks she quickened her steps to a run, not caring at the moment who might be watching. She was soaked through before she reached the Domus, her eyes scanning the shadows surrounding the door. Even searching she missed the lurking figure until their hand touched hers. Her scream was lost in another crack of thunder.

"I am sorry, my lady." The voice belonged to a man. Old and raspy. "I needed shelter from the storm."

Legs trembling she ushered the man into the vestibulum, where she could see him in the soft light. The man was dirty. His grey hair hung down to his shoulders, thick with mats while dirt clung to the wrinkles and folds of his skin. His tattered tunic had become nothing more than scraps. Her heart ached for the man. "Please, *domine*. You will stay here tonight. We'll get you some food and fresh clothing." The man followed after her. Always silent. "Layla!" Jubilee called as they entered the atrium.

Layla was there in seconds. "My lady we were worried!" The girl stopped in her tracks, her eyes wide at the sight of the bedraggled stranger. "Who is this?" She looked as though she were ready to jump between the two should the need present itself.

Ignoring her questions, Jubilee ordered she get the man food as well as honeyed water for her own still tangled nerves. "Afterwards, I want you to grab a tunic from my grandfather's things."

Layla frowned, her copper eyes watching the man. "Are you sure, my lady?"

"There is nothing to fear, Layla." She could not explain the calm she felt toward him, but she knew the man was to be trusted. With Layla gone Jubilee turned back to the man, urging him to sit. Taking up the pitcher she dipped the cloth in and wrung it out.

"Please don't." The man croaked, shrinking away from her touch. "You mustn't touch me."

"Please I-"

"Let me do it myself." Careful to avoid contact with her skin he slipped the cloth from her hands and began scrubbing at his face.

As the dirt disappeared, Jubilee felt her heart pick up. She recognized the face as though she had looked upon it all her life. "Leo?" She whispered.

Looking up at her he smiled miserably. Never had he seemed so old. "I am sorry to have frightened you, my lady."

Forgetting herself she threw her arms around the man and kissed his cheek. "Why didn't you tell me it was you?"

Leopold was gentle as he put her away from him. "I do not wish to get you dirty, my lady." There was something in the man's voice that made her look him over. He looked near lifeless. He had aged years in only months. "At least let me get a bath first."

...

The storm was slowing before Leopold reappeared in the peristyle, freshly bathed and clothed in one of her grandfather's tunics. His gray hair had been pulled back with string. Waving for her to stay seated he handed her a scroll.

Without a word, Jubilee took it and looked it over. "Your contract?" She breathed. "I don't understand?"

"I have had my taste of freedom, my lady. I do not care for it."

"It's only been a couple of months, Leo. I am sure it will take some adjusting."

The man shook his head. "I will never be free, my lady. Now please, rip it up."

"Leopold."

"I said rip it up, Jubilee!" The girl jumped at the harshness in his voice. He was quick to take her hands in his. "I am sorry, my lady. But please. I cannot go back out there."

"Why?" She breathed. "What happened to you?"

"I miss my home, my lady." His voice cracked, prompting Jubilee's tears.

"Then simply work for us, Leopold. Don't give away your freedom. You more than earned your right to be free."

"By the gods, Jubilee." The man snapped. "Stop acting so innocent. You and your mother sometimes, I swear it! You are not perfect."

Jubilee gasped before biting down hard on her lip. "Leopold, I-I never meant to act as though I was perfect. I am sorry if I made it seem that way."

The girl's lower lip wobbled and she turned away from him. "No, Jubilee." Leopold moved toward her. "That wasn't right. You have done nothing wrong. You are so much like your mother sometimes. She loathed the idea of enslavement. But, Jubilee, sometimes enslavement is better than freedom. I know that now and I do not want to be free. I have seen what freedom means for me and I do not want it."

Jubilee narrowed her dark eyes, still full of tears and hurt. "Why? What has happened to you?"

"Nothing happened to me. I only missed my home."

"If that were so, you would agree to work for me as a freeman. You would not come back here demanding that I revoke your freedom. Something that I cannot and will not do! Least of all without knowing why. You were not like this before. What changed you?"

"Nothing changed me, my lady. I simply came to terms with who I truly am. Someone I do not want to be."

"And who is that?"

"You must never know that, my lady. The things I have done in my life. The things I have done since leaving. They are despicable. You would never look at me again if you knew." Leopold's eyes met hers, recognizing the moment his words settled over her. "I am not half the man you believed me to be."

Jubilee lowered herself to the lounge as the pieces fell together. The truth she had so long feared. "You said you wanted to be free." She croaked. "But not from us." The realization felt like a weight against her chest. "You didn't just care for my grandfather."

"I do not know what you mean, my lady." Leopold kept his back to her. He knew the look the girl would carry. The same look Juliana had given him when she discovered them—the look of betrayal.

"Leo."

"Stop, Jubilee. I know what you will say and do not want to hear it."

"You don't know me, Leopold. How can you know what I will have to say?"

"I have heard your stories, Jubilee. I have listened to every word you and your parents ever spoke to me. I know what your kind think of me. I know what your grandfather did to me before he even knew what Julius and I were." There was a coldness to his voice, the sort she had never heard in him before today. "I can see it written all over your face."

"I am not my grandfather, Leopold. I never met my grandfather and I know that I would never want to react as he did." She gripped his hand, refusing to let him pull away. "I love you, Leo. Knowing this about you doesn't change that. Now please don't push me away. I can't lose you too."

"You lost me when you set me free and you will lose me again if you don't tear up that contract."

Jubilee stared down at the scroll. "Tearing it up won't make you a slave, Leopold. Not to anyone but sin and Satan. You do not have to be enslaved to me, Leo. Or anyone. Stay with Atticus and me. Just because you are free doesn't mean you have to leave."

"If I am free I will have to leave, my lady. I am not strong enough to deny my feelings on my own. I will not subject you to that."

"You can, Leo. I know you can." *But do you want that?* A dark voice whispered. *Do you want a man like him around your husband?* Jubilee shook her head. Of course she trusted Leopold —the man had lived with Atticus for months and had never proven untrustworthy.

"You do not understand, my lady. I have wanted to stop for so long. I tried to follow your God when your mother told me about him. I tried to follow his ways and yet the feelings never left. I thought with Julius gone things would change. But still, the temptations stay even now. I gave into many while I was away." He couldn't look at her as the memories of his time in Germania came back to him. Nights with men and drink. In the first few weeks, he had felt alive. Free from the guilt he had always carried for what he was. There was no judgment in the tavern, where men and women alike shared pleasure, and he had enjoyed that pleasure.

It was when the euphoria of freedom had faded that he had been left with an ache worse than the one that had pushed him from Rome. He missed Jubilee. He missed the purity and the stories she shared. Whether they were true or not they brought a hope to his chest that he couldn't find on his own. No matter how much pleasure he partook in. He wanted God and he would find the truth.

"They may never truly go away, Leopold." Jubilee held his hands to her chest. "They are your weakness. We all have them and no matter how strong our love for God may be we will always have to fight them. My mother has the strongest faith I know. Jesus himself laid His hands upon her, showing just how loved she is, and she still fights with the feelings she had before she came to know Him. She still at times believes she is unlovable. In those times she becomes so wholly convinced of it, that she is almost unrecognizable. She pushes everyone away, including the Lord. She even grows angry at Him. It takes so much sometimes for my father to convince her she is more than love."

Closing her eyes she took a deep breath before continuing. "After what happened. I had lost all faith in God. I hated Him for what he allowed to happen to me. I hated my father and my brothers for getting help when I wouldn't stop bleeding. I hated my mother and her constant, unending belief that any good could come from that day. Because all I wanted was to die. I didn't trust the Lord to take care of me anymore. I admit I still don't." She bit down hard on her lip, fighting back tears. "I do not pretend to be perfect, Leopold. Because I am not, and I will not judge you for sinning differently than I do. The evil one knows our weaknesses and he will use them to turn us away from the Lord. Do not let him win, Leo. *Placere. Pugna.*"

Leopold slumped to the floor. A cold sweat had broken over him the moment the realization had fallen upon Jubilee's face. He wiped it from his brow. "And if I lose?"

"I will never lose hope. I will continue to pray on your behalf." She bent down and kissed his cheek, ignoring the subtle way he jerked. "But I will love you all the same." She pressed the contract into his palms. "Please accept this. I want you free in every way."

Leopold brushed her cheek, wiping away the tears that had fallen. "No, my lady. I must be subservient to you. Then you will order me to stay within the confines of the Domus. You will order me to stay on the path I set out upon."

"I will never give such an order, Leopold. It must be a choice."

"I will make the wrong one, my lady. Always I do." He took a deep breath. "I stopped a long time ago. I have spent over thirty years fighting what I feel and have always failed."

"Because you didn't have someone to support you. I will be here, Leo. Just as my father is for my mother."

"These things are not for the ears of a lady."

"Have you forgotten what was done to me?" Jubilee demanded. "My ears are no less soiled than my body is, Leopold."

Leopold frowned at her. "All the more reason to keep you from this." Pulling his hands free of hers he turned to the fire.

"Galilee," Jubilee shouted. "Go to Galilee."

Leopold froze, his hand only inches from the fire. "Galilee?"

"You know they would have you, Leo. So go there. Let them guide you where I can't." Moving his hand away from the fire, Jubilee held his hands in hers. "You can speak with my father. See my mother healthy."

"I don't think I can, Jubilee. It will break your mother's heart to know how far I have strayed."

"It will break her heart more to know you died in your sin. That I failed you as I failed Julius. Don't let me fail again, Leopold. Go."

…

Leopold left the following week. Despite his early fears, the man had nearly tripped in his hurry to board the ship. How many years had he longed to see his Juliana once more? Even if only to see that the words were true. To see her healthy and glowing as she had never been before. But fear was mounting as the ship neared land. He had written to Juliana that he had found the Lord years before and had left his sinful nature behind. What would she say when she learned he had not only lied but had worsened in the months since her father's death?

To ease his mind he read again the letter Jubilee had written to him, filled with words of encouragement and love. Silent tears had fallen down her cheeks before he left, so unlike the tears she had shed when he had been freed. Her face was all he needed to push him toward that ship. Always reminding him all too much of who waited for him across the sea. His Juliana. As much his daughter as Julius's. He had kissed both her cheeks and assured her that he would write.

Reaching Galilee he looked at the map and instructions Jubilee had left him in finding her home. His heart pounded painfully in his chest the nearer he came to Nazareth. Would she even recognize him? Would he recognize her or would they be strangers to each other after so long apart?

The house stood empty when he arrived, but he felt certain he had found the right one. Stepping into the garden he sat upon the crescent-shaped rock that Jubilee had clarified would make it stand out. The sky was darkening before a woman walked up the street. Her dark hair was pulled away from her face and as she neared he could see the wide, unmistakable black eyes of his Juliana. She had seen him as well. She had come to a stop, her head tilted curiously and then her lips parted. "Can you even recognize me?" Leopold asked as she neared him.

Tears leaked down her cheeks. "Oh, Leo! Of course, I recognize you." The old man took her up in his arms, turning her in a circle as he always had when she was growing up.

Back on her feet, she looked up at him as he touched her cheek. Gone were the ever-present shadows beneath her eyes. Looking her over he noticed the way that her bones no longer poked against her skin. She even had healthy fat in her stomach —the product of the children he had always feared would be the end of her. "Hello, my beautiful girl." Taking her back in his arms he savored the wholeness of her. She was whole and healthy, just as she had always promised.

XXIV

Jubilee pressed the letter to her chest, a steady stream of tears tickling her cheeks. She hadn't realized the full weight of her homesickness until Regulus had pressed the letter into her palms. The delicate curve of her mother's handwriting carved fresh grooves into her heart.

"Is everything all right?" Atticus asked—a light concern saturating his soft voice. "Everyone is doing well?"

She nodded. "*Imma* thinks *Abba* will have to stop working soon, she says his pain and stiffness have nearly taken over his hands. He struggles now to even hold a spoon when the weather gets too cold." She bit her nail. "He had to hire an assistant to train."

The slight resentment that filled her tone made Atticus sit beside her. "That was supposed to be you."

"I have you now, and the shop. I always thought it would be though." She was quiet for a moment, silent tears streaming down her cheeks. "I won't be there, Atticus. I won't get a proper goodbye before he dies. *Imma* won't be there when I have children." She shook her head. "I don't even know where Nathanael is. He was in Germania the last we heard but that was over a year ago. He could be anywhere by now. He doesn't even know that I am here, Atticus. With you."

Atticus touched her cheek. She and Nathanael had been inseparable from the time they were children, Jubilee's hand always held tight in her brothers. "Once we have had the shop going for a time, I'll see that we can visit them. But as of now, we can't afford to close up that long."

Her eyes met his, a small smile playing at her lips. "Do you mean it?"

"Can you give me a couple of years?"

She nodded enthusiastically. "Thank you, Atticus." Pulling him to her she kissed him before tucking the letter away.

Atticus watched the skin of her arm as she did so, visions from his dream overwhelming him. "Jewess?"

Her eyes met his, soft and sweet, still blurred by unshed tears. "Hmm?"

Bleed for me, Atticus. "I love you." He said quietly, pushing back the memories that had trickled their way back into his mind.

Jubilee's eyes narrowed. "I love you too?" She took his hand. "Atticus, are you all right? You've been acting strangely lately."

Atticus laughed weakly. "I'm fine, Jewess. Don't start worrying about me now."

"Don't give me a reason to." She mumbled before turning away. He could see the way he hurt her by denying her the truth, but he couldn't tell her everything now. The truth was too pathetic.

Atticus could feel Jubilee's eyes on him as they worked. She wanted to ask. He could see it in the way she held herself. When they made their way up to bed she slipped her hand into his and walked close to his side. "I'm sorry." She said quietly. "You have been so patient with me. If you need time I won't push you."

"Thank you, Jubilee."

Getting into bed, Jubilee curled into his side where he could feel the quick beat of her heart. *I bled for you.* And she had. How often had she put her fears aside to raise him up? And he couldn't do the same for her?

Jubilee lay against Atticus's chest, her eyes growing heavy as his fingers drew circles on her back, sending delicious shivers down her spine. "I don't want you to push yourself, Jubilee." He said suddenly. "I like this too. This right here." Propping herself on her elbows she found him staring upwards. "Aelia never wanted to simply lay like this. It was all about mindless pleasure."

Laying back against his chest, Jubilee closed her eyes. "Did none of the other women do this?"

"I have only ever been with two women, Jubilee." He said quietly.

"Oh." Atticus felt the gentle curve of her lips against his skin. As easily as the smile came it was gone. "I was so horrible to you. I accused you of it."

"It doesn't matter, Jewess. You had no way of knowing."

She was quiet for a moment. "Was she truly that terrible to you?"

"She was hurtful in many ways." He closed his eyes. "She was bored with me and she wasn't afraid to say so. I would see the way she looked at other men and the way she looked at me. Like they were gods and I was nothing more than a puppy." He laughed mirthlessly. "That was what she called me. Her little puppy. *No one wants a puppy, Atticus. Least of all a fat puppy.*"

Jubilee's lips twitched. "I happen to love puppies." She laughed tearfully. "Especially the fat ones."

At her smile, Atticus felt the tension melt away and he kissed her. It continued to marvel him, how the wife who had fought him for so long could hold more love for him than the one who had chosen him.

· · ·

Jubilee woke to dawn's light breaking through the cracks of the board that covered their window. Atticus's steady breaths filled the room. He was still on his back, his arm slung over his face. His mouth was open and he snored loudly.

Rolling onto her side she smiled. She loved him so much. Her body cried out for his, but each time it was quieted by the memory of *him* and *his* touch. "Jesus, help me."

At her words, Atticus stirred. "What?" Opening his eyes he frowned. "Where are you going?"

"I thought I would take a walk around the peristyle." Leaning in she kissed him. "Just go back to sleep."

The summer air was crisp at this time of day. Wrapping her cloak tight she enjoyed the cool air on her hot face. *She was bored with me and she was not afraid to say so.* Jubilee pressed her palms to her eyes. It had been two weeks since they had shared their pasts and despite Atticus's reassurances she still felt a heavy weight on her chest. Did he believe her when she said it had nothing to do with his body? Or did Aelia's cruel words haunt him each time she pulled away, unable to do a wife's honor?

She had settled on simple pleasures. A pleasure that never fully satisfied the hunger she felt in herself, growing ever so steadily until it was roaring inside her, rearing its head in anger when she pulled away at the last moment, terror flooding every part of her. Why after so long was she still so overcome with terror? She trusted Atticus with her life—she overwhelmingly loved him. Why must she freeze even when her body yearned to be one with his?

You're weak, Jubilee. The voice made her shiver and she quickened her step, unsure of where her feet lead her until the door was opened before her.

"Jubilee? Are you all right?" Solaris's surprised, yet soft voice quickly brought the tears that had been building on her walk and she collapsed at his feet, aware of how she must have looked. "Oh, child." He took her gently by the arm and led her inside, where Tamar bounced their screaming child on her hip. "Simon is teething, I am afraid." He explained.

When they had settled in the church room, Jubilee looked up sheepishly. "I am sorry to be bothering you so early. I didn't know where else to go. Truthfully I didn't even know where I was going until I was knocking at your door."

Solaris smiled kindly, not looking the slightest put out. "It seems as though the Lord wanted you here."

"Right." She whispered.

"Do you not believe so?"

"I don't know what the Lord wants anymore, Solaris. I haven't in years."

"Is that what you came to speak about? Your faith?" Solaris asked. Since her first meeting, she had been an adamant visitor. All the while seeming a faithful follower. She had introduced their newest member to them only weeks before.

The girl shook her head. "Something happened. It was a long time ago now, but I still find it interfering in my life."

"Is it a sin? A temptation?"

"No." She cried. "No."

"Child, I am afraid you are not being very clear. I do not know how to help if I don't know what it is that grieves you."

Having calmed Simon, Tamar found her way to them, a mug of honeyed water in her hands. Seeing the great distress the girl was in, the mother in her took over. Wrapping an arm around the girl's shoulder, she dabbed gently at the tears. "Come now, sweet girl. What is it?"

The story seemed to burst from the girl like water from a dam. Solaris and Tamar found each other's eyes, finding the very thoughts that were in their own. How had the girl gone so long carrying so much inside of her?

"Can you ever look at me the same again?" The girl whispered.

Solaris squeezed the girl's hand, still held tight in his own. "I will look upon you the way you deserve to be looked upon. As a woman who has faced unquestionable pain and survived." His eyes found his wife once more, following the thick scars that marked her beautiful face. "Much like another I know of."

Tamar smiled at him, wiping away the tears that had begun to spill during Jubilee's story. He knew the story would have touched her differently.

"You will find a way to be with your husband, Jubilee. I do not doubt this. If it were not so, would God have led you into his arms in the first place? Would he allow you the desires you say you feel?" Seeing the uncertainty in her eyes he smiled. "Would you be willing to share your story with the congregation?"

Jubilee frowned. "Is there reason to?"

"So God has put the body together such that extra honor and care are given to those parts with less dignity. This makes for harmony among the members, so that all members are for each other. If one part suffers, all the parts suffer with it, and if one part is honored, all parts are glad.' We are one, Jubilee. If you suffer. We suffer. Let us help the best we can."

Camila was the first to arrive, rushing to Jubilee's side, her face flushed with concern. Sibyl arrived next, followed by Mathias. Within the hour, the church was full of members of the church, many carrying sleepy-faced children in their arms. But not a single one held a sour face as Solaris gave a brief explanation before letting Jubilee take over. Sibyl stood by her side, her hand rubbing circles on her back as Jubilee spoke. She kept her head down as she spoke, sensing the different emotions in the room. While the women cried, those with daughters holding them closer, the men mumbled angrily under their breaths, many spitting words that earned them stern but overall agreeing looks from Solaris.

When finished, Solaris allowed the room a brief moment before explaining in full why he had called upon them so early.

Before the embarrassment could leave her face, Jubilee was on her knees in the middle of the large group, a dozen hands touching her while the room filled with their prayers. Some, like Solaris and Tamar, spoke in tongues, others in Aramaic, Hebrew, and Greek. But no matter the language, Jubilee felt each word settle onto her heart, bringing to it an ease she hadn't felt since *he* had taken her.

XXV

Sibyl stared into the lararium, the old urge to make an offering picking at her conscience. Many times she had made to throw it out, but something held her back. It wasn't until that moment that she realized what it was. Fear. What if Jubilee's god was a farce?

An unseen god, Sibyl? The voice was low and seductive. *Stick to what you know. To what can be seen and proven.*

She ran a hand over her rounding stomach—what can be seen and proven. It had been a month since she had discovered the life growing within her. The question had been brought up after a week-long bout of sickness and an even longer fatigue that had Regulus worrying over her.

"Perhaps you should see, Jubilee." He paced in front of her, his eyes watching her nervously.

"It's nothing, Regulus. Just a little nausea."

"It's not just the sickness, Sibyl. You can barely get out of bed in the morning. I haven't seen you this tired since—" Regulus put a hand to his mouth. "Sibby?"

Seeing where his mind had gone, Sibyl scoffed. "Oh please, Regulus." She pushed the man away from her. His touch only made it worse. "You know I am too old for that."

She pinned her hair back as her stomach churned again. She squeezed Regulus's hand when he set a basin before her, her only way of thanking him as the nausea became too much. His hand moved up and down her back as she was sick.

"Plenty of women have given birth at your age." His own mother had been forty-four when he had been born.

She turned to face him, the sickness momentarily forgotten. "You aren't angry, are you?" She breathed. "I couldn't control this."

"We controlled it for twenty-nine years, Sibyl. But we got reckless. You were getting older. We stopped being careful because of it." Seeing her upset, he sighed and kneeled next to her. "I am not angry." He brushed the few tears from her cheeks. "A child is a blessing. But you have to understand my hesitancy. You know what we went through last time."

Sibyl looked at her hands. "We don't even know if it will last that long, Regulus. We have a history of losing children, and that is when I was young."

"Is that what you think I want, Sibby? To lose it?"

"Of course, that's not what you want, Regulus. I'm only stating that we have no idea what is going to happen. Why don't we just take a breath? We don't even know if I am with child."

Sitting back beside her, Regulus took hold of her, wanting her close. "I don't want you to lose the child, Sibby. I know what that would do to you. I wish I hadn't been so selfish before, but I couldn't lose you. You know I can't lose you."

"I know that, Regulus. But if you do," She turned to face him, taking his face roughly in her hands. "Don't you dare do anything stupid, you understand me? Don't do that to our son."

"Sibyl, you know that I would never do something like that. Not after-"

"Just promise me, Regulus. Please. I need you to promise me."

Regulus touched her cheek. "I promise, Sibby. No matter the qualms I may have with our son I would never abandon him."

She had visited Jubilee in the afternoon when she could no longer deny what she had so previously thought impossible.

"Sometimes the Lord rewards you for your works." The girl said quietly. "You never questioned Regulus. You took his command and accepted without fighting him." She took a shaking breath. "You were content with it."

"Because I understood where he came from. I couldn't risk leaving him alone. But now it seems as though that is just what I am doing." Sibyl lowered herself into the seat. "I want to be happy, Jubilee. But what we went through last time? It was a week of pure agony. Twenty-four hours of pushing before anything happened."

"Just because you struggled last time doesn't mean you will struggle now, Sibyl. I have seen women who struggle with one child and not another. I have seen women who had multiple children without complications die giving birth to their next. We have to believe that God has something special in store for you and this child."

Sibyl watched the girl a moment, noting the way she blinked back tears. "I'm sorry, Puella. I know how terribly you want a child."

"I am still overjoyed for you, Sibyl. You deserve this."

Sibyl looked at the lararium. How could she have earned a child? She had fought against God all her life. Even still she felt the draw to give offerings to the gods she had always worshiped. She felt her fingers twitch, tempted to pick up the reed. Jubilee's stories were confusing. She knew her gods. She had followed them since she was a child, making her daily offerings the moment she woke up. It was easy and familiar. It was comfortable. She wrung her hands in her tunic. She couldn't betray Juliana. She couldn't betray Solaris and Tamar and all the others who had poured so much into her. Jubilee, who had spent countless hours in their year together telling her of the Lord. She had given up her time in the shop in the hopes of saving Sibyl's soul. She couldn't abandon her now.

One more time, Sibyl. Just once more and never again.

Once more. The pleasure the idea brought was delicious. Picking up the reed she lit it with the skilled hand of one who had worshiped many gods in her time. Her heart pounded painfully as she moved toward the emblem.

Beloved.

Sibyl gasped and let the reed fall to the floor where it sizzled out pitifully. She glanced around, certain it must have been a servant. The words had been so clear. Finding no one, she turned back to the *lararium.* Filled with a sudden anger that shook her body—anger at herself. At the worthless idols that seemed to hold so much power over her. Anger at the mother that had so adamantly pushed her daughter towards the gods. It had been the only likeness she had to her mother and she had clung to it like a lifeline, even long after her mother had left her life forever. She would not do the same with the child that grew within her. She would not fail them as she had failed Atticus.

Taking the candles from their holders she threw them to the floor and crushed them beneath her feet until they were nothing more than dust. Taking up one idol, she smashed it into the pillars of the *lararium.* Into the wall with the carefully done painting again and again, until at last, the metals were bent, the pillars were down, and the painting was chipped and unrecognizable.

Dropping to the floor, she let her tears consume her. With each passing day the weight that pressed upon her soul was growing heavier. The weight was crushing her now, like a vice. *Can you truly forgive me, Lord?*

Her forehead pressed against the tile, the very weight of it all bending her spine. Her arms stretched out before her. *Oh God, if you are there, make me believe. I want to believe.*

Sibyl, Beloved.

An unnatural calm came over her and suddenly it was no longer the weight of her sin holding her to the floor, but an overwhelming presence that made her tremble in both fear and a jubilation that filled her entire being.

God, I need you. I want you.

...

Regulus did not understand his wife's sudden fascination with their daughter's god, but the effects it brought were undeniable. He had hoped that bringing a piece of Juliana back to Rome would help his wife in some way, any way, and his hopes were proving worthwhile. After each visit, he could see the pieces of his wife returning. The Sibyl he had fallen in love with came back to him. Even finding the destroyed *lararium* had not aroused in him the concern that it would have only months before. For it was after that moment that the true change within her had come. Her nightly terrors had ceased to exist. The light that had once filled her eyes was slowly returning, bringing with it something he had never seen within her. Peace. She was happy, joyful, and by all accounts back to her old mischievous self.

From her spot at the harp, she watched him with a curious look in her eyes. "When was the last time we spent a week in Pompeii?" She asked suddenly.

Regulus raised an eyebrow. "I think it was about the same time we stopped visiting Galilee."

Sibyl's face fell for a quarter of a second before she was smiling again. "I think it would be wonderful to visit again. We could shop. Visit the sights." Seating herself next to him she took his hand. "The children are coming up on a year of marriage, it might be nice to treat them to something in celebration, and I don't believe Jubilee has ever seen a show before. I think she would love it, I know Juliana did."

"Are you going to feel up to it?" Though the fatigue had left her, the woman still woke with sickness each morning. "I don't want to see you pushing yourself." His eye went to her stomach, already rounding. With his initial shock past, he couldn't help but smile at the thought of the child she carried. She had loved her time carrying their son, and he could see that same joy in her with their newest child.

Sibyl set a hand to her stomach. "I think we can manage."

"Then I am willing to make the plans if that is what you want."

"It is." She smiled. "It will be good for us all to get away from the Domus."

Lifting her to her feet, Regulus kissed her. "I'll get things all in line."

XXVI

J ubilee watched Atticus's precise work as he removed the sutures from her palm. Due to the placement on her palm, she had been forced to wear the sutures longer than she would have liked and she was starting to feel claustrophobic. After much begging and a threat to remove them herself, Atticus agreed to take them out. When he finished he kissed her palm. "You're free."

Jumping down from the table, Jubilee flexed her hand and winced. "I still can't move it very well." She said quietly.

Taking her hand, Atticus opened it and pressed it flat. "It was deep." He replied. "I'm afraid it may have done more damage than we had hoped." He continued working on it, folding and unfolding her fingers—stretching it until she felt her stomach turn. He kissed her palm once more. "It won't affect you, Jubilee. You will still be able to work, just as you have been."

At his kiss her arms wrapped around his waist, her eyes closing. She had taken Layla's word and studied him. She studied everything. From the way he moved to the way he spoke. When they prepared for bed at night, hands trembling she would slip the tunic from his shoulders and let her fingers graze the grooves of his skin. She had never seen a man's body but *his*. Lean and muscled and rough to the touch. His very skin had felt dangerous. Atticus had gained weight and already he was thicker than the body she had known. Rounder if only slightly. His skin was smooth against her fingers, not a single switch scar to blemish it. Always she would hear his breath sharpen when she reached his stomach, soft, rather than hard and muscled from gathering wood, and always she would kiss every part of him he deemed unfit.

The same desire was there, but she quickly pushed it away. She couldn't move forward until she knew most certainly that she was ready. She wouldn't hurt Atticus again.

"Someone help!" The two jolted apart at the curdling scream.

Moving toward the door, Atticus found a young mother stumbling as she carried her son through the streets. As she went, others moved aside—none offering a hand as she nearly sagged under the child's weight. Atticus rushed out the door and quickly scooped the boy from her arms, just before she stumbled to the ground. "Please help my boy. He can't breathe."

Back in the shop, Atticus set the boy on the table. "His name is Marcus." The mother cried as she entered the room. "He was fine and then he started choking."

Jubilee's body went hot at the explanation. "Was he eating?" Atticus asked.

"No. He was helping me prepare dinner but he didn't eat anything. He just went white and started coughing."

Pushing Atticus aside, Jubilee opened the boy's small mouth and tried to look into his throat. "Oh, dear Lord." She whispered.

"Jubilee?"

Her cheeks had lost their earlier pink and had taken on a sickly green pallor. "I think I have seen this before."

"Well, what do we do?"

She shook her head, her eyes wide. "I don't- I-" She closed her eyes. "Get some water over the fire." She said at last. As

Atticus moved to do so she glanced around the shop. "I need Helichrysum powder."

Atticus pressed a bundle into her hands. "You'll have to grind it."

With that done, she poured a small amount into a cup of water. Going back to the boy she tilted his head back. "You'll have to drink this now. Come on." The boy did so obediently. "Very good." Taking him up in her arms, she handed him back to his mother.

"Will my boy be all right? Please, his father died before he was born. He is all I have."

Jubilee squeezed her hand. "I will do whatever I can, but you must trust me. Can you do that?"

The woman nodded tearfully, holding the boy close.

"Atticus remove the water and pour it into a bowl." He did as he was told and Jubilee mixed in the remaining Helichrysum powder. "Cut down the curtain." Tossing her a confused look, Atticus handed her the curtain. First placing the bowl in the woman's lap, Jubilee tossed the curtain over the boy and the bowl.

The woman glanced up at her. "Now what?"

Jubilee pursed her lips. "We wait. The hope is that we can break down the clot that is caught in his lungs." Sinking to the floor, she listened to the child's labored breath. *Please, God. Let this work.*

She jumped as something brushed her shoulder. Turning she found Atticus sitting next to her. "Are you sure you know what you are doing, Jubilee? Do you even know what this is?"

"I don't know what to call it, but I have seen it once before. In a woman back home."

"And did she survive?"

Jubilee glanced back toward the woman, too focused on her son to pay them any mind. She shook her head. Suddenly very tired she set her head on his shoulder. The minutes passed like hours, the only sound coming from the boy's labored breathing. It was his mother's scream that broke the silence. "He isn't breathing."

Jubilee pulled back the curtain to find the boy's lips blue, his eyes wide and frightened. "It's blocking his airway." Clearing the table she ordered Atticus to lay the child face down, his upper half hanging over.

Atticus watched Jubilee work. "We need to get him to cough." She began patting his back, gentle at first and then in quick succession. "Come on, Marcus." Tears spilled down her cheeks. "Please, God." She groaned before slipping once more into that strange language.

The boy coughed violently, his body tensing as the clot left his body and fell into the bowl.

The woman began to sob as the boy began to breathe once more, rough but clearer than before. Scooping him up she kissed his hair. "Oh, Marcus."

When the boy and his mother had gone, Jubilee sank to the floor, her heart still pounding too fast. "I didn't know what I was doing." She whispered. "I could have killed him. I didn't think about it and I-" Her eyes were wide and frightened.

Atticus set his forehead to hers. "But you did it. You were amazing, Jubilee."

She laughed shakily. "I suppose that is why we do this, isn't it? The intrigue is in the mystery. Each day is like a new adventure. Some dull. Others are magnificent. But an adventure all the same." She grew serious, her eyes distant. "I just want to learn as much as I can in the time I am given."

"I just wanted to help people," Atticus said quietly.

"A very noble reason."

"It's what keeps you going on days like today when fear nearly paralyzes you."

"I guess I am a bit more selfish in my love for it. But it is all I have ever wanted since I was a child." Jubilee smiled, her eyes a million miles away. "I never told you about that did I? When I fell in love with it?" When Atticus shook his head she continued. "I was maybe two or three when a sixteen-year-old girl was attacked and brought to our home late one night. Nathanael screamed when he saw her—Abel had to rush him out. I think my parents forgot I was there, they were so focused on the girl. I was fascinated watching my father work. She should have died, but she didn't. I remember thinking how my *father* did that and all I wanted was to be able to do that too." She laughed. "It was soon after that I began sneaking into his shop. I have never been in trouble so many times in my life as I was then. I refused to listen. I didn't care so long as I could be a part of it."

Atticus smiled. "It was your father who first made me want it. I always loved the look in his eyes when he would speak of his patients and what he did for them. I knew I wanted to do that."

"I think it was him most of all for me as well. I loved watching him work. I loved the sound of his voice when he spoke of his work. I used to make him sit and tell me everything when he got home at night." She sniffed and buried her head in his shoulder before she could cry. "I miss him. I just wish I had one of them here. A little piece of family."

XXVII

Augustus

The trip to Pompeii was a two days journey from Rome. Though Sibyl had tried to fight it, Regulus breathed a sigh of relief when Atticus announced that he and Jubilee intended to take their own carriage. When he had agreed to the trip, he had been blinded by his Sibyl's reappearance. He had thought nothing of the week he would be spending within the same confines as his son. The two were unable to go an evening without arguing.

He could not say what it was about his son that managed to break the level head Nehemiah instilled at him at a young age. *"It is easy to get angry, Regulus. It takes great strength to hold one's tongue."* He had built his life around those words long before Nehemiah left him and he had clung to them through it all. Fights with his father. With Sibyl. But it was his son who squashed the words and its importance into the ground.

Sibyl could see the agitation in her husband as the carriage rolled forward and she frowned. "Please, Regulus. One week. I spoke with Jubilee and asked that she speak with Atticus. I asked that he be on his best behavior and now I ask the same of you."

"You will have no trouble from me, Sibyl."

Sibyl noted the point of his words but chose to ignore them. There was no point in causing problems now. She would have to trust that the two could remain adults, rather than the children they turned into around one another. Taking his hand in hers she smiled. "Jubilee could hardly contain her excitement when I told her about the shows. It seems Juliana spoke very highly of her trips there." Since their first meeting, Sibyl had refused to hear of leaving Rome without her dearest friend in tow, and therefore Juliana had never missed a trip with Sibyl's family. The two had always found ways to create mischief, even with Amma, Juliana's nurse in tow. From a young age, Juliana had begged the woman to blind herself to certain areas of trouble. So long as their adventures didn't bring a threat to Juliana's health, the nurse was as tight-lipped as a well-practiced mime.

...

They reached their villa, along the outskirts of Pompeii, just before dawn. Roused by Regulus, Sibyl got reluctantly to her feet and followed after him. Her back ached from sleeping on the hard carriage seats. Sleep dragged her eyelids down. Laughing, Regulus scooped her up and carried her the rest of the way.

After a few hours of sleep, the four made their preparations for the day. It seemed Atticus had already laid claim to his wife for the day, anxious to show her the sights he had explored as a child.

Taking Sibyl's hand, Jubilee smiled. "You and I will make a day of it tomorrow. I want to see all of my mother's spots."

"Tomorrow then." Kissing her on each cheek, Sibyl sent the two off.

Stepping into the summer air, Jubilee leaned close to Atticus. "Should I have gone with your mother?"

Atticus glanced at her. "Do you want to?"

"I do." She replied quietly. "I think I should. It was her idea to bring us here and it's where she came with *Imma*. I think she might be missing her."

"If that is what you want then we can take the day tomorrow."

Jubilee met his eyes. Since the meeting at the church, she had felt the change within her. Slowly she felt the fear trickling away drop by drop. "Tomorrow." She smiled. "Then we can take the whole day without guilt. Just you and me. Tomorrow is more important anyhow." The marking of their one year.

Sibyl was exuberant when the two returned to the villa. "Are you sure, Jubilee? I don't want to tear you away from your plans."

"Please, Sibyl. I want to do all the things you and my mother did, and finally hear more about the trouble she got into." Grabbing her coin purse she turned to Atticus. "Behave please."

"I will if he will." He mumbled, so quietly only Jubilee heard him. Tossing him a quick look she hurried after Sibyl.

Sibyl left nothing of the city unseen. She showed Jubilee the Temples. The theaters and amphitheaters. Sharing stories of her and Juliana as children. Reaching the Palestra Grande, the training grounds of gladiators, Sibyl smiled. "Your mother and I never missed a chance to watch the gladiators train. We were never allowed to watch the games of course. But the men were fun to watch. Your mother took quite a fancy to one once. I believe his name was Jacob." She laughed. "It seems your mother had a taste for the Jews from the beginning."

Moving past the training grounds, Sibyl hurried her to the Fora Triangolare, overlooking the sea. "We could spend hours here just talking. If Amma had her choice we would have spent every second here. Some days we did, if your mother was having one of her bad days. Juliana refused to hear about staying in when we were here." Sibyl took her to the shops next. "On her good days, we could spend hours at a time here. Amma used to grow irate waiting for us. Though it was one of the few things she truly felt comfortable letting Juliana do." Sibyl frowned. "I have spoken of Amma as if you know her. Your mother did tell you about Amma?"

"She has told me some," Jubilee said quietly. "But not much. She always became very emotional when she mentioned her."

"Of course. I think she and Amma were closer even than she and I were. Your mother could act as though Amma was such a bother, but even when they fought the love they had for each other was without compare." Sibyl put an arm around Jubilee's shoulder like her mother would. "You know, Amma is where she got her name for you. *Love*. It was nearly all Amma ever called her. It was a rare moment to hear Amma call her anything but her Love." Lapsing into silence, Sibyl examined a row of child-sized blankets.

Looking around, Jubilee felt her heart pick up a pace at the sight of a shop, the image of the Star of David carved into the wood. Moving through the crowd, Jubilee looked over the merchandise. Jewish pendants and rings decorated the walls. Along the side hung a tapestry, carefully woven in browns and golds and blues. Jubilee heard herself gasp as she made out the blurred image of the sea.

"What is it?" Sibyl's voice came behind her.

"The Sea of Galilee." Jubilee breathed. Her fingers grazed the tapestry. "How much." She asked in their native tongue.

"Four denariai and a Sestersi." The man replied.

Jubilee felt her lips part of their own accord. "I'm afraid I do not have that much." She had not expected to find much and had decided against taking more than she felt she would need. With the much-needed shoes for Atticus and the tunic he had insisted she brought back for herself, she was left with a single denariai.

As she looked, the tapestry was gently pulled from beneath her touch. Glancing up she found Sibyl paying the man. "If you can have that delivered to the Albanus Villa." She said. Turning to Jubilee, she took a handkerchief and dabbed the girl's cheeks. "Consider it a gift."

Realizing what she meant, Jubilee gasped. "No, Sibyl. It's too much."

"Nonsense. That home of yours still has the essence of Julius. You must make it your own now and I am thrilled to provide you with that start." When Jubilee opened her mouth to protest, Sibyl popped the handkerchief into the girl's mouth, silencing her. "The Albanus Villa." She repeated to the man. Giving her thanks she hurried down the street, making Jubilee run to catch up.

"Let me at least make it up to you, Sibyl."

Stopping, Sibyl looked at her seriously. "You gave me new hope. You gave me new life." Taking her handkerchief back, she dabbed her own cheeks, unconcerned with where it had been. "You have made it up to me a hundred times over, Jubilee Aquila."

...

The villa was quiet when the two returned. Separating, each woman went in search of their husband.

Jubilee found Atticus in their cubicula, pouring over the list of items the shop was in need of. When she walked in he smiled. "Did you have fun?"

She returned his smile. "I did. Your mother told me all sorts of stories I never knew about *Imma*."

"Did you bring back something pretty?" He asked, the dimples in his cheeks revealing the smile he fought to hide.

Unfolding the peach-colored fabric she held it up to him. "Your mother approved the color."

"She did well. Now why don't you put it on for me."

Jubilee raised an eyebrow before tossing the tunic at him. As she undid the clasp of her tunic she thought of King Solomon and the way his bride had danced for him. *Simple pleasures.*

Atticus felt a smile ease across his face as he watched his wife move in the dim light of the room. Letting her hair fall loose she looked like an angel. When her arms outstretched in invitation he felt himself drawn to her without conscious effort. Stretching onto her toes she wrapped her arms around his neck. "Dance with me." She whispered in his ear.

Atticus felt his mouth go dry as he took in her naked form. She wanted him to dance with her, showing her all the parts of him that brought him shame. No matter how often she saw him, he still felt that same jolt of fear at what she must think of him.

Seeing his hesitation her head tilted. "It is just us, Atticus." She breathed.

Atticus swallowed. There was something to the way she said it. *It's just us.* She was inviting him in. Drawing her to him he kissed her. There was no fear in her as he set her on the bed.

A sharp knock at the door made him swear as Jubilee dived for the blankets. Sighing, Atticus cracked the door open. "Yes, Layla?"

"I am sorry to bother you, my lord. Lady Sibyl has requested the two of you come for dinner."

Five minutes later the two entered the triclinium, Jubilee dressed in her new tunic.

Regulus smiled. "You look radiant, Jubilee. I hope Atticus has told you."

"Every day," Atticus mumbled.

Nudging Atticus lightly, she smiled. "Thank you, Regulus, and you mustn't worry. Atticus doesn't let a day go by without a compliment."

"Good."

As he helped her into her seat, Jubilee took Atticus's hand, urging him to kneel. "Don't let him get to you." She whispered. Her thumb grazed his chin. "I know. That's what matters."

The room was silent as everyone picked at their food. Baked Dormouse, *globuli*, and *libum* for dessert.

"What do you plan on showing Jubilee tomorrow?" Regulus asked quietly.

"I was thinking I would introduce her to Remus." Turning to Jubilee he explained. "He is someone I played with as a child."

"Do you think that is a good idea?"

Atticus frowned. "Why wouldn't it be?"

Biting back his retort, Regulus took a bite of food. *One week. Just one week.*

"Remus owns a tavern here." Atticus continued. He felt his father's eyes on him. "He can be a bit much at times, but he is a good man."

"He's a ruffian." Regulus spit. "I don't want Jubilee anywhere near him or that tavern."

"Jubilee is my wife and I will decide where I am comfortable taking her."

"What sort of uncivilized man takes his wife into a tavern?"

"I wouldn't take her in." Atticus spit, ignoring Jubilee's hand on his leg. "I am not so brainless as you like to see me."

"Neither one of you is seeing that man. Am I understood?" Regulus shook with rage. "The last time you walked into that tavern you came out with an opium addiction and a harlot wrapped around your neck."

Jubilee gasped, the hand at his leg tightening. Atticus glanced down at her, his eyes shining with tears. Turning back to his father his chest rose and fell quickly. "We're done here." He choked.

The room fell silent as the angry words settled. Finally, Jubilee stood.

"Jubilee," Regulus said quietly. "I am sorry. But you must understand, I am doing this to protect you. Both of you. You must believe that."

She met his eyes. Unsure of what to say, she shook her head before running after Atticus.

Sibyl glared at her husband. "Just a few days." She whispered. "All I wanted was a few days of normalcy. You two can't even make it one day."

"That boy is impossible, Sibyl."

"Don't start that." She spit. "This is all on you, Regulus. You are a completely different person when you are with him. Honestly, you remind me of my mother when you are with him."

"Perhaps I have to, Sibyl." Regulus hissed. "Seeing as you refused to parent."

Sibyl bit down on her lip, her hand going to her stomach. In all their years of marriage, Regulus had never aimed angry accusations at her. "I parented him." She spit weakly. "Just because I refused to be my mother does not mean I let him run wild. He was good. He was perfect before he met Aelia."

"There it is, Sibyl. You refuse to see any blame in him. We cannot blame Aelia for everything."

"I hold that wench accountable for everything." She seethed. "My boy was sweet. Perfect. He was everything a mother could want before she defiled him. I hope she burns in—" The words caught in her throat, burning like fire. *Oh God forgive me. I do not mean it. I do not mean it.*

She deserves it, Sibyl. Say it.

"He was addicted to opium." Regulus continued. He seemed unaware of the war in her mind. "Can we blame Aeila for that? Even if he started as a way to soothe himself, he was still stupid enough to begin in the first place, and now I am stuck paying the price."

"I have nothing for that, Regulus. But I choose to see more than his faults. If you stopped being angry for one moment you would see the pain he is in."

"Pain he brought on himself."

Sibyl shook her head. "Who are you?" She croaked. "I feel as though I lost both of you the moment she entered our lives."

Taking a deep breath, Regulus moved towards her. "Sibyl."

At his touch, she went to him. "We aren't supposed to fight like this." She said tearfully. Only once in thirty years of marriage had they spit such harsh words at each other. Pushing the memories away she hugged him tighter. "Come back to me."

XXVIII

Jubilee entered the room quietly, alerting him of her presence only when she pressed her fingers into his shoulders, massaging the knot that was building. Taking her hand he pulled her down into his lap and held her close. His face was buried in her hair.

The room was silent, Jubilee's fingers toying with the small tuft of hair at his neck. "Atticus." Her voice was small. Unsure, as though she feared upsetting him further. When he urged her to continue she took a deep breath. "Was it because of Aeila that you became addicted to opium?"

"What do you mean, Jubilee?"

"I know you, Atty. I know that you wouldn't do anything like that on purpose. You wouldn't do any of those things, and-and you said that she made you think you wanted it when you didn't." She hesitated before spitting out the words he had known would worm their way into her mind. "Atticus did she force herself on you?"

"Of course not, Jewess." He let out his breath in a feeble attempt at a laugh. "Don't be ridiculous."

"It's possible." She whispered. "If you weren't truly there." Turning in his lap she met his eyes. "I know what that looks like, Atticus. I know what that feels like in every way. So why do you hide it from me?"

"Because it's not the same, Jewess." His chest rose and fell quickly. The woman saw things in him that even he had forced from his memories. "No one can know, Jubilee. Please."

"But your father, Atticus. If he knew the truth of it."

"If he knew the truth of it he would be ashamed. I would rather him hate me than be ashamed of me. What man allows something like that to be done to them, Jubilee?" He closed his eyes, his breath coming in quick spurts. "I told her no. I knew I would be going back to Galilee the moment I could. I only wanted you. I think deep down I always knew it would be you. I don't remember much after that. All I remember is wine. A lot of wine." And fear. He remembered fear and the gentle way she coaxed him. He remembered the hint of anger in her voice and the slap when he mentioned Jubilee's name.

"And then I woke up the next morning and she was next to me." He noticed the way Jubilee flinched but the words wouldn't stop pouring from his lips. "I tried to stop it after that but it kept happening. Wine and then nothing and then her. Always her. Once I realized what had happened it was too late. I only married her to make myself feel better. I wanted to believe I loved her. I convinced myself that opium had simply given me the courage to go after what I wanted. It wasn't as if I could go back to you. Not after everything. You deserved someone clean."

"But I wasn't clean. I was never really clean. We were the same, Atty."

Moving her off of him, Atticus stood and began to pace. "You are not the defiled one, Jubilee. You aren't weak. You were a girl who couldn't fight back against someone twice her size. I was a *man*, Jubilee, and I let her take advantage of me. I could have stopped her and I let fear overrule me. Again and again." He sent a chair into the wall, watching as it splintered and shattered.

His tears came slowly at first and then all too quickly as Jubilee took his hand. He sobbed into her chest with the rawness of a wound that refused to heal. His fingers clasped onto the fabric of her tunic as though he feared her backing away.

When he knelt to the ground, she held him to her, feeling the way his body shook as he worked to stifle the tears, unwilling to show the extent of his grief, but unable to fight them any longer.

Jubilee kissed his cheek as he would her, tasting the salty tears on her lips. Finally, she rested her cheek on his hair and let him rest against her chest.

"Don't leave me." It was the whispered plea of a boy who had been taken and then tossed away like the runt of a litter. Inhuman and unworthy. The confession of one who had suffered alone for far too long, and knew he couldn't continue. "I need you."

"I will never leave you, *Amica Mea*."

Solaris's voice echoed. *You will know when it is time, Jubilee. Do not be afraid.*

Her eyes met her husband and she knew. She was ready for this. When she kissed him, Atticus hesitated. "Are you sure, Jewess?" His hand was gentle on her cheek, one expectant hand at her hip. "Don't do this for me."

"I'm not." She kissed him before he could protest, not wanting to waste another moment.

She felt only a small trickle of fear as he laid her across the bed. "Can I see your face?" She breathed, pushing away those old, horrid memories. He set his forehead to hers and she smiled, her hand touching his coarse cheek. This was Atticus who held her—a man who knew the same pain as she. A man who needed her in the very ways she needed him. With him, she was no longer the girl who was raped at fifteen—used and tossed away. In his arms she was safe. Just as she always had been.

Part III

50 AD

XXIX

Ianuarius

The world came back to him in parts. The dark, star-strewn sky. Mordecai hovering over him, his hazel eyes wide and frightened. He was vaguely aware of himself being lifted off the ground as the pain washed over him in violent waves. He opened his mouth and knew he screamed, though he couldn't hear it over the pitched ringing in his ears. He had always seen giving his life for the Lord as honorable. But the pain was blinding. *Oh God, if this must be my end, let it be quick.* He sighed in relief as he was lowered back to the ground. No, it was a plank of old wood. As he was lifted once more, he felt a hand slip into his, and once again Mordecai was in his line of sight. He said something he couldn't make out. *It's going to be all right.* Was that it?

The rock of the wood as the men moved jarred his aching bones. Something wet dripped down his cheeks. Was he crying? The pain was overwhelming. *Oh God, please! End it now. I do not fear death but this is too much!* As the men stumbled he felt himself roll to the side of the plank. He was on the ground again, pain seizing his limbs. He screamed again, longer this time. *Jesus! Jesus!* Would this agony never end? As they lifted him again onto the plank his vision blurred and graciously felt himself fading into a sleep.

He roused to someone's touch. Though gentle, the pain it caused sent his stomach rolling. The air was full of shouting.

Metal clanking on metal. And one voice rising above it all. "Nathanael?" The voice was small—panicked. "It is all right. You're going to be okay, you hear me?" The woman's thumbs brushed his cheeks. "Don't leave me now."

Don't leave you? I don't know you. Or did he? The voice sounded so strangely familiar. It made his heart ache for home.

He couldn't open his eyes. His head ached. He wanted the darkness. He had felt nothing in the darkness. Now the pain was consuming. And it was only worsening as they messed with him. His moan turned into another cry as someone pressed a hand to his ribs.

"His ribs are broken." The woman cried.

Why do you cry for me? He wanted to ask. But he couldn't work his tongue around the pain.

His head was lifted and a cup was pressed to his lips. "Drink this. It will make you sleep." He gulped the bitter liquid greedily and waited for the darkness to numb him from the pain. As he floated into that restful oblivion, he felt a hand take his own. It was the woman's. Small and soft, save for a rough, curved scar that ran the length of her palm. With the other, she gently brushed the hair from his forehead. She was speaking quickly. Too quiet for him to hear the words but he knew. She was praying. In his native tongue.

...

When Nathanael roused again he found himself in an unfamiliar room. When he tried to sit up he groaned and plopped back onto the bed—overcome with pain. Laying back he breathed deeply as his head spun, his eyes closed tight as snatches of the previous night came back to him. Sharing God's word. The shouting and swearing. The pain that followed. And that voice. He remembered the soft voice, so familiar it almost hurt. He could have sworn it had been... but no. It couldn't be. It was simply his pain-fueled delirium. Or homesickness.

Pushing the thought from his mind he took in the room around him. The light was dim, the only source being the moonlight. How long had he slept? Despite the minimal light, he managed to make out the room well enough. It was large and unlike any he had seen before. In the far corner sat a small dark vanity, its possessions scattered neatly across its surface.

A small sigh brought his attention to the window, where a woman had just turned over, her short frame tucked comfortably on the small lounge. His heart thudded in his chest. "No." He moaned loudly. He was losing his mind. He had thought he had seen her in Pompeii as well, disappearing into a crowd. But it couldn't be. "It's not her." The throbbing in his head worsened. Perspiration dripped down his forehead.

At his words, the woman had stirred. "Nathanael?" She walked through the darkness and stopped beside the bed. Her dark hair concealed her face as she leaned in to light the candles. Up close he could see her hair was a mess of pitch-black curls against honey-brown skin.

"Jubilee." He croaked. It had been four years since he had left Galilee. His sister had only just turned sixteen. Now three months shy of twenty, she had changed. Her round face had thinned, adopting their mother's mature features. But even still her eyes were the same, too wide and innocent for her to ever be more than the little girl he had grown up with. "Is that you?"

"You're awake." She breathed. A pleasant smile graced her face and he felt warmth spread through him. It was Jubilee. Helping him lean forward she placed another pillow behind his back, allowing him to sit up. Sitting beside him, she touched his hair. "You made me worried. You've been asleep for a week." As she went through the list of everything he had broken and bruised, lacerated and cracked, his head spun. He had always despised medical talk. Seeing his discomfort, Jubilee smiled. "Sorry. No more of that." Shifting, she rested beside him, her head on his shoulder.

At her closeness, Nathanael felt tears prick in his eyes. Four years had felt like nothing until he thought he had seen her in Pompeii. Now he felt the lonely parts of those years close in on him. He held Jubilee's hand in his as he let the tears fall. "Where are *Imma* and *Abba*?" He asked. "Are they here too?"

"No, Nathanael. They are still in Nazareth."

"You're here alone?" He turned to look at her. "Jubilee, what are you doing here?" He couldn't fathom it, his tender-hearted sister in a place like Rome—without even their parents.

A small smile curved her lips. "I married Atticus."

Nathanael blinked. The last time he had seen his sister she could hardly stand a man's eyes on her. "You're married? How long has this been? I mean," He squeezed her hand. "Are you happy?"

"It's been a year and a half, and I am very happy, Nathanael."

Nathanael smiled at the way her cheeks filled with a happy blush. "Then congratulations are in order. You finally got your hands on him."

Jubilee laughed softly "Something like that."

Born only ten months apart the two shared a bond that had often separated them from those around them, preferring to spend their time in the other's company. They had understood one another from the time they were infants and four years couldn't change that. Nathanael took her hand. "What is it, Joy?"

"It's nothing, Nathanael. Truly. The marriage just didn't happen as I had always expected it. Things have only just started to settle into place."

Nathanael stayed quiet as she told the story of her coming to Rome. "Well, it seems *Imma's* feelings win out again."

Jubilee frowned as she glanced toward the window, where the sun had long since risen. "I suppose I should go help Atticus in the shop." Standing she kissed his forehead. "I'll check in on you as often as possible." Hesitating a moment she smiled. "I am really happy you are here, Nathanael. I mean not like this but...I've missed you."

Nathanael nodded. "We'll talk later, Jubilee. Go and help your husband." She had only reached the door when he called her back. "Where are we?"

"The Aquila Domus. It was passed down to me after Grandfather died." She glanced around the room. "This was *Imma's* room."

When she was gone, Nathanael settled back into the pillows, taking in the room that now held a new meaning. His mother's room. After four years apart from his family, finding Jubilee, and staying in a room that once housed his young mother, he felt the ache he hadn't realized was there begin to fade.

...

Nathanael dozed most of the morning, craving the relief that sleep brought him. By mid-morning, he was woken by the door opening and closing softly. Expecting to find Jubilee, confusion blossomed as his vision cleared, revealing a tall Egyptian woman.

The woman kept her eyes down as she set the tray beside him. He took in the assortment of fruits and eggs and felt his stomach rumble. He couldn't remember the last meal he'd had that didn't consist of stale bread and fish. His mouth watering, his eyes fell on the cup of milk. Milk had always been his favorite. He drank it in one long series of gulps. Setting the cup down once more, he thanked the girl.

She nodded. "Would you like more?"

He would. But said he wouldn't. He was a guest in their home and he did not want to overindulge. "May I ask your name?" He asked, helping himself now to the eggs.

"Layla." Her accent was thick. He had to listen carefully to make out the words. "I care for lady Jubilee."

"Lady Jubilee?" Try as he might he could not see Jubilee as anything but his little sister. The girl had never been afraid of dirt and didn't shy away at the sight of blood. "Lady Jubilee."

Layla felt unsure of herself as she watched the man eat. Jubilee had requested that she stay with her brother until she could check in on him herself. He resembled his sister. Only taller and slimmer. She couldn't explain the sudden discomfort that had come over her as she stood over him. Like his sister, there was a kindness in his eyes that outshined any she had seen in another and yet she couldn't rid herself of it—the gnawing feeling that too much time with him and she would find herself unraveling.

Nathanael frowned as the girl stared straight ahead. Was she always so serious? Only in her almond eyes did he see the obvious pain that dwelled within her. She looked as though she could not have been much older than himself—too young to be so cold. "Is my sister good to you?"

"Lady Jubilee is all that a slave can ask for, my lord." Her tone softened at this, the love she held toward his sister clear in her very posture.

"Good, and please, call me Nathanael."

"You sound like your sister." She said quietly.

Nathanael smiled. "I take it she asked you to stay with me? Well, then I ask you to sit. You cannot stand all day."

Her eyes flashed to his and then she moved silently to the lounge. No further words were spoken between the two.

XXX

Jubilee felt Solaris's eyes on her as she moved toward the door. Moving with her, he touched her arm. "Are you all right, child? It has been some time since you stayed after the service. Tamar has been missing your visits."

Avoiding his eyes, Jubilee readjusted her stola. "I have been busy. My brother is staying with us now and he needs caring for."

Solaris nodded. "Perhaps we might be of assistance? I'd love to meet this brother you've spoken so highly of."

"You will—when he can move around. But as for now, I need to get back to him."

"Jubilee." The man's voice was gentle and coaxing. "Whatever holds you back now, know that you can always come to me or Tamar."

Jubilee turned her back to him, hiding the tears that broke free and trailed down her cheeks. "Why can I believe it here?" She whispered. "With all of you, I can feel His love and believe there is new life in Him. But on my own, I feel nothing at all."

"Because you are trying to find a reason for your suffering. Rather than accepting that you may never truly know his reason, you fight against him. Questioning him. Doubting anything that may come from it."

"What could come from this, Solaris? What good can come from something so violent?"

Solaris touched her cheek. "It may not seem so now, child. But God is doing great work in you. You know my wife. You have seen her scars and you have heard her story. You know the good that came from that violent act."

"She was stronger than me, Solaris." Jubilee's eyes found the woman. "She was always stronger than me. She never questioned it." Freeing herself from his gentle grip on her shoulder she stepped outside. "Thank you again, Solaris."

Tamar wrapped her arms around her husband's waist, watching the girl until she disappeared. It had taken only days before she had realized where she had known the girl from. That God-filled little girl from so long ago—an angel in a time of despair. "She'll find her way back, love. Just give her time."

"That girl is holding on to too much." He replied quietly. "Until she learns to leave it be she will never know the peace she yearns for."

"That sounds like someone else I know." Tamar kissed his cheek. "She reminds me of you when we first met."

"And I had you to guide me. That poor girl is caught between two worlds."

"She will find her way, Solaris. Just as you did. Now come. We have other visitors to entertain." Letting her take his hand in hers he followed after her.

...

Atticus watched the way Jubilee's fingers grazed the skin of her belly. Fat tears rolled down her cheeks. "Prima is expecting." She had noted after returning home from church. Tears had choked her voice. Prima, he knew, had been married a mere three months.

Pulling her hand from her stomach, Atticus kissed it. "It makes no difference to me, Jubilee."

"How can it make no difference?" She cried. "Prima is barely married and already she is giving her husband a child. It's been nearly two years for us and I have nothing to offer you."

"I have you, Jewess. That is enough."

She shook her head. "We're not truly married until I give you a child. Not in the eyes of Rome, we're not."

"Forget Rome, Jubilee." The words came out harsher than he had meant them and her lip trembled. "You are my wife, Jewess. Child or no child. Rome cannot change that."

"Aelia could give you a child."

"And she chose to murder the both of them, Jubilee. Don't ever compare yourself to her."

"Are you going to leave me?" Her voice cracked miserably, threatening to bring tears to Atticus's own eyes.

"Why would I leave you?"

"Because I can't give you a child." She sobbed.

His patience was wearing thin. Their months of bliss had ended and with no child on the horizon, it seemed as though they would never find their way back to it. "You may still be able to have children, Jubilee. Some women take longer. You know this."

"But if I can't, Atticus? Isn't that why you agreed to another marriage? To give your mother grandchildren?"

Atticus stuttered. "How do you know that?"

"It wasn't difficult to guess, Atticus. You didn't marry a prudish Jewess so that they could continue to point out your mistakes. I've seen your mother's face when she thinks I carry a child only to learn that I do not. You did it for your mother, didn't you?"

"Jewess, I said those things when I was angry. I didn't mean them."

"Do you mean to tell me they aren't true? That your sole purpose wasn't for children?"

"Perhaps it was in the beginning."

"And now?" She demanded. "What is to stop you from leaving me? From finding someone who can give you what you want?"

Atticus swore softly. "You are what I want, Jubilee. I love *you*."

She lowered herself back into his arms. He could feel the way her heart beat fast against his hand. "Do you promise?"

"I promise you, Jubilee. Child or no child, you are mine."

But no amount of comfort could rid her of the hollow ache that filled her being. She longed for a child like one longed for air. Every expectant mother who walked through the shop brought such quick tears to her eyes that she was forced to flee the room. To see Sibyl's round stomach brought an ache to her chest that made it hard to breathe. Her dreams brought her visions of a child in her arms and she woke to a feeling of terrible emptiness.

Atticus despised watching his wife try so hard. She was slowly killing herself in her efforts. Her efforts to please him. Her efforts to conceive a child. And most of all to please the devil she called a loving god. It was sickening the way she relied so heavily on an unseen god. A god who, if he existed, clearly held no love for her. He wanted to grab her. To shake her. Even slap her if that would wake her up to the truth. But what sort of monster would he be if he denied her the right to worship freely? He knew she would blame him. Not cruelly of course, but tearfully. *Why can't you understand?* She would cry. There would be no blame on her lips toward the very thing that caused her so much misery.

Night after night he watched her in the gardens, her distress clear in the way she hugged herself tightly, her hands clenching her tunic. Tears trailing down her cheeks. With a soft moan, she would fall to her knees and sob.

That is when he would intercede, unable to watch her tear herself apart for nothing. Taking her hands in one of his own, he brushed her cheek with the other. At his touch, the tears would halt and she would fall back on her heels. Her eyes finding his. Each time the desperation grew in him. "Please, Jubilee." He cried. "Open your eyes. What sort of god would allow you this pain?" When she opened her mouth he covered it with his hand. "Don't ask me to understand, because I won't." Kissing her hard he pulled back. "Let *me* love you." He whispered and that was all it took for her to fall into him, relying on him the way he wished her to.

XXXI

Regulus couldn't understand his wife's adoration of her new god. In all the years he had known her she had worshiped gods loyally. But he had never seen her as dedicated as she was to this newest god. He was all she spoke of. She spoke of the church. Her prayers. She spoke of the friends she had made. She had taken most to the pastor's wife, who had become a frequent visitor to the Albanus Domus—her four boys in tow. Sibyl told him of the stories she had learned from Jubilee and what she continued to learn each week at church.

"Do you truly believe those stories, Sibby?" Regulus asked as he got into bed.

"Yes."

"Water into blood." He questioned. "A simple man parting the sea? They are like stories you used to tell Atticus. Doesn't it seem childish to you?"

Sibyl smiled calmly. "The Lord parted the sea, Regulus. He simply used Moses to do so."

"So you have said. It all just seems too absurd to be real. I mean honestly, Sibyl. They are the sorts of stories you tell children to make them sleep at night. They aren't meant for grown adults."

"Do you wish for me to stop telling them?" She asked quietly.

"No, Sibyl." He brushed her cheek. "I love the sound of your voice when you tell them. I don't have to believe them to enjoy hearing you tell them. But I'm trying to understand."

"I wish you believed." She had tried many times in the beginning to make him believe. She begged him to come to church or to speak with Jubilee as she had done. It had taken only a few short weeks before he had snapped at her to leave him be. He had heard the stories all his life. Why must he hear them again?

It had been Tamar who had eased her heart. *"It doesn't mean you are leaving him on his own, Sibyl. You can still pray for him. Being a witness is more than sharing the Lord's stories. Simply behaving as the Lord calls you to can be enough. Let Regulus see the Lord within you through your actions, rather than your tongue."*

"Is that how it was with Solaris?"

"It was." Tamar smiled. "The curiosity is there, Sibyl, and soon enough it will drive him to ask questions."

It had taken only a month for Regulus to encourage her to begin telling him the stories once more. Though she knew it was simply out of guilt, she had taken it as a sign of hope that he was willing to listen.

Regulus was quiet as he slipped beneath the covers, letting her say her nightly prayers in peace. When she mentioned the child he closed his eyes. Any day the child would come. The nearer the day drew the sicker he became. Memories of Atticus's birth threatened to overwhelm him. But no fear showed in Sibyl's eyes. She was ready. When she got into bed he let her rest against him. "I wish you wouldn't do that." He said quietly.

"Do what?"

"Pray like that for the child. Those people are breeding false hope in you, Sibby. You know the odds of a child surviving."

"As do they, Regulus. But worrying will not change whatever God has planned for this child. We have made it this far. Why can I not believe we will make it all the way?"

Regulus frowned. "Because I can't stand to see you fall apart. I only just got you back."

Sibyl sat up. "Don't you see that it is this very thing that will keep me from falling apart should we lose the child? I had no one to lean on in those days, Regulus. I believed that it was my doing that caused me to lose them. I know the truth now. Should the Lord take them it is not because of me. Should I lose the child, I will have the church to lean on." She touched his cheek. "But I won't lose it, Regulus. Tamar is like Juliana with that strange sense. A gift, Solaris calls it. She believes that all shall come to pass without trial."

"I am sure that Tamar has your best interests at heart, Sibyl. But she is only a woman. She isn't a prophet."

"She isn't prophesying, Regulus. She isn't stating facts, she is simply stating what she feels is truth. Like Juliana has always done. I have to believe her." The tears were sudden. "This our second chance, Regulus. I won't fail this child. I have to have faith or I will fail this one just as I did Atticus."

"Hey now." Regulus took her chin. "Where did that come from?"

"We couldn't protect him, Regulus. We let that woman take him and defile him." She closed her eyes tight, her fingers gripping Regulus's. Whether from pain or grief he didn't know. When she could finally speak her voice was weak. "I know we all have our reason for our distaste for Aelia." She said quietly.

"But I think my biggest was how much she reminded me of my mother. It was terrifying to see our son going through the motions I was forced to go through. Never pleasing her. Always being made to feel as though we weren't good enough." She took a deep breath. "I hated the change in him. But I couldn't blame him for the way he gave in to it because I knew what he was feeling, and I had failed him. I didn't have the words for him that my father did me. My mother always criticized me for the looks I carried. I stood out. If it wasn't for my father I fear I would have fallen down the same path Atticus did."

She shifted uncomfortably, her hand held to her stomach. Her face contorted but still she didn't complain. "I know that he might not have been here now. But it is just as it was when I was expecting Atticus. I miss him even more. I can't help but think that all of this trouble with Atticus could have been spared if he were here. He always knew what to say. What to do. He would have known what to say to Atticus when he brought Aelia home. Daddy always knew how to ease the pain my mother caused in me. He always had the right words to make me feel like the most beautiful girl in the world."

"Because you are, Sibyl."

Sibyl laughed tearfully. "I think you will be singing something different if you're right and this little one turns out to be a girl." Final tears shed she rested against him.

"You didn't fail him, Sibyl. What happened to Atticus was a horrible mistake. But it had nothing to do with you as a mother."

"Even so. We need to raise this child in the light of the Lord. I know you do not understand it, but I need you to try. For me."

...

Regulus stumbled over himself as he hurried towards the servant's quarters. Sibyl's water had broken briefly after her first pain had started and only after an hour had she allowed him to send for Jubilee. "We don't want to get her here too early. Let her sleep and when I feel it is time you can go." Regulus had nearly gone mad in the waiting.

"Rachel!" He shouted. The woman was with him in moments, sleep thick in her eyes. "The lady's time has come. Go and fetch Lady Jubilee." As an afterthought, he added. "Afterwards fetch Lady Tamar." Sibyl would want the woman there. Ensuring the rest of the servants knew their duties, Regulus hurried back to his wife.

Climbing behind her, he let her rest against his chest. Her fingers curled through his, squeezing tight when contractions came. "It's going to be all right, Sibby." It had to be. He pressed his lips to her hair, pushing back the memories of Atticus's birth. It wouldn't be the same. It couldn't be. *Oh God, if you are true do not take my Sibby. Let her live and I will listen.*

"Jubilee." Sibyl's voice brought him back to the room and the realization of what he had just done. Her hand released his and reached for Jubilee who took it willingly. Giving it a reassuring squeeze. "Thank God you are here.

Jubilee wasted no time in preparing. "How long has it been?"

"My water broke in the night. But the pains are already close together." She shook her head. "It didn't happen this fast with Atticus. I labored for days with him before my water broke."

"This is good, Sibyl. Don't worry." Jubilee smiled up at Regulus. "Don't you worry either. We can worry when and if we have reason to."

"Does Atticus know?"

"He's waiting outside. I couldn't have kept him home if I tried."

Tamar came as Jubilee finished her examination. Sibyl blinked hard at the sight of her. "Tamar?"

"Your husband sent for me." The woman smiled before seating herself beside Sibyl. "It'll be all right, Sibyl. Trust in him."

Sibyl closed her eyes as another pain came, stronger than the ones before it. "I'm trying." She breathed. The pain of Atticus's birth was blinding in her memory, undermining all the peace she had been instilling within herself. Though she had loathed to admit it, she had been left traumatized after Atticus. It hadn't been Regulus's plea that kept her from growing their family, but her fear.

Tamar brushed Sibyl's hair from her face. "It's different this time. Already it is different." She glanced back at Jubilee. "Jubilee is different. She isn't the woman who assisted you before. She is kinder. Gentler."

Sibyl focused on her daughter as the next pain eased. The midwife who had assisted her with Atticus had been cold, only increasing the fear she had felt at that moment. There had been no gentleness as she had examined her. No patience when the hours of labor turned into days. Sibyl wasn't trying hard enough. She had to push harder. Longer. Stop crying like an insolent child and push. "Jubilee." Sibyl held a hand for the girl to take. When the girl submitted, Sibyl motioned for her to sit. She kissed her cheek. "Thank you for agreeing to this, *Puella*. I know it isn't easy."

"I would never leave you alone in this, *Deliciae*." Jubilee kissed her forehead. "It's almost time." She assured. "Just breathe."

Sibyl didn't speak as the minutes passed. She was pale and sweating and her teeth remained clenched as one pain rolled into another. Taking a cool cloth from Jubilee, Regulus dabbed at her face. It wasn't like the last time. She didn't scream but simply moaned quietly, her eyes closed tight against the pain.

When at last it was time, Jubilee found Regulus's eyes. "Are you staying?"

Sibyl's hands clenched his, holding him in place. "I am not leaving her now." He had listened to the screams from behind closed doors when Atticus was being born. He knew he couldn't stand that torment again.

Sibyl's face contorted as she pushed. She squeezed Regulus's hand white but still, she never cried out. Tamar kept the wet rag ready to dab at the woman's pallid forehead, her lips always moving in silent prayer.

"I can see its head, Sibby!" Jubilee announced joyfully. Sibyl let out a small sob as her legs came up, giving one last push. The next sound that broke the air was the infant's screams. Followed by Jubilee's soft laugh. "A girl, Sibyl! Oh, a perfect little girl."

Sibyl began to sob as the girl was placed against her chest.

Jubilee cleaned Sibyl first, careful to avoid causing her any more pain than necessary. When she had finished she eased the baby carefully from its mother and washed her before letting Tamar swaddle her.

Regulus touched the girl's cheek as she was passed back to her mother. "She has good lungs."

Sibyl smiled tearfully. "I think even Atticus was tired after he was born." She explained to the others. "He barely cried at all."

With her own family to get back to, Tamar kissed the woman's hair. "She is beautiful, Sibyl. And congratulations to you, Regulus." She took the man's hand. "Thank you for thinking of me."

Jubilee hurried to finish her cleaning before paying her respects to the two. Finding them sleeping she smiled. She kissed them each on the cheek before slipping from the room. Atticus was pacing the corridor.

"You have a little sister." He jumped before rushing to her. She had to take his hand to keep him from entering the room. "She is the most beautiful little thing. Perfect in every way."

"A girl?" Atticus glanced toward the room. "And Mama? Tamar said she was all right but I didn't know. I didn't hear anything."

"She is perfect, Atticus. She did wonderfully."

He seemed to hesitate a moment. "And my father?" He knew his father had spent more time worrying about the outcome than his mother had.

"Your father is fine. Everyone is fine, Atticus. Just tired."

Suddenly Atticus smiled. "You said it was a girl?" At her nod, he laughed. "Well let's see her."

"Wait, Atticus. They were sleeping when I left. We'll come back later. When they have had time to rest."

Jubilee walked close to his side as they made their way home. He could see the joy in her. But the farther they separated themselves from his parents Domus the quieter she became. The quicker the tears fell. Nearly six months since Pompeii and still no sign of a child. He slipped his hand into hers. "Someday, Jewess."

She didn't look at him but buried her face in his side. "Someday."

...

Atticus couldn't get enough of his sister and already the child seemed to have attached herself to her brother. Child mid-scream, Atticus would take her into his arms and watch as she hushed, a wide smile gracing her small face. When her eight days had passed they called her Tauria. After Sibyl's father, Taurinus.

"She looks just like you did," Regulus said quietly. Atticus glanced at him for only a moment before his eyes went back to the child. "Perhaps a little smaller." He couldn't help but watch the way his son held the child, kissing the small hand that clung to his finger. His heart ached for his children and their struggles to conceive. He had seen the way Jubilee watched her husband with the child, silent tears blurring her dark eyes. Why fate had seen it fit to give he and Sibyl a child, rather than their children, he would never understand. "Your time will come, Son. If their god is true, I cannot imagine him denying a woman like Jubilee a child. Women like she and your mother were made to be mothers."

"You don't think I am the reason for her lack of conception?" Atticus eyed him darkly. "The opium. The wine. The food. You're not going to tell me I destroyed myself when I did those things?"

"Please, Atticus." Regulus sighed. "Let us enjoy this moment." The two drifted back into silence. Since Pompeii, he had made an effort to look past the anger he felt towards his son —to see the pain that Sibyl spoke of. Since his daughter's birth, it was becoming easier. Atticus was his child. A boy he had held in his arms just as he did Tauria. Each time he looked into her face he wondered if he could ever look at her as he had so recently looked at his son. The more time he spent in his presence the clearer it became to him what lay beneath the surface of things the boy had done.

His last trip to Ostia burned in his memory. Aelia's confessions of her actions with his son made him sick. *Remus thought he could use a woman.* She had breathed, her lips always quirked in the coy smile that never left. *He was always held up on that Jewess. Get him tipsy and show him what a real woman can give.* The images the words conjured near brought him to his knees.

"Atticus." When the boy turned to face him, Regulus stumbled for the words. "I don't think you are undeserving of a child. You have made mistakes, but I have never seen you as undeserving of Jubilee or any children she may give you." He squeezed his shoulder. "I want to see you as a father, Atticus. I don't deny you will be a good one when that time comes." No matter what darkness lay in his past, the boy had his mother's heart for children.

"What am I supposed to say to her if it never happens?" Atticus's voice was so small Regulus almost missed it. "She'll hate herself, Papa. She already does. I can see it in her eyes every time another month passes. She already thinks she is failing me."

"You think it's Jubilee?"

"I don't want it to be." He moaned. "I wish it was me. By the gods, I wish it was me. But I know it's not."

"How can you know that, Atticus? I do not want to lay blame on you, but your past was harmful."

"Aelia conceived twice in our marriage and we were only married nine months." His eyes found his father's. "You can never tell Mama of that. It would break her to know what Aelia did to them."

"Are you sure they were yours?" Regulus asked. "I know that you are no stranger to the things she was into outside of you."

"They were mine, Papa. They were mine and she took them without even a thought for me."

Regulus pressed his fingers to his eyes. Papa. It had been years since Atticus had called him such. Using it only when Regulus knew he was breaking. "I don't know what to tell you, Son. I don't know why a woman like that would get a child where Jubilee doesn't. But that is the world. It may just be something Jubilee has to accept."

"It will break her," Atticus whispered. "That will be what finally breaks her."

XXXII

Jubilee lowered herself onto the bed—her legs suddenly weak. "He's dead?" She whispered. "You are sure of this?"

"He's dead, Jubilee. I saw him carried out."

"Dead." The word repeated itself again and again. *He* was dead. "Is it terrible to take comfort in that?" No matter the probability, she had always feared running into the man again. There was no doubt in her mind what he would do if they were to see each other again. The thought made her shiver and Nathanael patted her knee. "I don't mean it as it sounds." She said quietly. "I don't wish him a painful eternity. Not anymore. But to know that I do not have to look over my shoulder for him anymore? I never thought that day would come."

"It is not a selfish thought to want to be free from fear, Joyous. I harbored enough feelings towards that man that I know were not of the Lord." Tears dripped down his sister's cheeks, and he knew that the guilt would still cling to her long from now. Taking her hand he squeezed it. "It's all right, Joy. It's over now."

"I'm sorry." She wiped at her face. "I didn't realize it would it would affect me like this. When it first happened—until a few months ago really, I wished him to hell, Nathanael. I prayed for it even. I know how terrible that sounds, but I was angry. I hated him for ruining me." She pursed her lips. "It's odd though. I am happy to be free of the fear, but to know that he may be suffering now? I don't like it."

Nathanael said nothing. He had not shared with her how he knew of Jude's fate—nor did he plan on ever sharing that information. He could see her moving forward. Inching herself away from what was done to her. His sister did not need to know of the things he had seen and heard while in Jude's presence.

"Do *Imma* and *Abba* know? Have you written to them?"

"I wrote to them shortly after." He had needed his father then more than ever and had been able to settle only on sending his father a letter asking for prayer. The guilt of what he had done was near overwhelming—even the words of those he traveled with had served no help in easing his mind. Pushing the memory away he looked at Jubilee. "How is our father?" He had been staying with Jubilee for nearly a month and the time between them had been limited to short visits that had left no time for speaking of home.

"*Imma* said his pain has worsened. She says that as horrible as it is, she does enjoy having him home more."

Nathanael smiled. "And Abel and Rebekah? What of them? Do they have children?"

Abel's wife had conceived and miscarried more than four children in the first two years of their marriage. After a stillbirth and the loss of their two-month-old son, the two gave up on the idea of a family of their own. "They took in two boys about a year after you left. Rebekah's nephews."

"Anna's boys?"

"She and Jacob got sick," Jubilee explained. "They had a newborn daughter who died with them."

Nathanael shook his head. He had missed so much since he left. "I didn't realize how much I missed everyone until now." He said quietly. "The idea of leaving is almost too much."

"Do you have to leave?" Jubilee's eyes were hopeful. "Couldn't you stay? Maybe there's a reason God led you here?"

"I would have to pray on it, Joy. To be honest, I am ready to be still, but not if God wants me to keep moving." Nathanael loved traveling. He loved sharing the word and seeing people transformed through it. He loved the men he witnessed beside. But the months were long and cold. Where he had once found joy in those trials, he now longed for something more. Something he could only pray was from God and not the evil one creeping in. Something had led him back into the heart of Rome. He wasn't supposed to be preaching that night. The other men had urged him not to. They were supposed to be heading to Capua, and yet something had drawn him to that street. *Oh God, what does this mean? Have I lost my will to serve you?*

"Perhaps God let this happen for a reason?" Jubilee took his hand and pressed it to her chest. "I've been praying every day since I came here that your travels would bring you to me. I need you, Nathanael."

"We have plenty of time before I can move, Joy. We'll see what happens between then and now." He touched her cheek. "Have faith, Joyous."

...

When Jubilee had gone, Nathanael took up one of the scrolls Jubilee had placed within his reach. He had taken to studying his writings when Jubilee was not with him. Reading the scrolls he knew it was not a lack of desire to serve that kept him. If the Lord called him out once more he would do so with joy. But he couldn't rid himself of the new desire to remain still. "God." He said aloud. "There are so many people here who need your word." He thought of Jubilee. Of the slave girl he seemed unable to shake from his mind. "I have moved for so long. Has the time come for me to be still?" As he spoke the door was opened and Layla stepped in, her head down. Hearing him speak she looked up, her eyes grazing the room.

"I will never understand you and your sister." She said quietly. "Speaking to yourselves all the time."

"Not to ourselves, Layla." Her eyebrows raised in scrutiny but she remained quiet. "I suppose we do sound a bit mad." He agreed.

"At least I can understand you. Lady Jubilee speaks in a tongue I have never heard of when she prays."

At that, Nathanael laughed. He had seen the wide-eyed looks of those witnessing tongues for the first time.

Head down once more, Layla made her way toward the man. If she had it her way she would leave the room and never look back. The man was unsettling. He was just as she feared, calling out in her all of the things she had for so long hidden behind a stone-cold face. But as it was, Jubilee didn't allow him to be alone, fearing his need for something and having no one nearby to help. Avoiding his knowing eyes, she set the tray before him. Setting aside his scroll and quill he thanked her, said a quick prayer, and began to eat.

Layla eyed the scroll curiously. From the time he could sit up, he had poured over his scrolls day and night, his hand moving quickly across the parchment. Assuring his attention was elsewhere, she turned one toward her. It was written in a strange language full of squiggles and lines she couldn't recognize. Not that she could read it anyhow.

"It is Hebrew." He told her. She jumped, jerking her hand from the page. "I am willing to translate them into your language if you would like to read them."

She blushed. "That won't be necessary, my lord." No master she had served had ever seen it fit to teach a slave to read.

Understanding, Nathanael didn't press it. "I like to write things down." He explained. "My sermons. How people respond and who is saved."

"Why?" She asked. "What does it serve you?"

"I like to remember. In harder times, when I begin to question what I am doing and all I want is to go back home, I look back on all that has come about from it. I may suffer at times, but it is all worth it in the end."

"You want to remember this?" Her hand gestured over him. "Being beaten and broken by worthless men?"

"No one is worthless in the eyes of the Lord, Layla. If that were so we'd all be worthless."

She looked unconvinced. "If I may say so, my lord, there are plenty who walk this world who don't deserve to see the light of day. The man who did this to you is one of them."

Are you any different, Layla? Look at what you did to a man.

Layla swallowed hard. *That was a mistake! I didn't know.*

Nathanael smiled the way one might smile at a naive child. "You see the world from the view of one who has been hurt. You're angry."

The shaking was starting within her. As it always did in his presence. She turned away from him, hoping he wouldn't notice.

"You believe that the man who raped Jubilee has worth?" The words were out before she could stop them, hiding none of the hatred she held toward the man.

"The man who hurt my sister was human. I do not approve and I will never understand why it had to happen. But it doesn't change the fact that he needed God."

She shook her head. "I refuse to believe that you truly think that. I see the way you look at your sister. I can't believe that you can love her like that and not hate the man who hurt her."

Nathanael frowned. "I did not say that hatred never filled my heart, Layla."

"And you forgave him?" Cynicism coated her tone. "Just like that? Because your god told you to?"

"It isn't easy, Layla. It took time to truly forgive him, and I stumbled in it recently. I made a mistake in doing so. It's not a mistake I will make again."

"He doesn't deserve forgiveness. Least of all yours or Jubilee's. If such a place as hell exists, I hope he burns in it."

"To which he might be, Layla. Does that truly bring you peace?" Nathanael's voice was pleading now. "Knowing that he will spend eternity in agony?"

Layla's teeth ground. "Jubilee didn't deserve what was done to her. I have listened to her screams night after night. I watched her suffer for months trying to love her husband in the way she was supposed to. I had to hold her and listen to her cries when she believed herself a failure to her husband. All because of that wretched man. So yes," She hissed. "I will sleep well knowing that man will forever pay for his doings."

Nathanael took a deep breath. An ache was beginning to form as he learned of his sister's most recent struggles. "I am sorry you had to witness those things with her. I know firsthand what those look like. But, Layla, even Jubilee does not wish Jude an eternity in hell. Not anymore."

"Because she is afraid. She has been raised to believe that your god will do the same to her if she fails to submit." She scoffed. "What sort of foul being would submit a girl like Jubilee to an eternity of misery after all that she has suffered in life?"

"God does not submit people to hell, Layla. He doesn't wish for anyone to suffer. It is by our sins that we consign ourselves to hell." Seeing she wouldn't listen, he switched tactics. "You do know that it was the Lord that freed Jubilee from those fears? It is because of Him that she no longer struggles."

Layla's eyes met his, softening now. "She is still struggling, my lord. Maybe not with her husband—but her struggles are tearing her apart, and it is all due to her belief in an unseen god."

Nathanael let the tears fall when she was gone. He couldn't fathom the sudden emotion that had come over him. No matter the time he spent praying, the answer he longed for wouldn't come. To stay in Rome or continue his travels? "God, how can I leave knowing the pain that haunts this home?" The thought of leaving was nearly crippling. He couldn't leave Jubilee. Not if she still struggled. He had not wanted to believe that she remained in that pain. But it was becoming increasingly evident that something still clung to her—the pain hidden behind bright smiles. And Layla—as cold as stone and just as hard. Hatred seemed to seep from within her. Each word she spoke dripped with anger at the world that caused her pain. But what was it?

...

Layla dragged the razor over the soft fuzz that covered her head. A field of cotton against the rough terrains of the desert.

As the jagged razor cut into her scalp she was reminded of the first time her head had been shaved. She had been eight and beautiful—too beautiful. An unacceptable truth to her mistress. The woman had been known for her beauty since birth, and at eight, the small, insignificant slave girl and her little sister were being noticed—pushing the aging woman toward the outer corners of the villager's minds.

Layla had sobbed then as she watched her beautiful hair fall in a circle around her. How could she be a true girl without it? How could she be beautiful? Now, as she blew the loose hairs from her face she reveled in the smooth curve of her skull. When her sobbing had subsided, she swore she would never again let a mistress's cruelty hurt her so deeply. She would walk those steps to her mistress with her head held high—a complacent smile on her small face.

The same smile pulled at the corners of her lips as she slathered the soothing aloe onto her burning scalp. Her hair had been allowed to grow back after being sent away but had again been cut after her voyage to Rome, after the discovery of lice. She preferred it as such. In her mind, she saw it as a statement to Eurydice. *You cannot shame me.* It cried. *I will not allow it. Not like Mama.* It was the very attitude she had carried as she passed from home to home. Foul mistress after foul mistress. It carried her through beatings from her masters and the gropings from the ship's crewmen.

Nathanael could see it as something to be remedied, she saw it as her strength. Her protection against the world his god created.

XXXIII

Martius

Where Atticus leaned more towards his mother's Germanic roots, Tauria was becoming the image of her father. Her hair had already grown darker than her brothers—a shining black, rather than the blond Atticus had carried as a child. Her almond eyes were darkening to the rich brown of her father. Scooping her up, Sibyl kissed her daughter's full lips. Another blessing from Regulus. At her mother's touch, the girl cooed, revealing the dimple on her right cheek. "Good morning, *Dulcis*." As she spoke the girl began to suckle, signifying her hunger.

As she had done with Atticus she refused to hire a wet nurse. She wouldn't have her child attaching itself to a stranger as she had done as a child, and never once had she regretted her decision. Throughout all of the pain and adjustments, she had looked forward to the blessings it would reap. She loved the quiet mornings when she stole Tauria away to the gardens to feed, and the late nights with the moonlight shining on her beautiful face, lighting up her dark eyes.

Despite the tired ache that rested behind her eyes she had never felt so alive. Even when she first came to the Lord couldn't compare to what she felt as she looked into her daughter's face, for the child only strengthened her joy in the Lord. What had she done to deserve such a blessing?

The girl was an answer to a prayer she hadn't realized was in her heart. An answer to prayers she had prayed before ever knowing the Lord. Before even accepting him as truth, she had prayed to God that the rift between her husband and their son would wither and die and she had received just that in the shape of a child. The anger that had filled her husband's eyes when he looked upon their son had fallen away and instead, guilt had found its way to them. Though she hated to see his pain, she could see the work of God in him. He was asking questions. At last, he was asking about the Lord. Another prayer was answered. All because of a child.

...

With their last patient gone, Jubilee made to prepare for church before Sibyl came for her. Jubilee visits had been becoming fewer and fewer as she grew to prefer Atticus's presence over the ones she found at the church. She wanted to feel loved rather than blindly accept that she was loved by a being who sat silently as she suffered.

Atticus was waiting for her when she entered their room. At the look he gave her she nearly forgot what she had come for. As he took her in his arms she moaned. "I have to go."

"Stay with me." He whispered.

She wanted to. She wanted nothing more than to forget everything but him. "I can't. Not this time." She had missed the last two services already and to miss another would leave her with a deeper ache than she could bear. "I promised to walk with your mother tonight."

Atticus frowned at her. "Why must you choose him, Jubilee?"

Jubilee chewed her lip. "Because He deserves more than what I give Him."

"Do you truly believe that?"

"Please understand, Atticus."

Atticus felt irritation prick at him as she ignored the question. It was just as he had known it would be. She would never blame the one responsible for her pain. "Fine. Go."

"Don't be upset." She cried.

Atticus sighed. "I'm not." He kissed her to prove it. "Now go before you're late."

Tears blurring her eyes she let her hand slip from his and hurried away.

As he watched her leave, Atticus felt himself reaching out to her. He wanted to stop her. To apologize. But a dark voice stopped him.

She chose to leave. Why should you feel guilty? You should have known it wouldn't last, puppy.

No. She loved him. That he was sure of. She was faithful. But still, the thoughts persisted. Thoughts of Aelia and her deceit nearly choked him and the only person who held the power to ease his racing mind had walked away, leaving him defenseless against the demons.

When she returned, she crawled into bed without a sound and lay in silence. "Are you still angry?" She asked at last.

"No."

"Then why won't you look at me?"

By the gods the woman was relentless. Could she not leave him to himself for just one night? "Just go to sleep, Jubilee."

"Not until you tell me what is bothering you."

Atticus cursed himself and the vulnerability that she brought out in him. "I can't lose you." He whispered. "I won't."

Jubilee wrapped her arms around him, tucking her chin in the crook of his neck. "Why would you lose me?"

The confusion that filled her voice, rather than giving him comfort, grated on his nerves. How could she be so blind to the truth of the thing she called a god? "Your faith will get in the way. Some way. Somehow."

"You don't have to let it, Beloved. God doesn't wish for us to be separated."

"So it would be my fault?" He demanded. "I will always be the bad guy to you."

Jubilee blinked. "Atticus where is this coming from?" She shook her head. "Atticus, God lead me to you for a reason. He wants you to see. He wants you to love him."

And yet he denies you your only heart's desire. How can I believe in someone who would gleefully cause you sorrow? But he couldn't bring himself to remind her now of her lack of a child. Instead, he glared back at her. "You say your god lead you to me? Who is to say he won't lead you away?" When she didn't offer a response he scoffed. "You see, Jubilee? He will get in the way. All he is is an invisible force ready to push you to do his will whenever it suits him. No thought of you and what you want. You call that a loving god?" He demanded. "Honestly, Jubilee. He doesn't care for you, why can't you see that?"

"I do see it." She whispered. "But I am trying not to."

The words were spoken so quietly, he couldn't be sure he had heard her correctly.

XXXIV

Layla hated him—by the gods she hated him. But she couldn't bring herself to stay away. Nathanael was kind and enthralling. Infuriating and intrusive. He called out in her all the things she had hidden for so long. He made her hope. His gentle approach brought to her lips the stories she hadn't even told Jubilee and always she was forced to swallow them. This man wouldn't understand—no matter how much he pretended to.

She hated herself for the way she let him break away the pieces of herself that she had built as protection. And all without even trying. All it took was his soft smile and she felt herself weaken. He was too kind. The man even spoke with her in her native language, bringing the flavor of home to her tongue.

"Would you go back?" He asked. "If the offer was given to you?"

She considered it a moment. She had never allowed herself to think of Egypt or the possibility of freedom. She had never known freedom and though she loathed to admit it, the idea brought fear to her chest. Who was she outside of a servant's clothing? "No." She whispered. "Egypt holds nothing for me now." How long had it been since she had walked the hot sands of Egypt? It seemed like a lifetime ago. "You have been there? On your travels?"

"It was the first place I traveled to after leaving Israel. For that reason, it will always have a special place in my heart."

Layla shrugged. "All I remember is the vile nature of it."

"There is a vile nature in every place you visit, Layla. That is why God sends his people."

Must he always mention his god? "How can you still believe in those things? Being like this?" She waved a hand at his broken body. "And it isn't the first time it has happened, is it? What will it take for people like you and Jubilee to realize that it is hopeless?"

"I suppose it will take an eternity and more. I have had my share of doubts, Layla. But I have seen the truth. As has Jubilee."

Layla couldn't help but laugh bitterly. The man didn't know his own sister. Seeing where her mind had taken her, Nathanael spoke softly. "Just because Jubilee doubts does not mean she doesn't know the truth. It is normal to have periods of doubts."

"Is it normal for your god to torture his people?" She spit. "Always expecting them to believe he does so in love?"

"Have you always been so bitter?" He demanded. It was the first time she had seen any sort of anger in him. Even his anger was too kind.

She glared back at him. "Have you always been so naive?" She couldn't understand herself. That she could speak so freely with him without fear of repercussions. "We all have our ways of protection. Clearly childish innocence is yours."

"I tell you the truth." He was speaking in her tongue again, the words penetrating deeper than they had before. "Unless you turn from your sins and become like little children, you will never get into the Kingdom of Heaven.' God calls us to believe with the innocence of a child, Layla. Living as you do will only get you so far. Eventually, the walls you have built will be torn away and you will have to face the world beyond it. Do you truly want to be alone when that happens?"

"I have always been alone, my lord. It makes no difference to me." And if you would leave things in their place that wall would stay. She didn't say the words, but oh how she wanted to. Why must he insist at picking at the mortar of those walls?

"You do not have to be alone." He took her hand, only realizing his mistake when she pulled away from him.

"I will never accept your god." She whispered. "I will not become a puppet on his strings. Do this. Go here. Forgive this worthless, vile creature." Tears were building behind her eyes and she beat them back. "I will not."

Nathanael was quiet, allowing her time to gather herself. "Who aren't you forgiving, Layla?"

She glared at him. "That is my business."

Nathanael frowned. In the short time he had known her he had never seen her smile. Even with Jubilee, whom she seemed to hold most dear. "Don't you wish to find freedom?"

"I gave up the hope of freedom when I was a child."

"I do not mean physically, Layla. I mean from whatever holds you captive inside. Because something tells me the one you aren't forgiving is yourself."

Layla began to shake. By the gods, she hated this man. How could he see so much while knowing her so little? How could he fill her with such a strong desire to share those things with him? She wanted to run from him. She wanted to hide and yet she found herself slipping to her knees. Reaching up, she pulled the wrap from her head and wound it tightly. "There is darkness in my very blood, my lord."

"You are anything but dark, Layla."

"You do not know me. You do not know where I come from or what I have done. Do not tell me I deserve your gods forgiveness."

"I won't," Nathanael replied. "You don't deserve it." The girl's copper eyes met his. Though he couldn't be sure, he thought he saw her lip tremble. "No one deserves it, Layla. What he offers is a gift, not a privilege."

Her eyes fell back to her hands. "Then it is a gift I will not accept." Standing she hurried from the room. Leaving behind her wrap.

…

When she returned to Nathanael, she kept her eyes on the wrap, still laying in the sun that shone through the window.

"Layla." Nathanael started. "I am sorry if I offended you earlier. It's been four years. I am used to preaching, I suppose. But I do not mean to push my beliefs onto you if you do not want them."

The girl pursed her lips. "Your sister is the same way. Always speaking of your god. It does not offend me, my lord. If you believe it, that is your choice. I can't stop you from speaking it."

"Well, I won't speak on it now." He knew well enough that to force someone to listen was a way to push them further from the truth. "But so long as you are made to look after me, we should get to know each other. Should we not?"

Layla's lips parted. "I suppose." She sighed.

"Don't look so terrified, Layla, I don't want to know your life story. I just want to know you." He gave her a crooked smile. "We can start with a simple one. How old are you?"

She was quiet a moment, her eyes narrowing uncertainly. Her lips moved silently. "Twenty-three, I think."

"You don't know for sure?"

"The years have run together, my lord." She turned the wrap over in her hands, running the faded fabric through her work-worn fingers. "And you're nineteen?"

"Twenty." He corrected.

Her eyes flashed to meet his, narrowing in confusion. "You're not twins? Jubilee said you left when you were both fifteen."

Nathanael smiled. "It is a common misconception. No, we aren't twins, but it often times felt that way growing up. Jubilee was born only nine months after me."

"Is that even possible?"

"In our case." Seeing her confusion he smiled. "It is a strange circumstance."

"My sister and I were close in age but not that close. Did your father not give your mother time before forcing himself on her?"

"Well," Nathanael said quietly. "It isn't like that. My father would never force himself upon my mother. The situation in which my sister came to be is an unusual one, but she came to be in an act of love."

Layla kept her eyes down. "I'm sorry, my lord. But I have heard of women dying after childbirth because their husbands were too greedy and impatient."

Nathanael eyed her curiously. "I assume Jubilee has told you of our mother?"

"That she was healed by your god?"

"Yes. The day I was born. When the Lord laid his hands on my mother he didn't simply bring her from the brink of death. He healed every part of her. Meaning our mother was in perfect condition when Jubilee came to be."

Layla felt herself blush. "I am sorry, my lord. I never meant to offend you."

"You didn't. I simply wanted you to know the truth. You will never find a more loving husband than my father is with my mother."

"Jubilee has always spoken very highly of him."

"For good reason." Hoping to bring the conversation away, Nathanael smiled. "You said you have a sister?"

Layla's body jerked harshly. "Had, my lord. I had three."

"I am sorry." His hand reached for hers before thinking better of it. Turning away from her he went back to his scrolls. "We do not have to speak of your family."

"We spoke of yours, why should you not bring up mine?"

"Speaking of my family brings me joy. If it does not bring you the same joy to speak of yours, then we will leave it alone."

Turning away from him, Layla replaced her wrap. "Thank you, my lord."

"How long have you been in Rome?"

"I came when I was eighteen. I worked for lord Albanus and his first wife until Lady Sibyl took me in."

Nathanael's quill scratched across the page, drawing a thick line through the words he had written. "Atticus was married before?"

Layla inhaled sharply. Why did she always say the wrong things? "Jubilee hasn't told you?"

"Do not look so guilty, Layla. I don't think Jubilee is keeping it from me. We mostly speak of home."

"I know she won't be angry, my lord. Jubilee has never once grown angry with me. But it is not the first time I have let my tongue slip where the master's first wife is concerned. Jubilee asked that we keep them off limits."

"Well then, we'll just keep this slip between the two of us." Nathanael's smile was warm, easing the tension in her chest in a way even Jubilee couldn't. He was so much like his sister. Without trying he knew how to rid her of the constant ache in her chest, even if only for the briefest of moments.

XXXV

Jubilee couldn't understand it. So long as she made no mention of her faith, Atticus remained silent. He was as he always was—kind and loving. But any mention of church or God and it was as though something turned in his mind. He was cold. Withdrawn. He spit words of blasphemy toward her God and then pulled her in. Whispering words of love to her. He loved her. Why fight so hard to win the love of another when she had him?

Jubilee couldn't stand it. When he pulled her in she could nothing but let him. He was right, wasn't he? He loved her. He showed it without fear-so unlike the God she had been raised to know. It made her head spin and her heart ache painfully. When she gave into him, choosing him over prayer and church, she was lost in him, knowing nothing but the love he gave. But the moment it was over and Atticus slept, guilt overwhelmed her until she was sick. When she found her way to the gardens she could do nothing but sit in silence. There were no words that could change the truth. She was falling away from the Lord and she was not sure she wanted to fight it.

...

Atticus noticed the change in her. She was withdrawn. Her eyes were downcast. She had gone back to pinching the flesh of her wrist, a habit she had given up since Pompeii. She no longer spoke of her god. Nor did she attend church as she once had. She made excuses as to why she couldn't go to the gardens to pray. When she did drag herself to her prayer grounds she did nothing but lay curled tight as her sobs echoed through the corridors. *Jesus. Jesus. Jesus.*

He couldn't understand it. Why she tortured herself over a being so cruel? She deserved so much more than what she was given and to see her struggle only reinforced the idea that what she served was nothing more than a devil disguised as a deity.

Pain seared in Atticus's temples as he and Jubilee prepared the shop. Jubilee moved silently, her eyes avoiding his. Tears slid lazily down her cheeks. For one perfect week, they had thought that their time had come. After nearly a month of a missing cycle, they had finally allowed themselves to hope in what they were steadily believing to be impossible. For the first time in months, Atticus had seen Jubilee smile in a way that lit up her dark eyes. Despite her fear, she had been hopeful and in a single moment, he had watched it all crumble.

He had woken to her shaking him. "Get up, Atticus." She shoved at him. "The bedding needs to be cleaned."

It took a moment for his eyes to adjust as he stared at the blankets. When the blood became clear he felt his heart skip. "Are you losing it?"

"It's not a miscarriage, Atticus." She wasn't angry. She didn't even cry. She simply seemed empty. "We were wrong." She hadn't allowed him to touch or even help her as she stripped the bed before tossing the blankets into a basket and setting it outside. "We have to get to the shop."

"Do you remain blind to it, Jubilee?" He demanded. "Are you still blind to what your god is?"

She froze—her hand on the door. As tears flowed down her pale cheeks, a dark look filled her eyes. But behind the anger was a pain so raw he felt his own anger buckle. "Stop saying *my* God. He is not *my* God. He is *your* God too, even if you don't believe it."

Atticus glared down at her—new anger washing over him. How much pain would her god have to put her through before she realized that he wasn't who she thought he was? "How can you still think to praise a god like that, Jubilee? Tell me. What has your god done for you other than bring you grief?"

She hesitated, her lips quivering, struggling between truth and what she had been raised to believe. "Everything."

"Nothing, Jubilee. He has given you nothing. I see how you struggle to try to please him. Putting yourself and your own needs aside to please a god who repays you in misery. He doesn't deserve you."

Her mouth opened and closed again. "Just forget it." She spit.

Atticus watched Jubilee's sharp angry movements as she left. No matter the pain it caused her, no matter the anger, there was something to that wretched god that kept her going to him. Giving her the hope to keep going despite the pain. He wanted to understand it and yet every time he saw her in those gardens, her body curled in on itself, he couldn't help but hate the thing he had so previously thought a myth.

He had watched her in the gardens that morning—begging her god for mercy. To end her suffering. As he watched he had fought every urge to go to her. To pick her up and take her mind off that god. But he had been unable to move, his own grief paralyzing him.

"Is there anything I can do for you, my lord?" Though spoken softly, the sudden voice had jolted him. Looking up he had found Layla watching him.

"I am failing her, Layla." The words were out of his mouth before he knew what he was saying. "I am failing my wife and I don't know how to fix it." He had hoped Nathanael would be able to fix her. If she had to cling to her faith perhaps her brother could mend it. But her visits with him, though beneficial at the moment, always brought her back to Atticus in tears. She was slipping away from the both of them. The girl had begun to sleep longer and longer to avoid the day. Even work no longer brought joy to her eyes.

"She'll find her way out, my lord. Somehow."

"She is killing herself, Layla. And I can't stop it." He swore. "By the gods how am I any better than Aelia? Tearing my wife apart for her beliefs?" Taking a shaking breath he turned away. "I deserved a woman like Aelia. I do not deserve Jubilee. Not when I can't even comfort her."

Layla glanced around uncertainly before taking his hand. "If you deserved a woman like her, do you think you would have been the way you were with her? You have to remember that I saw you with Aelia. No matter what she did to you, you treated her with kindness. I know of men who deserve someone like Aelia and you are not one of them. Jubilee is who you deserve, my lord."

Seeing Atticus made to argue, she continued. "Jubilee spoke with me after she told you about the man. She couldn't face the night alone, so we stayed up half the night waiting for you. She told me about her life in Galilee. After him and before you. She said that even a man looking at her for one second too long would send her to her knees in tears. She couldn't handle male patients. She said she tried once and fainted. But she didn't with you. She told me her fear was so strong that first night but she never reached the point where she wanted you to back away. She wanted you. Despite the fear it caused her, she wanted you. And it was all in the way you handled it."

"Did she tell you how I tried to force her to say my name?" He demanded. *"I could see how terrified she was and I didn't care."*

"She understood why you did it. It wasn't in the way he did it. You were desperate and just as broken as she was. Unfortunately, I know more than others what Aelia did to you."

Atticus watched Jubilee move now. She had dried the tears from her cheeks but her breath still hitched. When she caught his stare she turned away.

Comfort my lamb.

"What?"

Jubilee glanced at him. "I didn't say anything." The tears had started again, blurring her dark eyes.

"Jubilee." At his touch, she folded herself into his arms. He let her ease her tears before speaking. "Don't push me away, Beloved."

Her fingers curled in his tunic. "I need you to understand." She cried. "I need your support or I am going to lose."

"Lose what, Jubilee?" But as the words left his lips he knew. "Your god?" He had seen the way she dragged herself to church. The excitement she had once had was gone. When she returned home, rather than speak of what she learned she stared up at the ceiling or else curled into his side, relying on him as she had once relied on her god. "Because you are questioning it, aren't you?"

Fresh tears poured down Jubilee's cheeks. "Yes, all right?" She cried. "Is that what you want to hear? That I am questioning everything I have ever believed?"

Before Atticus could answer a man burst through the door. "Can you take a man?" He shouted.

"No, not there." Another man screamed. "Not there. Please, anywhere but there."

Jubilee glanced at Atticus before making her way to the door. Outside a man was struggling against another, his feet digging into the dirt with a force that didn't match the tattered state of him. "Not there." He screamed. "Don't take me to her."

Jubilee shook her head. "No." She whispered. It wasn't him. It couldn't be him. She stumbled back as the group of men dragged the other forward. With Atticus's help, they got the man onto the table—his friends holding him down.

"Atticus." Jubilee felt sick as she took in the man. "Atty."

Atticus met her eyes and seeing the state of her kneeled before her, his hands at her waist. "What is it?"

"Cyrus." Atticus shook his head. "Cyrus!" She cried. "*His* brother."

Atticus's hands tightened on her waist. "Jude?" At her nod, Atticus turned back the man. "Get him out."

The men with him looked him over. "You're the physician! You are supposed to help him."

"He's already dead," Atticus replied. "There is nothing we can do."

Jubilee watched Cyrus. He no longer fought—he couldn't. He had exhausted the little energy he had. Instead, he now watched her with wide, dark eyes. The man's skin was yellow and covered in deep bruises. Even where she was she could smell the wine on him. As she watched tears began to spill down his cheeks and he looked away from her.

Tend to him, Beloved.

No. She shook her head. *No, God*! The memories of that day were pressing in on her so she couldn't breathe. Her knees buckled beneath her and she fell to the ground. *God, please! He is dead already! What can I do for him?*

Care.

She let out a sob as she watched the men carry the man toward the door. "Stop." Her voice was nothing more than a croak. "I'll care for him."

Atticus turned to her. "You won't, Jubilee."

"I have to, Atty."

"He's a drunk, Jubilee. Look at him. He's too far gone."

"But I can still help him."

Atticus glared at her as the words settled between them. "This is your god, isn't it? You think you can save his soul?"

Jubilee's voice shook as she choked out the very opposite of what she wanted. "I have to try, Atticus."

"No, Jubilee. You don't. Let him die! Let him face his eternity." He took her arm as she made to move around him. "I forbid you to touch him."

"I am helping him, Atticus. Now you can help me or you can leave." Freeing herself, she moved toward Cyrus. Her hands shook as she examined him, taking in the spidery veins that covered his skin. Cutting away the tunic she found his stomach swollen and distended. Up close the smell of wine was overwhelming. "I can't do anything but make him comfortable." She said quietly.

The men said their goodbyes quietly before leaving.

Pulling her aside, Atticus held her arm roughly. "You are not bringing him into our home, Jubilee."

Jubilee spun on him. "Of course, I am not. Do you think I want to do this? I don't want to touch him! I don't want to look at him."

"Then don't, Jewess. I'll take him somewhere else."

"No, Atticus. I have to do this. I spent four years of my life wishing his brother to hell and now that is where he is. I am not making that mistake twice."

"If you think I am staying out here while you care for him."

"Then go, Atticus." Jubilee snapped. "Let me do this."

Glaring at the man, Atticus left the shop. He wouldn't watch her cater to a man like that. It was disgusting.

What are you? To make her care for him? She breaks herself for you and you demand this? This will break her.

Or mend her.

Atticus snarled at the voice. He wanted to go back. To drag his wife from the shop and that man she claimed had worth. He knew why she did it. To save the faith he now knew was slipping through her fingers. There had been no satisfaction at Jubilee's confession. He didn't want her to lose her faith, but he also couldn't accept her working on the man who had assisted in her undoing.

...

Jubilee paced the shop, listening to Cyrus's labored breathing. *Oh God, I can't do this. I can't do this.* That morning was harsh in her memory. The vision of Cyrus holding her father by the hair, forcing his eyes on his daughter, threatened to smother her.

Tend to him.

Jubilee sobbed as she sat before Cyrus. She didn't touch him —she couldn't touch him. Not again.

Cyrus kept his eyes off her. "I heard this was your shop." He croaked. "People talk about you. About the way you tend to people. Like in Galilee. They say you know how to ease people's minds even when they are dying. That's how I knew it was you. That you made people smile even when they felt like this."

Jubilee said nothing.

"You said Jude is dead?"

That made Jubilee move as the name brought bile to her lips. She glared down at him. "You dare say his name to me?" She breathed. "Knowing what he did?"

Cyrus bothered to look sorry. "I'm sorry. I should have known. But my brother? You said he was dead?"

"Yes. Nathanael stumbled upon him in Greece as his body was being carried from an apartment."

"How?"

"How what?" She demanded. Why did the man insist on speaking?

"How did he die?"

"I don't know. Nathanael didn't say."

"I wouldn't blame him if he did it." Cyrus breathed. "If he killed him."

"My brother didn't kill him. My family isn't yours." Jubilee wrapped her arms around herself. She wanted to leave. She couldn't breathe in here. She wanted Atticus—she *needed* Atticus.

In the silence, the man began to sob.

Comfort, Beloved.

"No." Jubilee breathed. To sit with him was one thing. But to comfort him? To hold the hand of a man who sat by as his brother destroyed her? Who forced her fathers eyes on her as her virtue was stolen? Could she truly do that?

"I know you hate me, Jubilee." Cyrus breathed. "I hate myself. I hated myself in that moment. But what was I to do? I didn't know. I didn't know just how far he would take it. I thought he would do it and be done with it."

"And you thought that was okay? So long as he was quick about?" Jubilee felt sick. *You want me to comfort this? He doesn't deserve it!*

"I was young-"

"I was young!" The words came in a scream. "I was a child the first time he touched me. Too young to truly understand and still I knew that it was wrong. I knew the sin he was using me to commit." She stood, her legs threatening to send her to the floor. "I can't do this."

"Jubilee please! Not a day has gone by that I haven't thought about it."

"Good." Leaving him alone, she hurried into the main house. *I won't comfort him! I will not save him! He doesn't deserve you, God!*

She found herself in her grandfathers room. Sinking onto the bed she held herself. "Why are you doing this to me?" She cried. "Why make me talk to him?" Her father's face filled her mind, the way her level-headed father had sobbed that day. She slid from the bed, her forehead touching the cool stone floor. "Don't ask me to do this. Let him join his brothers."

Beloved.

She sobbed. "I can't. I can't."

She lay against the cold floor until her tears lessened and she could breathe again. Blinking back the tears, she focused on a shape beneath the bed. Breathing against the sobs that choked her she pulled out a scroll. Sitting up she unrolled it. She felt the tears roll quicker as she took in the unfamiliar script. It was written to her mother and it was signed her Tata. *Daddy.*

XXXVI

Jubilee read the letter through twice—taking in the words her grandfather wrote like they were the very air she breathed. Like Cyrus, he made excuses for the things he had done to her mother. But she couldn't deny the truth behind his apologies—the desperation behind his plea for forgiveness. She remembered the tear-splotched letter she had received in response to the letter she had sent her mother, telling her her father had died unsaved. The man had beat and belittled her all her life and yet she had loved him. She mourned his eternity.

"God, I need you." She breathed. "I can't stand being near him." Gathering herself, she made her way back to the shop. Taking Cyrus's hand in hers, she stared at the wall. Ignoring the bile that rose in her throat—the memories that turned the edges of her vision black.

"Jubilee-"

"Don't. Please." She couldn't hear his excuses. Not again.

The minutes passed slowly. Painfully. The feel of his hand in hers made her sick and she wanted nothing more than to be wrapped in Atticus's arms.

"Why?" Cyrus demanded. "I know you hate me. You have every reason to hate me. So why?"

Because unlike you, I refuse to sit by while another suffers. But she couldn't say it. "I don't hate you, Cyrus. At one time I did. At one time I wanted you dead as much as I wanted your brother dead. But it wasn't right—what you did. It was no better than what your brother did to me. The Lord wasn't in you that day, and he isn't in you now. Is he?"

Cyrus watched her, incredulity in his eyes. "You care about my soul? Even now?"

"I don't know why," Jubilee replied honestly. "I would be lying if I said there wasn't a part of me, a large part of me, that wants to see you join your brothers in eternity."

"So why do you help?"

"Because I don't want to be that person, Cyrus. I refuse to let hatred run any deeper within me. I have brothers, and if they were capable of such a thing, I would hope that others wouldn't wish them to hell. I would hope that they would save them if they came to them as you did me. If not for my brother, then for those of us that love him."

"I have no one left who loves me, Jubilee. I haven't had that since Ira died."

"You have the Lord—Who doesn't wish for any to suffer. Even men like you. Even men like your brother, and how could I ever face God, knowing it is by my hand that he is missing you?"

"My soul is lost—I know that. I don't deserve anything more than the deepest pits of hell."

Jubilee said nothing. Did he want her to deny it?

Of course he deserves it, Jubilee. Think of what he did. Think of what he sat by and watched. Think of Abba.

With the voice came another image of her father—his hand clutched in hers.

"No." Snatching her hand from Cyrus's, Jubilee paced the cramped space allowed to her. *God, what do you want from me? How can I speak of you to him when it is by his hand I now question you?*

Forgive and be forgiven. Refuse and be refused.

Oh God, I don't know if I can! Slipping to her knees, Jubilee began to pray. *God give me something. Show me any good in him.*

The image of her father was back—struggling against Cyrus and Ira, his eyes glued to Jubilee. *Abba* had begged to simply let them hold her hand. The only comfort he could offer, and Cyrus had relented, freeing one hand so her father could hold her. His hand in his daughters, he had thanked the man who still held him back, forcing his eyes on her.

It was small. But it was enough. Her father's hand in hers had kept her with him.

Standing she went back to Cyrus and took his hand. "You gave *Abba* and me the simplest comfort we could be given at that moment." She said quietly. "You had the simplest bit of mercy. And for that, I can forgive you." Resting her forehead against their hands she prayed aloud.

...

She stayed with him for three days, relying on Layla and Atticus to provide her meals as she listened to the man's breaths grow shorter. Speaking always of the Lord until at last the man cried out for him. When at last he took his last breath she stumbled away from him, freeing her hand from his lifeless grip.

Back hitting the wall she slid to the floor, feeling the weight of those days press in on her until she couldn't breathe. The sobs threatened to break her from the inside out. Her ribs ached. Her stomach burned. Her lungs screamed for air that wouldn't come. As though sensing her pain, Atticus found her and carried her to their room. In their bed, he let her cry against him, his hand on her back.

When at last her tears subsided he kissed her hair. "Why, Jubilee?"

"I had to." She buried her face in his neck. "What if it was your father? Or my father? My brothers? What they did was vile but what if you learned your father had done something so foul? No matter how disgusted you may be, no matter how horrified, could you ever simply stand by and let him die?"

"My father would never-"

"Of course, he wouldn't, Atticus. But just imagine for a moment that he wasn't who you thought he was. Could you let him die? Could you let him burn?"

Atticus was quiet, his mind showing pictures of his father suffering. "No." He whispered. "But he's my father, Jubilee. Cyrus was nobody. He had no one."

"He had God."

"Jubilee, please."

She looked up at him. "Why is it I can forgive him and you can't?" She cried. "I was the one they ruined! Me. My father. My family. We were the ones who lived with it. We were the ones who listened to the rumors and accusations. I was the one called a harlot and liar. Not you! Me."

"I love you, Jubilee. That is why I can't forgive him. Do you think that because I didn't witness it that it doesn't affect me? Do you remember our entire first year of marriage? Do you think I enjoyed seeing you struggle?"

Jubilee glared back at him. "I had to forgive him, Atty. I had to save him."

"Because you think it will save your faith?"

"Because I know that if I walked away from him, I would also walk away from God. That would be the final nail, Atticus."

His conversation with Layla came back to him, driving away the words he had to say about her faith.

"If I may say one thing, my lord." Layla had been quiet before continuing. "Don't let her abandon her faith. Not to please you. People like Jubilee can't stay away from what they know for long. She'll go back to Him and even if she doesn't blame you for the things that conspired while she was away from it, you will. You will hold that blame within yourself forever."

"How do you know this, Layla? How do you know she wouldn't be happier without it? She wouldn't be so focused on pleasing Him."

"It doesn't matter how I know. All that matters is that you encourage her in her faith. Even if you don't understand it. Even if you hate it."

Swallowing the words that had formed at his lips, Atticus gripped her chin. "Jubilee, I-"

"I don't understand why a God who loves me like I believed would do this." Her hands tangled in her hair. "It has been two years. Two years of trying and nothing. He gives children to women who choose to abort them. But after everything we've been through, we get nothing. Haven't we suffered enough?"

Atticus felt sick as anger and fear warred in his mind. He had known Jubilee all her life, watching as her faith grew each time he saw her. She had loved her faith. Had held it to be of the highest importance. Since her coming, he had watched her struggle with it. Faltering when her god's name came up. But never had he thought she could truly leave it. "Jubilee, you are grieving. You don't mean what you say. Remember what you believe."

Isn't this what you wanted? A voice mocked. *To see that ridiculous faith sapped out of her?*

He pressed a hand to his eyes. *I didn't want to hear about it. I didn't want to see her struggle. But I don't want her to lose herself.* And he knew the truth in it. Her faith was what made her who she was in Galilee—the woman he fell in love with. It was her very faith that was missing in her.

She looked away from him. When she spoke, she spoke with the tone of one who had lost all hope. "I don't know what I believe anymore, Atticus. I want to believe in a loving God. But for the past five years, all there has been is pain. Every time it gets better, every time I believe my test is finally through it all falls away once more."

Atticus felt as though he had been hit in the stomach. "Are you so unhappy here? Have I continued to fail you?" He flinched at the vulnerability that coated his voice.

"No, Atticus." She took his face in his hands. "I love you." She kissed him softly. "I love you so much. But I have also given up so much. My country. My brother. *Abba.*" Tears streamed steadily down her cheeks. "And the one person I need most now is an ocean away and I may never see her again." The truth of her words stabbed at her chest and she gasped, collapsing into his arms.

Atticus felt unsure of what to say. She needed her mother. Not the man who had taken her away. "I don't believe, Jubilee. I can't. But I don't want to see you lose yourself. Promise me you won't give up on him."

Jubilee met his eyes, a hundred questions in them. "Why? Isn't this what you wanted?"

He wanted to deny it. "Yes." He admitted quietly. "I hated that you loved him more than me. I couldn't understand how you could put so much love and faith into something you couldn't see and I despised him for it. I wanted you to turn to me. To somebody you could see and feel and touch. I didn't realize your faith was what held you together all this time. I don't want you to lose your faith. Your faith is what I love about you. The way you clung to it so tightly. Even if I don't understand it, even if I question it. It is still something I admire about you."

She blinked at him, fighting to see him through her tears. "I don't know how much longer I can hold on, Atty. I know that I won't be happy until I find him, but I don't know how to do that anymore."

Wrapping her tighter in his arms, Atticus held her until she fell asleep.

XXXVII

Layla was growing attached. She brought Nathanael his food and tended to his needs and rather than leave, Layla found herself staying—watching as he wrote endlessly in his scrolls. She wondered at what he could be writing after so much time in bed. When she garnered the nerve to ask, she noticed the light blush that filled his brown cheeks. "My prayers."

She wanted to ask what he prayed about, that he needed to write them down, but the way he had blushed told her enough. She felt the way Nathanael's eyes followed her as she moved and she knew the thoughts that filled his mind. Did she bring men to sin simply by her figure? She wanted to be angry. To curse him for his staring. But there was something so innocent about the way he did it. There was none of the hunger in his eyes that she had seen in the others before him. He looked upon her the way only one other man had looked upon her and it sent delicious shivers down her spine. But with her blossoming feelings came other emotions. Guilt that pressed so strongly against her heart that she felt sure it would be crushed. The walls were crumbling. Just as he had said they would.

Will you lead another to sin, Layla?

So she beat the feelings back. When at last Nathanael was allowed to walk she felt an almost relief. Once he was fully healed he would be leaving and that would be the end of things.

He didn't do anything in halves, she noticed. The moment he was told to move about he was walking the length of the Domus —perspiration beading his brows and pouring down his cheeks.

"You should rest now, my lord." She fretted. "Do not push yourself."

"I am not ready to go back to that bed, Layla." Even with the hint of frustration that tinted his voice, he gave her a crooked smile. "I need to move."

Layla swallowed back her retort. She could see the pain he was in by the way he held his ribs. His teeth clenched tight. But still, he walked on, circling the peristyle. He was as stubborn as his sister. When at last he was ready to stop, he looked as though he would be sick. When she touched him, his skin was hot. As she helped lower him to the bed, he groaned loudly, curling in on himself. "Nathanael?" Her hands fluttered over him uselessly.

He waved her off as she settled in. "Only sore is all."

Layla pressed a cloth to his forehead—all too aware of the feeling of his skin against her hand. "You should have listened to Lady Jubilee. You pushed yourself too hard. Push yourself anymore and you will only serve in injuring yourself further." She was well aware of the anger in her voice, and she hated herself for it. *It's only because you want him gone faster.* She told herself. *He'll stay longer if he injures himself.*

"Could you stand another moment in bed if you were me?" He asked quietly. "I have been moving for nearly five years."

Layla remembered her earliest days with Jubilee when the girl had shied away from using her. She had been bored with nothing to occupy her idle hands. "No." She conceded. "I suppose not." After so many years of work, to rest seemed wrong. Was that how he felt after so many years of travel?

Suddenly Nathanael smiled. "You called me by my name."

She glanced up at him, finding in his eyes the very things that burned for him within her. They were closer somehow, their breath mingling. "You scared me." She breathed.

"Is that all?" His voice dripped with disappointment, and if not for the years of practice she'd instilled within herself, she would have taken it back—confessed every pathetic thought she'd had for him.

Moving back she dried her hands on her tunic. "I am a slave, my lord. It's inappropriate."

Nathanael took her hand. "Why do you hide from me?"

"I am a slave."

"So you have said. But I don't think that is why you push me away. No one in this home treats you like a slave. You fear something. What is it, Layla? Please, I want nothing more than to help you."

Nothing more. Until you've given him what he wants. Then he'll want more.

"I don't deserve your help." She said harshly. "Now let go of me, my lord." Tears bit at the back of her eyes. "Please?"

He did as she asked. Dropping her hand, he leaned back against the pillows. "Whatever it is that binds you, Layla? You must release it. You can't keep blaming yourself."

"I can, my lord, and you would too if you knew." Holding herself tightly she hurried from the room. Why did he affect her so strongly? She didn't love him. She didn't want to love him. Love was dangerous.

Stop fighting it. It is in your blood to destroy. He wants you, Layla. Take your pleasure.

Pleasure. If love was dangerous—pleasure was deadly.

···

Nathanael prayed unceasingly for the wisdom to know where God called him. He had always dreamed of sharing the Good Word. When at last he set out on his journey he had believed he would serve until the day he died. Bringing his Father's words to the ends of the earth. He had traveled from Galilee to Jerusalem. To Greece and Germania. But still, he had so much to reach. Their travels had yet to take them to China and Britannia. India and beyond.

When he thought of how much they had yet to cover he felt the desire to go out once more into the unknown. But one look at his sister and he knew the damage his leaving would do to her. Her faith was small. Upon finding her in Rome, he had hoped to see her faith strengthened, no longer bound by the fears Jude had instilled in her, and yet her faith seemed to slip from her fingers more and more. Even her time with Cyrus, easing him into the hands of the Lord hadn't been enough. She asked questions she hadn't before. And then there was Layla. The perfect stranger who occupied his every waking thought.

He prayed. He fasted. Until at last the small voice whispered. *Be still.*

Nathanael felt his heart beat uneasily as he watched Jubilee's eyes scan the scroll. "What do you think, Joy?"

Jubilee pressed the scroll back into his palms. "It's wonderful, Nathanael. I can't believe how much you have done. How much you've seen—how many people you have reached. It's incredible."

Nathanael smiled. "I was speaking with Solaris. He thinks it would do me well to publish my works. All I have to do is say the word and he'll begin the work."

"Are you going to do it?"

"I want to." He admitted sheepishly. "To be honest I would love to. If I am going to stay, I still want to be able to do my part, and writing has come as a sudden source of joy for me."

"If you do this, you will stay?" Jubilee's voice was hesitant.

"I have already decided to stay, Joy. I don't think the Lord would approve of my leaving you where you are with him. Nor would *Imma* and *Abba*." He took her hand. "I am here to stay, Joyous. As long as you will have me."

"You have a home here as long as you want it, Nathanael. But I don't I can ever get back to where I was." She had begun attending church once more, at Atticus's request, and though the words didn't come, she spent each morning in the gardens simply listening to the silence. "I want to believe all of this has a purpose, but I feel so lost. It seems as though no matter how hard I try, I still fail."

"You will get there, Jubilee. So long as you don't give up. Even if you don't feel him—even if you have no words, you are still trying. You are still taking the time to be with him."

"But it's forced, Nathanael. I do it because I have to. Not because I want to." She shook her head. "It is so much easier to rely on Atticus. Atticus is who I trust. God doesn't make me feel safe anymore, Nathanael. Atticus makes me feel safe. Atticus makes me feel loved." Her love for Atticus was beginning to overwhelm her very senses. Filling her body, mind, and soul. He was her life. Her breath. Her savior. She clung to him to rid her mind of the monsters that haunted her. All he had to do was touch her and the memory of *him* and *his* touch fell away. Leaving only Atticus. And so it was with him. She could see within him the change when the insecurities Aelia had instilled in him drew him away. It was only a touch. The whisper of his name and she drew him back to her and she knew there was only her.

"I know it's wrong." She whispered. "But I don't trust Him anymore. After it happened I tried so hard to do so—to lean on Him as I once had. But I never felt Him, Nathanael. I never heard Him. It was like God disappeared the moment *he* touched me." Tears cascaded down her cheeks and she struggled to spit the words around her sobs. "I haven't turned my back on Him, Nathanael. My mind is just so muddled. I need to sort it out."

Nathanael waited until he knew he could speak, knowing his own emotion would only upset her more. "What is it, Jubilee?"

Jubilee was silent as she worked to get herself under control. "I need *Imma*." She sobbed. She buried her head in his shoulder, her tears soaking into his skin. "I need *Imma*."

XXXVIII

Atticus hesitated at the door of Nathanael's cubicula. The man had been with them for four months and he had yet to step foot in his room. He had adapted his mother's old vanity into a desk, at which he seemed to be working tirelessly. Dozens of scrolls were stacked around him—many dangerously close to rolling onto the floor.

Setting his quill down, Nathanael turned and smiled in surprise. "Good morning."

Atticus nodded and looked back toward the corridor. Both prone to timidity, he and Nathanael had never been more than mere acquaintances at the expense of Jubilee, who was rarely seen apart from her brother. As he stood in the doorway, he felt that old reserve returning. He knew nothing of how to raise the questions that had led him to the man's door.

Nathanael frowned, understanding the man's prolonged silence. "Why don't you come sit down? I can answer whatever questions you have."

Conceding, Atticus sat at the edge of the bed. When Nathanael didn't pressure him to speak, Atticus tried to get his thoughts in order. He had come for Jubilee but instead, he found accusations at his lips. "You knew." He said quietly. "About Jude."

"I was a child, Atticus," Nathanael replied, unfazed by Atticus's anger. "I had no reason to believe that he wasn't simply coming back from the bathroom all those times."

All those times. The words echoed in his head. How often had Jude taken her in that way? "But you knew. You saw it that last time. You watched."

"I didn't know what I was seeing and when I finally understood, I was in as much shock as Jubilee. Believe me, Atticus—I wanted to stop it. But you must understand that I was a child, watching a man hold a knife to my little sister's throat. All I can say is that I froze."

"And after? You knew as she did and yet you didn't tell your parents."

There was no frustration in the man's voice as he defended himself. "I was no older than she was, Atticus. I believed the lies he told her. Do you think that at thirteen years old I wanted to see my little sister stoned?"

Atticus shook his head. "What I don't understand is how no one noticed it happening in the streets. She said he would grab her whenever he could. From the time she was a child. And even after. When she was watched constantly."

"We couldn't see her every second, Atticus. We were working. Buying food. Talking with friends. We did the best we could to keep her safe and in the end, it wasn't enough."

Sighing, Atticus dropped his head into his hands. "I'm sorry." He muttered. "I never meant to make it seem as though it were your fault. I know how much you love her." Even as a toddler, Nathanael had been protective of his sister—keeping an eye even on Atticus as the two had grown closer in their final summers.

"We all watched Jubilee after that night. She never left the house without my father or Abel. Even my mother couldn't go out with her without a man with them."

"She's right." Atticus spit. "I should have been there. I may have been able to stop him."

"No one could have stopped him, Atticus." When Atticus made to counter, Nathanael held up a hand. "Do you not think it would have been worse, had you been there? Atticus, Jude was twisted and I do not doubt in my mind what he would have done to you had you been there. Do you think that would have made it better for Jubilee? Or worse? To watch you die? God knew what he was doing he put you on that ship."

"He knew and yet He let Jude-"

"Jude knew what he wanted, Atticus, and he wasn't going to stop until he got it. One way or another." Nathanael stood and paced. "I don't know what Jubilee has told you, but my father said Jude tried to give her a way out. That if she agreed to marry him he would let her go to their bed a virgin."

"And she refused."

"She told him she would rather face him once than let him abuse her day after day for the rest of her life. She told him to do whatever he wanted to her and enjoy hell when he was finished." Nathanael met Atticus's eyes. "Do you see the significance in that, Atticus? There are a dozen choices that led to the events of that day—personal decisions. We can't hold the Lord accountable for that, but we can thank Him for the good. He may not have stopped Jude, but He gave Jubilee the courage to say no and He kept you from being hurt in the process."

"Why?" Atticus demanded. "Why protect me and not Jubilee?"

"Because whatever you might think, there's purpose in your life, Atticus, and He knew Jubilee would need you. I don't agree with the idols the two of you have made of one another, but I can't deny that Jubilee would have been gone entirely had you been lost."

An idol? Was that what he had become to her? He knew what she was to him, but had he truly sat by and let her do the same?

You made it happen, Puppy. Love me. Come to me.

"It isn't entirely your fault what she has done with you, Atticus," Nathanael said. "Her faith was slipping long before now, and she would have turned you into an idol whether you encouraged it or not."

"Is that when her faith began to slip? It-" He closed his eyes. "It wasn't me? It had nothing to do with that night?"

"It is not uncommon for even the strongest of faith to question God in times like this. They are hurting and they need someone to blame. Unfortunately, it is easiest to blame him."

"She is doubting, Nathanael. She doesn't believe that she is loved. I don't believe in what you do, but I can't see her stop believing. Not if this is what I am left with."

"How much has she told you about what happened?" Nathanael asked softly. "About what Jude did to her?"

"All of it." Atticus breathed.

"So you know that afterward, she couldn't stop bleeding? We had to rush her to the local Jewish physician. When she arrived, Jubilee refused to be touched. She screamed. Cried. Begged." Nathanael closed his eyes, trying to block the memory of the horrid screams that had come from the house. "My mother tried to reason with her that if she didn't stop bleeding she would die. But she didn't care. She wanted to die, Atticus. She begged my mother to let her. In the end, she had to be held down while she screamed that she wouldn't forgive any of us for this."

Atticus pressed his palms to his eyes, dark pictures choking him. "Why do I need to hear this?" He had barely survived the first time.

"Because she survived, Atticus. For many days she was broken. She didn't speak. She didn't eat. She stared at a wall without even blinking. The only time she made any noise was in her sleep." Nathanael forced himself to breathe. "But she came out of it. Her faith was weakened. She questions. She doubts in ways she didn't before. But she still clings to him."

"What can I do for her?"

"Your father's ship is set to sail to Galilee, is it not? Send her back. Let her see our family."

Send her back? To the very place she had been broken? "Jubilee said that Jude is dead. Is that true?"

"It's true."

"You can be sure of this—that if I were to let Jubilee go, she would be safe?"

"I saw him, Atticus. He was dead. I ran into him in Greece." Nathanael swallowed at the memory. *Oh God, I am trying to forgive.* "Believe me, Atticus. I would not let Jubilee go anywhere alone if I were not certain he was gone."

"And the other brother? The one who helped?"

"Dead. He killed himself three days after the incident. They are all gone, Atticus."

Atticus pursed his lips. "Do you think it would help to send her back? Won't that only make it worse when she has to leave?"

Nathanael nodded. "So that is what this is about? Jubilee loves you, Atticus. She will want to come back simply for that reason."

"I can't risk losing her. I won't." He needed her.

"So you would prefer to keep her trapped in her pain?" Nathanael took a deep breath, working hard to keep his patience. "I can see you love her, Atticus. I have always seen it. But you are selfish. Jubilee has left everything behind. She gave up all that she knew. She loved you even when it hurt, and you refuse her this. She is breaking, Atticus. She needs a mother. Her mother."

...

Atticus watched Jubilee over the days that followed, praying to whatever being might be out there that there might be change. He couldn't give her up. He couldn't stand the thought of even a night without Jubilee beside him. But though she didn't worsen, she didn't improve and every night he found it harder to deny the truth. If he wanted her back he had to let her go.

Bringing her closer one night, Atticus pressed his lips into her hair, breathing in the scent of her. Curling into him, Jubilee's eyes closed, her breath trembling, and he knew she was fighting off memories of Jude. It happened sometimes—the memories of Jude trying to press back in on her at his touch.

"Did you never struggle?" Jubilee whispered. "After Aelia?"

"For a time." He replied quietly. "There were women in Greece who flirted or tried to get my attention. I might have found it flattering once, but all I saw was Aelia. Their touch and even their eyes made my skin crawl." He touched her hair. "I never thought about a woman in such a way until you. There was no fear with you.”

“I wish I could have been better to you. I wish I had been clean.”

“You are not unclean, Jewess.”

“I have never felt clean.” She whispered. “I don’t think anyone ever knew that. I never let them know it. But I did with you.” She toyed with the front of his tunic. “I always loved you. I always imagined marrying you. But when it came to what marriage entailed, I was terrified. All I knew was his touch and I feared to be touched in that way. Even by you. But then you did touch me and it was like you were washing it all away. Every memory of *his* touch, until I knew nothing but you.” She smiled. “It’s why I thought I could do this. Marry you. I thought it would be like that. That you would touch me and make love to me and erase what *he* had done to me, just as you did before.”

“Only it didn’t work out that way.”

She shook her head. “Even now, and I don’t know why.”

Atticus sighed. “Don’t you, Jewess?” Even he knew. She had still been strong in the Lord then. She had trusted Him and it had enabled her to trust Atticus. She held no trust now. “I think you should go to Galilee, Jewess.” The words burned at his throat.

“We will.” She replied. “Someday.”

“Not we, Jubilee. I can’t leave the shop, and I don’t think you can go another year without your mother.”

Pulling away from him, Jubilee’s lip quivered. “You don’t want to go with me?” She whispered. Tears choked her voice. "I don't want to leave you. I don't want to go back. Not without you. Please, Atticus. Don’t send me away now."

The woman was beginning to reach hysterics. "Jubilee, it is only for the summer. Come August you will be right back with me."

"You still want me?" Tears pooled in her eyes and spilled over.

"Jubilee." Bringing her to him he kissed her gently. "I will always want you, Jewess. Always. That is why you are going. I don't want you bound by your thorns forever."

"Can't you come with me? I don't want to be apart from you."

Atticus buried his face in her hair, unable to stand the look in her eyes. He had never known Jubilee to be needy. *God, if you are true. Let this work. Let her find you again.* "You must do this on your own, Jewess. But I will always be here, waiting for you."

"But what of you? Will you never be free of your thorns?"

"Not until you have taken care of yours. Go back to Galilee. Reform your faith and then come back to me."

"You'll listen?"

"I will."

Jubilee kissed him then, her first true smile in weeks dancing across her lips. Holding each other close, they took all they could from each other before three long months could part them.

. . .

The preparations were done in haste, Atticus's father seeing that she was comfortable and well taken care of. It had been decided that his mother and the baby would accompany her, Sibyl desperate to see her old friend after so many years.

Atticus felt a deep ache settle in his chest as he entered their cubicula that night. The small bed they shared felt large and empty. How was he to make it three months without his Jewess? Without her sweet smile and gentle touch to bring him out of the darker depths of his mind? His nightmares still haunted him nightly. Always the same and yet always different. Night after night Jubilee tore at the thorn-covered wall until—through the cracks in the mortar, a light could be seen glowing just beyond it. Growing steadily brighter with each dream. They were horrifying and yet beautiful. *Make it worth it.* Make what worth it? Her suffering? "How?" He wanted to scream. "Tell me how and I will."

You'll listen? Jubilee's voice whispered.

He had said he would. He had said it to appease her. It hadn't been until she smiled that he realized how deeply he truly ached to hear her stories. He hadn't realized how much he missed the stories she had once shared without any doubt in their author. He had heard them all his life, paying them no mind.

There was only one other time that he had felt a draw to the strange being Jubilee loved so deeply. Kneeling before the chest, he pried it open, revealing a bundle of old scrolls. Taking one up he sat at the edge of the bed and unrolled it.

"I appreciate your honesty, Atticus." Malachi's voice echoed. *"That is a character I want to see in whomever my daughter marries."*

"But you are going to say no." Atticus had felt the rope constricting his chest tighten.

"I am saying yes, Atticus. If you can only do one thing for me."

Atticus's fingers grazed the scroll. His heart pounding as it did that day. *"Study the word, Atticus. Do that and next summer I will give my Joyous to you."*

It had seemed an easy task. Read the scrolls and Jubilee would be in his arms forever. He had begun to study immediately. The words were difficult to understand and yet he had found himself reading more and more, yearning for something beyond Jubilee. After only a month, he found himself reading them for simple enjoyment. Could a thing unseen truly be out there, fathering the world? Loving the world? Loving him?

It was Aelia who had ripped away the strange hope that had taken root in him. The moment he had woken and realized the truth of what had been done, he knew the words he had read were false. But as he stared down at the stilted penmanship, he felt that same draw from before. A desire to know more.

XXXIX

Iunius

After two years, the streets she had walked for eighteen years seemed like a stranger's land to her. As she started down the path, Jubilee found herself longing for the home she had made for herself in Rome. The busy streets. The Domus she had despised for so long. They were home. Atticus was home.

As they grew closer, Jubilee unleashed her hair, letting it fall as a curtain between her and her neighbors. She did not want to be recognized now. She knew the thoughts that would cross their minds. She could feel the eyes on her as she entered the street. She could hear the whispers. Hiding her face would do nothing for her here. Biting her lip, she threw her head back, tossing her hair behind her back. Staring straight she could see her childhood home. Nearing it, she could see her mother through the window.

Her mother glanced up for only a moment before turning her attention back to her work. After a moment she looked back up, her lips moving. She was at the door in seconds, just as Jubilee came to it. "Is it you?" She croaked.

"*Imma!*" Jubilee dropped her bag and threw her arms around her mother. "*Imma.*" She said again, loving the feel of it.

Juliana clung to her daughter, afraid she would wake any moment to find it was all a dream. "Oh my love, what are you doing here? Where is Atticus?"

"He is back in Rome. He couldn't leave the shop."

But Juliana had seen Sibyl. Moving around Jubilee she wrapped the other woman in her arms. "And you." She laughed, her hand gentle at Tauria's head. "You have some explaining to do, my dear."

"And I will explain everything," Sibyl replied.

"Oh my." Juliana cried, feeling overwhelmed. "Please come inside." Taking Jubilee's hand, she led the two inside.

...

Jubilee lowered herself to the floor beside the bed. Taking his hand she pressed it to her lips. "Hello, Leo." She croaked.

Her mother had warned her of the man's ailing health before leading her inside. Though her mother had made sure he was shaved and clean, he looked much as he had when he returned to the Domus. The skin of his face sagged miserably and the dark circles under his eyes had deepened. He was so skeletal that Jubilee feared touching him.

His hand reached up shakily, his fingers grazing her eyelashes as he made to touch her face. "My Juliana." He rasped. "Where have you been?"

"It's Jubilee." She whispered. "Do you remember?"

His eyes narrowed in confusion. "Juliana." He repeated.

Her mother set a hand on her shoulder and squeezed. "His mind appears to be stuck in the past lately. He thinks Abel is your father." Her lips wobbled. "He keeps asking for Sonali. *Amma*." She explained. "And for my father. I don't think he even remembers his baptism."

"Is he still-"

"Of course, Jubilee. He is not in his right mind now. The Lord knows and understands."

Jubilee nodded. "He doesn't have much time, does he?"

"Your father thinks it will be in the next few days."

"That soon?"

"It isn't as soon as it seems, Jubilee. His mind started going shortly after he arrived. He was baptized six months later and had forgotten about it two days later. We thought he was having second thoughts until he asked who I was." Juliana turned away as fresh tears cascaded down her cheeks. She had known the man all her life. To have him look upon her as a stranger had nearly broken her heart in half.

Turning back to the man she knelt beside him and wrapped the blankets tighter around him. Even in the humid summer air, he shivered violently. "You sleep, *Tata.*" *Daddy.* She had taken comfort after Amma, knowing the woman had gone to her grave knowing Juliana's feelings, and she would do the same with her Leo.

Juliana felt flustered as they roamed about the house. She hadn't expected visitors.

Jubilee grabbed her hand and pulled her down next to her. "The house looks lovely, *Imma.* As always. Stop fretting." She sat close to her mother, her hand in hers. She refused to let her go and she knew her mother to be doing the same.

"Now." Her mother demanded. "What are you doing here?"
"I have been having some trouble lately. Atticus felt it would be good for me to come back for the summer." Jubilee could see the concern that filled her mother's eyes, but she didn't press it. They could share everything later when they were alone.

Instead, her mother pressed a hand to her cheek. "You look sick, Joy. Are you all right?"

Jubilee smiled. "Yes, *Imma*." She had spent the week's journey bent over the side of the ship and the nausea had yet to leave her. "I just have to recuperate." Turning the subject away from her, Jubilee retrieved Julius's letter and pressed it into her mother's hands. "I found this after *Avus* died."

Juliana pressed a hand to her lips, careful to keep quiet as Tauria slept. "Still Julius Aquila." She laughed tearfully. "Even apologizing he still makes it sound as though it's another's fault."

"But he recognized his wrongs," Jubilee said. "I'm sorry I couldn't reach him fully, *Imma*."

"Oh don't blame yourself, Jubilee. My father was stubborn. That you reached him in any way is everything to me." With the sun starting to dip in the sky, Juliana jumped up—the letter forgotten. "I forgot all about supper."

"We'll help you, *Imma*." Following her, the three quickly went to make a stew.

"Your father will be home any minute." Juliana sighed. "His arthritis has been paining him more lately. I hate for him to have to wait."

"*Abba* won't mind," Jubilee assured her. As the words left her tongue she heard her father's voice drift in through the open door. "*Abba*!" Jubilee hurried out the door. "*Abba*!" She threw herself at her father and kissed his cheek.

Righting himself on his cane, her father hesitated before hugging her back. "Joyous?" He cried. "What are you doing here?"

"I'll explain inside." Offering her arm, she led him inside and helped him sit painstakingly.

After the hellos and welcomes had been given, as well as congratulations to Sibyl, Jubilee gave him the same brief explanation that she gave her mother.

Malachi smiled. "Well, you will have to thank him for us. We have missed you, sweet girl." Like her mother, he noted the pale look of her skin, his fingers grazing her forehead. "Are you feeling all right?"

"Yes, *Abba*. Just tired is all."

Coming to sit next to him, Juliana kissed him. In all the busyness, she had neglected to welcome him home. "I got so busy with everyone I forgot all about dinner."

"That's all right," Malachi assured her. "If I had known I would have been home sooner." As the table was set he explained his reasoning for being late.

"I would never have imagined Matthew as a physician." Jubilee smiled, remembering the day the boy had come in with his father, who had cut himself chopping wood. The boy had been green.

"He doesn't come by it like you, Joy. But he is dedicated." Her father replied. "He should be ready to take over soon."

"Will you miss it?" Sibyl asked.

"I think I am ready." He admitted. "My back aches too much to stand all day."

"But how will you earn a living, *Abba*?"

"Your brother is building me a stall that will sit outside the house. I'll sell oils like my father did when his pain got him."

"I'll finally get to help." Her mother smiled at her father. Juliana's heart had always been too tender to hear the cries of those who came through the shop. The few that had been brought to their home had always left her in tears, wanting to comfort, rather than assist her husband.

Her father smiled. "Are you sure you are ready to deal with me day in and day out?"

"Don't be ridiculous. I have been waiting for this day."

Seeing her parents together made her ache for Atticus. Glancing toward Sibyl she could see the same yearning for her husband reflected in her green eyes. The woman held her daughter closer, making Jubilee ache more.

When dinner was finished, Malachi read Julius's letter to Leopold, Tauria bouncing on his knee while the women worked together to wash the dishes.

"I won't take no for an answer this time, Juliana." Sibyl had said when Juliana tried to protest. "I can imagine you must be doing a lot more of Malachi's chores now."

"I don't mind it." Juliana smiled. "He had to take care of me for so many years, it's the least I can do to return that love."

Jubilee watched her mother carry a large bucket of water toward them, trying to imagine her as anything less than healthy and strong. The way she had always known her. Though growing up she had heard many stories of her mother's delicate health, she had never seen her mother take on so much as a common cold. Not since she had been touched by the very hands of Jesus.

Jubilee had always loved that story. Of how her mother, weak and dying after childbirth, risked her marriage and friendships alike to walk the nine-hour trek to Capernaum, to ask the man her people called a devil to save a premature Nathanael, only to find not only her son brought back from the brink of death but herself with him, all the frailties she had carried in life falling away. Fresh guilt washed over Jubilee at her lack of faith. She was a black mark upon their faith-filled family.

…

Jubilee woke to the gentle sweep of a hand across her forehead, the nightmare that edged the outskirts of her mind fading away. Opening her eyes she found her mother standing over her, a candle in one hand, a thin blanket slung over her arm. She nodded toward the door.

Careful not to wake Sibyl, Jubilee eased her way off the mat the two shared. Taking her mother's spare hand, she followed her out to the small garden situated behind their home. Sitting next to her, her mother wrapped the blanket around them and let Jubilee rest her head against her shoulder.

"No nightmare?" Juliana asked.

"It was coming." Jubilee took a shuddering breath. The dreams had started again on the ship. "I always sleep in Atticus's arms. He keeps them away." Breathing around the lump in her throat she buried her face into her knees. "I don't know how I am going to do this. I need Atticus."

"You can't rely on Atticus to keep the dreams away forever. You can't rely on him to ease your mind. Not entirely. You need to learn to rest in God first." Juliana tucked the girl's hair behind her ear. "Atticus shouldn't be your god, *Amica Mea*. He should act as God's arms."

"I tried that for three and a half years, *Imma*. Praying every night. Asking Him to be with me. But it wasn't until Atticus was with me that they stopped."

"But you know it isn't right, Joy. The Lord gave you Atticus to be the answer to those prayers. You must recognize God in that."

Jubilee shrugged. "I did. Once. Now I am just confused." She closed her eyes, breathing in the night air. "I don't think I can have children, *Imma*." At her mother's understanding eyes she began to sob.

Juliana said nothing as she held her daughter. Words would not give the child comfort now. Nothing would. The most she could do was hold her close and let her spill her grief.

"You must have patience, my love. I believe that it will all be made right in the end."

"Will it be all right if I never have a child? If I never give Atticus an heir or am never truly married in the eyes of Rome?"

"Do the eyes of Rome matter more to you than God, Jubilee?" Juliana demanded. "It does not matter what Rome thinks of your marriage. It is God's opinion you want, and child or no child you are married under His law. Now look at me." When Jubilee met her eyes, they were stern. "You will be a mother, Jubilee."

Pulling the blanket tighter around herself she curled closer to her mother. "I fear that I will never know the feeling of having a life grow inside of me, *Imma*." Jubilee's voice was small. "I fear that I will never get to feed a child. That I will never know what it feels like to have a child feed at my breast." She glared into the darkness, tears streaming down her cheeks. "Why is this happening, *Imma*? Every time I think that things are moving up it all comes crumbling down again."

"Perhaps He is simply waiting, Joy. You and Atticus are still recovering from all that you have been through." Pressing a hand to Jubilee's clammy skin, Juliana frowned at the pallid look to her. "You are a physician, Jubilee. You of all should know what all this worrying can do to you."

Jubilee bit her lip. "Let's not talk about it anymore." She whispered. The sky was beginning to show the early sign of sunrise, its pinkish glow kissing the horizon. Laying her head on her mother's, she felt her kiss her hair. The garden at sunrise was theirs. She only had so long with her mother and she wanted to enjoy this moment.

XL

Jubilee's absence was a hole he found himself sliding into. She had been by his side near every moment for two years, and to find himself without her left him empty. He studied the scrolls her father had given him each night, relying on their words to keep his mind off the space beside him.

Like the time before he felt their words etching into him—beckoning him to believe, and he wanted to. By the gods, he wanted to. But each time a question was answered he was left with another. Their scriptures spoke of a loving God. A father of the earth and those who resided there. But what of Jubilee? Why had she suffered so hard and so long if this being loved her as he said? Why had He allowed Jude to take her in the way he had? Destroying her not only mentally but physically?

Nathanael insisted that the Lord's heart broke when Jude took Jubilee. That it continued to break in her struggles. So why didn't He stop it? *"Because the Lord gave us free will, Atticus. Jude knew what he wanted and he took it." Nathanael said. "But God does not allow pain without purpose. If He is letting it happen, He is working on her. Preparing her."*

Atticus couldn't understand it. Preparing her for what?

"Time will tell, Atticus. Now is the time to trust that Jubilee is in His hands. Now is the time to focus on your walk with God."

Atticus had found himself splitting his spare time between Nathanael and his father, over time finding the two overlapping as his father joined him in his discussions with Nathanael.

Only a week into the summer, his father had invited Atticus to join him at the gymnasium—aching for a piece of his family. Though the first few days had found them working in silence they had quickly found their way back to the quiet relationship they had had before Aelia's disruption and within days Atticus found himself confessing to his father the things that had transpired within their marriage, feeling the weight ease from his shoulders with each day that passed. "You must remember that you can never tell Mama any of this." He always began. "It would break her to know of even half of these things."

His father set a hand on his shoulder. "You do not need to remind me, Atticus. Your mother is best kept in the dark about some things."

The way his father watched him unsettled him. "Do you know?" He asked. "What she did to me?" At his father's nod, Atticus felt sick. "How?"

Regulus made himself busy before answering. "I have been meeting with her regularly ever since she left."

"Meeting with her? Why? Does mother know?"

"She knows. It became too big of a secret to keep from her."

"But why?" Atticus demanded. "You hate Aelia."

"Did you think she simply let you live where so many others didn't?"

Atticus nearly dropped the weight he held. "You paid her to leave?"

Regulus tightened the boy's grip on the weight before it slipped from his fingers. "No matter how angry I might have been, do you think I was going to sit back and watch her abuse you? My hatred of the situation had nothing to do with her dragging our name through the dirt." Regulus frowned. "You are my son, Atticus. I will never sit by and watch another hurt you."

"How long have you known about how it started?"

"Since shortly after Pompeii. There were things said on that trip that made me wonder. I asked her when I next saw her."

"And she told you? That easily?"

"She saw no shame in it." Regulus's fist curled. "A real man wouldn't have needed so much coaxing."

"A real man wouldn't have let her use him." Atticus breathed. "Not like I did."

"Atticus." Regulus squeezed his shoulder. "You weren't in your right mind. But you should have told me. After the first night. I should have insisted you talk that morning. We could have avoided so much." The boy had been unusually quiet the next morning. His fingers tapping restlessly at the table. When Sibyl set a hand to his forehead he had lurched away from her.

Sibyl had urged Regulus to speak with him but he had assured her he was fine. Too much wine was all. Let him sleep it off and he would be back to normal.

"Do you think I wanted to tell my father what I had allowed a woman to do to me?" Atticus asked. "It was shameful. It was terrible enough having Jubilee know it."

"I would not have been ashamed of you, Atticus. I know what opium does to a man. Especially when mixed with wine."

"And now you are stuck paying her off?" Atticus demanded. "Because of me?"

"It's the only way to keep her away from you, Atticus. And now we have Jubilee to think about. I most certainly don't want her coming near Jubilee."

Atticus shivered at the thought. "Does she know Jubilee is here?"

"No," Regulus replied. "I had no desire to hear the things she would say over her. I hear enough about you and your mother. There was no need to drag Jubilee's name into it."

"I understand all of that," Atticus said quietly. "But you can't keep yourself tied to her for me, Father. Or Jubilee. I'll understand your cutting ties. As would Jubilee. "

"I won't risk her coming back, Atticus. If demons are true, that woman is riddled with them, and one way or another you and Jubilee will have children. Do you want her coming near them?"

"Of course not. But I also don't want to see you bowing to her every whim. I don't want to see you in her home. I know what Aelia can do to you." Atticus watched his father shiver and knew he had felt it. The way being in very presence could make you feel small. "We have to simply trust that we will be all right."

"Trust God?" Regulus asked. The man was struggling to grasp the idea of any god, let alone one unseen.

Atticus smiled. "That is what Jubilee would say. Perhaps she is right?"

"Yes, it's what your mother would say as well. She has been saying it ever since she found God. But I think she might say differently if she knew what Aelia did to you."

"But she will never know. And even so, Jubilee knows everything, and I know she would not like what you are doing."

Regulus watched him a moment. "Does she? Know everything?"

"Yes. She figured it out in Pompeii." Atticus smiled, his eyes distant. "Surprisingly that was what she needed to move forward."

Regulus felt a new rush of appreciation for his daughter. Loving his son even in the darkest moments. Lifting him when he was low, many times by Regulus's hand. "Atticus, about Remus. I know I went about it wrong but you must know that I truly had my misgivings about him."

"Misgivings that turned out to be right. I know it now. Jubilee didn't like him. It was obvious the moment he laid eyes on her. She said he reminded her of Jude."

"I wondered if he might." Regulus frowned. "Remus played a part in Aelia's use of you, Atticus. He thought you needed a woman. To get your mind off that Jewess."

"I did wonder," Atticus admitted. "He was the one to introduce Aelia. He kept the wine coming. And the way he looked at Jubilee that day. It made me uneasy. She says that is how Jude always looked at her. Like he was figuring out how he could get to her." Regulus watched the boy shudder. "Do you think she is all right now?" Atticus asked. "Do you think I was right sending her there?"

"I can't say how she is doing at the moment, but I know you were right sending her away." He set a hand on his son's shoulder. "You have done well by her, Atticus. I'm proud."

...

"Auntie!" Jubilee found herself on the ground as Isaac and Caleb rushed her, their little limbs entangling as they hit the dirt.

Fighting his older brother off, Isaac wrapped his arms around her.

"Boys." Her brother's deep voice rose above their screams. "Let her breathe." Removing them from her, Abel offered his hand. "Welcome back, little sister." Tossing Isaac onto his shoulders, he guided Jubilee inside, Caleb's hand in hers.

"Joy?" Rebekah met her with a hug. Urging the girl to sit, Rebekah worried over her, checking for the fever her parents still worried would appear alongside her pallid skin. Rebekah and Abel had been friends since they were infants, the girl spending more hours at their home than her own. At eleven years old, Jubilee had been the first birth Rebekah had assisted in during her training. She had taken to looking after Jubilee and Nathanael like an older sister long before she and Abel had married. When she asked the question on her mind she was hesitant, her fingers inches away from the girl's stomach. "No children?"

"No children," Jubilee replied. "We're having some troubles there."

"But you haven't lost any?" Jubilee knew she was thinking of her lost children. Rebekah was another faith-filled member of her family. Though she had lost every child she had carried, the woman persisted in bringing other women's children into the world with joy. Never letting her pain get in the way of what the Lord called her to do.

"No, Rebekah. We haven't lost any. That's one consolation, I suppose." Turning to her brother she took his hand. "I was hoping we could talk?" Understanding, Rebekah stood and readied the boys. "My mother is already expecting you," Jubilee told her. "You can meet Sibyl's daughter."

Rebekah's face lit up at that. Kissing Jubilee's cheek, she ushered the boys outside.

When they had gone, Abel came and sat next to her. Jubilee rested her head against his shoulder. Taking the quiet comfort he offered her. Her relationship with Abel had always been so different from the one she had with Nathanael. Nathanael was a friend. Too close in age to be much of a big brother. She and Nathanael had gone through life together, hitting each milestone together. But Abel had been married and in his own home before she had turned six. He was no older than Atticus and yet he had always seemed so. Their mother had been sick through the first ten years of his life, and where Jubilee and Nathanael had been allowed to play and get loud, Abel had been taught since birth that he was to be quiet around their mother, to avoid worsening the ever-present ache in her mind. He took care of her while their father worked. Leaving him old, even as a child.

"What is it, little one." He asked. "Is this about children?"

She nodded. "Have you ever blamed her? Because she can't give you a child?"

"I didn't marry Bekah for children, Jubilee. Just as Atticus didn't marry you for children."

"Abel, Atticus married me because he had to. He didn't want it any more than I did at the time. Who is to say he won't change his mind again?"

"Atticus married you because he loved you, Jubilee." Abel tucked her hair. "There may have been underlying reasons for the timing. But he loves you. Just as he always has."

"His first wife gave him children. His first wife gave him children and she murdered them. Now I can't give them to him. What sort of cruelty is that?" Jubilee was only vaguely aware that she was telling another's secrets. "He deserves children, Abel. More than anyone he deserves a child."

"As do you. And you will, Joy. Have our mother's feelings ever steered us wrong?" When she didn't answer Abel tapped her nose, just as he had done when she was a child. She shrugged. "She felt the need for you to go to Rome and look at you with Atticus? I admit I thought she was mad for sending you there. I thought Ju- I thought that day had taken that sort of future away from you. Even with Atticus. But I was wrong. Of course, I was wrong betting against our mother." Taking her chin he turned her to face him. "She was right about Rome and she is right about this. Even if it comes in the way it has for Rebekah and me. Those boys are our boys, Jubilee."

"I wouldn't even know what it's like to carry one, Abel."

"But you also won't know what it's like to lose one." Allowing her to rest against him once more, Abel took her hand in his. "It gets easier, Joy. There comes a time when you forget that they aren't truly yours. That you didn't give them life through your blood. You will be a mother, Joyous."

"Do you think that day will ever be forgotten, Abel? I'm finally able to move on mentally, at least somewhat. And now this?"

"I don't think it could ever be forgotten, Joy. But in time it may become easier. It has gotten easier." Against all odds, it had gotten easier for him. It had been Abel who had carried her to Judah. He had thought her dead when he and Nathanael had finally found them—held tight in their father's arms as her blood soaked the cloak she had been wrapped in.

Wrapping an arm around her, Abel pressed his face in her hair. It had been years since he had allowed himself to think so clearly of that day. But his sister's sudden reappearance was overwhelming. "The Lord has a plan for you, Jubilee. A reason for all of this. I do not think you would be sitting here if that weren't so. Joy, you were dying. You should have died. I watched the color drain from your face. Listened as your breath grew weaker. And then came the voices."

Even his parents had been drawn to the window as the sound of a hundred voices filled the home. Outside Rebekah stood with their neighbors and friends, Jew and Christian alike, all locked in arms as they sent out prayers for his sister. For the girl who had healed their husband. Their child. The girl who knew how to bring a smile to even the bitterest of people. For that one moment in time, the two groups had become one, putting aside the rift that had existed since the Lord had walked the earth, and together, he and his family had watched as color refilled Jubilee's face.

...

Despite her reassurances, the pallor never left Jubilee's skin. Nor did the nausea that had accompanied her on the ship. The longer her discomfort went on, the more her parents worried about her. Each morning her mother ran a hand over her forehead, always expecting a fever but finding none. Each time she was sick, her mother's eyes would find her father's.

When she was sure she was done, she laid her head in her mother's lap, letting her brush her temples. "It's been two weeks." Her father said quietly.

"I'm fine, *Abba*."

"I am sure you are, Jubilee. But still, we must pay attention." Kneeling beside her, her father brushed a hand over her forehead. "You may have picked something up on the ship, if that is the case, you need to rest."

Above her, her mother watched her, her eyebrows furrowed. Jubilee knew the thoughts that ran through her mind and she refused to acknowledge them. She had given into that belief once and she wouldn't do so again. Not until she could be sure. "I don't want to hear it right now, *Imma*. Please."

Her mother peered down at her. "I am not the only one who thinks it is a possibility, Jubilee. Rebekah believes in it wholeheartedly."

Jubilee shook her head. It was impossible. Two years without a child only to find herself with one only weeks after her husband had sent her away?

"When was the last time you had a cycle?"

Jubilee glared at the ceiling. "The end of April." She admitted. "Into May."

Her father squeezed her shoulder. "That's nearly two months, Joy."

"I have been late before, *Abba*. In March, I believed I was with child and then I was let down. I will not do that to myself again. Not until I know I can be sure."

Juliana pursed her lips. "What if there was a way you could be sure?"

Jubilee met her eyes, hope rising despite herself. "How?"

"There is one way I knew early on with all three of you," Juliana replied. "It's how your grandmother and Rebekah knew with each of theirs." Urging Jubilee to sit up, she ordered Malachi to borrow a cup of wine from Abel.

When Malachi returned, Juliana pressed the cup into her daughter's hand. "You think this is the way to tell?" Jubilee questioned.

"It hasn't been wrong before. Not in our family."

Eyebrows raised, Jubilee lifted the cup, a silent, uncertain prayer on her lips. She wanted a child. But she couldn't take the disappointment again. And should she truly carry a child now, Atticus should be there with her.

The moment the cup reached her lips she knew. Her stomach lurched miserably at the bitter scent. Coughing she passed the cup back to her mother, nearly splashing the blood-red liquid onto their tunics. When her stomach settled, she spoke. "Can that be enough to tell though?"

"That with everything else." Her mother replied. "I enjoyed wine when I was young, Jubilee. But I had the same reaction as you each time I was I was with child. You must think about it, Jubilee. The aversions. The missing cycles. Nausea but no fever. You have always been prone to fever. If you were merely sick you would have been burning up since the beginning."

Jubilee felt a smile easing across her face. It was true that even the simplest things caused her temperature to rise and yet her skin had remained cool to the touch. "Do you believe that I could be?"

"Joyous, I had a feeling the moment I saw you. I just didn't want to be wrong." She brushed the girl's hair. "You kids are where I struggle the most in trusting what I feel."

From the table, Sibyl smiled. "You called out the existence of Atticus during our first visit here."

"Really?" Jubilee breathed. At the woman's nod, Jubilee laughed tearfully, her hand at her stomach. "I only wish Atticus could be here." None of Regulus's ships would be docking in Nazareth until August. It would be almost two months before he would know about the existence of his child.

XLI

Layla frowned as she watched Nathanael kneel in the garden. From where she stood he could see the way his shoulders shook. Edging closer she could hear the tremble in his voice as he prayed. "God forgive me. Forgive me." As she watched, he leaned forward, setting his forehead on the floor.

Her heart ached for him. What could he have done that followed him even now? Unsure of herself, she set a hand on his shoulder. At her touch, rather than dry his tears as she expected, he set a hand over hers and finished his prayers.

Turning to her he smiled self-consciously. "You were crying," Layla whispered. "What awful sin can you have in your past?"

"We all have sinned, Layla. I am most certainly not exempt from that." Nathanael pursed his lips, feeling the story bubble up in him. "I ran into Jude in Greece." He said quietly. He knew the story was better kept to himself. A woman as bitter as she would not understand the magnitude of his guilt, but the story was eating away at him, dying to be released. "I didn't want to, but I could feel that I was supposed to talk to him. So I followed him back to his home. Only he didn't want to talk about God. He wanted to talk about Jubilee and what he had done. About where she was. He didn't regret for a second what he had done to her. He was proud of it. All of it. He would do it again and he admitted it." Nathanael set a hand to his mouth. "So I walked away. Not caring at all that God was near screaming at me to go back. His head fell into his hands and he began to sob. Why had he not gone home with Jubilee? He needed their father's words as much as she needed their mother. "I tried to go back later but he had been killed."

Layla raised an eyebrow. Anger replaced sympathy and reminded Nathanael why he had felt compelled to stay. "You feel guilty for this?" She spit. "Why should you? If there is a hell he deserves to rot in it."

"Layla, please. You shouldn't say things you don't mean."

"I mean it, Nathanael. People like him deserve to live an eternity in misery. As for you still feeling guilty, you said it yourself he was proud of his sin. Nothing you said would have saved him."

"Perhaps not." He admitted. "But there is always a chance, Layla, and no matter how small that chance is you should take it. Instead, I let anger and hatred blind me, and because of that God lost one of his children. A child who may have been saved if I had listened to him."

Layla glared at him. "I don't feel sorry for him, Nathanael. I refuse to pity a man who would do such a thing."

"I wish you felt differently about that Layla." Sighing Nathanael stood and walked away.

Oh God, can she truly be the one? She is so full of anger. So full of hatred. I don't know how to reach her.

Comfort, Beloved.

How can I comfort her when she closes herself off to me?

Patience.

...

Nathanael couldn't get enough of Layla. The more time he spent with her the more he craved. Without Jubilee to tend to, Layla had found herself with little to do and they found themselves spending the better part of each day in the peristyle, more often sitting in comfortable silence as Nathanael poured over his scrolls.

He had felt it the moment he had seen her. That still small voice. *Her*. His heart raced wildly in his chest each time he looked at her. Could she truly be the one? The exotic beauty with the face of stone? She had asked him once what he wrote. He told her his prayers. What would she say if she knew the prayers were about her? That God would soften her hardened heart? That she would look at him from more than a servant's eyes? Would she be angry if she knew how he prayed for control? Wisdom to know when their time was right?

Slowly he could see the change within her. The cold that had hardened the already harsh planes of her face was beginning to soften. But with it came a hollow look of guilt that pooled in her eyes. She had spoken little of her time with different owners, but the few stories she told made his heart ache for the childhood she had lost.

Entering the peristyle, he could see the girl at the fountain. Her wrap was off, showing the dark peach fuzz that covered her head. She had shared with him the story of her first mistress' hatred for her and the day her hair had been cut and her head shaved. As he watched she dipped the wrap into the water and wrung it out over the nearby plants.

Nearing the spot, she glanced up at him and blushed. Hurrying to put the wrap back on she explained. "It's hot today."

"You don't have to explain." He wiped away the water that dripped down her face.

She stiffened at his touch but she didn't move. Instead, her eyes fluttered shut. "My lord."

"Nathanael." He said miserably. "Nathanael."

"I am a slave."

"Stop that. I have heard you call Jubilee by name. You have used mine when you let your guard down. Why do you avoid it when we ask for it?"

She met his eyes, finding only kindness and she felt the words leaving her lips before she could stop them. "To look at you as anything more than a master is dangerous." She whispered.

"What do you mean, Layla?"

"Everyone I have ever loved has left me." Her back slid down the wall and she wrapped her arms around her knees. "I was not simply born into slavery, my lord. My mother was born into a wealthy family." She closed her eyes—her breathing harsh. "When my mother was thirteen she was traveling to Alexandria to meet a potential husband, when the men hired to escort her killed her maids and raped her before leaving her for dead. She was found three days later by a man who took her in and nursed her back to health. When she was well enough to go home he told her that her family would never take her back now, that to go back would only bring them shame, and that it was best she let them believe she had died." Layla sniffed. She hadn't cried in years but she couldn't stop the tears from falling now. She hid her face in her knees to hide the shameful tears. "He offered her a job. His wife couldn't have children and they needed someone to provide a child for them. He was a handsome man. Charming.

He convinced her that he was different from the men who had hurt her. That he wouldn't mistreat her. So she *let* him."

"And she had you." Lifting her chin, Nathanael wiped away the tears that cascaded down her cheeks.

"I look like him." She said quietly. "Mama said I am just like him. She and Nawa were timid. Naive. But I wasn't. He couldn't manipulate me. Nawa and the others called him Papa, as he asked. But I refused." Running the wrap through her fingers she continued. "The mistress didn't want a daughter who could grow to be more beautiful than she, so she ordered her husband to kill me. My mother begged him not to. She would keep me down with her. She bore three more girls, each one rejected before she gave them a boy."

Nathanael waited silently for her to continue. Now that she had spoken, she seemed unable to stop.

"Afterwards, Eurydice refused to even let my mother serve as his wet nurse. She had her son and she didn't need any reminder as to where he came from. My mother said she wouldn't let us be separated, so she mixed mandragora into our water. She told us it would only make us sleep, but I knew. Nawa and I were old enough to refuse, but Habibah and Anat were only six. They didn't know any better."

"Of course not, Layla." Nathanael kneaded a knot in the girl's shoulder. "It's not your fault."

"We were put aboard a ship to Greece two days later." Layla let out a harsh sob before continuing. "Nawa was like my mother. She was timid. Meek. She didn't fight back when the men wanted her. After three weeks she threw herself overboard."

"Layla."

She swatted his hand away. "I started with four family members and came out with none in less than a month." Her voice was distant. "And you'll leave too. Once you say goodbye to Jubilee. Jubilee will send me away one day. Like Sibyl."

"I am not leaving, Layla."

"I don't want to love you." She screamed. "I can't feel that pain again. I won't. I let Jubilee break me. I let myself love her. But I will not love you." She couldn't. "Because the pain of it would kill me."

"Layla."

"Please, Nathanael." She moaned. "Don't make it harder."

"I am not going anywhere."

Together they sat in silence. As Layla cried, he fought the urge to pull her to him. To comfort her.

At the feel of Nathanael beside her, Layla felt her resolve wavering. She wanted to know what it was like to be wrapped in his arms. To feel his comforting kiss on her skin. Could he mean what he said? Would he stay?

Do they ever stay, Layla?

Shaking, she leaned into him and felt him react. His arms wrapped around her, bringing her closer. She was weak. Had she not cursed her mother for her weakness with her father?

...

Nathanael felt the shift after that day, though he could see the fear in her. She watched him as if she expected him to leave her at any moment. She continued coming to him in the peristyle each morning, watching silently as he spent his time in prayer.

When he finished she would sit with him, her knees drawn to her chest as she watched him write. Silently. Always silent.

Where he had once loved the silent moments with her, he now felt restless. Silence left time for him to think. Time to worry. After her story, a gnawing fear had taken root in his heart. *She didn't fight back when men wanted her.* Nathanael found himself watching her, taking in her dark skin and the high set of her prominent cheekbones. She was so beautiful it almost hurt to look at her. Had those men who took her sister felt the same way? *Please, God! Not two of the women I love most.* When the worrying became too much for him he asked.

"No. There was one man who tried but I-" Her cheeks reddened. "It doesn't matter what I did. They whipped me near death but no one touched me again." Her face was set angrily now.

"You would think that look of yours would be enough to keep them at arm's length." He felt his own heart thump in his chest when she looked at him like that. "I myself seem to invite them in."

For the first time, Layla's lips twitched just slightly, revealing dimples in her cheeks. "I do not think many people fear you, my lord."

Nathanael laughed. Given all his father's height and his mother's build, he had a lanky look to him that made him less than menacing in the eyes of those he preached to. He was nothing like Abel who had taken their father's sturdy build. Even Jubilee had grown new curves that suited her petite height perfectly. Where his siblings had known their future spouses from childhood, he had remained on his own—always planning for the moment he would leave Galilee, rather than marriage. It had been a truth he had taken comfort in. He had seen the hardships his mission could put on marriages. But it was in the cold nights, as he fell asleep that he became only too aware of the empty space beside him and ultimately in his heart.

Layla's presence only served to deepen that desire. Should God ever call him out again, he knew he could never go alone. "Perhaps these scars will do me some good."

Layla frowned back at him. "It isn't your looks." She said quietly. "You have peace about you. They know you won't hurt them back."

Nathanael frowned as she looked away from him. He almost missed the angry set of her jaw. Without the anger shielding her she simply looked miserable. "I attacked Jude once." He watched the way her eyebrows raised.

"Did you?" She asked. Again her lips betrayed the smallest hint of a smile.

"The morning after Jubilee found him in her bed." He said quietly. "When she woke and saw he was still there—when she realized it hadn't been a dream, she was sick all over herself. My mother sent Jude and I to get her water for a bath." Nathanael pressed a hand to his eyes. "I don't know what came over me, but all I could see was Jubilee. I was so angry with myself that I didn't stop him from touching her. I didn't do much, I was only thirteen. He was nearing sixteen. But I took him off guard."

Layla shook her head. "How did no one know what he was?"

"I believe my father might have suspected something after he pulled Jude off me. It wasn't like me to fight, nor for Jubilee to be so despondent. But I don't think he wanted to admit it and he knew Jubilee and I had never cared for Jude. It took everything in me not to tell him as we got the water. But as it was, Jubilee didn't want them to know, and for all I knew at that moment, I didn't either. What would they say if they knew their daughter wasn't clean? What would they say if we told them it wasn't the first time he had touched her?" He was quiet for a moment. "What would my father say if he knew I had sat by and watched, too scared to move?"

"You were a child, Nathanael. You wouldn't sit by now."

"Perhaps not. But that doesn't change what I felt at the moment. I thought my father would be ashamed to know what had been happening behind his back. What had happened in his own home while I let it happen."

"Was he?"

"No. He was as he always was. He held me as I cried and then told me that he has had many moments in his life where fear kept him from doing what he knew he should have done. I couldn't keep tearing myself apart over it. Jubilee didn't hate me for it, he and *Imma* didn't blame me, so why should I hate myself?"

"Was it really that easy?" Layla's voice was small. "To forgive yourself?"

"Not at all. I still struggle at times when I think about it. That is why it was so easy to walk away from Jude that day. Because he made me remember all the times I had let Jubilee down. It made me blind to Christ and what he could have done in him."

"Your god would truly forgive a man like Jude?" At Nathanael's nod, Layla bit her lip before looking at him. "Can I ask you something?"

"Of course."

"You have said your god is loving. Forgiving. Is that true?"

"All I have said is true, Layla."

"What would your god do if you fell away? If you sinned greatly against him?"

Nathanael turned her question over. "Have I realized my wrongs and made them right?"

She nodded.

"Then there is no need to dwell on those sins. God does not expect perfection, Layla. He knows there will be times when we fall. All he asks is that we get back up and right our wrongs."

"It seems too easy." She mumbled. "No one can forgive that easily. Not when someone hurts you. Surely what Jude did hurt your god?"

"What Jude did to Jubilee broke God's heart, Layla. He did not wish for it to happen. But would you hold something over a child's head? If you had a child who went against your word, would you turn your back on them?"

"No. Of course not."

"Because you love them? Because you recognize that they are only human? Layla, it is the same with our heavenly father. Only his love for us is so much stronger than we can even imagine feeling toward another human being."

She nodded. "I want to believe that. But some people don't deserve your god's forgiveness."

"Do you mean you? Layla, what could you have done that you see yourself so terribly?"

Her eyes fell to her hands. "I took someone from him, my lord."

"Who?" She shook her head, her lips pressed tight. "Layla, you can't heal what you hide. I can't help if you do not tell me what is bothering you." Seeing the tears that had begun to spill down her cheeks he sighed, "I'm sorry. You have shared more than enough. I don't want to force it." She had questions. It was all he could have hoped for in the beginning.

XLII

Iulius

With Regulus's blessing, Sibyl had Tauria dedicated by the Sea of Galilee. Six months to the day of her birth, she let Malachi take Tauria and watched as he sprinkled the water over her head—a prayer at his lips. Sibyl wouldn't let her daughter walk onto the same path she had single-handedly set her son upon. Her daughter would be raised in God's light, following His words as Sibyl so desperately wished she had lived her own life by.

Wading in to meet them, Sibyl wrapped her arms around the man. "Thank you, Malachi."

"It was my honor, Sibyl." Kissing the child's cheek, he passed her back to her mother before letting Abel assist him out of the water.

Returning to the house, Sibyl laid the girl down before sitting with Juliana. "I don't suppose you had a feeling about her?"

Juliana laughed. "I didn't know with this one, Sibby. I think this one truly was a special surprise."

"She was an answer to prayers, Juliana. Prayers I didn't even know I had." Sibyl glanced back at the girl. "I truly thought my days of even being able to conceive were behind me. I hadn't thought about children of my own in years. To be honest I didn't want more after Atticus, not after what we went through." She laughed. "In the end, Tauria only took three hours in all."

Juliana smiled. "Looking at my children I can't help but think sometimes that their births are little omens of the kinds of trouble they will give us. The boys were easy enough for me considering. It was Jubilee who was the most difficult of them all. She was the easiest to carry and I spent nine months thinking her birth would be the same. I was stronger—healthier. But hers was the longest. Both the boys only lasted a couple of hours each. I labored for three days with Jubilee." Juliana frowned suddenly. "I know how it will sound, but it all gave me the strangest feeling. That she would be the one to bring us the most pain in the end. But I never expected this. It wasn't until that first night with Jude that I knew. I just knew what we were facing and I couldn't stop it."

Sibyl's eyes narrowed. "What first night, Juliana?" She had never heard anything more than the morning of the incident.

"That morning was not the first time he laid hands on Jubilee. She woke up to him in her bed. He only touched her then but she was only thirteen, and Nathanael tells us it wasn't the first time." Juliana rubbed her eyes. "We never told you and Regulus because Malachi and I agreed it was best kept in our little family. We didn't want Jubilee coming up with those whisperings in her head." She laughed humorlessly. "Turns out what was coming was far worse. He was obsessed with her, Sibby. We often found him just watching her as we walked through town. Malachi could hardly let her out of his sight. You know Malachi, he doesn't anger easily. But I have never seen Malachi so angry as he was the night Jubilee confessed to what had happened. I thought he would kill the boy where he stood. But as it was we couldn't let him know that we knew." She had never been so angry with her husband as she had that night, listening to him tell her of Jubilee's confession.

"So you exiled her?" She'd spit.

"She is with Abel, Juliana. She isn't being punished. But I had to make it look as though she is. I won't have her sleeping under the same roof as that boy."

"Then send him away. Why should we reward him with a bed? I will not sleep with him under our roof, Malachi. Not when Jubilee is forced to sleep away with us. Where is the fairness in that? What does that tell Jubilee? That she is hurt and subsequently punished for it?"

"Would you be quiet?" Malachi had hissed. Calming he knelt to her level. "I know you want to be with her, but for now you have to trust Rebekah to care for her. If we let that boy know that we know, if we send him away, he will turn around what was done. He will say she coerced him. That she wanted what was done to her. Do you want her living with that in her head? With her world believing she is corrupt?"

She had dissolved into tears then and he let her cry against him for only a moment before setting her away from him. "I need you to dry your tears, Juliana. Be angry if you must but do not let him see you cry." He took a shaking breath, his teeth gritting as he spit the following words. "Our daughter embarrassed us after all."

"But you knew it was coming?" Sibyl's voice brought her back to the room.

"I knew something with Jude was coming. But not this. I thought she would marry him at worst. He was always asking and I thought one day she might give in. I didn't suspect this until that morning when I woke up with this gut-wrenching feeling. I had never felt anything so strongly in my life. It was suffocating. But I couldn't warn them, by the time I woke up they had already gone. I spent hours that morning waiting before I finally sent the boys looking for them. Nathanael was the one to come running for me. Nathanael." She whispered.

"He could barely get the words out he was crying so hard. I think we all felt our faith slip that day, even if only a little. The difference was that we found ways to get it back. Malachi did what he had always done best. Leaving it to God. Trusting him. Abel stayed away until he was sure he could look at her without wanting to curse God. I fasted until I was sick.

"I never would have thought it possible, but Nathanael's struggle lasted the longest of us four. His faith was always the strongest of our children, I don't think he ever doubted before Jubilee. It is why he chose to leave when he did. He knew that if he stayed any longer he would never leave, as his faith continued to waver." Juliana swallowed. "And then we were left with Jubilee. We could see the struggle in her as she tried to continue in her beliefs, but the relationship she had once carried with him had been broken. She still loved God but I know she no longer trusted him."

Sibyl shook her head. "All those years I let you beg me to come. You needed me and I couldn't spare even a letter to explain my absence or wish you condolences."

"It's in the past, Sibby."

"It isn't for me, Juliana, and I don't think it is for you either. I need you to tell me the truth, Ana. Was there ever any anger in you for my abandonment?"

Juliana frowned. "I suppose there might have been some anger. I never realized until I saw your letter and I wondered what you could want after all these years. But don't let that get to you, Sibyl. It was only for the briefest of moments that I felt it. We have been through too much to remain angry over something so trivial."

"I should have trusted you. Perhaps if I had confided in you earlier our children wouldn't have fallen so far. Perhaps we could have united them sooner."

"But that wasn't the Lord's plan. We have to believe in time, Sibby. He knew what He was doing bringing them together when He did."

...

Juliana watched her daughter at the window, her hand on her stomach. Despite the initial joy she had felt at the discovery, the excitement had slowly drained from her eyes until the lifeless look had filled its place once more. The lack of trust she held towards the Lord had stifled even that joy.

"Sibyl, would you mind leaving us a moment?" Perhaps some time to themselves would loosen her daughter's tongue. Taking Tauria, Sibyl excused herself. Turning back to Jubilee, Juliana held out a hand. "Love."

Jubilee went instantly into her lap. "I missed that." She whispered, setting her head on her shoulder.

"I missed saying it." She rested her head against her daughters. "Now that we are alone, we can finally talk."

"I don't know what's wrong with me." Jubilee breathed. "But I can't get excited. Not really." Tears dripped down her cheeks. "Why am I so bad at this, *Imma*? You and *Abba*. All of you are faithful. Even before God, you were good."

"I am far from perfect, my love. And I was even further from it back then. There is still so much to my past that you don't know. Things you will never know."

"Why? Do you think that I wouldn't look at you the same?"

"Jubilee, what sort of example would I be to my children if I kept anything from you out of shame? Everyone who deserves to know about those areas of my past knows. But some things are better left in the past. So they don't cause any more pain. If what you were struggling with went with what I did, I would tell you. But it doesn't." Juliana kissed her cheek. "I wish so much I could take all of your pain for myself."

"I want to be excited. But I can't help but feel as though it will all come crumbling down once I do. I have been praying for a child for so long. Now I have it but I still feel so wrong. Like no matter how hard I try I just can't be happy."

Juliana pursed her lips. "Perhaps because you are still questioning him, Jubilee. Instead of taking what he has given you since it happened, you can't move on from it." Juliana pressed her lips to her daughter's forehead. "Do you remember what I told you after-" She hesitated—Jude's name on her lips. "After what happened? When you asked the same questions?" Jubilee was quiet. Reluctant. "Love."

"I don't feel his love anymore, *Imma*. I haven't since that day. All I feel is lost and alone. It is dark and I am alone." She took a shaking breath. "There is no light, *Imma*. Not anymore."

Juliana took her daughter's face sternly. "You survived, Jubilee. When you shouldn't have. That is the light. Look at all that you have experienced in the past five years." Loosening her grip, she brushed back Jubilee's hair. "Tell me. I want to hear you say it."

Jubilee frowned. "At first, every time Atticus touched me I felt as though I'd be sick. But then it got better. Wonderful." Her cheeks flushed red and she turned. "I forgot about-about *him* and it was just Atticus."

"And what did you get from that?"

A shy smile touched Jubilee's lips, her fingers going to her stomach. "Atticus."

"And has that been taken away from you? Jubilee, you have fallen so deeply into your pain and distrust of the Lord that you have become blinded to the things he has given you." Seeing the look Jubilee gave her, Juliana continued. "I'm not saying that I blame you, Joy. But you will never be happy if you don't face it."

"Face it?" Jubilee whispered. "How?"

"That is for you to decide."

Jubilee let out a small sob. "I don't know how to move on from this. I want to, *Imma*. I have tried to give it to God. Over and over but the pain stays." She shook her head before turning back to her mother. "That day? That day you told me that that morning was just one event. One horrible event that would one day be history. Only it wasn't true, *Imma*. It wasn't just one event. It will never be history. Things happened that day that will follow us forever." Taking a deep breath she continued. "It wasn't one event, *Imma*. It's a lifetime." Standing she moved toward the door.

"What was the rest of it, Jubilee?"

Jubilee stopped in the doorway. "You said that I can't change what happened. But I can decide how I move forward."

"And?" Juliana pressed.

"That in the end I would find new strength." She closed the door behind her.

Out of sight of the house, she quickened her pace until her feet were pounding against the dirt. Ignoring Sibyl's call as she passed her. Ignoring the stares of neighbors. She ran until the well came into sight. Slowing, she walked the remaining steps, her heart pounding as though trying to escape its cage. She hadn't been here since that day. No one had. After all that had taken place, the town elders deemed it unfit ground to walk on. By the grace of God, water had been discovered closer to town and the well was fixed immediately.

She had loved this place once, as quiet and peaceful as it was. It was there that she had first kissed Atticus. It was there that she had first felt his loving touch and it had all been taken away in one hideous moment.

The scream tore through her like a shard of glass. All the pent-up frustration from that horrible day until now came out in one long, pain-filled scream. When she was finished she fell to her knees, her chest rising and falling in quick succession, her sobs ripping her apart as they tore their way out.

She hated this place. Pain haunted it like a ghost in a tomb.

I was with you, Beloved. Always.

"Why did you let it happen?" She cried. "All of it? Please tell me why?"

For you.

"For me?" She screamed. "You let him take me for me? You let them make *Abba* watch for me?" She laughed maniacally. "You beat and broke and left me on the rocks for me?"

So you may be made new, Beloved.

Juliana felt the need to move. To do anything that would keep her restless mind from watching the dark window, looking for any sign of Jubilee's return. The moon was high, the sky having darkened hours ago. Standing she poured Jubilee's bowl back into the pot and moved it over the fire. With that finished she gathered the other bowls from the table and readied them to be washed.

"She will not give it up, Juliana." Came Sibyl's soft voice. "These last years she has endured so much and always she has clung to her faith, no matter how difficult it may have been." Moving to be with her, Sibyl took Juliana's hand. "She is letting her pain blind her, but she will see again. That is why she is here."

Juliana nodded and turned back toward the window.

At the table, Malachi's fingers drummed the wood, the fears he refused to speak filling his throat like a thick, dark smoke threatening to choke him. He knew the thoughts that ran through his daughter's mind. Questions that had haunted her since the beginning.

His daughter had spoken words to him that had clung to his very soul. *"Should I have married him, Abba?"* *She had spoken so quietly he had almost missed them. "Would it have been easier? Would he have been..." She trailed off, not needing to finish the sentence.*

"I don't know what he would have been like with you." *Malachi breathed. "But I know you made the right choice."*

"It doesn't feel like it." He had been unable to speak. What could he say that would make her see differently? "I want to die, Abba."

"I know." He whispered.

She was silent a long moment before she could choke the words. "Would God truly count it against me if I chose to take my own life?"

"You know the answer, Jubilee." She had dissolved then into tears.

Malachi swallowed. She still had some faith then. She was ready to give up now. Would she give in to the pain that haunted her? He shook the thought from his head. She was with child. A child she had waited and suffered for. That would be enough to keep her mind from its darkest pits.

Sibyl, unable to bear the silence spoke again. "Your daughter is something very special, you know? It's because of her dedication that I now know the Lord. Leopold is experiencing great joy with the Lord now because of her love." The woman covered her mouth as she worked to staunch her emotion. "She brought my Atticus back to me. She welcomed my daughter into the world with joy, no matter the pain it might have caused her. I will forever be grateful to you and Malachi for bringing that sweet girl into the world." She took a trembling breath. "I hope you know that."

Malachi laid a hand lightly on her shoulder. "We thank you for taking care of her these last two years. The knowledge that she was in such loving hands is what got us through."

At that moment there was a soft knock against the door. Juliana was out of her seat before the door could fully open. "Jubilee!" She wrapped her arms around her, afraid to let her go.

"Do you have any idea of the time?" Malachi demanded. "Where could you possibly have been?"

The girl met his face with red-rimmed eyes. "At the well."

"What in heaven's name could you have been doing there?" Dear God, what could have led her to such a horrid place?

Jubilee stared down at her hands, twisting in her tunic. "Crying." She said softly. "Screaming."

Juliana raised an eyebrow. "Did that make you feel better?"

"It did actually. There were things I needed to get off my chest." She had screamed until her throat was raw. She had worshiped and screamed again. Just as King David had. She spoke in truth until long after the sun had set and even then she could not move, but kept on until she had emptied herself of it all. "I am not saying it will be easy. But I am trying to believe." She glanced at her mother then. "I don't want to give up, *Imma*. I can't."

Jubilee found herself passed among the three, each one kissing her with tear-soaked lips. When she reached her father she held him a moment longer. "I have stumbled a lot, *Abba*, and I think it would be best if I started over in my faith."

"How do you mean, Joy?"

"I want to be baptized again." She pressed her forehead to his chest. "I was a wholly different person then. That girl was naive and innocent. I want to rededicate my life to him as I am now. Knowing all that I do now."

Malachi smiled tearfully. "We'll go down first thing in the morning."

"If it is all right, *Abba*. I think I would like to do it now? With you."

Jubilee was baptized by moonlight. As her father lowered her into the water she felt the residual pain and sorrows she carried fall from her shoulders, washed away by the water and the overwhelming, all consuming love of her Father.

XLIII

At daybreak, Layla rose and hurried to the peristyle. She had slept later than she had intended and the sun was already inching its way up in the sky. Nathanael would be halfway through his prayers by the time she reached him.

She found him on his knees, his hands folded in front of him. She couldn't help but watch him curiously. She had never known anyone so dedicated to their god. As though nothing could tear him away. When he finished he stood and turned. Seeing her he smiled and she found herself smiling back without conscious effort. She walked toward him, her stomach fluttering ever so slightly.

"I missed you." He said with that crooked grin. "I hope your beauty sleep was worth it."

Arms wrapped around herself she followed after him. Without even trying he had managed to work out of her everything she had ever dreamed. The things she had forgotten after so many years in servitude. As they walked their hands found one another's of their own accord and she felt herself drawing closer to him. She no longer fought the feelings that had settled in her. They were there and they wouldn't leave no matter how much she wished them too. The feelings roused in her were warm and comfortable, easing the ache that had burdened her for so long. She knew the pain of his leaving would be her undoing but why not enjoy what he gave until that moment came?

"Layla." Nathanael sounded miserable. Stopping he pulled her close to him.

"My lord."

Nathanael's heart pounded in his chest. Looking into her eyes he found the same longing in them. *"Nathanael."* He whispered.

Layla set her forehead to his. "Nathanael." She whispered. The name was like honey on her lips and he saw it.

"Why do you still fight it?" He reached up and ran his thumb along her cheekbone. "I am here to stay, Layla. So long as you want me."

"Do you promise?"

"I promise, Layla."

Though he smiled she felt the seeds of doubt creeping in and she swore softly before pushing away from him. "I'm sorry." She cried.

"It's all right, Layla." Bringing her back to him he kissed forehead her softly. "Marry me, Layla."

The idea made something in her unfurl. "I can't." She breathed.

"You can. If you want to. Jubilee will free you."

"I don't doubt that she will, Nathanael. I know she would." She let him kiss her again, too weak too deny him. "I want to, Nathanael. I do. But you don't know me. You don't know all that I have done." She closed her eyes. "You're a Christian, Nathanael. Your family. They wouldn't accept me."

"They would love you, Layla. Just as their own."

"No. I don't believe as you do. As they do."

"You believe, Layla. But you think that you are unworthy." Nathanael took up her hand, refusing to let her go. "Why? What could you have done that you can't forgive yourself?"

"I cannot give you what you deserve. Someone clean. Someone whole."

He gripped her arm. "Do you think that because you have known love before that I couldn't love you all the same, Layla?"

She couldn't look at him as she spoke. "I didn't just love him, Nathanael."

"I know what you meant, Layla." There was no betrayal in him as he looked at her. "Tell me about him."

"No." She spit. "I won't hurt you further."

"I want to know all of you. All the things that made you happy once. All the things that have hurt you. That continue to haunt you. I want to know you, Layla."

She watched him a moment. Uncertain. If she told him everything, would he finally see the truth of her? "I met him in my first home after leaving Egypt. I think I was fifteen. Maybe sixteen." She whispered. "He was selfless. The most selfless man I have ever met. Within my first week I had managed to anger the mistress. The master was set to whip me before Noah stepped in and took it for me. He and his father did it for all the women. When they could anyway. Noah said he would take a hundred lashings if it meant keeping one from that sort of harm."

"That's very noble."

"It's very stupid." She replied. "He was always being beaten. I was always afraid they would send him away. I think the master only kept him because he knew that our watching was so much worse than taking it ourselves." She buried her face into his chest, hating the way she relied on him even now. "You shouldn't want me, Nathanael. I went to his bed. I started it."

"Why do you cry that?" Nathanael breathed. "I don't hold your past against you. Why must you hold it against yourself?

"He was a Jewish boy, Nathanael. He was like you. He believed in your god. He loved him more than anything and I drew him away from it. I led him to do things he could never get back." Her legs gave way and she slid to the floor. "I loved him and I defiled him. I will not allow the same to be done to you. Because you are so much more."

Nathanael knelt beside her. "What happened?"

"He woke up—realized what he was doing and tried to rectify it. He told me what we were doing was wrong but I was stubborn. I refused to listen to his preaching. So I gave him the choice between his god and myself. He chose his god."

"Layla, the blame does not fall wholly on you. He played a part as largely as you did."

She shook her head. "I started it. I led him to it. Would your god accept him back?" Her voice cracked miserably. "Please, Nathanael. Tell me he would not turn away from him for things I led him to do."

"If he was true in what he said and repented of his sins then yes, Layla. The Lord most certainly accepted him back. Layla, no one is too far gone. No matter how far they go from Him they can always find their way back."

He brushed at her tears and she pushed his hand away. "You shouldn't touch me. After my father I swore I would never let anyone use me the way he used my mother and I didn't. Don't you see, Nathanael? What I did was worse. I *became* him. I used someone else the way he used my mother."

"What you did and what your father did do not go hand in hand, Layla. What your father did was rape. What you did, however misguided, was done in love. You made mistakes with Noah but you did not use him."

"Then why do I feel as I do?" She curled in on herself, her arms wrapping tightly about her knees. "I can't do it anymore." She sobbed. "It hurts too much."

"Give it to him, Layla."

She shook her head. "What if he rejects me?"

"He won't."

"You can't know that."

Nathanael took her face in his. "He died for this moment. For this very moment right here, he gave his life so that you may be saved through his blood. How can you deny his love for you after something like that that?"

"I don't know what to do. I don't know what to say to him."

"Say what is in your heart. It will come, Layla."

Her heart beat miserably, the ache growing stronger as Nathanael took her hands in his. "Promise me he won't reject me."

"I promise, Dove."

Layla shook as she turned her face to the heavens. "I have done so much, Lord. Can you ever forgive me?"

It came quietly, a voice so small yet more powerful than any she had ever heard.

Seventy times seven.

XLIV

Augustus

Jubilee's feet pounded the hard packed dirt, her heart pounding painfully in her chest. "Jubilee!" Atticus's voice echoed through the woods, guiding her through the thickly packed trees.

"Atticus! Where are you?" His pain filled scream echoed around her. The trees slashed her face as she ran but she hardly felt it. She had to find Atticus. Running faster she stumbled and fell. She scrambled back up and continued, screaming his name until her throat was raw.

Coming up on a clearing in the distance, she could see him at last, bound in a knot of thorns. "Atticus!" She tried to run toward him but her feet refused to move. "Atticus!"

"Jubilee." His screams were strangled as he struggled against the thorns that dug into his flesh. As she watched, a dark misshapen shadow closed in on him.

"Atticus." Jubilee woke with a start, a cold sweat soaking her hair. Atticus's pain filled screams echoed through her mind, making her stomach roll. Sitting up she set her face in her hands, feeling the way the bed shook beneath her.

At her side, Sibyl turned. "Jubilee love, are you all right?" She eyed the girls stomach.

"It was just a nightmare." Jubilee breathed. "Go back to sleep."

"You're trembling." Sitting up, Sibyl pressed a hand to her clammy cheek. "You're burning up. Are you sure you're all right, lovey?"

"I promise, Sibyl." Her voice was weak even in her ears. "I am sorry I woke you."

Still frowning, Sibyl relented and lay back. Within moments her breathing steadied and Jubilee knew she was sleeping.

Laying back on the pillow, she stared up at the ceiling. *Oh God, what is this? Tell me what it means.* She shifted uncomfortably. Sweat had soaked through her tunic as well, making it chaff against her skin.

Easing from the mat, she changed into a fresh tunic before stepping out into the cool night air. The moon was high. It couldn't be later than midnight. Moving through the dark she found the barrel of water and scooped some in her hands. Splashing her face she forced herself to breathe. "It was only a dream." She said aloud.

"Joyous?" Jubilee jumped. She had forgotten her father walked at night, when discomfort kept him from sleeping. "What are you doing?"

"I had a nightmare." Her fathers face pinched in concern. "It wasn't that, *Abba*." She assured. "I haven't had those in weeks. Not since the baptism."

"Do you want to tell me then? I haven't seen you this upset about any other nightmares but Jude."

Jude. The name caused only the slightest turn of her stomach now. Hugging herself tightly, she moved to sit next to him, wanting his comforting arms around her. He did just that and finally she could breathe. "I don't know, *Abba*. It's strange." Doing the best she could, she explained Atticus's dreams of her before explaining her own. "Does it mean anything, *Abba*?" She whispered.

Malachi was silent as he thought it over. "Your brother has always been better at this sort of thing, hasn't he?" He asked at last. "You have both been through so much, Jubilee. Both alone and together. All I can say is that both of you still have a long way to go before you are free of those thorns."

The feeling that something was wrong refused to leave her. "But why am I tearing them away in his, while he is being hunted in mine?" She swallowed, remembering the beast that had circled him. The lioness stalking its prey, waiting for just the right moment to lunge. A laugh like growl had filled the air, low and menacing and then it was lunging at Atticus's neck.

...

Atticus walked the dark corridors of the Domus, following the haunting sobs that filled the air. Stepping into the garden he walked the maze of overgrowth and found Jubilee on her knees before the wall of thorns. Her shoulders shook from tears.

"Jubilee." He whispered. She turned to him, a snow-white rose in her hands.

"Make it worth it." She cried. "Make it all worth while." As he watched, the wounds in her hands began pouring blood, turning the white rose red. It had been the same now. Night after night. The sobbing. The rose and then the blood. So much blood.

"I can heal all wounds." The voice, though spoken softly, rang through the darkness and pierced Atticus's heart. "Give it all to me, Atticus." From behind Jubilee came the same glow from the dreams before it. Atticus raised his hand to shield his eyes as a man stepped from it. No. Not from it. The man was the light. Bright and blinding.

Stepping before Jubilee, the man touched her cheek, a sort of love in his eyes that knocked Atticus to his knees. Jubilee's eyes never moved from Atticus. Did she not see the man? "I have always had a fondness for this one. The moment I woke was the moment she came into the world. I felt great joy in it."

Atticus felt his stomach tighten. Was this truly Him? The risen Lord Jubilee loved so dearly? The man took the rose from her hands then. As He touched her the wounds were sewn closed, leaving her hands clear of all wounds, save for the scar from the scalpel.

As he watched, the blood poured from the rose and to the mans scarred hands, staining the fabric of His pure white tunic. "Just as I have loved her, I have loved you, Atticus. My daughter has given me her pain. Will you not do the same?"

"I don't know how." Atticus breathed.

Holding out the now white rose, the man smiled. "All you must do is reach out and take it, Beloved."

Atticus felt his feet stumble forward and then he was awake in bed, his heart pounding furiously. Breathing deeply he sat up and massaged his eyelids. He missed Jubilee so deeply it ached. She had seemed so real, as though he could have reached out touched her. And the man. Why did he have to wake up? He wanted to go back. To see her again. Sighing he laid back against the pillows and replayed the dream. What had it meant? He knew not what the rose symbolized, all he knew was that he had wanted it. He ached for it. And those words. *My daughter has given me her pain.* Could that be true? Could his Jewess be in

Galilee, enjoying the faith she had so previously suffered in? *Oh God, if nothing else, let that be truth.*

Pulling the blankets up to his chin, he felt his blood run cold as something shifted in the shadows. He wasn't alone. Swallowing hard, he turned his eyes to the body that rested on the lounge. The room was too dark to see their face but he knew even before they spoke.

"Hello, Puppy."

XLV

Jubilee's heart felt as though it were about to burst from her chest as she threw things into her bag. The moment the words had come to mind she had known it to be truth. Aelia was coming back and Atticus was alone.

"Jubilee, you cannot go racing off to Rome." Her mother cried. It was her third time in the space of only minutes. "He is two thousand miles away."

Of course they didn't understand. How could they when only she knew the truth of all that he had suffered at Aelia's hand? Ignoring them, she continued packing. She would find a way back to Rome if she had to swim there.

"You need to relax, Joy." Her mother's hand went to her stomach. "Just breathe."

"No. I need to be there." She cried. "You don't understand! You don't know what she did to him." Her stomach lurched and it took all she had to breathe deeply. "I have to go."

"Jubilee." Taking her hand, her mother lead her back to the table. "What will your being there serve? This is something he must face alone, just as you did at the well. What you need to think about now is your child."

"*Imma*, she-" She choked on the words. It was his secret to tell, not hers, and he wanted it hidden. "She hurt him, *Imma*. I didn't have to face Jude. How can I leave her alone with him?"

Sibyl sat beside her, Tauria held tight against her. She had woken and clung to her daughter the moment Jubilee's words had settled over her. "We can't go, Jubilee. The ship won't be back for another two weeks."

"So you're giving up? Sibyl, he's your son."

"I know that, Jubilee." Sibyl spit back. "Do you think I like this? Knowing my son will suffer all over again and I can't be there to stop it?" Her voice cracked and she began to sob.

"Oh Sibyl." Juliana took her in her arms. "It will be all right."

"Did your feelings tell you that, Juliana?" Sibyl's voice was cold and full of cruelty.

"Now there is no need for such cruelty." Malachi stepped in. "Arguing will get us nowhere. Now, we don't even know if Aelia is truly there. It was a dream. That may be all it was."

"It was real, *Abba*. I feel it."

"You feel it?" Sibyl asked. "What is it with you and your mother and your feelings about everything? Clearly they are not all right or you would not have needed to come back to Galilee—leaving my son alone."

"Sibyl." Juliana could do no more than breathe the word. She had always known her friend to express her fear and grief with anger, but never had she spoken so cruelly.

Sibyl's face had already washed white. "Jubilee, I didn't mean that." Getting up she moved to the girl, who turned away, hiding her hurt tears. Her hand protected her stomach. "Oh *Puella*, I am so sorry." She took the girl in her arms and they clung to each other.

. . .

Atticus felt as though he would be sick as Aelia's stood and made her toward him. "I missed my puppy." She smiled. "Did you miss me?"

"Not for a second." Moving away from her, he stood up. Her dark eyes and the bright silks of her tunics held no power over him now. Her beauty paled in comparisons to the wife who touched him with a gentle hand and had only words on love for him on her lips.

"Has my puppy grown into a man?" She smiled.

Holding her off, he stood and reached for his tunic. He felt her eyes follow him all the while. "You've gained weight." She pouted. "After all my hard work."

Slipping the tunic on, he grabbed a toga, wanting to hide everything from her scrutiny. Scared to lose sight of her he kept his eyes on her. He tried to remember the previous night. He had spent it with Nathanael and Layla before falling asleep reading the scrolls. No wine had touched his lips—as it had been since he and Jubilee had shared their secrets. His eyes went to the pitcher of water beside the bed.

Aelia smiled, her head tilted seductively. "Relax, puppy. I didn't touch you. I did watch you though. You seemed quite peaceful. It was sweet. Though you were always sweet weren't you, my little puppy?" She laughed. "You did cry out for Jubilee once. Still pining after your Jewess, are you?"

"We're married."

"Married?" Standing, she walked to him and unfastened his tunic with quick fingers. "Does she like this?" She took the fat of his stomach roughly between her fingers and pinched.

"She is the one who encouraged this." Atticus spit. "Jubilee doesn't look at the outside."

"Which means she must be horrid looking."

"She's beautiful. More so than you will ever be."

Aelia laughed. "My puppy has bite. What happened to my sweet boy?" Releasing him, she stepped away.

Fetching up his tunic once more he dressed quickly, keeping his distance from her.

She scoffed. "You wouldn't have to hide if you took care of yourself. I showed you what to do."

"This has nothing to do with shame."

"Ever so modest. Is only your Jewess allowed to see you now? Has she converted you, puppy?"

Atticus watched her move about the room. Her fingers grazed the tapestry Jubilee had acquired in Pompeii. "What would you say if she had?"

"I would say you were weak." She spit. "Much like the puppy I knew." She had moved to the chest now, where she pulled out the bundle of old letters he and Jubilee had passed in past summers. Looking through them she smiled. "She wasn't very subtle was she?"

"She was a child." The letter she held was written when Jubilee was only seven.

"Is this her?" She held up a finely detailed picture Juliana had drawn. It contained him and Jubilee during their last summer, tucked close at the table as they reconnected. Atticus had not realized their hands had been linked until Juliana had pressed the paper into his hand on his last day there. In the picture, Jubilee's eyes were bright as she looked at him. "She's bug-eyed." Aelia drawled, her voice betraying only the slightest discontent.

Tossing the things away from her she stood. "Where is your Jewess anyway?"

"She is in Galilee visiting her parents."

"And yet you are here? Are you having trouble? Life with your Jewess not everything you thought it would be?"

Atticus bit his tongue. He wouldn't give her the satisfaction of belittling him further.

Turning to him fully, she smiled. "I don't see any children. Are they with her?"

"Yes. She took them to see their grandparents." He would give her no reason to mock his wife further.

"I look forward to meeting them. And your little bug."

"No." Atticus breathed. "You will never set eyes on her."

She laughed. "Did you think I came back just to visit, Atticus?" She made her way back to him. "Slow, slow boy. You're still mine."

Atticus swallowed the bile that rose in his throat as she neared him. "I would die before I left Jubilee."

"Don't be so pathetic, puppy. I'll let you keep the bug." Aelia smiled, her fingers toying with his tunic. "Does she know? About how often you cried for her? Like a little boy crying for his mommy?"

"Jesus." He breathed. *God, please.* He begged inwardly. *If you are there, give me strength. I can't do this alone.* Memories of that first night in the tavern were overwhelming him, making his knees weak with fear.

I go before you. Let your fear go.

With that soft voice in his ear, Atticus looked at Aelia. "Jubilee knows everything. Every minute detail." Atticus smiled as the woman looked puzzled. "Did you think I would be too ashamed? Did you think that you would leave me so broken that no other woman could look at me?"

"Something like that." Shrugging, Aelia stood straighter. "Though, perhaps that is why she's in Galilee?" She smiled. "Or does the bug exist, Puppy? What a coincidence she just so happened to be gone tonight?"

Scoffing, Atticus started for the basin of water—clinging to scriptures he'd read to keep his mind free. "You may think what you want, Aelia. But you can no longer break me." Not with that voice in his ear and the love-filled memories of his life with Jubilee.

He frowned at the way she watched him, a small smile pulling at the corners of her lips as he filled a goblet with water. *No, Beloved.* Atticus froze, the goblet halfway to his lips. Bringing it to his nose he sniffed. The bitter scent burned his nose and made his stomach churn.

Pouring it back into the basin he turned to find Aelia watching him. "What?" Her dark eyes were wide and innocent.

"You're mad." He spit. "So that is what you came back for? To finish me off like the others?" Despite the earlier peace, fear was beginning to creep back in. "Jesus." He breathed. Remembering all the days Jubilee had cried out to her God. "Jesus. Jesus. Jesus."

Aelia sneered. "You haven't changed at all have you, puppy?" Aeila smiled. "Still weak. Still calling out for your Jubilee to save you." She gripped her arm, her nails drawing blood. "This is why people leave. It's pathetic."

Yanking his arm free, Atticus stepped away from her. "Get out."

"You almost sounded like your father." She smiled. "Did he not tell you? He and I have been doing business together for years."

Atticus's fist twitched at the meaning behind her words. The disgusting little liar. "My father would never touch you."

She rolled her eyes. "I wasn't talking about that, puppy. Though I did offer him such a pleasure, your father is strangely devoted to that mother of yours." She rolled her eyes. "I can't imagine why."

Atticus pressed his nails into his palms as she mocked his mother. Finished, she laughed. "I was talking about money, puppy."

"I know what he did." Atticus spit. "I am the one who told him to end it."

"Did you?" She drawled. "Didn't want Daddy fixing your problems anymore. I am surprised he listened. He was quite adamant, you know. Bringing me money when I needed it. All I had to do was write to him about how much I was missing my sweet puppy and how lonesome Ostia was without you." She smiled. "He made sure I was comfortable. He made certain I was keeping my promise to stay away from you. He never told me you were married though. The only time he mentioned you was when he told me you were in Greece, studying medicine under Aretaeus. How does your bug feel about such a menial occupation?"

"She works with me. She is the reason I chose to study medicine."

Aelia raised an eyebrow. "A lady physician. Is she any good?"

"She's incredible. More than I could ever hope to be." The ache for her was too much.

"You really are your father. *She's beautiful. She's incredible.*" She mocked. "You two are like women."

"We love our wives as we are meant to. If that makes us such then I am glad to be."

Aelia frowned. "You never loved me like that."

"Perhaps because you drugged me?" Atticus spit.

Aelia set her arms around his neck. "Did you love me at all?" She pouted. "Even a little?"

"No." Atticus's heart picked up again at her touch. Sweat beaded his forehead as Aelia pressed closer. *If demons are true, that woman is riddled with them.*

Atticus shuddered at the thought, as though he could feel the creatures around him.

I am with you, Atticus.

Clinging to the power of that voice, Atticus forced his lips to move. "Get out." The words were choked and little more than a whisper, but to his surprise, the woman back away.

Aelia looked back at him with a strange fear in her eyes.

"Get out." He repeated. "Before I go for the magistrate."

The woman let out a small laugh. "The Magistrate?" She whispered. "And what will he do?" But even beneath the sneer, Atticus could see the fear building in her.

As the reason for her fear dawned, Atticus spoke. "It doesn't have to be this way, Aelia."

"Oh?" She whispered. "Are you going to tell me about your god now?"

"If you are willing to listen."

Aelia laughed breathlessly. "You people are sick." Grabbing her stola, she hurried past Atticus, avoiding his touch.

XLVI

Atticus couldn't remain still as he watched the ship roll in. In just moments Jubilee would be where she belonged—in his arms. He couldn't wait to hear about her faith and what it was that had refined it as he knew it had been. But most importantly he couldn't wait to share his own with her, knowing the smile that would grace her face.

His heart beat anxiously for her, but an uneasiness was beginning to bubble in his stomach. He knew he would tell her about Aelia. Would she believe his innocence? Or would she believe he sent her away for Aelia?

Do not fear, Beloved.

Since that night the voice had been there, always so small and all-powerful.

"I want to believe it, Nathanael. But I don't know that I do."

Nathanael had smiled patiently. "Can you tell me what else it would be?"

Atticus had tried and couldn't. "Why would he come to me, who has denied him for so long when he ignored Jubilee's desperate pleas?"

"He has never ignored Jubilee. She was simply too lost to hear it. Just as you once were."

. . .

Jubilee bounced on the balls of her feet as the ship docked. Through the crowd she could see Atticus and his father.

Sibyl slipped her hand into hers. "He is all right." She breathed.

Feet touching ground, Jubilee hurried through the crowd and slammed into Atticus. "Oh." She cried, as his arms went around her. Three months was too long to be apart. "Oh, you're all right."

Atticus breathed her in. She fit him so well, as though she were made just for him. Taking his face in her hands she kissed him.

Her eyes bore into his, his face still in her hands. "Aelia came back didn't she?" Tears spilled down her cheeks. "I knew it. I hated not being here with you. It nearly killed me not knowing if you were all right. Not knowing if you were scared or if she-"

She was rambling. Atticus kissed her to quiet her. "Jewess. We have all the time in the world to explain. Let's go home."

. . .

Atticus set his forehead to Jubilee's abdomen. She had wasted no time in sharing the news she had learned while away. His arms wrapped around her waist. "Of course you would find out when you're away."

"Just over a month later." Jubilee laughed. "They will be here in February. At least I believe so."

Letting him pull her down beside him, Jubilee curled closer into Atticus's side, her head in the crook of his neck. After three months apart she couldn't get close enough. Her eyes closed contentedly as Atticus's thumb stroked her stomach. "How did you know she came back?" He asked quietly.

She explained her dream to him. "I can't explain it, but somehow I just knew. It was horrible."

"It's all right, Jewess. It is over now." It was his own turn to share his side. "She called you the bug." He said quietly, explaining the picture Aelia had found. "My precious bug."

"Puppy and the Bug?" Jubilee smiled. "Does that make me a flea?"

Atticus laughed as he continued. "I had never seen Aeila afraid before. Not truly and there she was, white as death when I ordered her out."

"She wasn't scared of you, Atticus. It was God. She could see the Lord in you."

Atticus considered that a moment. It made more sense than the alternative. Men didn't scare Aelia. Aelia scared men.

Holding her closer, Atticus listened to her tell him of the well and her baptism. "That's all?" He asked. "Being baptized again?"

"No. I still had to work to get here, Atty. And it had to be the right moment. I was ready then." She looked up at him. "I just couldn't do it anymore, Atty. And weirdly the well was what I needed. When I stepped foot there I knew I couldn't keep fighting everything that I had felt since Jude. So I stopped. I stopped fighting my anger with God and just allowed myself to scream. I stopped fighting the pain and just let myself feel it. And after that I was ready."

"I'm not sure I like the idea of you there." Atticus breathed. "At that place."

"I wasn't alone, Atty."

"Of course not." He whispered. They were quiet and as the minutes passed he listened to Jubilee's breaths turn rhythmic. He had been there, the first time she had been baptized. She had been six and unable to contain herself. She had gone into the water shivering with excitement and had come out crying, overwhelmed he now knew, by the presence of God. It had been shortly after that that she had began praying in that strange tongue. What had she felt this last time she came from the water?

Atticus nudged her. "Jubilee." When she turned to look at him he hesitated before whispering the words. "I want to be baptized."

A small smile played at her lips. "You do?"

"Can you do it? Does it matter who does it?"

"Usually men do it. Pastors."

"But God wouldn't forbid it?"

"I honestly don't know, Atticus. Baptism isn't required by God to be saved. It is simply a choice we make ourselves. It symbolizes a new beginning as you are being washed clean." She watched him with unexplained tears. "Let Nathanael baptize you, Atticus. I want to do something else for you." Her voice was thin.

"Did I say something wrong?"

"No, Atticus. I am proud." Grabbing his hand she pulled him out of bed. "Come. We will get Nathanael now."

Layla was baptized as well. Letting her go first, Atticus watched the gentle, loving way Nathanael held her as he lowered her into the water. The two had confided in him the news a few days after Aelia had gone. Turning to Jubilee, he wondered if she could see it. But she had eyes only for him.

When it was his turn, Atticus entered the water with Jubilee at his side. Her hand held tight in his. "Do you give yourself and your life to the Lord?" She asked tearfully.

Atticus smiled at her before turning his eyes skyward. "I do." Nathanael lowered him back and the water rushed over him, washing away all the filth that had ever covered him.

…

Layla's hands wrung at her wrap as she stood outside the triclinium. "Are you having second thoughts, Layla?" Nathanael's voice was soft behind her.

"Not of you." She whispered. "I wasn't born a free woman, Nathanael."

"Nor am I a Roman citizen." He replied. "Their laws do not restrain me."

Her tear stained eyes met his. "I am not a virgin. I can't give you the gift you deserve. Can you truly accept that? I don't want you waking up after and wishing for something else."

"I do not hold your past against you. You are no longer that lost girl." Pulling her to him he kissed her wet cheeks. "I love all of you, Dove. Thorn strewn past and all."

She set her head against his chest. She loved him so much. The idea of losing him felt like ice to her soul. "Would you like me to go with you?" He asked.

"No. No, this is something I need to do on my own." Taking a deep breath she stepped into the room. "My lady?"

Jubilee turned to her. "Yes, Layla?"

Layla shook her head. "I-" The words caught in her throat. What if she was wrong? What if Jubilee didn't wish to free her? What if she hated the idea of a slave marrying her brother?

Jubilee smiled knowingly. "Nathanael." She breathed. "You wish to be freed."

Layla's heart skipped a beat. "Yes, my lady."

"Jubilee, Layla. If I am to free you and call you a true sister, you cannot go on treating me as a mistress." Smiling at the look on Layla's face, Jubilee continued. "Why do you think I insisted on you staying with him? I could have stayed with him, you know. I wanted to give you a chance to know each other."

"Does Nathanael know this?"

"Not that I know of." Jubilee laughed. "Do not be impressed, Layla. It was highly selfish on my end. I hoped that if Nathanael found love he would stay. The fact that you would be a sister was a lovely benefit."

"I do love him, Jubilee. But your family. Will they approve of this? I'm not like you." She took in the girl's skin. "In any way."

"Layla, my family does not think in such ways. You must remember that my father was a Jew who married a Roman, in a time when that was very looked down upon." She took Layla's hands. "My parents will love you, Layla. As though you are their very own."

Keeping Layla's hand, Jubilee led her into the tablinum and approached the desk. Reaching into the drawer she produced a tightly bound scroll. "I almost signed it the moment you came to me." She admitted sheepishly. "I wanted to. But something told me I was supposed to keep you with me. I guess now we know why." She signed the contract carefully before pressing it into Layla's hands. "And one more thing." Rifling through the drawer she pulled out a bag of jangling coins. "A year and a half of weekly earnings. It should be enough to afford you and Nathanael an apartment. As well as give you time for Nathanael to find work."

"Oh, my la-Jubilee." Layla held the purse gently as though afraid of it. "This is too much."

"It isn't a gift, Layla. I have been saving this since the day you came to me, for the moment the Lord told me to let you go." She placed the girl's hand over the bag. "You were never a slave in my home, Layla. You earned this."

Layla looked the bag over. "Do you think he would still let me work?"

"If you wanted to."

"I do. I have never not worked, Jubilee. Those few weeks here, having nothing to do were miserable."

Jubilee smiled. "I suppose we can work something out. I don't plan to continue working once the baby comes, but I am sure there will be days when Atticus needs assistance. It would give me a lot of comfort in those moments, knowing they were with someone like you. And their cousins someday."

Layla laughed. "I would love that, Jubilee."

…

Regulus walked the expanse of the Domus, unwilling to remain still. The gnawing guilt thrived in an idle mind. He had despised his son for so long. His son. How could he forgive himself for the things that he had said in recent years? He had been blind to the pain that had consumed his child and he was paying the price for it now. A price he wasn't sure he could survive.

"Give it to the Lord." Sibyl had told him. "Atticus has forgiven you. You mustn't let guilt destroy you. He doesn't want that."

Give it to the Lord. The idea was ludicrous. He had tried to follow his promise after Tauria's birth. He listened. He asked questions. He had spent the summer in church and listened to Nathanael speak, but he couldn't grasp how something unseen could be the answer to his guilt. He could see the forgiveness clearly in Atticus's manner. The two had spent their spare moments without their wives in each other's company, and still, he couldn't forgive himself. Nothing could rid him of this guilt. Not when he deserved it.

But still, his wife's words echoed in his mind. *Give it to the Lord.* Sighing, he picked up his pace until he found himself in the very place Sibyl so often came to pray. He sat on the bench and placed his head in his hands.

"Lord?" He laughed at himself, feeling like a child with an invisible friend.

"Does that not feel strange to you?" He had asked Sibyl after discovering her praying aloud in their room. "As if you are talking to yourself?"

She had smiled. "It can feel a bit odd at times." She admitted.

He sighed. "God if you are there." *No.* He stood and began to pace.

It becomes easier over time, Regulus. Sibyl's voice encouraged. *Just ignore the unbelief.*

Fear still strong that he would be found out, Regulus slipped to his knees. Tears threatened to fall as he fought for words. "Lord, my heart has been heavy for so long and I now know why. I have denied you all my life and I see now what it has cost me." He pressed his palms to his eyes, doubt flooding him once more; dispelling from his mind all other words. "I believe." He roared.

Heart pounding he took a breath. "God, I believe. I believe. Free me of my unbelief."

He felt gentle hands press into his shoulders and with them came the long withheld tears. Rather than the embarrassment he had so worriedly expected, he felt relief. This was Sibyl who held him. From the day he had known her, he had loved her with a strength that filled his body, mind, and soul. Never would he allow himself to feel shame in her presence. For it was in her that he had found his strength so long ago and it was in her now that he found new confidence.

Taking her hand in his he squeezed, drawing on her strength. "God, I give this to you. No longer will I dwell on my grief."

XLVII

Februarius 51AD

Their child came to them in the early hours of a crisp, winter morning. A boy they called Hosea—for what better example could they be given of their Father's restoration power? As the boy was laid upon his mother's chest, she looked to her husband who beamed with a pride she had never seen in him before. "He's perfect." She told him.

Sitting beside her, Atticus stroked her wet hair away from her face before taking one of her trembling hands in his. "Was he worth the wait?"

"Worth every moment." She breathed.

The days that followed were a tired, love-filled ecstasy as they acquainted themselves with the small life entrusted to them.

Jubilee smiled down at him as she fed him, his tiny hand curled into her hair. The child suckled contentedly, a dimple forming on his cheek as he smiled. He looked like his mother, with a tuft of thick black hair and wide eyes—already showing tints of green that hinted towards his father. "I don't see how I deserve this." She said quietly.

Atticus squeezed her shoulder. "Don't think like that, Jewess. He knew what he was doing. Now," Easing the boy from his mother's arms, Atticus kissed his cheek. "I think it is my turn to hold this little angel."

Jubilee watched him hold their son close, his nose to his. She had not thought it possible to love him more and yet in the short few weeks they had known their boy she felt as though her heart could not hold an ounce more of love.

She gasped. She had nearly forgotten her promise to him. *I want to do something else for you.* Smiling, Jubilee stood on her toes to whisper in his ear. "I'll be back in a moment." She returned as he was laying a sleeping Hosea down in his cradle.

Turning to her he stopped short. She stood dressed before him in one of her old tunics—tight and worn thin. His lips quirked. "What are you doing?"

"Please, let me serve you." She breathed. Her heart thumped in her chest in fear and excitement. She wanted to lower herself before him completely. In a way, no one had before. She said nothing as she sat before him. Placing the bowl before her, she took one of his feet. She felt the way he stiffened at her gentle touch, confusion sweeping over his face.

Atticus sat stunned for a moment as the woman poured water over his feet. He could smell the oils she had added. Sandalwood and frankincense—his favorites. As she worked she spoke in that strange language he now knew to be tongues. She went on without pause as tears slid down her cheeks and mixed with the oils on his feet. Her voice shook as she unleashed her hair. With now trembling hands she pressed her hair to his feet and dried them. He felt the air rush from his lungs. He knew her hair to be her only true pride. Something she treasured and there she was treating it as nothing more than rags for the pile.

When she had finished she kissed each one and finally, he understood why she had done it. *I want to do something else for you.* She wanted to humble herself before him in a way the wife before her never had. Taking her in his arms, he set her on the bed and knelt at her feet, kissing each one as they were before pouring the water. He sang as he worked, a sweet song his mother had sung all his life. If anyone deserved to be served it was his Jewess. The girl he had loved all his life. The woman who had sacrificed herself again and again to better him.

When he was finished he took her in his arms and held her to his chest. His lovely, delicate rose.

XLVIII

Epilogue
64 AD

Jubilee Albanus watched the distant shore of Galilee roll closer, the ache in her chest deepening. After sixteen years in Rome, they had been forced to leave their home after Nero's persecution of the Christians had become a danger too big to ignore.

Though her heart had always longed to go back and stay in Nazareth, she could not imagine a Galilee without her parents. It had been a year since her parents, their love unable to be broken even in death, had died only an hour apart—Juliana still clutching her husband in her arms. Jubilee had not been back since.

In her arms her four-month-old gnawed at her finger, bringing her wandering mind back to the present. Turning away from the shore she watched her family bustle about the deck. Her eyes first found thirteen-year-old Hosea, holding his seven-year-old sister, Julia, as she leaned over the side of the ship. She could hear the girl chattering about the animals that swam beneath them. Smiling she glanced over Nathanael and Layla and their six children, scattered around the ship. A gray-haired Regulus was lying back in the sun, Sibyl in his arms. Tauria sat with Tamar and Solaris's son, Simon.

Jubilee's eyes found next her girls—eleven-year-old Hadassah and ten-year-old Livia, heads together as they shared secrets. Finally, she found Atticus, running playfully after a five-year-old Aquila. Eyes landing back on Malachi, now resting against her chest, she felt a smile ease across her face. She pressed her lips to the boy's forehead.

Though the pain she felt was strong now she was looking directly upon the truth that from the thorn do roses bloom.

Acknowledgments

I want to start by thanking my beautiful grandma! This story never would have seen the light of day without you! Thank you for kind kind words and encouragements.

Thank you to my parents who keep my eyes on Christ!

A special thank you to my editors, Caitlin Miller and Christina Smith! You make the editing process so much easier!

Thank you to my writer friends who have been so encouraging throughout this process.

Thank you to my sweet little dog-child, Oliver! I love your sweet snuggles when you sense my stress.

Finally and most importantly, thank you, Jesus! Without you, I would have nothing. Thank you for being close to the broken-hearted!

About Author

Faith R. Mathewson grew up in Oregon and has been certifiably obsessed with stories for as long as she can remember.

She tried her hand at writing at sixteen and hasn't stopped since. Faith loves Jesus and seeks to create stories and characters that glorify Him. Photography, coffee, and snuggling her dog-child Oliver, are just a few of her favorite things.